WHEN SHE SAW THE MAMMOTH STONE, EVERYTHING STOPPED . . .

Just like that, Old Magic went away. Maya couldn't see him anymore. She couldn't see the tiny, ever present fire, or the shadowy piles of furs, charms, and implements that lined the curving walls of the Spirit House.

She couldn't see her own hands, or the caribou coat she wore. It seemed she'd become wholly eyes, that all there was of her was what she could see, and all she could see was the Stone. Somehow the Stone moved closer to her, and then it hung in glimmering darkness just beneath her eyes.

She could see every detail. The stone was about the size of her palm. It was a mammoth, lovingly carved, softly polished, never touched.

From far away, low and rolling and almost bell-like, words slowly rose up beneath the Stone like great, dark bubbles, each bubble bursting in a single event of sound.

Take . . . the . . . Stone. . . .

THE
MAMMOTH
STONE

BY
MARGARET ALLAN

A SIGNET BOOK

SIGNET
Published by the Penguin Group
Penguin Books USA Inc., 375 Hudson Street,
New York, New York 10014, U.S.A.
Penguin Books Ltd, 27 Wrights Lane,
London W8 5TZ, England
Penguin Books Australia Ltd, Ringwood,
Victoria, Australia
Penguin Books Canada Ltd, 10 Alcorn Avenue,
Toronto, Ontario, Canada M4V 3B2
Penguin Books (N.Z.) Ltd, 182–190 Wairau Road,
Auckland 10, New Zealand

Penguin Books Ltd, Registered Offices:
Harmondsworth, Middlesex, England

First published by Signet, an imprint of New American Library, a division
of Penguin Books USA Inc.

First Printing, February, 1993
10 9 8 7 6 5 4 3 2 1

This is for Tom Winger:
Oldest Friend

The spring has less of
    brightness
Every year;
And the snow a ghastlier
    whiteness
Every year;
Nor do summer flowers quicken,
Nor the autumn fruitage thicken,
As they once did, for they sicken
Every year.
        —Albert Pike

All that we see or seem
Is but a dream within a dream.
        —Edgar Allan Poe

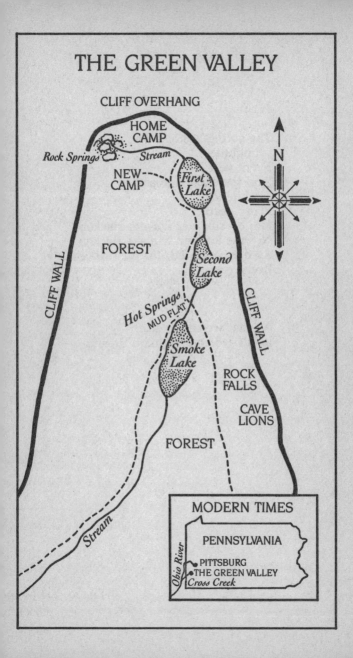

Chapter One

Dyukhtai Cave, Siberia: 21,466 B.C.

Blood.

Ga-Ya wrapped her coat of tightly stitched fur closer around her frail shoulders and shivered. The wind bit at her like a wolf. From her perch fifteen feet above the Siberian plain, she could see the distant forms of the Great Hairy Ones, their tusks flashing in the wintry afternoon sun. "Good," she grunted to herself. She guessed the main body of the herd would approach her position in less than an hour. The leather straps that bound her to the wooden saddle atop the pole on which she sat had begun to cut into her thighs. In her lap were the magic instruments of her calling: a short flute carefully carved from reindeer horn, a rattle of similar material, and the carven ivory shape of a mammoth.

Blood.

The smell filled her nostrils and sent red fogs through her brain. None of the mammoths in the distant herd had yet felt the sting of the People's spears—but she could smell and taste their animal blood with every cell of her being. It was part of her magic. There would be blood, a lot of it. And soon.

The pole on which she sat guarded the entrance of a narrow, ice-coated defile which led down to the

1

river. Mammoth had traversed a nearby trail as long as she could remember, both in her own mind and in the songs of the People she carried within herself. Of late, however, despite her own powerful magics, the great beasts had not been seen. Three springs had come and gone without a single beast falling to the spears and axes of her People. This time, though, as the days grew slowly longer, she had held the carven mammoth to her withered breasts and Dreamed. She had fasted, and on the fourth day the Dreams had begun.

In the Dream she spoke to the Mother of a herd and the Mother lowered her great, hairy skull, as if listening to the songs Ga-Ya sang to her in the Dreamtime. When the old woman awoke, she summoned the hunters.

"Send Ku-Yak and Be-Dag out." The two men she'd named, the most proficient trackers in the tribe, had nodded as she'd given them directions for their search. The area she sent them toward was somewhat different from those they'd hunted before, slightly north of their usual grounds, but they didn't question her. Nobody of the People of the Mammoth questioned Ga-Ya. She was their soul, their Mother.

Ten days later Be-Dag had loped into camp. "Mammoth!" he'd shouted, and within an hour a full party of hunters had departed the half-buried long house which rested beside the river. After they had gone, Ga-Ya directed the women in their tasks— attaching ropes to the carved Spirit Pole and dragging it toward the deep hole in the frozen tundra, and making ready the saddle Ga-Ya would ride high atop the pole after it was set upright.

Now she watched the hunt unfold from her traditional seat, the sky overhead as empty and blue as ice on dark water, and gently fingered the worn ivory side of the carved mammoth. Soon she would send her magics through that shape into the mind of the Great Mother, and thence to the Mother who ruled the approaching herd.

She touched the rattle and the flute. The wind chugged and huffed at her cheeks. Her thin fingers curled inward against the cold.

She waited.

Blood!

Ku-Yak leaned on his spear, careful to avoid the sharp edges of the meticulously chipped point that was bound tightly to the wooden shaft. He had no fear that the relatively nearby herd would notice him; he was safely downwind, and the eyesight of the big animals was notoriously poor.

He turned to Be-Dag and said, "That one, just behind the Mother."

Be-Dag nodded. The two men, along with ten other hunters, had stalked the herd since the previous afternoon. Now, as the sun neared its zenith, they watched the Mother turn her path sharply and begin to lead the herd toward the shadowy opening into the ice-covered river cleft.

"If Ga-Ya's magic is still strong, we may take all of them," Be-Dag said. "If not, then I agree." He grinned at Ku-Yak. "You and me—we'll get the young one ourselves."

They had watched their intended prey—a young male not fully grown or tusked—meander away from the safety of the herd several times. Each time the Herd Mother had followed him out, trumpeted, and bumped and nudged him back into the security of the larger group. Now, as the mammoths and the hunters approached the circle of Ga-Ya's magic—the two men could see her now, fixed atop her Spirit Pole like a tiny black crow—perhaps the young male would wander again. But this time the Herd Mother would be too busy to rescue the young one. Be-Dag licked his lips at the thought of the kill. He could almost taste the hot blood streaming into his mouth.

"Come on," he whispered. "Let's get closer."

Ku-Yak nodded and shouldered his spear. Together, the two hunters loped forward, crouched low against the thick carpet of steppe grass. In the distance they heard sudden, thin cries. The Mammoth Mother paused, then lurched into a slow gallop.

Ku-Yak shouted with joy. Right toward the river-cleft!

And now the young one, panicked, began to turn away from the main herd.

"Eeee-yah!" Be-Dag shouted, and waved his spear.

Ga-Ya straightened sharply and raised her right hand to shield her vision. The herd had begun to move. Too soon! Then she saw the cause. The wind had shifted and carried the smell of the hunters to the lead cow. Ga-Ya strained against her binding straps, leaned precariously forward, calculating furiously.

Yes! The Mother had panicked, but the direction of her flight was toward the defile and the trap that awaited her there.

Quickly Ga-Ya closed her eyes, picked up the bone flute from her lap, and raised it to her lips. For a moment, in the windy darkness, she sensed something long and awesome, and she paused. But then it was gone. She rubbed her tongue against the hole of the flute, spat, and began to play. The song blew long and plaintive, weaving in and out of the greater song of the Wind Spirits. A few moments later the ache of the pole beneath her scrawny buttocks, the distant cries of the hunters, the trumpet shriek of the Great Beasts, all receded from her consciousness. In the enfolding dark, wrapped in the magic of her song, a door opened and Ga-Ya entered the realm of the Dream Mother, whence all came and, eventually, all would return.

As he ran, Be-Dag tried to imagine what the scene looked like from above, as if he were a sharp-eyed bird. The herd, with the Mammoth Mother in the lead, now spread out and lumbering with ever-greater speed toward the river trap. The tiny forms of the hunters, widened into a broad skirmish line, forming a long semicircle behind the herd itself. And now the terrified young male, head tossing, eyes wild, galloping at an angle away from the herd, directly toward himself and Ku-Yak. He glanced at the other hunter and shouted, "Circle around between him and the herd! Drive him toward me!"

Ku-Yak nodded and veered away, his black eyes intent upon the lurching form of the young male. There was great danger in this maneuver; if the Herd Mother took it into her head to change the path of her charges, Ku-Yak might be caught between the tusks and feet of the stampeding animals and the wild thrashings of the young male.

Be-Dag spared a moment to search for the lonely figure of Ga-Ya atop her pole. His lips stretched across his teeth as he ran. They had come much closer to her now, and he could make out her features above the flute she held in one fist. He could even hear the faint whisper of the tune she played. Her eyes were closed. She was in the Dreamtime now, with the Great Mother, sending her magics out to the Herd Mother. It was Ga-Ya's job to prevent the Herd Mother from swerving away from the path of her death. Ga-Ya was the only protection the hunters had from such a disaster.

He turned back to the young male, now less than a hundred yards away. The sharp stink of the male's fear reached his own nostrils. He stood up straight, waved his spear, and shouted his hunting cry.

"Aaaayaagh!"

The young mammoth shied suddenly, stupefied by the sudden apparition that had appeared in his path. His huge forelegs dug into the tundra as his massive weight brought him almost to his knees. Be-Dag shrieked again and rushed forward.

The mammoth regained his feet and whirled, trumpeting loudly. His head swiveled wildly as his rolling, reddened eyes sought safety. Dimly he saw the rest of the herd, now receding rapidly toward the river, but as he sought to join them Ku-Yak sprang up from the grass and shouted a long, ululating cry.

"Wooeeeoooeeeeooooo!"

The mammoth turned again and Be-Dag surged forward, his spear extended before him, almost within reach of the terrorized animal's tusks.

Paralyzed with fear, the young mammoth froze for an instant back on his haunches, with one massive foreleg upraised. Be-Dag waved his spear in the animal's face, dodging to avoid its wildly thrashing trunk. The curving tusks, white against the blue sky, waved above him like a pair of knives. Not yet fully grown, the tusks still measured more than a meter in length, easily capable of impaling the hunter with a single bloody thrust.

"Aaayaagh!" Be-Dag shouted.

The animal twisted away, but as he did so he exposed his soft underbelly to Ku-Yak's hungry spear. Ku-Yak leaped forward, the thick muscles of his shoulders bunching and unbunching as he put all his weight behind the thrust.

The mammoth screamed.

Ku-Yak fell away, rolling, his furs covered with a sudden, steaming gush of blood. Be-Dag laughed with the mad joy of it all, his own blood-lust singing in his veins. While Ku-Yak readied his second spear,

Be-Dag danced forward, searching for his own strike.

Dimly he was aware of other shouts, other cries, and over all the mad trumpeting shrieks of the rest of the herd as the other hunters drove them into the ice-covered defile from which they would never escape.

Blood, thick and red, sprayed from the gaping wound, which opened like a mouth around the haft of Ku-Yak's spear. Some of the crimson liquid spattered against Be-Dag's face. He licked it from his lips, and at the hot, red taste of it he went completely berserk.

He screamed and plunged forward, directly into the wounded animal's face.

Blood!

In the darkness of the dreamtime, Ga-Ya felt enfolded by the warmth of the Great Mother. She'd never seen the Great Mother's face, only felt Her limitless compassion, the sense of individual care the Great Mother felt for each of Her creatures. Ga-Ya knew the Great Mother cared as deeply for each mammoth as She did for each one of the People, and that the Great Mother would allow the People to destroy the mammoths only because it was part of some greater scheme only the Great Mother could know. And so she approached the Great Mother humbly, riding the thin, shining rope of her song, her hands outstretched and pleading.

"O Great Mother," she sang. "Give my People the boon of Your love. We have not eaten of the mammoth for a very long time. We love the Mammoth Mother too, and will pray her spirit on to You when the time comes."

She paused in her chanting, and it seemed that some vast presence in the dark smiled upon her. A distant flash of light appeared. Ga-Ya knew it was the spirit of the Mammoth Mother. She bowed toward the spark, and sang to it as well.

"Mammoth Mother, who succors the People with your flesh, we sing the songs of praise to your spirit. We honor you, your might, your great soul, the life you give willingly to our tribe. The People love you, Mammoth Mother. We call to you, and beg the ultimate gift."

Now other sparks appeared, each representing the spirit of one of the Mammoth Mother's children. It was an enormous sacrifice she was asking, Ga-Ya knew, but it was a part of the wider circle only the Great Mother Herself could see.

The wail of her flute surrounded her in the darkness as she gazed upon the sparks soon to be snuffed. She felt tears upon her cheeks. Then, in slow, rolling words that were not words, the Great Mother spoke to her: *Go now, Daughter. I will hear your prayers. I will pass your pleas to the Mammoth Mother, and she will hear me. Go now. . . .*

The sparks glowed brighter only for a moment and then, one by one, winked out. Finally only the brilliance of the Mammoth Mother remained. Ga-Ya faced that light, her heart full of love for the sacrifice that would be made, and for the Great Mother, who ordered all things.

"Thank you," she whispered, first to the Great Mother, and then to the Mammoth Mother. It seemed she felt a distant reply, sadly accepting, and then the spark was gone. The warm darkness began to dissolve around her. The sound of her flute grew loud in her ears.

Finally, just before her eyes popped open, when she hung suspended in that space between the Dreamtime and the World, she heard the cries of the hunters calling her back. Blindly her fingers sought the rattle which rested in her lap. She lowered the flute, took the rattle in one hand, and let the fingers of her other hand rest on the worn ivory of the mammoth carving. She fancied she could feel the spirit of the Mammoth Mother there, coursing up from the bone to her fingers and thence to her heart.

"Thank you," she prayed a final time. She opened her eyes, shook the rattle, and began to chant the death song of the Mammoth Mother, calling her to her final grave.

She didn't notice the small, frenzied group lurching toward her precarious post, the young mammoth and his two blood-crazed attackers. But even if she had, her song of respect would not have faltered. The Mammoth Mother had given up everything to the People; she deserved her final ode of respect.

The rattle made a soft, rushing sound in her ears. She sang on, of blood, and death, and love.

The women and children had gathered along the crest of the defile to watch the carnage below. Outlined against the sapphire sky like a flock of carrion crows, their black eyes flashed with delight as the end of the hunt unfolded in the deadly cleft at their feet.

The Mammoth Mother, her mighty feet pounding the soft, swampy earth on the floor of the small canyon, had stormed in first. Her ears were spread wide like fans, as she lifted her huge head and trumpeted again and again in fear and desperation. Behind her followed the rest of the herd: three full-grown females and half a dozen smaller females and young males. The women who watched their passage into the canyon felt the pounding thump of their broad foot pads as a low, thrumming vibration through the soil. They waved sticks and scrapers, heavy hand-axes, and stone skinning knives at the beasts as they lumbered past.

Now the hunters appeared at the mouth of the declivity, shaking their spears, dancing and shouting. The noise sent the maddened animals further into the narrow canyon, where they bunched together as the walls pressed in on them. The ground beneath, soft and mushy from ice melt seeping into the earth, began to slow them down. Their huge bodies slammed against each other and against the rocky walls that imprisoned them, until the entire herd was a thrashing, slashing mass of screaming beasts. In the extremity of their panic, they hacked at each other with razor-sharp tusks. The women shouted and laughed as the smell of blood began to rise from the conflagration below.

Now some of the men left the main band at the mouth of the canyon and scrambled quickly up to join the women, who moved out of their way. The sudden dispersal revealed several piles of small boulders, the result of the work the women and children had labored at for almost a week after Be-Dag and Ku-Yak had first gone out.

Grunting with excitement and effort, each hunter lifted a stone from the pile and staggered to the edge of the cleft. As one reached the lip he would pause while he hoisted the boulder overhead and then, with a long, triumphant howl, hurled the deadly projectile down into the heaving mass below. The mammoth herd, trapped by the walls and slowed by the swampy ground underfoot, had nowhere to flee to. Those few animals who managed to turn themselves end around, in an attempt to retreat the way they'd come, met the rest of the hunters and their terrible spears.

Crack!

The women shouted and cheered as an old female, her skull split wide, showing white bone and aqueous gray and red beneath, collapsed beneath the deathly rain. Her huge body completely blocked any further retreat toward the mouth of the canyon. Now the only way out was down, toward the river, and the People knew that was no escape at all.

The tiniest children scampered to the edge of the canyon, chattering with glee. Even as young as they were, they understood that the terrible slaughter meant food for them—huge piles of hot, steaming meat and bowls of fresh, warm blood. Their mothers watched them carefully, but didn't try to shield them from the sight. This was the life of the Mammoth People, intertwined inextricably with the lives and deaths of the mammoths whom they both worshiped and hunted. The children must know these truths in their bones if the People themselves were to survive.

The hunters in the canyon rushed upon the still heaving carcass of the old female and thrust their jagged stone spear points into her belly with terrible strength. Though wounded unto death, and with blood streaming from a dozen terrible rents in her flesh, she managed to thrust herself up, six-foot curved tusks slashing a swath before her. But then an especially brave hunter, Ko-Bak by name, shouted his battle cry and sank his long spear into her throat. He twisted the haft of his spear as he thrust, sending the stone head on a curving path upwards into her brain. It was the death stroke; her body convulsed in a dreadful shudder and then collapsed entirely. The marshy ground around her was slippery with her blood as the hunters, their noses full of the smell of blood and intestines and suddenly released animal dung, clambered over her corpse to continue their assault on the rest of the herd.

As the appalling massacre continued its inexorable way down the canyon, a kind of tenuous silence, a momentary pause, descended on the final resting place of the great old mammoth. Then came other sounds: the slip of rock, the scrape of wood, breath hard-drawn. The women and children descended into the canyon, sharply chipped hand-axes and butchering knives grasped tightly in eager hands. A moment later, as the Mammoth Mother led the rest of her band deeper into the canyon of death, the People began to strip the flesh from the first victim's bones. Even the children soon were covered with blood, and when one of the women, shouting triumphantly, reached deep into the mammoth's chest to withdraw her dripping heart and wave it overhead, everybody cheered.

Ga-Ya slumped forward. The sun seemed unbearably hot. Even her old nose could scent the smell of blood. The sounds of the hunt had receded, muffled by the walls of the canyon and the marshy decline toward the river. She sat like this for several moments, her head bowed, an unutterable sadness filling her heart. She had no illusions about the necessity of what her magic had accomplished. The People first must eat; above all else, the People must survive. Yet she felt a kinship with the doomed Mammoth Mother. Each of them led their tribes in their own ways, and each of them wanted the same thing. It was only by the twisting rope of fate woven by the Great Mother Herself that their two destinies were so intertwined.

"Aaieeee! Spear him! Spear him!"

The sudden, terrified shout jerked her from her reveries. Her eyes shot wide. She swiveled her head on her ancient, scrawny neck, momentarily confused. Then she saw it; Be-Dag and Ku-Yak and the mammoth they hunted, a single shouting, screaming mass less than ten yards from her post atop the Spirit Pole. As she watched, Ku-Yak raced along the wounded mammoth's side and hurled his spear wildly. The heavy point glanced off the thick hide of the mammoth, leaving a shallow, pulsing rent almost a foot long. The mammoth shrieked in pain, but slowed not at all. His maddened charge took him directly at Be-Dag, who danced awkwardly backward, trying to avoid the raking tusks and the flailing trunk of the dying beast.

"Be-Dag!" she called. "Get out of the way! Get back! It will die soon! Get away from it!"

But the young hunter, emboldened by the success of his friend's earlier attacks, was determined to score his own kill. Either he didn't hear her or he ignored her warnings, for he lunged forward a final time and tried for the fatal throat penetration. The young mammoth whipped his formidable head back and forth, perhaps not even able to see his attacker; but one of his youthful tusks, flailing without direction, touched Be-Dag's shoulder.

To Ga-Ya, from her excellent vantage point, it seemed that time momentarily slowed down, as it often did when she entered the Dreamtime. She blinked in wonder as, frame by frame, the tragedy unfolded.

The needle-pointed tusk sank through Be-Dag's caribou coat and penetrated the flesh beneath as if it were melted fat. The tusk tore a path down and across, eventually exiting near the center of Be-Dag's chest.

The young hunter bellowed in agony, hooked like a fish on the curving tusk. The young mammoth tossed his head up and back. The force of the movement thrust his tusk completely through Be-Dag's body until the side of it ripped its way out through his rib cage. The hunter's body went flying through the air, perhaps ten feet above the ground. Clearly visible to Ga-Ya, the great hole in Be-Dag's chest sprayed blood like a fountain. The mammoth trumpeted once again and lurched forward.

Ku-Yak cried out in anguish at the death of his

friend as he retrieved his thrown spear. Ga-Ya could see his contorted features as he surged forward a final time and plunged the long, heavy weapon between the ribs of the thrashing mammoth.

It was a lucky stroke. For once, the wounded beast's rib cage didn't deflect the spear point, which slid easily through skin and muscle and exposed white tendon to reach the soft, vital organs beneath.

The mammoth essayed a final cry that ended abruptly in mid-bellow, as the destruction of its heart sent a message of death to its tiny brain. Already dead on his feet, the young male lurched forward, spinning crazily, and collapsed against the base of the Spirit Pole.

Craaack!

Ga-Ya felt her seat wobble wildly, then begin to fall. Her last fragment of vision was of the heaving, bloody, mammoth carcass beneath, rising to meet her.

Then, darkness.

She had no name, at least none that she knew as such. If she thought of herself at all, it was simply as Mother, for most of those in her herd had sprung originally from her massive loins.

Still in her prime, less than fifty years old, she stood eleven feet tall at her shoulders, and topped this with a high, massive head and broad, curving tusks nearly six feet long. In order to support her great weight the soles of her feet were thick and wide, filled with elastic skin, fat, and extendable toes. In ordinary times, she was a very difficult beast to trap in marsh or swamp. These weren't ordinary times.

Suddenly, in her dim brain she felt a flash of movement, as if she had fallen from a high place, and then it seemed as if a dark mask had been ripped from her vision.

She raised her head and saw with freshly cleared eyes the terrible disaster that had befallen her herd. Off behind her left shoulder stretched a long, bloody line: the huge, ripped carcasses that had once been her family. A part of her didn't understand; such concepts as "death" and "dying" were not part of her limited instinctual equipment. Were they asleep? But they didn't move, and small, strange animals swarmed over them, hacking and chopping at their flesh.

A sudden lance of pain spun her around. She found movement hurtful—things stuck to her, ground together in her insides when she moved. Even her huge head ached, and a red stream flowed down through thick hair to cloud her limited vision.

The air was thick with foreign smells. The stench of blood and entrails was frightening enough, but over all this the high, thin stink of man wove a melody of terror. More than anything else this bizarre olfactory song drove her wild with fear.

She turned away from the ruin of her herd and plunged forward, her berserk charge channeled and driven by the slippery walls of the canyon. Her wide, padded feet still found good purchase on the soft ground though, and she finally emerged beyond the end of the gauntlet of boulders smashing down from above. Since she'd led the herd into the canyon she had mostly escaped the spear thrusts, and what few thrown weapons had penetrated her thick mat of fur and fat-laden skin had not mortally wounded her. As the Mammoth Mother emerged from the declivity and descended to the rock-walled river bank she was still a mighty engine of destruction.

Ko-Bak knew this as he led his band of hunters over the still steaming bodies of the dead mammoths to the mouth of the canyon. He approached cautiously, darting from one pile of jumbled boulders to the next, his sharp, black, button eyes never leaving the great bulk of the Mother ahead.

His experience told him the wounds she'd already suffered were nowhere near being fatal; if anything they'd only maddened her further, while sapping her awesome strength little if at all. Clearly, killing her would call for different techniques than those that had already been successful.

Quickly he summoned the rest of his small band to him, and explained what was necessary. The rest of the hunters, men in their prime years, none less than sixteen, the oldest no more than twenty-eight, nodded agreement.

Up to this point they had herded the mammoths forward with shouts and movement and the waving of their spears. In the closer confines of the canyon they had killed with short, heavy thrusts, darting close to already dying beasts to administer the coup de grace. Now they reached into their packs and withdrew strange instruments; shafts of carved and painted wood nearly three feet long, thick at one end, shaped into a shallow hook at the other. These tools had been a gift of the Great Mother, taken from the Dreamtime by Ga-Ya and passed on to the People. They were spear-throwers, and they vastly increased the ability of the People to strike from a distance with great force.

Ko-Bak sent one of the hunters back to salvage any unbroken spears from the slaughter further up the canyon. They would need every projectile to bring down the wounded mother, and even what they had might not be enough. Briefly, in the heat of the noon sun, he debated dispatching some of the women downriver a half mile to their camp for even more spears, but decided to chance the kill with what he had.

He took out his own thrower and slipped the butt of his spear into the concave hook designed to hold it securely. He folded the length of the thrower back down along the haft of the spear and grasped both tools in his right hand. He crawled forward and peered once again at the great Mammoth Mother below.

Trailing a stream of blood, the Mother lumbered forward to the water's edge. Her wide foot-pads left huge, shallow depressions in the mud, which rapidly filled with water. Ko-Bak shook his head. He'd hoped the ground below would be soft enough to snare her, but it wasn't to be. If the People were to feast on the Mother's flesh, they would have to kill her themselves.

Momentarily he wondered why Ga-Ya's magic was no longer befuddling the wounded beast, but then dismissed the thought. The old woman had done her job. She'd brought the Mother and her herd to the canyon. Now it was the task of the hunters to complete the work.

He slipped forward quietly, crouching over, trying to get as close as possible to the Mammoth Mother, who had drawn back from the swiftly rushing deep water and now turned to face the oncoming hunters.

Wind breathed down through the canyon, carrying the scent of the men to her in greater strength as they approached. Ko-Bak sighed. There was no way to get downwind of her. He could only pray to the Wind Spirits that the Mother wouldn't suddenly decide to charge back up the canyon, trampling him in her thundering wake.

He halted less than ten yards from her, partially hidden by a hump of rounded black boulders. He knew her eyesight was dim, and perhaps, in her panic, she'd be unable to distinguish him from the background before it was too late.

"Now!" he shouted suddenly. He stood fully upright, his feet planted wide, and brought his arm as far back as he could. Then he whipped the thrower forward. The extra length propelled his spear with much greater power than a simple cast; the long shaft whirred through the air and struck the Mother's side. This time the point didn't glance off. The deadly tip buried itself a full foot into the Mother's heaving flesh. A moment later the noon was full of spears and the sound of the Mother's death agony. Mighty as she was, even she couldn't withstand so many wounds. Finally her strength ebbed out, blood soaking the thick wool of her pelt and running along the ground in narrow, glittering streams. As she sank slowly to her knees, the water behind her swirled pink and frothy.

With a long groan she collapsed, her tusks still facing the hunters. Their warily approaching forms were the last things she saw before a dark curtain descended across her fading sight.

Her pain was gone. She never heard Ko-Bak's cry of conquest, nor did she feel his final thrust. The night claimed her, and in the night a door opened.

Welcome, the Great Mother said. *Welcome home, most loved of daughters. Welcome.*

The hunt was over.

Ga-Ya awoke to the sound of wailing. Her head was full of confusing sounds and pictures—Be-Dag whirling through the air in a cloud of blood; the young mammoth lurching in his death throes beneath her; Ku-Yak's cries of rage and anguish; the last sadness of the Mammoth Mother—so at first she didn't know if she was still in the Dreamtime or fully awake in the world.

She blinked her eyes in confusion and licked her lips. The movement brought sudden soft sounds: "Shhh, Mother, it's all right." Something cool and wet touched her dry lips, and she sucked greedily at the bit of water-soaked moss.

As her vision cleared she made out details: a shadowy face looming over her, the sparkle of sunlight, an over-arching wall of bluish rock.

She sighed and settled back, her wits about her once again. She was safe in her cave, then, in the cliff overlooking the river, about a half-mile down from the canyon of the hunt. With the faint movement came a long, rolling ache from every part of her body. Experimentally, she tried to raise her right arm. The effort brought further agony, and the voice once again: "Lie still, Mother."

She waited until the white, painful flashes had crept away from the corners of her eyes. Now the face above her became clear: It was the face of She-Ya, the young man whom she'd trained for almost two years to succeed her.

"She-Ya?" she whispered.

His hand stroked her brow. He smiled down on her fondly, his sun-browned features full of love and concern. "I told you I should have ridden the Spirit Pole, Mother."

She felt a small flash of irritation, then thrust it away. She had always ridden the Spirit Pole, but She-Ya was young and eager. His two years of training had brought him to the place all young ones eventually reached—where they reached out for things they thought they understood, but could not truly grasp.

Or was that the truth? She-Ya had Dreamed with her. He was young, but his power was great. In some things he'd already surpassed her—his knowledge of the Spirits that resided in plants, for instance. She'd taught him all she knew of them, but he'd gone even further. As he now demonstrated.

"Here," he said gently, "drink this."

He gentled his palm beneath the back of her head and lifted her up. She ignored the sudden lance of agony and concentrated on drinking from the hardened clay cup which he had placed at her lips. The dark brew inside was warm and bitter, but she got most of it down. After a short time a delicious, balmy feeling spread through her body, and the pain went away.

Now, relieved of her anguish—the brew seemed to soothe her thoughts as well—she began to take further notice of her surroundings. The rhythmic chanting from beyond the cave mouth continued. "Be-Dag?" she asked.

She-Ya nodded. Ga-Ya gathered her muscles and tried to sit up, but his hand on her chest held her unmoving.

"She-Ya," she said. "I will have to sing him to the Mother."

He shook his head. "I will sing him, Ga-Ya. Already the People have built the pyre and brought their gifts." He glanced down at her legs. "You were very lucky, Mother. The body of the young mammoth broke your fall, or the fall would have broken you." He chuckled at the little joke, then leaned back on his haunches, his dark eyes serious.

"As it was, your left leg broke like a twig. You won't be able to dance, not in time, maybe never again. I bound it up, and put poultices full of the Spirits on your bruises, but, Ga-Ya—Mother—you are very old."

She sighed. It was true. She *was* very old. Perhaps her momentary flash of irritation with She-Ya was nothing more than that: the reluctance of the old to let go of the strings of their life, to pass on what must be passed on.

She-Ya reached behind him, then rocked forward and placed two objects on her chest, within easy reach. "When you fell, they came for me right away. I had you brought back here, and I searched for the sacred charms." Now worry clouded his thin, youthful features. "I found the flute, and the rattle. But I didn't find the Stone."

"What?"

He shook his head. "It is gone, Mother. I even had the People cut up the body of the young mammoth into tiny pieces, so that we could move it and search beneath. We searched a full day, Mother. But we couldn't find it. It is gone."

The Mammoth Stone? Gone? But it was the heart of her magic!

Fear clutched at her heart. What could have become of it? If it was truly gone, there was only one thing that could have happened to it. It was the Key to the Door of Dreamtime. Perhaps the Great Mother herself had reclaimed the Key.

Hesitantly, She-Ya spoke. "I Dreamed last night," he said. "I searched for the Stone, and for a moment I thought I had found it. But it was in darkness, and I saw it only for an instant. When I reached for it, it ran away from me."

She-Ya's dream sent a thrill into her heart. "And the Great Mother? Did she speak to you?"

He shook his head. "No. But the Stone is gone. I'm sure of it."

Ga-Ya was sure of it, too. She could tell, from the expression on She-Ya's face, that the young man feared that the loss of the Stone meant evil for the People. But Ga-Ya thought otherwise. Recently she'd begun to dream of strange things—of her daughters to come, of the Secret and their roles in it. The disappearance of the Stone might mean danger—or it might be a signal to her. There was only one way to find out.

Her voice was husky with age as she spoke. "Bring me the tusk from the young mammoth. The tusk on the right."

He nodded, sensing her sudden purpose. "We have it," he said.

"Good. And my tools."

His eyes met hers. "A new Stone?" he whispered. He didn't try to hide the awe that filled his voice.

"Perhaps," she replied. "If my magics are still strong enough. If the Great Mother wills it."

He knew better than to offer his help in the making. The making of a Stone was for Ga-Ya only. He rose to his feet and gazed down on her fondly. "Right away," he said, smiling.

She peered up at him, the death chants for Be-Dag ringing in her ears. "Sing him well," she told her apprentice.

"Not as well as you, but yes. His song will be good."

After She-Ya had gone, Ga-Ya stared vacantly at the chipped, smoke-covered ceiling of her cave. Animals danced there, red and blue and orange; mammoth, bison, caribou.

She wondered if she was right and, further, if she still had the strength. Then a great peace overcame her, and she understood finally that it was out of her hands. Not her strength, but the strength of the Great Mother. And She had all the strength in the World. And the Dream.

"So be it," Ga-Ya whispered, and sank back, waiting.

Walking.

She had been here before, many times, but never had things seemed so sharp, so clear. In the distance loomed a mighty range of mountains, their flanks swathed in green, their needle peaks rising to spires of ice. Before her stretched the endless plain, a tundra of green and gold. Bright lakes sparked light that seemed to come from everywhere. The air itself held a soft, amber glow. Nameless music surrounded her.

After a time, she discerned movement in the distance. Figures drifted closer and closer, until she could make out details.

A great crowd of beasts, all treading over the sacred earth together. And in the front . . .

Her breath caught in her throat. Never before had she seen *this*!

There was a huge Mammoth Mother there, and a mighty cave lioness, a graceful wildebeest, a comical tumbling Mother Bear. But at the forefront was Another, and it was on Her that Ga-Ya riveted her astonished attention.

A young woman whose belly was swollen with impending birth. She trod before Her herd naked, Her hands outstretched, and as She walked, the golden air about Her swirled like the finest moss in the breezes of spring. Where Her footsteps rested, the grass sprang up greener in Her wake. Ga-Ya felt her own ancient limbs warm, her muscles loosen and stretch, as She approached.

Ga-Ya bowed her head. She was afraid to speak, to move, even to breathe.

"Daughter," came the voice, and it was soft, yet strong and filled with thunder, "do not fear Me, for I am your Mother, always and forever, and you have served Me well."

Tears flowed down Ga-Ya's seamed cheeks.

"Look upon Me and rejoice, for soon I will welcome you Home," the Great Mother whispered, and there came a lowing and mooing and grunting of agreement from the beasts gathered around Her.

Joy! Oh, she'd never known there could be such joy!

"Ah, Mother! I am weak, but I love You! Take me now!"

"No, beloved Daughter. Soon, but not yet. A final task remains, and you are the tool I have chosen to begin it."

Ga-Ya felt puzzlement. What good could she accomplish, old and withered as she was? But she said nothing, and was astonished when the Great Mother seemed to read her very thoughts.

"It is My strength, not yours," the Great Mother said. "And I see far and long. Nothing is beyond My power, and that power I give to you, to do what you must for Me."

Then Ga-Ya knew great bliss, and fell on her knees, but the Great Mother came forward and lifted her up, and at that blessed touch, for a moment Ga-Ya was healed and made wholly new and young again.

"You shall begin a mighty line of women," the Mother said, "that will stretch down into the mists of time. And these daughters of yours, who will bear My Mark, the eyes of emerald and sapphire, shall also receive the Token of My powers, to fight My battles against My Ancient Enemy of old, He of Fire and Snakes.

"But they must freely choose, and the choice will be terrible, for my Power is not given lightly, and the Power of My Enemy is dreadful. Yet I will give them a Sign and a Token, that they may know Me."

Ga-Ya shivered in terror at the sound of Her voice, for it had become like hardened metal, and was full of the groan of ice and the howl of the winter winds.

"Look at Me, Daughter!" the Great Mother commanded, and Ga-Ya felt herself drawn up again. She gazed full upon her Mother's face, which blazed like the sun, and into its center—Her eyes, twin pools of emerald and sapphire—whence came the brightest light.

"Look and see!" commanded the Great Mother.

In that moment Ga-Ya lifted her eyes and understood many things.

Never had she felt such power!

"Command me, Mother, I am yours!"

"Hear My Promise!" the Great Mother thundered.

"My People shall journey away from Me, and know great need and face the ultimate danger. Yet even as they deny Me, I will be there. For in their greatest danger I will send the One who bears My Mark to make a choice, whether to wield the Token of My Power, or not.

"Hear Me, Daughter! None may know the full measure of My Power but She Who Will Be Waited For, and none may defeat My Ancient Enemy, He of Fire and Snakes, but She who bears My Mark. That is My Promise, that I shall never forsake My People."

"Ah, Mother! Tell me what you wish of me!"

In her anguish Ga-Ya thrashed back and forth, her eyes squeezed shut. But there was no further command. Yet even so, she felt herself filled with a flood of wordless knowledge, and gasped in awe at the intricacy of the Promise and its fulfillment.

When she opened her eyes the crowd of beasts had retreated, and with them, veiled now in the golden stillness, their Mother, the Mother of All.

A Promise, a Gift, an Ancient Enemy. Yes, she would do the will of Her who demanded it, without question, as fully as she could. And in the future . . . ?

But she knew her future then, and felt a pang of sadness that she must leave this place of Light for a time, to journey into the darkness of the Outer World.

Yet it was commanded, and she bowed her head. The Great Mother and Her cohorts had vanished into the mists, and only the mountains, topless and eternal, stood guard over the plain and the tiny woman who trembled there, so alone.

"I obey," Ga-Ya whispered. "I obey. . . ."

It took her nearly two turnings of the moon, but finally the carving was finished. She set down the

burin stone, carefully chipped, with which she'd
scraped the last traces of roughness from the finished sculpture. In the blinding glare of the Great
Light—high summer here came short, but sharp as
the eye of a bird—she squinted at her creation.

The bone, taken from the tusk of the young mammoth that had nearly killed her, made admirable
carving material. She'd worked and cut and smoothed
it, shaping each curve, each line, with painstaking
precision. The tusk, originally bow-shaped, was
now straight. Two small replicas of the great beast
faced away from each other, joined in the middle by
a narrow bridge of bone. Each tiny mammoth was
almost identical to the other; the bone-connector,
less than an inch wide, was so thin that when she
held one end of the carving and shook it up and
down, the other end vibrated like a leaf in the wind.

She nodded with satisfaction. It was the best work
she'd ever done, and she knew it would be her last.
The cold breeze of death blew in the heart of her
bones; the mammoth carvings, full of every potent
magic she'd ever known, would be her last gift to
the People of the Mammoth.

She smiled, a toothless expression of immeasur-
able warmth and love. The bone felt hot in her hand.
She glanced toward the gray line of horizon, nodded
at the blue and the Great Light, then brought the
amazingly sophisticated sculpture down sharply across
her knee. With a soft crack, the two carven beasts
divided precisely where she'd planned. Her skill had
been sufficient.

"One for me," she whispered. "And one for my
daughters, all my daughters."

She was thirty-six, and dying of old age.

Her future was past, yet the future stretched without end, a thin silver line she sometimes felt she
could play like an instrument.

Time had no meaning. Yet it meant everything.

She took the left-hand mammoth, wrapped it carefully in a soft bit of skin. The other she took into her hand, savoring the feel of it.

"For my daughter," she breathed a final time, and forced herself creakily to her feet. Her muscles cried out against the strain, but she was content. All her magic had gone into this final magnificent piece of carving. Some magic she would keep; the rest already bequeathed. Dimly, in the eye of her mind, she could see her daughter to come. She didn't understand her, but did not expect to; that her daughter would exist was enough.

Two stones. One to keep, one to pass on.

The universe balanced on it. She didn't understand, but that frightened her not at all. Understanding wasn't necessary, only acceptance.

She had accepted her burdens all her life. So would her daughter to come.

She smiled one more time as she limped toward the People. Her People. They called themselves the People of the Mammoth. She knew better.

They were the People of the Mother, but they wouldn't know that. Not yet.

Not for twenty-five centuries.

Strange. Not that it *wasn't* strange, but that she didn't find it strange at all. Nor would her daughter.

The sun caught her eyes, reflected crazily from green and blue, the colors of her gaze that made her what she was.

She held a mammoth in each gnarled, knowledgable hand.

"I love you," she whispered, as she stepped toward the grave. Only time awaited, but that wasn't a problem either.

Time.

She had all of that in the world.

It would be enough.

*   *   *

She-Ya's eyes widened as he examined the carvings. He held both of them, wrapped in soft hide, so that his male fingers did not touch their smooth surfaces. She'd already warned him about that.

"No man may touch the Mammoth Stones, lest all the magic go out of them, and the People wander in darkness," she'd said. It wasn't exactly a curse, more like a warning, but he sensed the truth of it and was careful.

He looked down at her. He'd been right; after her injuries, her leg had never healed fully, and Ga-Ya had never walked properly again. Now he thought she was failing. It was as if all her Spirit, all her magic, had gone into the making of these two small carvings.

Her eyes were slits, a faint line of blue showing from one, a clear, aqueous green from the other. Every time he gazed on her eyes he was filled anew with wonder. None of the People had ever had eyes like that. It was a mark of the Great Mother herself, which she gave to her chosen ones.

He thought she was dozing, as she often did now, sometimes in the middle of her conversations with him. During the Making they had talked long and often, words pouring from her mouth in an inexhaustible flow, as if she felt an urgency she couldn't reveal, and was determined to pass on everything, no matter how small, that he would need or she could give.

She seemed to be sleeping now. Her chest rose and fell faintly, but with regularity. Carefully he placed both carvings on her chest, where her fingers would find them easily when she awoke. Soon enough she would let go of the life she'd grasped so fiercely and, understanding this, he found himself reluctant to see her return to the Great Mother.

All his life he'd wanted her magics, but now, finally, he understood the responsibility that went with the magic. He was no longer himself alone, but of the People and the Mother, belonging wholly to them. The Secret—that a Great Journey would soon begin, sending the People into far places—was his as well as hers. He was uncertain exactly what role the Mammoth Stones would play in all this, but his instructions were explicit: The Stone—for on the Journey, there would be only one—could not be touched by man. Only a daughter of the Great Mother herself, marked with her signs—one blue eye, one green—could take up the Mammoth Stone and use its full power. But the mere presence of the Stone, carefully guarded and protected in the heart of the People, would be sufficient to guide them on the Journey.

She-Ya had dreamed this with Ga-Ya, and knew it to be true. But although he had shared the Dream with her, he hadn't shared it fully. She had clearly seen through the mists of time, where he'd had only a dim understanding of the millennia involved. When he thought of a long journeying, he thought in terms of the turnings of the Moon. The concept of "centuries" meant nothing at all to him.

As he gazed down on her, all of this departed from his thoughts. All that remained was his love for her. Softly he reached down and smoothed her ancient brow.

"Mother," he whispered.

Her eyes shot wide. Startled, he withdrew his fingertips. Her gaze burned him, but when he thought about it later, he didn't think it was him she had seen.

Like tiny fires, her gaze burned in her face. Suddenly her back arched, and just as suddenly she relaxed, like a small animal with its bones suddenly broken.

He knew what it was he watched, and a sadness as black as the night filled him.

Her lips moved, and he leaned close. "Mother . . ." she whispered. It seemed for a moment that she tried to say something else, but no more sounds came from her lips.

After a while he straightened. He stared down at her face, somehow softer, younger in death. Her eyes were still wide open, but the light had gone out of them. Carefully he reached forward and smoothed the ancient skin of her eyelids down, hiding the serene emptiness beneath.

He chanted softly to himself for a few minutes, then rose and walked out of the cave.

It would be a great Song.

Chapter Two

Northeastern United States: 17,997 B.C.

The great, booming noise shook the cold air as it had for thousands of years, and would for many thousands more. Skin glanced uneasily toward the north. He had grown up with that low, thunderous roar, had even seen the source of it, but still it frightened him. He raised one hand and the tribe, less than a hundred men, women, and children strung out behind him in a rough forage line, halted.

Old Magic, walking just behind Skin, came forward, his nut-brown face wrinkled with puzzlement. "Why do you stop?" he said. The furry ruff that surrounded his face whipped wildly in the wind, which blew also from the north and carried the booming sounds with it.

Skin turned and faced the older man. "Can't you smell it?" he asked.

Old Magic turned away, squinting his eyes against the wind. With slow ceremony he faced north, then east, where the Great Light was born every morning, then south and, finally, west. As he made the arc his broad, flat nose twitched. He ran his tongue over his lips, nodded thoughtfully to himself, then pointed directly ahead. "Water," he said. "There."

A low murmur of joy rose behind him. The tribe

31

had traveled for many lights and darks without finding a good source to replenish the rude skin bags they carried. Water meant more than merely assuaging their thirst, however. The spoor of mammoth and mastodon, bison and caribou had become unmistakable; a water smell this strong meant a creek or a large spring, a place where the great animals they hunted might gather.

To Skin, the possibility of water and meat meant even more. Perhaps, if the People of the Mammoth were very lucky, they would find a site where they could settle for a time. He wanted the time. His wife, Tree, was pregnant again. She'd dropped her last two, both boys, dead. Skin felt the first whispers of age in his bones. He wanted a living son, before it was too late.

Hope widened his black eyes as he brought his arm down in a forward motion. The People shouldered packs and travois poles and lurched ahead. Even the youngest could smell the misty scent in the air.

Tree jogged forward from her place with the rest of the women and younger children, until she was at Skin's side. A wordless question filled her shoe-button eyes.

"Maybe," Skin told her. "We'll see."

This trek had begun ten hand-spans of lights before, when the People had left the place of sand after its nearly barren spring had suddenly disappeared. With the vanishing of the water the game had departed as well; the women had been unable to snare the tiny, rodent-like rabbits and ground squirrels which nested beneath the tight-rooted tundra grass, nor had the male hunters found any trace of bison, mammoth, or the great-horned caribou which had once frequented the sparkling rivulet. The hardship-toughened knowledge of the people had told them it was time to move. When Old Magic had disappeared with the sacred bone for three days and then returned, they knew it would be soon.

The tribal structure of the People was very loose: there was no chief as such, not even Old Magic, with all his knowledge of the ways of the Spirits of earth and sky and fire. Instead, the one who was most competent to guide them in any task did so; Skin had led them successfully through arduous treks in the past. He had been the natural choice to do so again. Now, as the twenty-three-year-old middle-aged man (by *homo sapiens sapiens* standards of the time) trotted warily forward at the point of his people, he felt a certain diffuse satisfaction. His nose was full of the scent of water, and he fancied he could hear the soft chuckle of glittering liquid over round stone, even beneath the continuous rumble from the north. Once again his lore had contributed to the preservation of the People. Soon it would be time to lay down his responsibility and let another lead. Perhaps Spear, the best of their hunters, or Stone, who chipped the precious blades of flint and chalcedony which tipped the weapons of the tribe. Even Fire, who knew the secret ways of his namesake, would be a better leader for the settled tribe than Skin, who found nothing odd in so admitting. Soon Skin could settle into his more accustomed role of tracker and hunter, lie by the fire and tell stories, and wait for the arrival of his son.

Soon, he prayed silently, his vision questing out across the long, slow-rolling rise of short brown grass across which they marched. His nose was better than his eyesight here. He could smell the water before he saw it. It was one of the reasons he led the treks: There was no more precious skill than the water-sense.

As the Tribe approached the top of the long, surging hump in the endless brown tundra, Skin clearly heard the sound of water. It was no longer his imagination. The low, gurgling rill of it filled him with hope; a large spring, certainly, perhaps even a stream. He smiled to himself, an expression of happiness that revealed wide, thick, white incisors—the "shovel-shaped" teeth which marked as his recent ancestors the Dyuktai people of the Siberian steppes and the long, cold plains of Beringia, the continental land bridge.

He loped forward, eager to see the source of the water sounds, and so was almost three hundred yards in advance of the rest of the tribe when he finally crested the low rise and crashed to a halt, an expression of incredulous joy filling his flat-faced features.

His heart thudded in his chest. He could only stand and stare; the rumble from the north, the ever-present wind, even the People themselves, were momentarily forgotten.

"O Water Spirits!" he breathed softly to his personal divinities, a prayer of heartfelt gratitude. The rise subsided before him, brown and sere, but less than two hundred yards ahead the dry lands ended. Beyond, the earth fell away in a sharp drop at least a hundred yards deep, a broad cliff heading a wide valley running from the north to the south. The sharp projection of the cliff itself hid the water from him, but he knew a stream, at least, cut near the bottom of the overhang. Yet that knowledge wasn't what filled him with so much wonder—he'd seen cliffs and streams before. What shocked him to breathless silence was the contents of the valley itself.

Trees. But such trees as he'd never known before. He was a child of the tundra, accustomed to the sounds of glacial ice grinding the land. The roar of unceasing wind, and endless vistas of the low brown grass that fed the mammoth and bison were

all he'd ever known. Now he stood above an emerald island, a small sea of green-leafed oak, hickory
and walnut. He had no idea what these strange,
towering things might be, but they were green;
greener even than the tundra grasses in the spring,
when for a short time tiny blue and lavender flowers
made the wintry plains beautiful.

Old Magic glided to his shoulder and stood silent
for a long moment. Skin could hear him inhaling
and exhaling, the sound a slow, liquid rasp in the
old man's chest. He turned to face the Shaman and
said, "What is it? What are those things? They look
like trees, but I've never seen trees like that before."

Old Magic rubbed his chin, his eyes squinted in
concentration. He observed the valley as if it were
some strange animal. At last he shook his head.
"They are trees," he announced. He didn't seem
happy with his judgment.

Skin felt a momentary flash of irritation. Old
Magic wielded the power of the Spirits, but sometimes, particularly as he grew older, he spoke the
obvious, the plain truth that any man could see, as
if it were mystery.

"Yes," Skin said. "Trees. But they are new, different. What of their Spirits? Do their Spirits talk to
you, Shaman? Do they welcome the People?"

Old Magic answered with what was, for him, surprising speed. But first he spun a half-turn to face
Skin. His dark eyes glowed in the high light of
noon, and Skin thought the old man looked younger
than he had in years. He grinned, a gaping, crack-
toothed expression, and said, "You hurry too much,
Skin. We will camp here. When I am done, I will
tell you."

"What about the water?"

"I don't know," Old Magic said. "I will listen to
the Spirits."

Skin felt a thrill of happiness. "You can hear these Spirits?"

Old Magic grinned knowingly. "Of course," he said. "I am the Shaman."

Skin relaxed. Of course. The faint hint of doubt he had felt earlier floated away. A touch of warmth, of sun, caressed his back, even through the carefully stitched furs he wore. Overhead the sky stretched endlessly, a blue bowl. It was no longer his responsibility. He nodded.

"Of course," Skin said.

Old Magic turned away. Already the young man, Ghost, whom he had been training for many turns of the moon, was walking toward him, bearing the sacred bone and the pack with other implements of their trade. He tossed a thin smile in Skin's direction, then ignored him completely. Skin didn't care. He trudged back to the women and put his right arm over Tree's bulky shoulder.

The woman leaned her head against him and said, "We have walked a long way. Are we home yet?"

Skin nodded. "I think so," he said. He looked past her to the green carpet and the strange Spirits. Who knew what welcome awaited the People here? But Old Magic could speak to these Spirits. He said it, and if it was so, then all would be well.

As well as it ever could be. The sound of water spun loud in his ears. He squeezed Tree's warm brown shoulder, and glanced down at the prominent bulge of her belly.

Fifty miles to the north, the mile-high wall of the Laurentide ice shield moved forward one and one half inches. Thunder filled the crystal air. Skin's black eyes flickered.

"I hope so," he said.

Old Magic settled into his tent—a rounded affair of caribou hides stretched across a wooden frame, reinforced here and there with carefully selected reindeer horn. Since he intended to pause here only for a short time, he and Ghost had not dug into the earth to seat the tent more permanently.

Now he sat in the round, flapped doorway and gazed into the fire that danced in a small hearth before him. His gaze was troubled. He'd sent Ghost out earlier, to approach the cliff top which overlooked the strange new land below. Ghost, true to his name, seemed to possess a sharp affinity for the ghostly beings who dwelt in the places of earth, fire, water, and sky. Old Magic didn't begrudge him his talent, although in other ways Ghost was still callow, and not truly wise in the more mundane things of the Mammoth People. He disdained the hunters, for instance, and even Stone, who made the blades by which the People survived. He seemed to consider these things beneath him, as if he were, by concourse with the Spirits, somehow more exalted than they.

It was, Old Magic knew, a dangerous but seductive delusion. He himself, in his youth, had fallen under its tantalizing thrall—but the Shaman who had trained him had eventually shown him the true way, where the Spirits and the People worked in tandem, each in his own way, for the glory of the other.

But Ghost had returned with tales of jumbled whispering, of bizarre visions, of strange new Spirits. Old Magic didn't doubt the reports his apprentice had brought, but he didn't know what to make of them, either.

He was, now that he fully considered the situation, in a quandary. The People looked to him for instructions from the Spirits, and he had no answers for them. When he had first gazed upon the waving sea of green beyond the cliff, he'd felt only puzzlement. The exotic trees, the bright green colors, even the silvery-white clouds he'd glimpsed in the distance were like nothing he'd seen before. Moreover, the mere presence of all this in the middle of the long, brown tundra shocked him more than he cared to admit.

In the long memory of the People, much of which he carried within himself in songs and stories, there were hints that the People had faced other such disturbing events—many of the tales of heroism he knew dealt with the methods the People had developed to deal with such things. Stories of the Great Ice Canyon, and the mighty hunters who had succored the People in their time of need came to mind, as did other, more secret accounts of the doings of his own ancestors, the shamans who stretched in unbroken line back to the beginning, to the Mother of the People Herself.

He shook himself and bundled his furs closer against the wind, which had picked up strength with the setting of the sun. Sharp, vagrant breezes whirled around his tent and whipped the small fire into sudden bursts of sound; coals popped and sticks snapped, sending up small clouds of sparks that reminded him somewhat of things he saw in dreams.

Which was exactly what he needed now, he decided. Although full entrance into the Dreamtime was barred to him, a male, he was still given the power to Dream. Sometimes he found what he sought there, sometimes not. But, as he considered the awesome decision he must soon make, he felt the call once again. Much as he feared to do it, he must take the ultimate step, and carry the Sacred Stone into the new place. If he could not decipher the secrets of these new, untrustworthy spirits, perhaps the Great Mother Herself would do so.

He rocked forward on his haunches, his fur-clad feet tucked neatly under him, and stared deep into the fire. A chant rose unbidden to his lips; "O Mother," he sang softly, "O Great Mother, hear me."

He repeated this over and over in tuneless rhythm, the beat of his words comforting him. Overhead the stars burned down in their millions; faint, silvery shadows betrayed the slow rising of the moon.

It was a time of magic; both his own and that of the new place, the Great Mother Herself. He could feel it all around him, like a vaguely glowing fog. Finally, as his chant ran down and nothing remained but the sounds of thunder from the north, the pop and sizzle of his fire, and the moan of the wind, he felt something else.

It came from behind him, a subtle tugging sensation, as if something were drawing him inward and outward at the same time. His face split into a slow smile. He knew the source of the summoning. Gradually, taking care not to burden his old sinews more than necessary, he rose to his knees, then squatted and hunkered his way back into the tent.

The calling was stronger there. He thought he could almost see the light of it, enwrapped in its fur and hidden in the carved box which sheltered it.

The Mammoth Stone.

So it wouldn't be his decision, after all.

Thank the Great Mother! She watched over Her People still.

Skin said to Tree, "Put the windbreak there." They stood just above a low hollow in the tundra, a depression perhaps two feet deep. About ten feet away, Stone gave similar directions to his wife, Grass.

Tree moved slowly, burdened by the heavy weight of her belly; after a moment, Skin grunted and stepped in to help. This was to be a temporary camp, only for as long as it took Old Magic to determine whether the People would enter the strange Green Valley. Skin had no idea how long it would take for Old Magic to make up his mind; the Spirits moved at their own pace.

The packs supported on travois poles that the women had dragged across the tundra lay scattered and partly open. Only Old Magic, aided by Spirit, had set up his entire round house—but Skin had expected that. The Spirits, it was known, were best dealt with in secrecy, where they could converse in private with the Shaman. The rest of the People saw no reason to set up an entire semi-permanent camp.

Skin reached into his own packs and withdrew several long, hardened wooden sticks. While he did this, Tree, panting with effort, gouged out several small holes in the barely thawed tundra earth; five holes, each spaced about a foot from the other. When she had finished, she plopped back on her haunches and blew a long strand of black hair away from her sweat-shiny features. "There," she said, and pointed at the holes. "Deep enough, I think."

Skin nodded and carried one of the wooden poles forward. He checked the ground, then licked his forefinger and raised it above his head. The side that turned cold first showed the direction from which the wind came. He had checked repeatedly, and the direction had not changed. Still from the north, although as the day grew warmer the strength of the wind grew weaker.

Satisfied, he slipped the thick end of the pole into the hole made for it. The fit was almost tight, but before he walked away to fetch another pole Tree grunted and leaned forward, to pack loose dirt around the wooden butt to hold it firmly.

The two of them kept at it until a sturdy line of five poles extended in a skeleton wall parallel to the force of the wind. When they'd finished, Skin removed several roughly cured skins from the pack.

The curing process had left the hides soft enough to fold, but still tough and stiff enough for her purposes. With long, thin strips of braided skin, she fastened the hides to the stick framework. Then she tied heavier skin ropes, strengthened with long lengths of braided mammoth hair, to the top of the newly built windbreak, and pulled it down in a shallow curve. She tied the other end of the guide ropes to stakes Skin had pounded into the dirt. Once the shelter was built, Skin set off for an outcropping of crumbly brown rock beneath a stand of wind-stunted shrubs; he sought two necessary things: stone and wood. The first for a hearth, and the second for something to burn in it.

When he returned with his first load, Tree had finished unrolling the jumble of soft, carefully cured bison pelts that they used for bedding. He nodded his satisfaction as he laid stones in a small circle before the windbreak.

"I'll have wood in a little while," he said. Then he looked at her hard. "Are you all right?"

Tree nodded. "It will be very soon, though," she said. "Your son moves like a hunter. He kicks hard." She smiled. "But very soon."

Skin heard an undercurrent of worry in her voice. Something was wrong, but she wouldn't tell him what it was. He wasn't surprised. The secrets of the birth time were the province of women, and the Great Mother herself. No man would be allowed to witness the sacred event, lest the birth be soiled by male eyes prying into the secret magics of the Mother. He hoped everything would be all right.

He gazed fondly at his wife. Tree had seated himself on the furs and loosened the ties which held her coat closed, so that her milk-swollen breasts, slick with sweat, spilled partially forth. He thought her beautiful, and for a moment his penis twitched partially erect beneath his own clothing. She read the thought in his eyes and shook her head. He could have taken her anyway, and in other times might have, but a curious thought had grown in his skull after the deaths of his earlier sons. Could the Spirits have been offended by such things? He wasn't sure, but this time, he had followed her wishes in the matter. He hadn't filled her with his seed in almost two turnings of the moon, after the time she'd tried to push him away in the darkness of their bed and said, "No, Skin. It hurts."

The wave of lust washed away as abruptly as it had come. The birth of his son was far more important than satisfying his momentary desire. "You sit," he told her kindly. "I'll fetch the wood."

Three days later, his worries would intensify.

Old Magic had gone alone, much to Ghost's displeasure. He'd carried only a few furs for bedding, some dried meat, a small pack containing the implements he thought he might need—and, of course, the Mammoth Stone, securely bundled in its wrappings.

What Old Magic did not tell Ghost, because he couldn't tell him, was that he was afraid. In all his long life—and it was a very long life; he was almost fifty—he had never faced a challenge such as this before. The Spirits with whom he'd spoken before had been much the same: Spirits of grass and trees, of ice, of mammoth and bison and steppe lion and wolf. All familiar Spirits. Now he was faced with something entirely new—and as he stood on the lip of the broad cliff over the valley, searching for a way down, his knees shook and his heart pounded. When finally, after walking several hundred yards to the west, he found a narrow cleft in the overhang and placed his right foot on the jagged, rocky path down, it was perhaps the bravest thing he'd ever done.

He slipped and scrambled down the face of the cliff, almost falling twice, certain that the strange Spirits that must dwell in this valley would destroy him before he ever reached the floor of their domain.

Yet several minutes later, when he'd reached the crumbled rock at the bottom, nothing happened. He stood tense and silent, waiting, but still nothing occurred. Finally, his breath whooshed out of him in a great sigh of relief. If the Spirits here were hostile, they hadn't shown it yet. *On the other hand*, he thought as he turned slowly around, trying to get his bearings, *the Spirits haven't shown anything*. He had no reason, other than his own current survival, to think they were friendly, either. Perhaps it was some kind of Spirit joke—the Spirits did show humor, sometimes in a manner as grisly as it was funny.

At last, as his old heart quieted and the strength began to return to his quaking legs, he began to take full note of his surroundings. Part of the secret of magic, he knew, was simply in observation; a Shaman was trained, and then all through his life trained himself, to see *more*. The first thing he noticed was the absence of wind. He blinked. Yes, the wind was gone. He could still hear its long, sighing moan, but down here, a hundred feet beneath the chilly tundra upland and shielded by the tall cliff overhang, the air was still. And warm.

Warm! For a moment he was puzzled. Then he stepped back and placed the palm of his hand on the rocky face of the cliff itself. The dark stone there was almost too hot for him to touch. He understood immediately. With no air movement to cool it, and facing south against the path of the Great Light, the rock soaked up heat like a sponge. He knew that even after dark, the cliff would shed heat like an animal shaking off water. He glanced up.

Even better. The rocky overhang of the cliff top

loomed far out over him. He made a quick estimate and guessed that perhaps twenty feet of ground beneath was so protected. It would be an ideal camp for the People, better than any he'd ever seen.

If the Spirits permitted them to camp here.

Finally he turned his attention out, away from the cliff, and stared down into the valley itself.

He stood on a broad ledge, which ended approximately thirty feet ahead. The sound of running water burbled loudly and drew him forward. Carefully he made his way across the rocky surface, stepping around clumps of unfamiliar, bright green shrubs which grew from cracks in the stone, until finally he stood just above the sound of the water. He drew in his breath sharply and took the final stride.

"Ohhh . . ." he whispered.

The ledge ended as if cut with a knife. It dropped, perfectly perpendicular, to a scene of great beauty less than six feet below. Off to his right, a tracery of springs bubbled directly from the rock of the low decline. The small streams wove rapidly together and fell perhaps another three feet into a broad, clear pool, which itself overflowed at its far end, to his left, in a briskly running stream. Without thinking about it, he knew that these springs would never run dry, nor would the pool freeze over in winter. Small, darting shapes glittered beneath the faintly roiled surface of the tiny pond; his thirst for knowledge made him wish to stop here and net them out, simply to look at them and see how they were made.

Again, almost automatically, his eyes picked out another wonderful feature: On the far side of the pool, the soft earth was muddy and without grass. He picked out the spoor of mammoth, of bison, and even—fearsomely—of lion. The trail paralleled the far side of the stream and eventually disappeared to the east.

Warmth, shelter, water, food!

Never had the People found any spot so perfectly suited to their survival. A sudden thought struck him; he spun slowly around one more time, searching for particular signs. Once he paused and stared long and hard, then shook his head. Those bones were old, and partially crushed by rock-fall.

Finally he breathed another sigh of relief. Nothing he could see betrayed the presence of other hunters or other tribes. Unless he found something to tell him otherwise, it looked as if the People had found this place first. It wasn't a surprising thought. He himself had seen another tribe only once, and that in his earliest youth, long miles and years ago. None but himself still lived who remembered it. All the rest of the People had traveled in the silence of the steppe. He knew the younger ones laughed at the stories of Others, and even the adults perhaps thought of those tales as half-myth, half-dream. He knew better, and was glad to find no evidence of competition.

Now he lifted his eyes to gaze across the stream to the land beyond. The trampled mud gave way to grass so green it made his eyes hurt, a broad swale that dropped slowly to the dark emerald silence of the strange trees. Trees they were, no doubt about it, but unlike any he'd ever seen. Their trunks, unlike the gnarled, thin-needled pines he'd known before, were thick and deeply wrinkled. The leaves— if that's what they were—hung rich and heavy, and broad as the span of a man's hand. And the trees were tall!

He tilted his head back until he could see the tops of them. From the cliff heights they had seemed like great green clouds, filling the valley like a bowl.

Down here, he saw for the first time what giants they truly were.

What Spirits these new trees must possess!

The thought brought him suddenly back to his mission. It was the Spirits of these trees, as well as the other new Spirits which lived here, that he must meet and speak with. Until he determined whether the new Spirits would welcome the People, he could not give them passage into what appeared, at first, to be a paradise.

For that was precisely what the valley was: a place of the Dream on earth, a realm of legend. It was, in fact, almost what the Secret—

He shook his head again. Too soon even to think of *that*. Even Ghost knew nothing of the Secret, though Old Magic judged the time was soon coming when he'd have to know.

I'm growing old, he thought. *Time runs out. But there must be a final sign, before—*

Again he thrust the thought away, though his heart thrilled with the possibilities.

First things first. He adjusted his pack and headed west, to bypass the springs and thus come down, the first of his People, to the floor of the Green Valley, and all that might await them there.

If, of course, the Spirits allowed it.

Yet even strange spirits, he consoled himself, must bow to the Great Mother and her will.

He entered the woods, pausing only to run his palm across the mossy corrugated surfaces of the trunks. But nothing spoke to him then, and so, still fearful but filled with growing hope, he continued into the stillness of oak and hickory.

From atop the cliff he had noticed something far ahead he wanted to look into. If the Spirits were anywhere, they would be in that place.

*   *   *

"Aieeeeee!"

Old Berry had gone to sleep thanking the Great Mother for her many blessings. At forty years of age, she was the oldest of the women of the People. In her knowledge of the lore of grass and rodent, of cooking and the ways of plants, she was nearly the equal of Old Magic himself. In fact, the old Shaman spoke with her often—they shared much in common, not the least aching muscles and fragile bones.

She'd returned three husbands to the Great Mother, and nine children. Even so, six of the People had come from her belly and one, Skin, was about to present her with a grandchild. Or so she hoped. But the sudden, anguished shriek which awoke her in the dark hour before dawn filled her with fear. She knew what it portended. Almost without thought she sprang from her bed in the women's shelter and began to bark orders to the young, unmarried women whose shadowy, sleeping forms surrounded her own bed.

"Get up! Awake! Get out of *bed*, you lazy girls."

Grumbling, the forms began to move. Old Berry paid no more attention to them. In the dark her hands found the pack she needed. She'd already prepared it in anticipation of what would come. Now it took her only a moment to hoist it to her shoulder.

She paused to kick one still unmoving shape. "Blossom! Get up. Help the others with the screens!"

Without looking back she rushed out of the shelter, her feet turning toward Skin's windbreak two small camps down.

"Aieeeee!"

Tree's terrible cry sent Skin rolling out of his furs, hand scrabbling for his spear. It took him several groggy seconds to realize the danger: not animals, not fire, but something he'd feared and hoped for. The time of birth had come!

He rolled back and stared at his wife. Another wrenching shriek came from her lips and he flinched away. She arched her back suddenly, high, like the bent branches which held a completed house. *Too* high! Her other births, even with their heartbreaking results, had never been like this.

Trembling, he touched her forehead. Hot! Dry as burning sand, too. Something was very wrong. And he knew he was as helpless as all men were, when the Great Mother began to work her will.

He scrambled out of his bed and lurched to his feet. He ran from the shelter, his path uncertain in the dark, until something slammed into him.

"Get out of the way!"

"Berry! Tree . . . I don't know. . . . She screams. . . ."

Old Berry shoved him sharply aside. In this matter she was supreme. No man could stand in her way.

"Move!" she snarled. "Go stay with the other men!" Then her voice softened. "Try not to worry, my son."

Wordlessly Skin nodded at his mother, then stood aside to let her pass. She spoke no more, merely brushed past him as if he no longer existed.

"*Aaaaaghhhhaaa!*"

His blood felt like ice in his veins as he staggered toward another tent. Already Stone was up, shouting for Fire to kindle a blaze. Skin joined him. Stone, a few years old, patted him gently on the shoulder. Neither man said anything.

It was in the hands of the Great Mother now.

Chapter Three

The Green Valley, Northeastern United States: 17,997 B.C.

"*Push!*" Old Berry commanded harshly, her lips almost touching Tree's ear. "*You have to push!*"

Tree, momentarily lucid, her face running with sweat, panted like a dog. "So hard . . ." she managed.

Old Berry took a bit of dry moss and swabbed at the tortured woman's forehead and at her cheeks, where thin rivulets of blood made a tracery down from the corners of her mouth. She had chewed her lips to gory meat.

The child was coming with bitter difficulty. Old Berry glanced across Tree's heaving chest at Leaf, who stared back with knowing sadness. The two women, oldest of the People, had seen such things before. Almost always, the result was death; either for the mother, the child, or both.

The rest of the women crowded round, shielding Tree from the sharp dawn winds which blew across the steppe from the north. Far away the Ice Wall grumbled ominously, a forbidding undertone to the hunting chant the men sang around their own fire.

Old Berry's lips curled with contempt. *Men!* She knew what was on their minds. They sang to hide

49

their fear. And as they sang, their eyes might slide in furtive glances toward the hide screens that shielded the women from them. *They are right to be afraid*, she thought. Hunters they might be, mighty trackers, spear-throwers—but the great mysteries of birth and death belonged to the women. Who else brought the newborn into the world, and prepared the bodies of the dead for their travels home to the Great Mother?

We do, she thought grimly.

"*Aahhhaaa!*"

Tree's low, choking moan returned Old Berry's mind to the task at hand. "Push," she whispered. "Push down hard." As Tree, her skin gone cold and clammy, tried to comply, Old Berry nodded at Leaf. "More furs," she said. "Try to keep her warm." She tilted her head sharply toward the other women. "Have those lazy girls stoke up the fire!"

Skin reached over and pushed Stone's shoulder. The men had gathered in a broad circle around two hearths, where Fire had kindled two blazes from the clay pot he carried everywhere. Inside the pot, fed and protected by bits of moss, rested the coals which kept the People warm.

The men had finally grown tired of songs, and now, as the ordeal a few feet away continued, they lapsed into the telling of tales. Stone had just finished a ribald recounting of Skin's first mammoth hunt and, still chuckling with appreciation, the rest of the men tried to ignore the sense of disaster they all felt.

"It's gone on a long time," Skin said.

Stone nodded, his brown face serious. He bit into a chunk of dried meat, chewed and swallowed before he replied. "Very long."

"I wish Old Magic was here."

Both men glanced toward the round hut which

stood lonely and silent beyond the circle of their own camp, next to Old Magic's Spirit House. Ghost had not come out today, not even to kindle a fire in the small hearth fronting his own dwelling. The men wondered at this. Ghost was different than Old Magic—sharper, quicker, more given to sudden inexplicable tempers. Yet concourse with the Spirits changed those who spoke to them, and Ghost's power with his namesakes was well known. Even so, it didn't make him any easier to deal with. In the privacy of his own thoughts, Skin was in no hurry for Old Magic to rejoin the Mother—although he would never have dreamed of voicing those thoughts aloud.

"Aaagghhhhh!"

Skin shivered. Already the Sun was three steps high in the blue morning, and yet the terrible sounds from his shelter continued. He felt a growing sense of doom; never had Tree suffered like this, even in the deaths of his two sons before. Old Magic was gone, and Ghost chose to remain hidden. The signs were dire. Even the discovery of the Green Valley no longer excited him. Who knew what news Old Magic would bring? Perhaps the new Spirits would be inimical to the People, and even if Tree survived to give him a living son, they would have to move on.

Stone said suddenly, "Remember the time when Fire and Spear got into that fight about whose Spirits were the strongest?"

Skin settled back against his furs. "Yes," he said, making himself grin at the others. "That's very funny. Tell that one."

"Ugh! Ughughugh!"

In the extremity of her agony and exhaustion Tree could only grunt—a series of short, liquid sounds that brought cold chills to Old Berry's heart. The woman's flesh beneath her hand felt cold as the belly of a fish, and as slimy. Tree's eyes had rolled back completely into her head, so that only the yellowish whites showed.

It will be soon now, Old Berry thought. *One way or the other*.

Two of the younger women held Tree's muscular legs apart, guiding them into a bent-kneed position and holding them firmly as the contractions came faster and faster. Outside the wind changed slightly and blew a gust of harsh, acrid smoke into the shelter. Though her eyes watered painfully, Old Berry ignored the distraction. Her eyes were riveted to the spot at the jointure of Tree's thighs—she'd seen certain signs, and wanted to make sure the younger girls, some of whom had never participated in the mysteries of birth, saw them too.

"*See*," she said sharply, "the way the opening changes—*there*. Look, you silly girls."

And indeed, the vaginal opening had swelled suddenly, as a small, dark, bloody, and membranous shape appeared there. "Ahh," breathed the two girls holding Tree's legs.

"Wider!" commanded Old Berry. "Give him room!" She had no idea yet of the sex of the child, but to speak of it as female might curse it forever, even as it exited its mother's womb into the World.

Tree arced back abruptly, her teeth grinding together, her eyes slitted in her face. When it happened, it happened with surprising speed.

"*Aieee!*" As Tree uttered the short, sharp cry, Old Berry leaned forward and pressed down on her belly with all her weight. The infant's head popped from Tree like a bit of meat spat from a hunter's mouth. Swiftly the rest of the tiny body followed, and Old Berry reached down to catch the child as it fell.

"The knife!" she commanded sharply. She'd had the sacred knife ready for several turnings of the sun; Stone himself had refined the beautifully chipped edge of it until it was sharp enough to sever one of Old Berry's hairs as it fell. Now Leaf handed the knife to the older woman, who took it and uttered a short prayer to the Great Mother. This was a moment of magic, the severing of the cord which had once connected the newborn to his mother.

For it *was* a him, Old Berry noted, as with a single sure stroke she cut through the umbilical cord and welcomed the child forever into the World.

"Here," she said, and handed the boy over to Leaf, so she could clean the blood and mucus and membrane from the baby and wrap it in furs already prepared. Then she turned back to Tree, expecting to see the relaxation that followed upon a successful birth. But when she glanced at Tree's face, her eyes widened. Tree's jaws were creaking wide, a slow yawn of torment. Her body was stiff as a stick.

Quickly Old Berry's knowledgeable hands sought Tree's belly, pushed and kneaded. She looked up once again. "Leaf!" she whispered. "There's another one coming!"

Leaf passed the newborn boy to another woman and bent over to assist. "Hold on!" Old Berry snapped at the two girls who had released Tree's legs. "I said *hold on*, you stupid girls!"

Ghost stared moodily at the tied-down flap of his tent. He was warm enough, reclining in his bed of fur and grass, but his mind was troubled.

He had Dreamed the night before, and he still couldn't make any sense of the message the Spirits had brought to him. Ghost was still a young man, only sixteen years old, yet he'd been apprenticed to Old Magic for over two years. His lips curved into a sulky pout.

You'd think the old fool would trust me by now, he

thought. *But no, he feeds me bits and drabs of lore, and holds all the great secrets for his own.*

There were, Ghost had no doubt, great secrets to be revealed. Many times, unnanounced, he'd interrupted the old man in his private rites, and seen implements quickly hidden, heard chants which he'd never been taught. Yet when he asked about what he'd seen and heard, trying to keep his face blank and full of innocence, Old Magic fobbed him off with vague word about "later," and "when the time comes."

The old man's secrecy ate away at him. What did the ancient fool think he was doing? Why wait? It wasn't as if the Shaman was getting any younger—he'd already lived far longer than any other of the People, even that equally irritating Old Berry. And that doddering old woman knew things that were kept from him. He was certain of it, and hated the occasional disdainful glance she spared him.

Now she presided in her glory over the birth of another child. The birth magics weren't his province, but as the only Shaman—well, apprentice Shaman, but Shaman nonetheless—present among the People, she owed him at least the courtesy of acknowledgment. Yet she'd ignored him completely, and when Tree had gone into labor not a single woman had been sent to his tent, to apprise him of the progress of the birth.

There were Spirits to be appeased, too. The birth might belong to the women alone, but once the child was in the World, only the Shaman could work the magics that assured a welcome to the new arrival among the Spirits who dominated the People's every living moment.

So Ghost festered in his tent and waited, hearing the agonized cries of Tree's labors, and thought, *Good. It serves them right.*

The birth was taking an awfully long time, though.

Could it have anything to do with his strange dreams of the night before?

An interesting thought. He settled back and considered it further.

The air inside the shelter smelled of blood and sweat and damp fur and smoke, a stench so strong that Old Berry's tough stomach twisted at it. But she fought back her growing nausea and, her hands slippery with blood, guided the second tiny head from Tree's birth passage.

"Good," she muttered finally, as the insignificant weight dropped finally into the waiting cradle of her fingers. This one kicked, unlike its brother. A girl. A gift from the Mother, then—for although only boy babies were valued in the masculine eyes of the People, Old Berry had a harsh and unforgiving knowledge about the role of women. Despised they might be, but they held the destiny of the People between their loins, no matter what some blustering hunter might say or think. Even her own sons, if it came to that.

She passed the child over to Leaf, who ministered to it expertly. The boy squawled in the background, a robust, healthy sound. The girl, however, though she kicked strongly, made no sound, her face red as the berries from which the old woman took her own name. Her tiny eyes were screwed into slits. She waved her minuscule fists back and forth in protest against her exit from the warm, dark comfort of the womb.

A fighter, Old Berry thought. Good. She'll need to be.

She reached down to help clean Tree's body, and that was when she discovered the disaster. Catastrophe came as a long, slow, pulsing flow of hot blood. The crimson fluid spread thickly, coated Old Berry's fingers, dripped down in stringy loops onto the furs beneath Tree's now relaxed buttocks.

Too relaxed. Old Berry knew that flaccidity. She reached up quickly and felt at Tree's neck, searching for the regular beat that ought to be there, but knowing what she would find.

A faint flutter, rapid as the wings of a bird—then even that winked out, like the last dying embers of a fire.

"Moss," she said curtly. "A lot of it."

She knew it was no use, but she had to try. She worked frantically, even as the baby girl finally let out a lusty howl.

It wasn't entirely a catastrophe, Old Berry told herself, dreading the moment when she would have to face her son. *At least there will be two new People. Even if their mother is dead, the Great Mother has been good to us.*

After several frenzied moments the smell of abruptly voided feces filled her nostrils, and she ceased her work. There would be joy and sadness among the People this day.

She rose slowly, feeling every day of her years in the stiffness of her spine, the crackle and pop of her knees and shoulders. "Clean her," she directed the younger women. "Make her ready to return." She sighed. "I will go and tell the men."

She trudged to the edge of their circle and paused. "Somebody go and get Ghost," she said, almost as an afterthought. "We will need him soon."

Privately, she wished that Old Magic were here, but certain things had to be done immediately. She neither liked nor trusted the Shaman's apprentice, but that had nothing to do with the necessity of appeasing the Spirits. And, grudgingly, she had to admit the young man was good at those vital duties.

"Give them to me," she ordered. Both tiny, squalling, fur-wrapped bundles were placed in her broad, ample arms. She joggled them a little, and smiled at their tiny features. At the movement, the boy's eyes popped open and stared at her blindly, two shiny black buttons in the center of his round face.

"Boo boo," she whispered softly, and blew a tiny puff of breath into his nose, for luck. The girl's eyes remained tight-shut.

Old Berry sighed as she carried the two infants out to meet their father. The girl would open her eyes soon enough—and later, as a woman, she might not much like what she saw.

But it was the way of the Great Mother, and despite all, Old Berry accepted it. She had to. She had no other choice.

As she walked a wailing arose behind her, and she hastened her steps—but not out of fear. Only acceptance. The entire short, sharp, brutal life of the People was shadowed by such wailing. It was their song. A song of life, for those who still lived.

And death—for those who didn't.

Ghost's lips curled into a bitterly triumphant smile as the sound of the death chant seeped through the walls of his tiny house. Most likely Tree, just as twice before, had given birth to another stillborn child. He wasn't surprised. In their refusal to summon him in time, such things became inevitable. The women, in their arrogance as guardians of the birth mysteries, forgot that without the magic of the Spirits, even the Great Mother's protection was sometimes not enough.

They would call him soon. Reluctantly he rolled out of his furs, shivering a bit at the chill. Unlike the rest of the People, Ghost was unnaturally thin, lacking the protective layer of subcutaneous fat which shielded them from the worst of the cold. It was only one of the many things that separated him from the rest, marked him as different. He took a perverse pride in these oddities, for they had rescued him from a life of true misery.

His earliest memories were of taunts and beatings from the other boys. Smaller than the rest and skinny as a blade of grass, he'd been the natural butt of cruel jokes and hard-fought games. That had been bad enough. But when, at the age of twelve, as the others grew skilled in the use of spear and axe, he fell down on the ground in the midst of a hunt and lay on his back and grunted like a hairy pig—his life turned into something horrible.

Worst of all, he remembered nothing of the episode. His father, a hulking man named Lion, already deeply ashamed of the woman-like son he'd created, told him nothing of what had happened. So when the other boys shouted, "Demon! Bad Spirit!" at him, and made warding signs behind his back, he'd been left totally alone, shunned and terrified in his misery.

That was when the dreams began. Since no one would talk to him, it wasn't hard to keep the dreams secret. But he would have done so anyway, for the dreams were the only wonderful things in his pathetic life.

The dreams! At first they'd been only flashes of color, so bright they took his breath away. Then, later, the dreams had grown, become gorgeous panoplies of strange beings who danced around him and sometimes even spoke to him, in tongues he didn't comprehend. He was too young and too ignorant to understand the meanings of the dreams. The bizarre creatures, half-human and half-beast, who came to him in his sleep and, sometimes, even in his waking moments, had no meaning to him beyond their willingness to treat him as an equal. At least they *talked* to him, when nobody else would.

His life of scorn and derision stumbled on for another year. He resigned himself to existence as a

despised outcast, and expected any moment to be
fully rejected by the People, left behind to hunt or
die in solitude, until the disaster occurred. He'd
taken to trailing along behind the other boys as they
hunted small game, aping their movements and pre-
tending in the secrecy of his heart that he was one
of them. The boys would dance along behind
bounding jackrabbits, shamming that they were
hunting the great mammoth or, even more fearsome, the long-toothed lion, with its claws as
lengthy as a man's fully extended hand. He followed
twenty or so yards behind, the sun beating down
on him, his mind full of anguished longing.

A huge rabbit bounded up out of the tight-woven
grass and leaped over the edge of a low arroyo, a
dry, jagged gash in the rolling steppe. Laughing and
shouting, the other boys surged after, waving their
spears.

When he reached the lip of the declivity, he
stood for a moment and watched the scene below,
which had degenerated into a playful wrestling
match. The rabbit was nowhere to be seen. Wist-
fully, he watched them frolic. In that moment he
wanted nothing more than to be invited down, to
join them as an equal.

Then blackness took him once again and, sightless
and twitching, he tumbled down into their horrified
midst.

He woke to heat and pain and darkness. The
sound of slow, heavy breathing, very close, terrified
him. At first he thought he had been dragged off to
the lair of some animal. Then, even more frightening, he decided he was dead and some malign Spirit
crouched nearby, waiting to eat his heart.

"Ahhhh!" he whispered, and tried to sit up. The
movement sent a white-hot lance of agony into the
swollen mass of his left knee. As he rose, still sight-

less, the thick, warm pad of a hand touched his forehead and pressed him back down.

"Rest, Little Boy," a gentle voice said. "You are safe."

He knew that voice. Old Magic, the Shaman of the People. But why was he here? And why was the tent so dark?

His lips moved to shape the words but Old Magic had begun a soft song, and the sound of it was so comforting, so peaceful, that with a grateful sigh, Little Boy—for that was his first name, and the hunters had never given him another—sank back down and slept, savoring a security he hadn't known for as long as he could remember.

"I want to talk to you about something," Old Magic said.

It was almost a week since Little Boy had fallen. The anguish in his knee had subsided to a dull, throbbing ache. With the aid of a rude crutch he was able to stand, even lurch out of the tent to pee and shit. Old Magic checked the huge poultice of foul-smelling moss he'd packed around the injured knee every day. and today he nodded his head, satisfied. "Not perfect," he said, "but you won't be crippled. Maybe limp a bit, and it will hurt when the cold and snow comes, but not bad."

The flap of the Spirit Tent was pegged wide so that thin yellow sunlight streamed in. The Shaman squatted on his haunches and regarded the boy thoughtfully. "You dream, did you know that?" Old Magic said.

A small, fearful fist clutched at Little Boy's heart. Dream? But that was his secret. How could the Shaman know?

Some of this must have shown on his pinched features, for Old Magic smiled reassuringly. "You talk when you sleep, Little Boy. I listen. That is one of the jobs of being a Shaman. Listening." He nodded to himself.

Little Boy shook his head. So Old Magic had learned his secret. What would it mean? Another mark of bad Spirits? Perhaps the final ruin of abandonment? Suddenly Little Boy didn't care anymore. A hint of defiance colored his voice. "Yes," he said. "I have dreams. Many dreams."

"Ah," Old Magic replied. "Tell me about them."

And thus did Little Boy find himself delivered from misery at last. The Shaman listened carefully—as he had said he would—to Little Boy's long and rambling discourse on the strange beings who peopled his moments of sleep. Old Magic seemed particularly interested in those times when Little Boy saw these creatures when he was open-eyed, by the light of day. Finally, the Shaman seemed satisfied. He leaned close to Little Boy's face, smiled, and said, "I will tell you something now."

A bit alarmed, Little Boy returned Old Magic's gaze. "What?"

"Your name isn't Little Boy any longer."

Confusion. If he wasn't Little Boy, then who was he? "I don't understand."

Now the old man's smile stretched more widely. "I will give you a new name. Now your name is Ghost. Do you like it?"

Stunned by the power of his new name, Ghost's mouth dropped open. He nodded slowly.

"Good," Old Magic said. "Your name is Ghost—and you belong to me. For when I am gone, you will be the Shaman after."

Thus was Little Boy raised from the lowest to the highest. It wasn't his fault the rescue had come a bit too late. Something once soft in his heart had already grown black and hard, and time would only burnish that nugget. He never noticed the loss, but later, Old Magic began to suspect it.

Ghost didn't care. He had the Spirits themselves, and would be mighty among the People. Someday. After Old Magic was gone.

Which might be sooner than anybody thought.

Old Berry faced Skin and said solemnly, "Tree has returned to the Great Mother, my son. I grieve for you."

She watched Skin's face carefully. The younger man nodded, as if what she told him was only what he had expected. The question in his dark, shadowed eyes grew stronger. Gently, she opened her arms and showed him her two burdens.

Now she smiled, for even though Tree was gone, her death had not been in vain. "Two, my son. Two strong children. A healthy girl—and a boy!"

Skin couldn't help it. He was saddened at the death of Tree, his long companion, but there would be other women. But a son! His Spirit would go on, in the bones and sinews of the tiny baby Old Berry thrust forward. Gently, he took the bundle in his arms and bent his face forward, his button eyes shining. Twins of those eyes gazed calmly back at him.

"Goo," he said softly. "Goo goo."

Behind him, one of the men laughed. Already, it seemed to Old Berry, Tree's death was forgotten, even as the women wailed her death song. She was but a footnote, fading quickly. The important thing was the boy that Skin held in his hands.

Men!

"You have a daughter, too," she said, a sheen of irritation on her words. "Here. Don't you want to see her?"

Skin looked up. "A girl?" He seemed dazed, his whole being riveted on the reality of the boy.

"Yes, a girl. Healthy, strong. She kicks like a lion."

Almost reluctantly, Skin shifted the weight of his son back to Old Berry's waiting arm and reached out for the girl baby. "See," Old Berry said. "She's smiling."

And indeed, the girl's tiny lips were curved like a bow.

Skin joggled her. "What's the matter? Is she asleep? Why don't her eyes open?"

As if on cue, the newborn girl's eyelids twitched and then, slow as a sunrise, slid wide. She gazed clearly into her father's eyes.

Skin's whole body jerked. Without thought he pushed the tiny girl back at Old Berry, who grabbed for the infant lest she fall.

"What's the matter?"

"Aiee! Her eyes! Look at her eyes!"

Old Berry tilted her face forward. Then she, too, gasped.

Though Tree had died giving birth to this child, Old Berry knew she'd done all the right things to appease the Great Mother. But now she saw that she had failed. Something had gone drastically, horribly wrong. Tree's death was only the first sign. She held in her arms the second.

Oblivious to the fear she caused, the infant girl stared sunnily at the dim, fuzzy shape of Old Berry's round brown face. She wrapped tiny fingers around the old woman's callused thumb and drooled prettily.

Her eyes, one green, one blue, glittered like tiny jewels in her face.

"Guh," she said.

Old Berry turned away.

"Where is Ghost?" she demanded. "Somebody get the Shaman! Quickly!"

Ghost watched with appreciation the sinewy rump of the girl who led him from his tent. Branch was her name. He had already marked her in his mind as the one to receive his precious seed, when the time came.

He had no doubt she'd accept willingly. To bear the child of one who spoke with Spirits was as great an honor as Branch could ever hope for. And even if she wasn't willing, he would take her anyway. Who would stop him?

For, although on occasion still uncomfortable with it, Ghost had no doubt of the great power he wielded. His life had truly changed, that day when Old Magic had given him his name. Suddenly his moments of darkness, when he lay on the ground and shivered, spit spraying from his lips, suddenly these were no longer marks of evil. Now the men drew back in awe, for they knew the Spirits themselves inhabited his body and spoke in their Spirit tongues.

The People thought themselves lucky to be so gifted with a future Shaman of Ghost's obvious potency. At first Ghost had gloried in his newfound stature, and had taken particular pleasure in the small revenges he was now able to work on those who had most heavily tormented him. Young Thrower, the obvious leader of the boys, woke one day in terror to find a strange sign painted upon his father's tent flap, and Ghost squatting just beyond the door, smiling at him enigmatically.

"I dreamed it," he'd explained to Old Magic. "A Spirit told me to put the sign there. I don't know what it means." And then, with a meaningful glance at Thrower, who quaked with terror a few feet away, he had said, "I don't think it was a good Spirit, though."

Eventually, such childish vengeance had palled. The more he grew to understand the breadth and nature of his abilities, the less he felt a need for tangible exercises of dominance. In fact, as he grew older and more sure of himself, individual members of the People had less and less influence on him. Some he regarded as no more than insects, pale and lifeless dolls to be maneuvered as he wished.

The immutable base of any Shaman's power was the Spirits, and through them, the Great Mother who had created them. But there were other, more mundane supports on which authority rested. Knowledge was one such, and Ghost's quick mind, long starved by rejection, soaked up lore like a thirsty sponge. He learned the secrets of roots and berries, bark and grass. He studied the entrails of animals, and the soft matter inside their hard skulls. He memorized songs and chants and lays that were really none of these, but simple bits of information passed down from Shaman to Shaman alone.

He learned how fear of the unknown could turn the strongest hunter's bowels to water, and the incredible power that was given him to create or allay that fear.

His ache for knowledge was frightening in its intensity, and more than once Old Magic had found himself wondering what it was he'd unleashed upon the People. But each time he did so, the old Shaman pushed his doubts away. Ghost truly did possess awesome skills. He would be a great Shaman.

If only Old Magic could gain a surer sense of what it was that was lacking in Ghost, and find some way to remedy it. In the end, he consoled himself with the knowledge that he'd really had no choice. It was the Spirits who had given him Ghost, and their ways could never be fully known.

He kept his apprehensions from Ghost, of course. There was still time.

Now Ghost approached the knot of sullen hunters and Old Berry, who faced them still bearing her twin burdens. A soft sigh greeted his arrival, for he came in full Shamanic regalia.

A beautifully cured reindeer hide covered him

from shoulder to foot. Atop his narrow head perched the skull of the same animal, polished as white as virgin snow, a great rack of antlers protruding three feet on either side. In one hand he grasped a rattle filled with lion's teeth, and in the other a small but perfectly chipped ceremonial spear.

He strode directly to Old Berry, noting the deep lines of distress etched upon her aged features. "You summoned me," he said curtly. "What do you want?"

Ghost's garb was not lost upon the old woman. The apprentice Shaman had come ready to deal with Spirits of all kinds. The spear he carried was a toy, but deadly nonetheless—for while it would cut human flesh like butter, in certain instances it could even wound a Spirit. The apprentice somehow already knew what would be required. Grudgingly, Berry's respect for his power, if not for his personality, inched up a notch.

"Here," she replied brusquely, and thrust the girl baby toward him.

Ghost leaned forward. At first he didn't understand. The child looked healthy enough, no obvious deformities or other signs of demonic possession. Then she turned her face and he saw her eyes clearly. He almost drew back, but caught himself with only an imperceptible movement.

Those eyes!

With a rush, his uneasy dreams of the night before returned to trouble him. His memories of them had been hazy at best. Sometimes the dreams were as clear as his hand before him, but others, infuriatingly, were chaotic jumbles of light and noise. Yet the eyes of the baby girl, watching him steadily, were familiar. Somehow, although he couldn't remember in exactly what manner, those eyes had been a part of the dream. And though he couldn't recall the specifics, there had been a general warning: Danger!

Danger to himself, to the People.

He looked down at the tiny, innocent face, then placed the rattle in the pack he carried and extended his now empty hand. "Give it to me," he said. After Old Berry had handed the girl over, he said, "Tell me what happened."

Old Berry slowly recounted the terrible agony of Tree's labor, and the brutal moment of her death. Ghost—who had learned many lessons well—listened carefully. When Old Berry had finished her tale, he nodded.

"I see," he said. He glanced down at the silent bundle in his left arm. "So it killed Tree. It is a demon, of course."

A low, sighing murmur went through the men gathered behind him.

Privately still full of his own dreams, Ghost knew he faced a crucial moment, a time that would do much to determine his future, and for a moment he quailed inwardly. This . . . thing was truly an evil Spirit, come to devil the People. Old Magic had spoken vaguely of such things—more particularly, of obvious signs like twisted limbs or malformed skulls—but the proper remedy, though complicated, was obvious.

Ghost turned and smiled at the men. "Do not fear!" he said loudly, ignoring a swirl of movement at the back of the crowd. "I will slay this evil Spirit!"

As if she understood the terrible fate that awaited her, the girl baby let out a sudden wail.

At that moment Old Magic pushed through the crowd and said, "What's going on here?"

Chapter Four

The Green Valley: 17,997 B.C.

Skin, his mind a numb welter of confused, conflicting emotions, stared dully at the back of Old Magic's head. Part of him mourned Tree; another part gibbered in nameless terror at the blue-and-green eyed apparition that had killed her; but a third leaped and danced for joy at the answer to his greater prayer: the little boy nestled in Berry's broad arms.

A son! Now his Spirit, reborn, could continue. In a dim and formless way, he savored the concept of immortality. Not with the Great Mother, but here—on the broad and rolling steppes that were all he'd ever known and, because of that, all he'd ever loved.

"It's a demon," he spoke to Old Magic's back. "A bad Spirit. It killed Tree."

"What?" Startled, the old Shaman turned. But before Skin could say more, Ghost interjected, "Welcome back, Old Magic." There was a formal, almost chantlike quality to his words, and the Shaman responded to them quickly, as if there were some challenge hidden in them.

He noted that Ghost wore the full trappings of Shamanhood, although, technically, the younger man did not yet have that standing. A warning coursed through his tired bones—this was the first skirmish in what could become a long and drawn-out battle. He nodded with ceremonial grace at Ghost, who seemed to sense an equal import in the moment.

No doubt he does, Old Magic thought. *He's not even willing to wait until I'm dead.*

In that moment all his ancient wisdom came rushing to his aid—this first challenge from his apprentice frightened him not at all—but the People themselves had, all unknowing, arrived at a vital crux in their history. He brought news of vast import from the green depths of the new Valley, and this adolescent confrontation with Ghost might become a needless but irritating distraction.

Not all of being a Shaman is magic, my boy, he thought grimly. *As you will soon learn.*

And now to business, he told himself. He stepped away from the crowd and planted himself between Ghost in his finery and Old Berry, who looked as worried as he'd ever seen her.

"What's this about a demon?" he said.

Ghost felt the momentum of the conversation slipping from him, and pushed himself forward. Old Magic's few steps had somehow changed the tableau, so that Ghost now stood beyond the circle of authority. He sought to enter it. "A demon, O Shaman. Come to bring death and bad luck to the People. Already it has killed Tree. But there is nothing to worry about. I have promised the People that I will destroy the monster." Slowly, he raised his right hand and brandished the spear over the tiny bundle he held.

Old Magic glanced at Berry, who returned the look with an opaque but meaningful roll of her black eyes. Ghost saw the movement and frowned, but Berry ignored him.

"Ghost has the child," she said softly.

"Ah," Old Magic said, turning smoothly. "Let me see it."

For an instant Ghost stiffened, as if loath to comply with Old Magic's command, but faced with the Shaman's full authority in front of the People, he finally decided that now was not the time to challenge him. Not publicly, at least.

Without a word, his face full of suppressed fury, he thrust the bundle forward. Old Magic took the infant in both hands and gazed down at it.

How his heart shook!

It was worse than he'd thought. *Why does it happen when I'm so old?* But the Great Mother gave no reply to his wordless question. He wasn't surprised. She never seemed to offer straight answers to simple queries. Then he chuckled inwardly. Of course she didn't—if she did, the People would have no need for Shamans.

Slowly, just to make sure his faded eyes weren't playing tricks on him, he bent his wizened face close to the tiny features beneath. The little girl smiled vaguely at him. Her squalls had ceased the moment Ghost had handed her over. Now a sunny, sweet expression suffused her features. Her eyes, with their peculiar, unmatched colors—*No wonder Ghost thinks she's an evil spirit*, Old Magic thought to himself—glinted cheerfully in the harsh morning light.

It was the Sign. H felt himself begin to tremble, as the full weight of the Secret took hold of him. He had never expected to see this, not in his lifetime. It frightened him. The responsibility was awesome, and he was in the winter of his years. Would there be enough time?

He saw the problem clearly enough. And Ghost, it seemed, was an integral part of the problem.

The Secret would have to remain secret a while longer yet. For him—he glanced at Ghost, who watched him like the black birds that picked at the leavings of the hunt, terrible and hungry—and for *her*, and for the People themselves.

He jiggled the soft bundle gently, and smiled at the faint noises the infant made in reply. First things first. He turned and faced the People, who stood stiff and uncomfortable before him.

"Be full of joy!" he spoke in a clear, ringing voice. "I bring you great news of the valley beyond! And now I tell you of another sign: this little girl!"

A stirring swept through the People. None of them missed the import of his words: not "demon," but "little girl."

"She is a sign, as well. Perhaps the two are twined together, this baby and the Green Valley. I have spoken to the new Spirits. Now Ghost and I must confer about this fresh wonder."

He lowered the child, turned, and gestured with his head toward his apprentice. "Come, Ghost. We have work to do."

Then, without a backward glance, he swept away toward the Spirit tent. All that was left for Ghost was to follow—unless he wanted to stand there like a stupid stick.

He was many things, but Ghost was not stupid. Tight-lipped with anger, he forced himself to smile—as if it had all been his idea—then whirled and followed, his coat of reindeer skin flapping behind.

Soon, he told himself. *Old fool, you won't live forever!*

Old Magic stood aside, still glancing down at the baby girl, as Ghost undid the flaps of the Spirit House. Old Magic watched him carefully, noting the tense stiffness of his back as the apprentice untied the sacred knots that held the flaps down. When he had finished, Ghost stood up and gestured curtly.

"Welcome back," he said, although there was no welcome in his voice.

"Thank you," Old Magic replied, as he ducked his head and stepped into the musty darkness of the tent. It took a moment for his vision to adjust to the change in light and he paused, blinking. The girl baby stirred faintly in his hands and he whispered, "Shhh, Little One."

Finally he could see well enough to make sure he didn't trip over anything and spill his precious burden. He was conscious of Ghost moving behind him, and for a moment felt uneasy. Ghost would be a problem—but nothing he couldn't handle.

Though I'd better handle it soon, he reminded himself.

The small ring of stones in the center of the House smelled dank and foul; low mounds of powdery charcoal, now reduced almost to black mud, disclosed to Old Magic's discerning eye that the roof had leaked in his absence. His eyes searched upward, and he saw glints of light where the smoke hole had been imperfectly tied down.

He'd been tying down that flap for thirty years. To do so perfectly was second nature for him. He didn't need any Spirit to tell him who had opened the flap in his absence, no doubt to burn his own Spirit Flame, and Magic was glad the heart of the Secret had gone with him to the Green Valley. Who knew what disaster might have come from Ghost's uninitiated fumblings?

The young man's pride was growing far ahead of his sense. It was time to take him down a peg or two. But carefully. Ghost must be brought to heel, but not made into an enemy. Old Magic knew he would not live forever, and too much depended on the younger man's good will—at least until this girl child was grown and able to use her powers fully. Maybe even after. Old Magic bore the Secret, but even he could not claim to know its full extent.

He moved across the Spirit House and settled himself painfully on the pile of furs there, ignoring the protest of his aged joints. "Ghost, would you light a fire, please? It's cold in here."

Without grumbling, but with the set of his shoulders plainly showing his feelings, Ghost said, "Of course, Teacher." He paused, then reached up and removed his ceremonial headpiece and laid it carefully to one side. Old Magic grinned inwardly—those antlers were impressive, but they *did* tend to catch on things. And they itched.

He sighed and shrugged out of his pack, letting it fall to one side within easy reach. Carefully he placed the still silent girl baby on a soft bed of fur near his right leg, then reached over and opened the pack. His fingers found the tight-wrapped shape easily. A moment later he drew it out, then placed it in his lap. It didn't weigh much, and most of the weight was in the softly cured skin and the thicker outer wrapping of fur which protected the precious thing inside. Bound around all were lengths of hide rope, each piece knotted in a secret way, so that it would be almost impossible to open the package without revealing that it had been done. He gazed down on the thing, remembering when he had first seen it, on the day when Great Dreamer, the previous Shaman, had given it to him. On that day many years before, Old Magic had been Young Magic, and had not fully understood the power of the Secret. Yet Great Dreamer's gift had also signaled Magic's full ascendance to office—Dreamer, ancient and bent as some steppe tree, had told him so.

"Now you are the Shaman," he'd said then, and Magic had wondered at the relief in the old man's voice. Now he understood the relief. Great Dreamer had passed on to the Great Mother within the week—and Magic thought, not without a grateful sigh, as mighty burdens finally were set down.

The essence of Dreamer's solace was fully open to him now, of course. The weight of the Secret was tremendous; he would be glad when he could release it. Then he shivered. Great Dreamer had only passed it on. It had fallen to him to bring it to fruition. Him and Ghost.

His gaze slid sideways. And the girl. The girl most of all.

So much power, in such a tiny, fragile thing. He marveled again at the work of the Great Mother. She worked in devious ways, her miracles to perform. With this thought he glanced at the reindeer headdress Ghost had let fall, and he recalled his wry thoughts at the inconvenience of the thing. Once, he would never have entertained such sacrilegious ideas for an instant; but the years had changed him. He fully understood the power of symbol and mystery on the People themselves, but age had warped his original faith. There were times when he wondered if the Spirits cared about the People at all. They acted so capriciously—and most often, the results of their actions were harmful in the extreme. The Wind Spirit blew down tents and cut the flesh like knives. The Spirits of Mammoth, Bison, Caribou were most conspicuous by their absence, so that the People starved as often as not. All the other Spirits acted with equal strangeness—and the messages they sent him personally usually made no sense whatsoever.

Yet he had faithfully interpreted what he'd guessed of their intentions, couched in terms the People could understand. Still, after thirty years of this, he knew he relied as much, if not more, on the vast store of learning he'd gathered for himself. And one of the things he'd learned was that reindeer antlers caught on things.

They had to be dusted occasionally, too.

Ghost clumped into the Spirit House with a load

of kindling and firewood, which he dumped without ceremony onto the hearth. Then he knelt and blew on a bit of moss, which flared into a tiny, flickering blaze. A moment later the kindling caught, and within a few more minutes a cheerful fire snapped and popped in the circle of stones, driving away the chill.

Ghost settled himself on the other side of the ring. He loosened the ties that closed the reindeer cape, moved his shoulders experimentally, then leaned back and closed his eyes, basking in the warmth.

Old Magic watched the younger man, waiting. Finally Ghost sensed the regard and opened his eyes. "It is a demon," he said flatly. "I dreamed about it the night before."

So it will be this way, Old Magic thought. *He brings his Spirits and his Dreams to me, to challenge my own.*

There was only one way to meet the challenge, without destroying his apprentice entirely. Reluctantly, he dropped his fingers to the securely wrapped bundle in his lap.

"There are other things than Spirits and Dreams, my son," he said softly. "There is, for instance, the Secret."

Ghost's black eyes glittered like bits of smoky quartz as he leaned forward. "The Secret?" he breathed. "What is the Secret?"

"That," Old Magic said, "is what I will tell you now. . . ."

"A very long time ago," Old Magic began, his voice dropping into a low, chantlike rhythm, "many, many lives and deaths of the People ago, the Great Mother gave the first Shaman a command.

"Go out from the heart of the country, leave your magic springs, leave your ever-bountiful hunting grounds. For you are My People, and I have chosen you.

"You will wander upon the face of the World, and stop only for a short time in each place. For I send you on a Great Journey, from which you shall not return."

As Old Magic chanted the beginning of the Secret, his eyes drooped drowsily. He lips shaped the words exactly as Great Dreamer had spoken them, and no doubt an endless line of Shamans before him. Ghost sat stone-still, listening raptly—at last, the old fool would pass over what was due him. He shivered at the intonations of power in the older man's song.

Old Magic noted none of this, as the song itself, the Secret, drew him deeper into its ancient web.

"The Journey will be long and terrible, but the People will go, because I wish it, and because the People are Mine forever. But when the Journey is ended, then I will give you a sign, and shower the People with great gifts. Then may the People rest at least, in a World of endless food and drink, where the game is always plentiful, and the water never-ending and fresh.

"But first you must Journey, and know great hardship, so that you may prove yourself worthy of such a mighty boon. For I do not give My gifts lightly, and even the People whom I love must earn what I bestow upon them.

"Yet you will not go alone in your Journey, for I will be with you, and I will guard you against the Spirits of Wind and Ice and terrible Wolf. And when your Journey ends, I will give you your Sign, as I have spoken.

"Thus I speak to you, Great Mother of All. Heed My words!

"And obey them!"

The final sentence rolled from Old Magic's lips with a sound like muted thunder. His eyes had turned back in his head, so that only narrow slits of white showed beneath the flesh there. Ghost's teeth chattered. He had no doubt of the truth of those words—his own experience with Spirit messages left him able to recognize the presence of divinity in others.

But the truth horrified him. A great Journey! An *endless* journey! The People doomed to wander forever in the World.

It was awful. The Great Mother's gift was poisoned.

"To wander forever . . ." he whispered, appalled.

Old Magic's eyes snapped wide. "Not forever," he said. "There will be a Sign."

Ghost, from the depths of his youthful cynicism, spat into the fire. "Of course, a sign. There are always signs."

"Yes," Old Magic agreed. "And this"—his hand gently stroked the forehead of the baby girl—"is one of them."

His gnarled fingers found the knots of the bundle in his lap and began to undo them. "This," he whispered, "is another."

It took several minutes for Old Magic to finish releasing all the knots. Ghost leaned forward, his eyes intent, trying to follow the rapid movements of Magic's fingers, but somehow, without seeming to do so, the Shaman's hands and arms shielded his work. It looked accidental, but Ghost was certain it wasn't. Nevertheless he kept silent. If the old fool had finally decided to give up the enigmas of his power, then Ghost decided he could wait to unravel the final details.

Nevertheless, as Old Magic finally laid the ropes carefully to one side, then unwrapped first the fur outer coverings and then the buttery skin of the inner, Ghost felt his heart begin to beat rapidly in his chest. It seemed to him that great forces were converging on this moment—and with his special senses, he felt Spirits crowd round him like a great flock of birds, chattering and flapping.

In the dim and flickering light of the fire Old Magic paused, the final unveiling put in momentary abeyance. He turned slightly, rummaged in his pack, and drew out a pair of strange, furry things, which he slipped onto his hands.

Mittens, Ghost saw, beautifully made things cut from the brown pelt of a Mammoth. Old Magic glanced up at him from beneath bushy brows.

"This is very important," he whispered. "What you are about to see is the heart of the Mammoth People. It must not be touched by human hands." He spoke this lie without blinking. Perhaps it was time to tell Ghost some things—but not *every*thing.

Even as he spoke, he felt a thrill. Every Shaman in the history of the People had known this moment, when the Heart was finally exposed to another. There was a great feeling of transition to it, as if one's own life's work was drawing to a close. Always, before, that had been the case. The Heart had not been revealed except as the final act in the creation of a new Shaman.

Now, it could not be. Not yet. Old Magic envied his predecessors, for the simplicity of their burdens. No other before him had borne what he now must bear. He only hoped he would remain alive long enough to do it—and that he would somewhere find the strength he needed.

"Here," he said. "Look upon the Heart of the People." Carefully he folded back the last wrapping, to reveal to his apprentice the force which had driven the People for at least two thousand years.

Ghost felt tiny muscles pop in the base of his spine as he leaned sideways to see around the smoky fire. Finally, his eyes watering, he inched himself around until he sat knee-to-knee with his aged mentor.

He looked down and waited until his vision cleared. He stared at the thing for what seemed an endless time. Then, finally, he spoke.

"It's small," he said.

Old Magic nodded. "Great things do not have to be large in size," he remarked. "A tiny spear can kill a huge mammoth."

Ghost stared at the small sculpture. It glowed faintly in the dusky light, a dark, warm golden color. Time had darkened it thus, although neither Old Magic nor Ghost had any true idea how much time it had taken. Nevertheless, untouched by human hands for more than twenty centuries, the details of the carving remained almost as sharp and clear as the day they were made.

The diminutive shape of the mammoth was perfectly proportioned, from the delicate tusks to the tiny twist of its tail. Hints of shaggy hair had been incised on the sides of it, and the shape of small, flappy ears. One eye regarded them calmly from the ages, and for a fearful moment, Ghost thought the eye looked at *him*. But the moment passed, and the object became only a carving again.

Even Ghost understood, however. Inside this bit of ivory resided terrible power. Old Magic had called it the Heart of the People, and Ghost's spiritual senses, now raised to fever pitch, could feel the silent beat of it. The carving was alive with Spirits, perhaps with some even greater force. It frightened him. Yet he desired it more than he'd ever desired anything else, with a lust so mighty it made him shake.

He reached forward, his fingers trembling.

"No!" Old Magic drew back, protectively. Then, in a calmer voice, he said, "I told you. No one may touch this. It is the Heart, and the Great Mother herself lives in it. Remember the words of the Song."

Once again he chanted softly, "Yet you will not go alone in your Journey, for I will be with you." He raised his eyes to meet Ghost's. "She is with us, in this bit of ivory, which She made with Her own hands and gave to the first Shaman. It is *sacred*, Ghost. If you touch it, She will leave us forever. Then the People will be truly lost. Do you understand?"

Ghost nodded in assent. He did understand. If the ways of the Spirits were often convoluted and hard to understand, so much more capricious were the ways of the Great Mother Herself, who had created even the Spirits. The younger man found it not at all odd that the Mother should lay such a stricture on Her People. And finally he understood the utmost care Old Magic took with the carving: the double wrapping, the wearing of mittens, the exaggerated consideration in each movement when he handled the Heart. If the Great Mother said She would abandon the People for such a sin, then no doubt She would. If anything at all was surprising, it was that her instructions had been so clear.

Old Magic sensed a change in his apprentice, noted well the awe that suffused his frozen features. He waited until the younger man had settled back in his earlier position. "She has been with us always," he continued. "And She will remain, as She promised, if we heed Her commands."

He stopped and licked his lips, gathering his thoughts and every wile he possessed for his next few words. This was the crux of the matter, after all—Ghost *must* be bonded to the task ahead, without knowing the true nature of it—for the protection of the People, for *her* protection.

The survival of everybody depended on it. For a moment he quailed at the enormity of what he must do, but then, as had Shamans before him, he summoned up the peculiar strengths that made him

what he was, and said, "Ghost. The Great Journey
is over."

Ghost rocked back on his haunches. *"What?"*

Old Magic nodded. "I have spoken to the Spirits
in the Green Valley. And I have seen the sign promised us by the Great Mother Herself. The journey of
the People is finished. We are home, Ghost. At long
last, the People have come home!"

Old Berry trudged wearily toward the gathering
of women around the shelter where Tree's body lay.
Wordlessly she pushed the swaddled boy baby into
Leaf's waiting arms. "We will have to find a mother
for him," she told the other woman. "I think Blossom. What do you think?"

Leaf nodded. Blossom, one of Stone's women,
was approaching her own time, and her breasts
were already swollen with milk. "I will tell her," she
said. "What about the . . . other one?"

Berry shrugged. "I don't know," she replied. "I
imagine Old Magic will tell us, in his own good
time." She knew better than to try to unravel the
doings of the Spirits in the world. That was the Shaman's job, and welcome to it. She had more press-
ing things on her mind, anyway. "Is she ready?"
she asked.

Leaf nodded, and stepped aside. Sighing heavily,
Berry plodded the last few feet to where Tree's body
lay waiting, still shielded by the clustered women.

Tree lay perfectly still on her bed of furs. The
younger women had already cleaned away the
bloody traces of labor and death, and the young
woman looked remarkably lifelike. But her Spirit
had departed, though Berry knew it remained close
by, and would so remain until released by Old
Magic, when he sang her back to the Great Mother.

She checked the corpse to make sure the girls had
done their work correctly. The furs were fresh; noth-

ing remained of afterbirth or blood, nothing to tie the Spirit to the World. Old Berry nodded her satisfaction.

"Cover her," she instructed. "I will see to the bindings myself." It was very important that the hide ropes which secured the furry wraps be done correctly, lest the physical body seek to escape the flame and follow the Spirit home.

A faint, squalling noise floated to her ears. She smiled. The boy was a lusty one, well formed, strong, and hungry. All good signs.

She glanced down. It was too bad about Tree, but such things happened. If not for the strange girl baby, Berry would even have felt an odd satisfaction in the balance of things: a life traded for a life, with the greater life of the People going on.

As it was, she wondered what would happen. So much had occurred: Tree's death, the births, and, most important, the discovery of the Green Valley. Old Magic had said he brought news, that he'd spoken with the Spirits there. She wondered what the Spirits had said—but that, too, was the task of the Shaman.

In any event, whatever happened would, in the end, follow the will of the Great Mother.

As always.

Blossom, a short girl with a curiously flat face, came shyly forward to where the men lay around the two large hearths. Her right breast was exposed as she knelt between Skin and Stone. Skin hitched himself up on his elbow to watch more closely, a wide smile brightening his face.

"See," Blossom said. "He sucks hard. He's very hungry."

Skin nodded. Indeed the infant, its tiny eyes squeezed tight shut, was fastened onto Blossom's nipple as if his life depended on it.

And it did, of course. Sometimes babies were born

who couldn't suckle, and there was nothing to do but sing them back to the Great Mother. But, Skin saw, his own son was not one of those. His miniature fists moved briskly back and forth as his tiny lips tensed and relaxed, tensed and relaxed.

"He's strong, my son," Skin said proudly. He glanced at Stone, who grinned in return.

"Very strong," Stone agreed.

The two men watched for a while, conscious of the approving stares from the others in the circle.

"He will be a mighty hunter," Spear offered from across the fire.

"Yes," Skin agreed. "I will teach him."

"Mightier than you," Spear added, to general laughter. Skin was a great tracker, but his skill at the actual kill was not as good as it might have been. The joke was well known, and Skin felt no offense.

"Maybe you could teach him!" Skin called. "Of course, he can't kill anything if he can't find it!"

More laughter greeted this rough sally. Spear had his own weaknesses, and finding and following spoor was one of them.

Eventually Blossom raised herself up, still cradling the tiny body carefully to her breasts. When she had gone, Stone glanced over at Skin. "You will need a new woman," he said.

Skin nodded. He knew what would come next, but he was honored. Stone was his brother, but with his indispensable skills at shaping the flint spear heads and knives and choppers which kept the People alive, he was held in much higher status.

"We will share Blossom," Stone said "Your son and mine will be the same."

Skin blinked. He'd expected the offer of sharing, but Stone's further statement shocked him with its generosity. Sharing a woman was one thing, but Stone offered more: to actually make the new baby a part of his own family, and, implicitly, to pass on his own skills to the newborn infant.

The child's future status would assuredly be far greater than Skin himself could offer, necessary though his own aptitudes were.

He lowered his head. "Thank you, Stone," he said.

"I don't know about the girl, though," Stone replied slowly, his features troubled.

Skin shook his head. He didn't know about the girl baby either. Old Magic had said the child was a sign. But Ghost said it was a demon. Now both had disappeared into the Spirit House, and showed no signs of coming out.

"I'll just have to wait," Skin replied. He glanced uneasily at the thin, silvery plume of smoke rising from the Spirit House. "The Shaman will tell us what to do."

Stone reached across and clapped him on the shoulder. "Who knows?" he said. "Maybe the Shaman will keep her."

Skin brightened. "Maybe," he replied hopefully.

The intensity of Old Magic's pronouncement took Ghost by surprise. He stared into the older man's wide black eyes and found nothing but utter and complete conviction. A thrill shot through him. A few moments earlier he'd cowered before the image of an endless, empty Journey the Shaman had conjured up. Now, the wonder of the Mammoth Stone fresh in his mind, he faced the knowledge that the Journey itself was over.

Magic had not yet spoken truly of what he'd discovered in the Green Valley. Plainly it was a place of great and strange magic. Was it to be the new Home of the People, as well?

"How do you know?" Ghost whispered finally. His voice felt dry and raspy in his throat. Smoke swirled in the tent and then, for a long moment, hung motionless like a veil.

"The Sign," Old Magic replied softly. He wrapped up the Mammoth Stone again, but did not tie it. Still wearing his mittens, he gently hoisted up the tiny, silent form of the baby girl. "Look at her!" he commanded urgently. He held her forward and shook her. Once again her eyes popped open, and Ghost found himself staring into the two vaguely shining orbs, one blue, one green.

"Her eyes," Old Magic said. "Her eyes are the Sign. They are the eyes of the Great Mother Herself. This child was made in Her image. I tell you, Ghost, we are home. The People have come home at last."

In the smoky relief of the moment, Ghost knew it was true. The Journey was over. And all because of this tiny girl child, whom he'd almost killed.

He shuddered at the enormity of the mistake he'd nearly made. To kill the Great Mother Herself! For the first time he understood that there were things he didn't know, and must know—for his own survival, if nothing else.

His mind a chaos of fear, and awe, and joy, he stared back into the eyes of the Sign. Inwardly, a thought began to grow, a new thought: *I must do better. I promise I will do better!*

And so he would. For a time.

After Ghost had left the Spirit House, Old Magic sagged back in relief. As far as he could tell, he had suitably impressed the younger man with his tales of ancient magic and wonder. He doubted Ghost would be able to separate the truth from the lie, for the lie had been as much in what he hadn't told him as what he had.

For there was more to the Secret, much more, and he would keep this to himself.

If it was true. If the primeval tales handed down

so carefully had spoken rightly. He looked down at the bundle in his lap. Those eyes gazed calmly up at him. She was so quiet!

It frightened him a bit. What he was about to attempt frightened him even more. If he was wrong, then ultimate disaster awaited the People. But if he was right . . .

Ahh, if he was right!

He retrieved the Mammoth Stone and its protective wrappings. His one actual lie to Ghost had been both small and great; he'd told him no one could touch the Stone, lest its power depart and the Great Mother turn away from Her People.

That wasn't exactly true.

The tales told of one, and only one, whose flesh could meet the Stone with impunity. Trembling, he raised the bit of ivory from its furry bed. His heart raced in his aged chest. Finally, sighing with fear, he lowered his hand.

"Here," he prayed softly, "if it is yours, take it."

Her tiny fingers slipped around the Stone, which Magic had placed on her chest. The little girl looked up, then down at this strange, faintly warm thing. It felt good. Dimly, she wanted it closer to her. Her lips parted.

"Ooohhh . . ." she sighed. A tiny droplet of shining spit appeared at the corner of her mouth as she gurgled happily.

Old Magic had to pry her fingers away.

Chapter Five

The Green Valley: 17,990 B.C.

"Hold still," Blossom commanded sharply.

Maya giggled. The fur at the collar of her coat tickled her neck and made her squirm, as Blossom tried to fasten the collar more securely on the seven-year-old girl. "It tickles," Maya complained.

"How can I get you dressed when you jump around like that?" Blossom admonished. "Do you want to freeze to death? It's cold outside."

Maya glanced toward the flap door in the front wall of their half-buried house. The flap was partly open, revealing the thin gray light of a cloudy morning. A sudden cascade of shouts and laughter sounded beyond the door. Maya squirmed harder, trying to see beyond the fuzzy bulk of her mother. She managed to make out the form of her brother, Wolf, and several of the other boys, rolling on the ground in some frantic game.

"Mama!" she wailed. "I want to play with them!"

Privately Blossom was aghast at her daughter's unwomanly impulses. She blamed Old Magic for them—the Shaman treated Maya differently than anybody else, although he wouldn't say why he did so. Already, far from befitting proper childish behavior, Maya was wont to run in and out of the

Spirit House as if it were her own. There was nothing Blossom could do about it, though, except do her best to teach Maya what she would have to know as a woman of the People.

"Little girls," she whispered into Maya's ear, "don't play with little boys. You'll learn, sweetheart. You have your own things to do. Don't you want to go with me today?"

Maya slipped back down, her lips in a thoughtful pout. "I don't know," she announced finally. "Are we going to dig in the mud with sticks again?"

Blossom smiled. The work of gathering roots from the soft, marshy ground along the stream, or from the Second Lake, was hard, sweaty labor fit only for women. She herself grew tired of it, though it had to be done. The men certainly wouldn't do it. But today she had something better to offer the little girl.

"No," she told her. "Today we go with Old Berry to the Lake of Smokes. No digging, I promise you."

Maya's oddly colored eyes widened. "The Lake of Smokes?" She'd heard often of this wonder, but had never seen it with her own eyes. At Old Magic's instructions, little Maya was never allowed to wander far from the Home Camp, though the younger boys often did, much to her dissatisfaction. At the thought of finally being allowed to see the mysterious Lake, all other distractions vanished. "Let's go!" she announced, and tried to struggle from her mother's ample lap.

"I told you to hold still!" Blossom scolded, as she pulled her back. "Do you want Old Berry to think I don't know how to take care of you, how to dress you properly?" She paused, then uttered a threat that, in her own mind, wasn't entirely playful. "She might take you away from me, if she thought that."

The threat worked immediately. Maya twisted around and placed her tiny, button nose on Blossom's chin. She twined her hands around her mother's neck and said, very seriously, "I wouldn't go. I'll never leave you alone, mama. Don't worry."

"I don't worry," Blossom replied. "Now, will you hold *still*?"

Obediently, Maya finally subsided, and waited patiently until her fur coat and legging wraps had been properly secured.

"All right, now you're ready," Blossom announced at last, and gave Maya a fond pat on the top of her head. "You stay with me—hold my hand and don't let go. There are many strange Spirits around the Lake of Smokes. Perhaps they would find a little girl tempting."

This warning, usually sufficient to put fear into the bones of even the wildest boy, swayed Maya not at all. "I'm not afraid of Spirits!" she announced loudly. "The Spirits are my friends!"

Blossom appeared to ignore this, although she quailed inside. The Spirits, even those best disposed to the People, were capricious in their benevolence. The Spirit of Wind, almost balmy in high summer, turned sharp and brutal with the coming of winter. Other Spirits were even more erratic, and some Spirits, fearsome in their power, were wholly evil. To hear her seven-year-old daughter, with her strange, multicolored eyes, make such cavalier pronouncements frightened Blossom profoundly.

It came, she supposed, from Maya's close, almost constant association with the Shaman. Why the old man took such an intense interest in the little girl was beyond Blossom's understanding—but he did, and what he taught her appeared not only unseemly, but unsettling.

Maya didn't speak much of what her times with Old Magic were like—particularly, she remained silent about the contents of the Spirit House, and the doings of Ghost and Old Magic therein. But Maya certainly didn't behave like other girls her age: properly silent around the men, shy and unassuming as they trained in the duties they would perform all their lives.

It wasn't that Maya shunned the knowledge Blossom and Old Berry had to bestow, it was simply that she didn't give it the attention it deserved. Only dimly could Blossom perceive her daughter's future, and it was beyond her powers of comprehension to envision a life much different than her own: a constant search for food—berries, nuts, tubers, small animals and fish—and the preparation and storage of that provender for the People as a whole. These things were what women did—there was no other life possible for them.

Yet Maya seemed not to understand this at all, and Blossom worried for her. The little girl's strange behavior marked her in the eyes of the People as different, and that wasn't good, either. Her bizarre attitudes were tolerated only because of Old Magic's—and, to some extent, Old Berry's—sponsorship. But those two wouldn't live forever, and when they were gone, Maya would have to survive within the closely knit system of rules and traditions that had governed the People forever.

She sighed heavily. It was such a burden sometimes, but one she shouldered gladly—for little Maya, at least when her erratic conduct was safely under control, was a joy to her heart. The girl was smarter than any of the other children her age, even her brother, Wolf, who was already the natural leader of his growing gang of companions. Her bright, sparkling eyes missed nothing, and perhaps because of that, her questions were endless. Sometimes the questions shocked Blossom, for they challenged the very bedrock of her own understanding of the World. Her lips tightened uneasily as she recalled the most recent example: "Mama, why do the men lie around the fire so much? Why don't they help us dig the roots?"

Deeply shocked, Blossom had for a moment been unable to reply. When she did, her voice was low and trembling. "The men do as they do, Maya. Don't ever let one of them hear you ask something like that. Terrible things might happen."

"What terrible things?"

But Blossom had only put her callused fingertips on Maya's tiny mouth and made her promise never to repeat the question again. Oddly enough, though she'd never thought of it before, the experience had planted the puzzle in her own mind like a small, sharp stone. Why *did* the men lie about all the time? But she sought no answer, for there was none. The roles of men and women were perfectly understood, totally accepted, to the point where even the thought of question brought a dizziness to Blossom's head and an acute pang of fear to her heart. She knew better than even to think such things, and wished her beautiful, precocious daughter had not implanted the nugget of doubt within her.

What was Old Magic teaching her, anyway? Whatever it was, Blossom decided, it would do Maya no good, and might even cause her great harm.

She sighed again, gave a final twitch to the leather thong that closed the top of Maya's coat, and said, "Come along, Maya. We don't want to be late."

Obediently, the little girl inserted her fingers into the warm, rough cage of her mother's hand, and allowed herself to be pulled through the flap door of their house. Once outside, they paused—Blossom looking around for the gathering of women she expected, Maya simply regarding her surroundings with wide, expectant eyes.

The brawl of shouting boys had tumbled like puppies to the edge of the overhang above First Lake. As Maya watched, her brother Wolf pushed Rabbit to the ground and sat on him, shouting in triumph. A moment later the fight was over, and the boys ran laughing along the overhang to a jumble of rock that rose toward the springs at the far end of the cliff.

She had no memory of the first camp the People had made here, nor of the woman whose death in childbirth had given her life. Her recollections only encompassed a time when the Home had always been—a jumble of houses built of bent wood, caribou bone, and rough hides, half-buried in the hard, graveled soil of the ledge, sheltered from wind and rain and snow by the great, overhanging cliff above.

Her world was quite circumscribed: the ledge of Home, First Lake beyond, the grassy sward beyond the small Lake, and a few hundred yards into the woods beyond that. She didn't understand why her mother guarded her so carefully; other little girls had penetrated the woods, even as far as Second Lake and the smoky places further on. The boys, of course, went almost where they pleased, though even they stayed away from the Lion Caves at the far end of the Valley, where a pride of the great beasts lived when they weren't hunting on the rolling steppes.

Maya lusted to see it all. Her boundless curiosity goaded her like a whip, to see, to smell, to taste and feel and *know* everything about the World. The mysterious limits placed on her by Blossom chafed unbearably, for Blossom never explained the reasons for them. Sometimes Maya wondered if it had something to do with her own strangeness, for she knew she was different from the other children. At first she'd been hurt by the difference—the way the children mocked her eyes, the way they pushed her out of the way, or threw rocks at her. But that time had passed long ago, and as she'd grown she'd finally become accepted as a part of the whole tribe, though even now she still occasionally noticed one or another adult making a strange sign at her back.

When she'd asked Old Magic about these things, his ancient, seamed face had wrinkled into a stern, forbidding mask. "Ignore them," he had told her. Then he'd asked, "Who made signs?"

She'd told him the names—Leaf, Spear, some others—and the Shaman had squinted and nodded. Maya had no idea what had occurred then, but afterwards, Leaf, even Spear had simply ignored her presence, seeming not to see her at all.

They were the exception, however. Most everybody else treated her as what she was—a little girl of the People. Perhaps a bit strange, but then all children were strange, weren't they?

Overhead, the sky loomed gray and chill, as it usually did. From someplace above the top of the cliff came a long, booming sound. The thunder of the ice wall to the north was so ever-present as to be completely unremarkable. Maya barely noticed it. She was much more interested in the activity she saw around the men's hearths, three of which fronted a long, low house buried like her own halfway into the earth.

She saw her fathers, Skin and Stone, standing next to Spear, part of a group that included most of the able-bodied males. Ghost was there, too, she noted with fascination; he was dressed much as the others, in warm furs and bound leggings, although he carried the carven wooden staff that was a mark of his office. He was speaking to the rest, and although she couldn't make out his words, she gathered a sense of urgency from the sharp, harsh gestures Ghost made with his staff.

Her attention hadn't been snagged by some childish mystery, however; the signs had been coming for weeks now. First Stone had disappeared for almost a turning of the moon. When he'd come back, his pack was full of dark, reddish stone, upon which he'd immediately set to work. Within a few days he'd produced a wealth of beautifully shaped points for the long spears of the hunters. He kept at it, chipping and polishing, until each man had several points, enough to arm two spears apiece, plus two more for backup. Moreover he created longer, thinner blades, which the men bound with leather and pine resin, creating extremely sharp knives.

Finally, as recently as the last week, Stone had begun to fashion heavier, blunter objects: hand-axes, choppers, butchering tools. The signs were plain.

Soon the men would hunt. No doubt that was the subject of discussion now, for no hunt could proceed without the blessing of the Spirits involved. She was mildly surprised that Ghost was there instead of Old Magic. The success of the hunters was of paramount importance to the survival of the People, and such a critical event had always been the province of the old Shaman. Still, she'd noticed that Old Magic seemed to stir about less and less, more content to laze by the fire inside the Spirit House, his eyes half-drowsy as he chanted ancient stories to her.

Age meant nothing to Maya, nor did she have any conception of death. Old Magic was old. That was all there was to it. Perhaps the old man was tired today, and so had sent Ghost in his stead. Ghost would someday be Shaman himself. She really didn't understand the difference between Ghost and the older man, but knew it existed.

Ghost was another story, anyway.

Now, as she watched, Spear raised both his arms in a praying gesture, then turned and pointed at the rocky trail which led to the top of the cliff. Ghost nodded assent, and everybody else slapped their hands together in a gesture of agreement.

Enthralled, Maya wanted to watch further, but

Blossom suddenly tugged on her hand. "There they are," Blossom announced. "Over there, behind the girl's house."

Prodded yet reluctant, Maya left off her observation of the men and turned obediently. Indeed, the gathering was well under way. Several women, dominated by the sound of Old Berry's sharp voice, had formed up into an orderly group. Maya made out smaller forms among the larger—other young girls would go with them, then. She wondered if her sister Bud would be among them. This girl, a year younger than Maya, had become her best friend.

"Hurry up!" Old Berry called stridently. "We don't have all day!"

"Come on, Maya,' Blossom said. "We're late. You shouldn't wiggle so much."

"Will we see the Smoke Spirits?" Maya demanded as she worked her short legs, trying to keep up with her mother. "Is Bud coming too?"

Blossom looked down, trying to appear stern, but a smile flickered across her features. "Yes," she promised. "Today, you will see the Smoke Spirits. You and Bud, both."

"Good," Maya replied, finally appeased.

Old Berry scowled at Blossom as she came up to the main party of women and girls. "Where have you been?"

Wordlessly, Blossom glanced down at Maya and shrugged. Old Berry's eyebrows shot up. Then she nodded. She too understood what sort of encumbrance the bright-eyed, active little girl could become. "Well," she said, her old, rough voice softening a bit, "everybody else is here. It's time we started."

"Don't let go of my hand!" Blossom warned Maya, who was already tugging at the restraint.

"I want to walk with Bud," Maya replied. She'd

seen her younger sister on the fringe of the party, chattering happily with two other girls her own age.

Maya had nothing to gauge it by, nor would she have consciously thought on it even if she did, but since her birth there had been many, many more children given to the People; more children than Old Berry could recall, certainly. Old Berry noticed it, however, and had remarked on the curious fact to Magic.

Magic had replied, "The Great Mother blesses us in every way. She has given us water, and abundant food, and shelter. Now She gives us the greatest blessing: more People."

Since that fit in perfectly with Berry's view of how the World operated, she questioned no further. The People had only a tenuous knowledge of the relationship between sexual intercourse and childbirth. They knew there was some sort of relation, but believed the sexual act to be only a sort of male-female magic, not absolutely necessary in itself to procreation. Since all women were more or less constantly subject to male sexual attention—the People didn't even have a word for "virgin," and only made distinction between girls, who hadn't yet passed their menses, and women, who had—babies seemed to come at the whim of the Great Mother Herself.

The second factor in the increase in the number of children was the Green Valley itself. Because of its near idyllic environment, more infants survived to grow up. After seven years, almost every fertile woman had given birth at least once, many more often than that. The upshot was that of this party of thirty women at least half showed signs of early pregnancy, and the rest were surrounded with rollicking packs of offspring. The People were undergoing a population explosion the likes of which they'd never seen in all their history, and though they didn't understand it yet, their very survival as a People was about to be subjected to a tremendous strain.

Maya only knew that there were a lot of children her own age. "Mama," she said urgently, "*please* let me walk with Bud. I'll be good. I promise."

Ever conscious of the burden laid upon her by Old Magic and his relations with her daughter, Blossom looked doubtful.

"*Please*," Maya said, and punctuated her appeal with another strong tug at her mother's hand.

"Well . . . all right," Blossom finally relented. "But you stay with Bud and the other children. Don't wander. You understand?"

"I promise," Maya said solemnly.

"Go, then." Smiling, Blossom watched her strange, quirky daughter bound joyfully away. Then, relieved herself at being, if only for a short time, free to mingle with those her own age, she padded steadily forward to join another group of women near the front of the party. It had been a long time since she'd seen the Smoke Spirits. She looked forward to it eagerly herself.

Maya skipped around the fringe of chattering women and screaming girls until she came up behind Bud, who was deep in conversation with Twig and Branch, two sisters. A mischievous expression crossed Maya's face. She crouched down low and pretended she was a jackrabbit, meek and mild, and thus crept up without being noticed to a spot only a few feet away from her sister.

"*Boo!*" she shrieked at the top of her lungs, and sprang onto Bud's shoulders. Bud screamed in mock-terror, half collapsing beneath Maya's unexpected weight.

"Maya! Where have you been?" Bud finally gasped, disentangling herself from her stepsister's grasp. Twig and Branch—though a year apart, as alike as two brown nuts—giggled at them.

"I'm a rabbit!" Maya announced. "I'm not Maya, I'm a big, jumping *rabbit!*"

At this Bud dissolved in fresh laughter and, a moment later, so did Maya.

"You girls watch where you're going!" one of the older women, a dour bird named Bush, called sharply.

Chastened, the little group pulled themselves together and took their place on the path. Old Berry, far to the front, led them forward, supporting her wide, bent back with a sturdy walking stick. Two of the younger women walked at her side, ready to catch her lest she fall among the jumbled rock between the ledge and the lower ground beyond.

Maya, now holding Bud's hand, frisked happily along, as the two girls inspected their surroundings with wide, happy eyes. All around them bubbled tiny, silvery springs, from which ran bubbling freshets in a wide, glittering net down to First Lake a hundred yards to their left. They stepped carefully here, for the black, volcanic rock was slippery and covered with gray moss. The group moved with careful gravity, for Old Berry, now nearly fifty, was much weakened with age, though her will remained granite and her lore was boundless. Almost all her days were spent teaching the secrets of leaf and shrub, furtive animal and glittering fish, nuts and the berries that were her namesake, to the women who would eventually succeed her. Even as they walked, the old woman stopped and gestured occasionally, pointing out a particular kind of moss and explaining how to harvest and dry it to some of the younger ones.

Maya paid no attention. Freedom was enough for her today, to be out from under Blossom's ever-watchful eye, laughing in the odd, clear light beneath the cloudy sky.

"Look!" she said to Bud.

"What?"

"At how the smoke rises from Home."

The two girls paused, looking over their shoulders. They had reached a broad, grassy sward beyond the rock jumble—the same place that had been mud when Old Magic had first made this same trek. Now the presence of the People had frightened away the game that had once come to drink from First Lake. The mud had gradually filled up with grass, and now exibited almost park-like features. From this clearing, Maya had an easy vantage of the ledge of Home behind, the great cliff wall above it, and the somewhat lower but no less imposing side walls of the Green Valley itself, towering hundreds of feet above the valley floor.

From this distance Home Camp looked like a village of doll's houses; the half-buried structures blended in with their surroundings, but from the front of each structure there issued great, white, feathery plumes of smoke—the hearths where the women who'd remained behind cooked, and the larger blazes where the men gathered in front of their Mystery House. The most striking effect was the way the smoke rose in a straight line until it reached the level of the cliff top. Then, as if chopped off by an invisible knife, the wind that always blew there blasted the smoke away. The effect was spectacular, and for a moment Maya shivered. Although she claimed the Spirits as friends, the Wind Spirits were formidable, and this demonstration of their power only served as a warning of their true capabilities.

After a moment the scene palled, however, and she tugged at Bud's coat. "Come on," she whispered. "We don't want Bush to shout at us again."

Old Berry led them across the grassy meadow and into the silent, massive forest beyond. It was like stepping from day into night. Maya looked up as they entered the woods, her eyes big as saucers.

Giant oaks towered on every side, fighting with spreading maple and gaunt, gnarled hickory trees. There was very little underbrush, for the canopies of the forest giants screened out almost all sunlight from their massive bases. Only patches of tough, gray grass sprouted here and there, up through a thick mulch of fallen branches, rotting leaves, and decomposing nuts. It was very quiet; Maya felt the same feelings she knew when Old Magic whispered ancient secrets to her, in the warm dark of the Spirit House.

"Scary," Bud remarked.

And though Maya felt some of the same awe shared by her sister, she forced herself to laugh. "There's nothing to be afraid of, Bud! Don't be a scaredy-rabbit!"

"Am not!"

"Are too!"

Bud arranged her features into a pout of bravery and stuck her tongue out at Maya. Maya, instead of replying, only squeezed the hand within hers reassuringly; Bud seemed to take heart from the show of support and a moment later the cloud passed from her face.

The noise of the party was unnaturally loud in the looming silence of the wood, but the rest of the women seemed unconcerned. They passed this way regularly. Off to their left the low, muted murmur of the stream sounded a continuous song; they didn't follow its banks for a simple reason. Treacherous marshes and spots where the ground turned to quicksand lined the water's edge; more than one of the People—even, once, a hunter—had been lost to the strange Spirits who lived there. The path they trod was well marked, however, and though not wide, had been tramped flat by the passage of thousands of feet in the last seven years.

The women marched two abreast in a long, strag-

gling line. Some carried packs filled with tools made
of bone and chipped flint, which they would need
when they arrived at their destination.

Maya glanced up at a sudden sound; a flapping
noise, like the sound door covers made sometimes
when the wind struck them right.

"Look!"

Bud glanced up just in time to see a disappearing
glint of motion. "What is it?" she asked doubtfully.

"A bird," Maya said. "A big black one." She
peered up with new interest, trying to spot further
movement. "I think we scared it away."

"I don't like the black ones," Bud confided. "Leaf
told me they were evil Spirits."

"What does Leaf know?" maya said scornfully.

"Hah! And you know more than Leaf, I suppose?"

Maya licked her lips thoughtfully. "Maybe about
Spirits, I do."

Bud was about to protest this example of over-
weening pride when she remembered whom she
was talking to. Only Maya entered the Spirit House.
Only her sister spoke regularly with Old Magic and
his apprentice, Ghost. Nevertheless, even this could
not repress her completely. "Well, then, what *are*
the black birds?"

Completely serious now, Maya said, "Just birds.
I think." Then, more cheerfully, "Anyway, it's gone
now."

Despite the cloud cover, the day had turned quite
warm. In this late part of the morning, the tempera-
ture was approaching fifty degrees—not hot by later
standards, but of such luxurious heat compared to
the frigid conditions the People had endured that
women loosened cords and let coats hang open,
their breasts exposed to dry the sweat gathered
there.

Maya felt it as well. And it seemed to be growing
warmer. "Hot," she complained.

For once, Bud had the advantage of her older sister. She'd been this way before, and, if only the one time, took the chance to show her superior knowledge.

"It'll get hotter, too," she said importantly. "You wait, you'll see."

"What are you talking about?" Maya demanded, but Bud only shook her head and looked smug.

Now the path began to descend somewhat, and the trees grew further apart. Undergrowth sprang up on either side—fat, thick-leaved bushes, under whose leaves Maya glimpsed tiny round shapes, still milk-white with their summer growth.

She knew the berries would become dark red by fall, and the women would add their harvesting to a host of other duties. They had a sharp, bittersweet taste that became muted when dried and mixed with the acorns the women would also gather.

As the underbrush grew thicker and more profuse, birds appeared, diving to pick at the berries. Flashes of color showed beneath their gray and brown wings, and the forest echoed with their sharp, impatient cries. Maya sighed with delight—she'd never come this far before, and though her legs had begun to ache with the walk, she was enthralled with the new sights and sounds. The World was such a wonderful place! Of course the Spirits had to be placated, but even so, the bounty that surrounded her took her breath away.

Her nose twitched. The air had become full of the thin, vinegary tang of berries fallen and rotting on the ground, but something else intruded, an undersmell she'd sniffed before but only faintly, and when the wind was right.

Now the stench billowed into her face, thick, heavy and ominous. The only thing like it was when she'd once found an abandoned bird nest in the Rock Jumble that contained two tiny, broken eggs.

Those eggs had smelled something like this, but nowhere near as strong.

"Phew," she said to Bud. "That stinks. What is it?"

"You'll see," Bud told her mysteriously.

"Come *on*, tell me."

Bud only shook her head.

The suddenness with which the forest ended was a complete surprise. One moment they trod the well-worn path, canopied by gigantic, rough-barked trees, and the next the full gray glare of day filled their eyes.

Just beyond the edge of the forest the earth dropped sharply, perhaps ten feet, down to the edge of a lake much larger than First Lake.

"Second Lake," Maya breathed. Off to her left, the stream broadened out as it emptied into the larger body of water. A brisk breeze stirred the silver surface of the lake, which glowed like mercury beneath the gray-white sky. From where she stood Maya could see the entire body of water, and she discerned that it was shaped like a teardrop, where she stood at the narrow end. There was a narrow beach of gravel around this side, no more than five or six feet wide and studded with larger, darker stones. Old Berry led the way down to this natural path, her stride resolute. The party didn't pause here, though Maya dearly would have loved to stop and explore. Nevertheless, conscious of the gaze of Bush, who marched behind her, she kept up her pace, only slowing momentarily to gaze at some fresh wonder.

An erratic breeze ruffled the top of the water and made it hard to see what she squinted at. A group of tiny black dots in the center of the lake, bobbing like bits of floating wood. But the dots weren't wood. When the sound of the women's passage reached them, the ducks exploded from the surface in a sudden spray of water and wings, and the air was filled with their honking cries. There were hundreds of them!

"Ohh," Maya breathed.

Speaking from her well of great experience, Bud sniffed, "They're only ducks, Maya."

"They're beautiful!"

More practically, Bud said, "They're good to eat, at least."

Which was perfectly true. The women occasionally managed to snare one of the wary birds, and when they did there was celebration around the lucky hearth. Ducks, rich in the fat the People craved, were considered as tasty as any provender found in the Green Valley. Maya's mother, Blossom, was not however particularly skilled in their entrapment, and so Maya had only tasted the birds a few times. Her mouth watered in remembered enjoyment as she watched the creatures, poky and awkward, turn into visions of grace as they climbed into the lowering sky.

Finally the group approached a point where the stream spilled again over a natural rock dam at the end of the lake. As always Old Berry led the way down, but this time she paused and called back, "Be careful now. Watch where you step."

Obediently, Maya switched her observations to the ground, which had become wet and muddy. Now they followed the stream itself, for the woods on either side had turned impenetrable, choked with bushes and saplings of every kind. As she walked, Maya continued to wrinkle her nose. The nasty smell was almost a physical presence, thick and dark on the air. She wondered what it was.

Then, finally, several hundred yards downstream, she made out a final wonder. A loud, sighing noise split the morning, and then, from the ground itself burst a long, curling feather of smoke!

*   *   *

The she-lion was full, and disposed to lie on the rocks with her two half-grown cubs, soaking up the heat stored in the dark stone. But the wind shifted suddenly and she moved uneasily, half rose, then sank down again, uncertain.

She knew that odor, had smelled it many times before. But it was a new thing still, and not one she normally associated with food.

Her two cubs mauled the bloody remains of a large jackrabbit they'd flushed out minutes before. They made soft, mewling sounds as their small, sharp teeth worried at the flesh and cracked the tiny bones.

Mother Lion rose again. The smell was stronger than any she could remember. Her first instinct was to retreat, but she had her cubs with her. Nothing could be allowed to threaten them!

She hissed a soft warning at them and then, with almost weary fluidity, slid from her perch on the rocky outcrop of the valley wall.

Not far away, she thought. She had penetrated well up into the valley, away from the series of caves she normally occupied, intent upon training her children to hunt the rabbit and squirrel that were more numerous here. The new spoor both frightened and intrigued her. This ambivalence made her uncomfortable and, hence, irritable.

Snarling softly, she padded off into the interior.

Chapter Six

The Green Valley: 17,990 B.C.

As noon approached, rents began to appear in the cloud cover overhead, so that the full heat of the sun burned down on the women who labored below. It grew so warm that some of the younger women threw off their coats entirely and let the golden rays play across the thick pads of muscle on their shoulders.

Old Berry was in her element. Many of the youngest girls had never gone on a trip like this, and were clumsy at their newfound tasks. Berry tramped among them, leaning on her stick, gesturing, explaining, criticizing.

"No," she said, "not that kind." She stopped near a small group of three, Petal, Moss, and Flower. The girls halted their work to listen.

The area where the expedition had finally stopped was eerie. To their left as they faced downstream was a long, narrow body of water: Smoke Lake. The waters of Smoke Lake bubbled continuously, and where the patches of roiled water appeared, smoke rose into the air: live steam, from vents that extended deep into the earth. The graveled path they'd followed disappeared just ahead, into an area of low, grassy marsh and brush, from which issued more smoke. Further on and a bit to their right a broad patch of dark brown mud made thick, gloopy sounds, and emitted a symphony of stinks: rot and decay, spoiled eggs, sulfur. Little smoke came from this area, however, only the smells, which made the women wrinkle their noses in disgust and cough occasionally. Beyond the mud flat and the marsh the ancient forest closed in again, dark and foreboding, although brightened a bit by the birds which nested there and flew about, cawing and shrieking at each other and the invasion of women into their territory.

The girls worked right at the edge of the marsh, with the forest less than ten feet from their backs. In their hands they held small, heavy choppers, blunt rocks shaped to a single edge by Stone's skill. With these tools they hacked at the base of a group of saplings perhaps two inches thick. The graceful, brown-barked shrubs bore leafy crowns of delicate green about eight feet above the ground; only a few twiglike branches extended out from their narrow trunks. They were youthful hickories; perfect for the role they would eventually play in the everyday life of the People.

Two of the girls had nearly hacked through their saplings; Flower, perhaps misunderstanding, worked instead on another kind of plant, a low, crooked, flowering thing with thorns and tough, dark brown bark. It was she Old Berry admonished.

"Why don't you listen, Flower? I told you what kind. See what Petal and Moss are doing?" She slapped Flower lightly on the top of her head. "Now leave that ugly thing alone and work on"—she pivoted, selected a likely prospect, and pointed—"that one."

Flower, a jittery, nervous girl given to giggles and not much else, abandoned her task and knee-walked over to the hickory Old Berry had designated. Berry watched her closely as the girl began to chop away at the delicate bark a few inches above the ground until, satisfied her instructions were being carried out, she nodded and said, "Good. Keep it up." Then, with a grunt, she wheeled and stumped away, toward the next group.

In mid-stride she paused and shaded her eyes. Her ancient senses had picked up . . . something? Slowly she scanned the forest wall, but saw nothing amiss. The birds still flew, and the other sounds she heard—the sigh of breezes (mostly deflected by the canyon walls, so that only the weakest remnants of the terrible steppe winds penetrated here), the chittering call of small climbing rodents and others that hid in the ground—all were normal enough. So what had she heard?

Faintly troubled, she hitched herself about and regarded Smoke Lake itself. Nothing unusual there; the bubbling and smokes had awed her when she'd first seen them, but now, after years of exploration, they were as familiar as any other part of the Green Valley. There were fish in the lake, she knew, but these were rarely caught, for the lake was deep, dropping off immediately from its banks. Once, she'd made a long line by tying lengths of leather cord together and fastening a stone the size of her fist to one end. She'd paid out the line from the bank, and when she'd reached the end the stone still hadn't struck bottom—and the line had been five double-hands of paces long. She shuddered faintly; any of the People who fell into Smoke Lake would never come back; the skill of swimming was completely unknown.

She still saw nothing untoward, and after a moment the faint hint of alarm faded. She shrugged and hobbled on, toward the next group of women.

Maya, too young to be entrusted with the actual work of chopping, had watched for a while and then, bored, wandered off with Bud to the fringes of the group, right at the edge of the forest. Here they rested, comfortable in the shade, on a fallen trunk whose far end extended back across a shallow ravine into the wood proper. For a time they sat and chattered at each other, as much at home in their surroundings as any other animal sheltered in the Valley. Then, as children are wont to do, they turned their attention to other things.

"Look, Bud," Maya announced, shifting herself about on the half-rotted top of the huge log, "it's like a bridge across the canyon." Carefully, she got her legs under her and stood, holding her arms out for balance.

Bud eyed her doubtfully. "You better not let Old Berry see you."

But Maya ignored the warning as, with childish calculation, she measured the distance of the log across the ravine. It *looked* strong enough to hold her. She couldn't quite make out the end of the timber support, for it disappeared into a loose thicket, almost like a leafy tent that had grown up around the shattered base of the forest giant.

"I can get across!" she announced finally. Then, without further ado, she took a step.

"Maya!' Bud squealed softly. "What if you fall?"

Both girls looked down. The ravine, while shallow, was perhaps four feet deep, and lined with a hodgepodge of sharp stones, partially concealed by a low growth of some kind of thorny bracken. It would be a nasty fall, but Maya didn't intend to slip.

"Shhh, Bud!" she replied sharply. "You'll bring Bush or Blossom down on us!" Then, ignoring the plaintive, whispered cries of alarm from her sister, she moved forward, lithely balanced. A few moments later she stood on the other side, looking back down the length at Bud.

"Well," she called, "are you coming, or not?"

Bud eyed her sister warily. "We'll get in trouble," she said.

"No, we won't. Just to the end of the tree," Maya replied. "Come on, scaredy-rabbit."

This slur was too much for Bud to bear. She sighed, then carefully got to her feet. She was smaller than Maya, but a natural acrobat, and made it across the mini-chasm with great ease. Once across, her black eyes sparkled. "There!" she announced. "See, I'm *not* a scaredy-rabbit!"

Maya nodded in approval. It was easy to talk Bud into doing things, even things she didn't want to do. Both girls got into a lot of trouble that way with the older women.

Now they re-seated themselves, short legs swinging over the edge of the log. Just beyond, the canopy of saplings that had grown up around the cracked roots of the ancient oak tree made an inviting, almost house-like arch. After a moment, Maya crawled forward until she was inside the small, leafy cave. Bud watched dubiously, but paused only an instant before joining her sister. Within seconds, both were engrossed in a childish game in which the natural tent was their home and they, grown up, were playing at mother and father, their imaginations inflamed with the mysteries of adulthood. So enthralled, whispering and giggling together, neither of them heard the low, harsh cough that issued from deep within the forest—and even if they had, they wouldn't have known what it was.

Neither girl had ever seen, or heard, a hunting cave lion before.

Mother Lion was a fearsome beast. Somewhat larger than a modern Bengal tiger, she stood three and a half feet tall at her heavily muscled shoulder, and weighed six hundred pounds. Her pelt was colored like honey, and much longer and thicker than that of her descendants of the far future, but her most distinctive feature protruded from her great jaws: a pair of backward-slanting fangs almost ten inches long, white and glistening and pointed like needles.

Now, teeth flashing as she yawned, she glanced back over her shoulder. Her two half-grown cubs, their own fangs just beginning to show, gamboled in a small, sun-lit clearing a few yards behind. They'd given off mauling the carcass of the jackrabbit and follower her, and her instincts had given her no reason to chase them away. The strange smells she'd tracked were upsetting, but not enough to make her afraid.

Mother Lion feared very little, as far as that went. She sat firmly atop the predator chain hereabouts. Nothing challenged her supremacy, for with claw and fang she hunted the huge mammoth, the bison, and most delectable of all, the tender caribou. She could be killed—a maddened mammoth mother defending her family might get in a lucky strike with her formidable tusks, and then finish the job with pounding feet—but it would be a very lucky strike indeed.

It was as much curiosity as anything that led Mother Lion toward the group of women who chattered by the shores of Smoke Lake. She had crossed the stream below the lake, taking the bubbling water in a single lazy, fifteen-foot leap. Her cubs, struggling, had barely made the same jump. One, in fact, had slipped backwards into the fringe of the stream and emerged moments later, hissing and spitting and shaking at the drenching he'd taken.

With a final glance at her cubs, Mother rose from her haunches and advanced for a closer glimpse. As she arose her yawn ended in a low, coughing grunt, a terrible sound. Old Berry had heard it almost subconsciously, but had not truly understood it for what it was, since it had been masked by the sounds of the women themselves, as well as the ever-present noise from the forest.

But as Mother Lion moved forward, a curious thing occurred: For a space of ten or fifteen yards all around her, everything fell silent. Tiny, burrowing animals disappeared into their holes; birds clung suddenly to safe branches high above the floor and regarded Mother Lion's passage with bright, beady eyes. Mother Lion noticed this silence not at all; it was her customary due. She, and all others like her, had moved in this respectful, appalling silence all their lives.

Her cubs tumbled after, batting and pawing playfully at each other.

Maya glanced up, suddenly afraid, although she had no idea what had caused the fright. "Bud. Did you hear anything?"

The other girl glanced around uneasily. "No," she said, her voice unnaturally loud, "I didn't." She paused, then continued. "I don't hear anything at all, in fact."

It was true. The forest had gone dead silent around them. They could hear the voices of the women in the distance, thin and high, but the sounds that they'd heard unconsciously all around them— birds, animals, even insects—had died away.

Maya stirred nervously. Finally, moving very carefully, she stood up and faced back the way they'd come. "I think," she whispered, fearful of disturbing the ominous silence, "we'd better go back."

Bud, her eyes narrowed and watchful, came to her feet in a single smooth movement. She didn't say a word, merely turned and started back across the ravine. Then she halted, paralyzed with panic.

Two huge, glittering green eyes regarded her with calm ferocity from the other end of the log.

Mother Lion opened her huge jaws and coughed.

Old Magic stared through lowered eyelids into the tiny flame that flickered in the hearth at the center of the Spirit House. It was quite warm; he'd been dozing, and something had half wakened him.

He was used to the cycle. More and more, lately, he found it easy to sit by the fire, immersed in ancient memories, singing songs to himself. He knew he was old, very old; his bones told him so every morning when he awoke. In other times he might have already passed his mantle on to Ghost—but these weren't other times. The weight of the Great Secret pressed heavily on him. Maya was barely seven now, a long way from womanhood. Somehow he must hang on—for though he wasn't certain, he was fairly sure the little girl could not wield her full power before the onset of her menses. Years yet— and Ghost growing ever more troublesome as he approached the peak years of his manhood.

Hoping to placate the younger man, Old Magic had relinquished more and more of his duties to him. For instance, this would be the first time Ghost had managed the Spirits of the Hunt. He could hear the younger Shaman's voice in the distance, rough with authority, as he conferred with Spear and the other hunt leaders.

He sighed heavily. He hoped it would be enough. The Secret spoke of many things, most of which he hadn't told Ghost. His years of experience warned him—Ghost was not yet ready to understand the full power of the Secret, nor his role in it. Old Magic was in fact afraid that if Ghost *did* understand the part he was to play, he might no longer be trusted at all. The safety of young Maya—he smiled to himself as his lips shaped her name, so different from the names of the rest of the People—*her* safety was paramount.

If he could keep on managing things. If he could live long enough to do what had to be done. He didn't want to think of the alternatives. They were too fearsome, not only for Maya, but for the very survival of the People.

The weight. The terrible weight.

Gradually, the feeling of alarm that had wakened him began to ebb. The sounds of the village outside the tent were a comforting hum, and the low snap and crackle of the fire soothed his tired brain. His head tilted forward and his eyes closed.

The dream took him with all the force of a thunderbolt.

He found himself walking, walking. All around him stretched long, rolling plains, covered with a thick carpet of bright green grass. Here and there within the grass glowed patches of bright blue. He smiled in recognition; those tiny flowers were called "Maya," and were the source of the girl's name. When he saw them he knew he was Dreaming, for he'd only seen them in the Dreamtime.

He kept on walking. He knew what would come next.

Sure enough, in the distance, he made out a grouping of figures. When he saw them, he understood that this was a Great Dream, for those figures only appeared at times of crucial importance for the People. Dimly, he wondered what had called them up; things had gone remarkably well for the past several years, and although certain changes he'd noticed worried him, they hadn't become a problem yet.

Finally he came near enough to make out features. The woman who stood at the forefront of the group raised her right hand, palm out, and smiled at him. "Peace, Brother," she said in a soft voice. It was odd. Her lips moved, but no sound came out. Rather, the words appeared directly in his mind.

When he'd first met her, in his youth, he'd thought she was the Great Mother Herself, but gradually had come to understand that she was not. The Great Mother, even in dreams, would never speak to a man. This woman, so calm, so full of potent magic, was only Her handmaid—though her powers were as far beyond his own as his were above the animals of the ground.

He thought she might be a Spirit, but since she never spoke of herself, he couldn't be sure. Nevertheless, he smiled in turn and replied, "Peace to you, Sister."

Directly behind her towered a huge female Mammoth, who regarded him peacefully across the immense curve of her tusks. Next to the Mammoth Mother loomed the great form of a female bison, a Caribou Mother, a huge wolf, and, finally, at the woman's left hand, the monstrous form of a she-lion, fangs swept back so far they almost grazed the soft fur of her neck.

He sensed the forms of others, invisible to his eyes, as if the woman fronted for a vast throng of which he knew nothing except one thing: All of those he faced on this endless, beautiful plain were female. Though the Great Mother chose not to reveal Herself to him, She was here in all Her strength and power.

The dreams frightened him, yet at the same time bathed him in an inexpressible calm.

He bowed slightly and waited. The woman, whose green and blue eyes flashed as she spoke, whose fingers lightly caressed the carving of a mammoth hanging from a thong around her neck, like but not twin to the one he kept safe in the Spirit House, conveyed to him the warning she had to give.

He awoke fully, covered with sweat, his heart pounding with terror. His muscles creaked in protest as he levered himself to his feet and stumbled

out of the Spirit House, not even bothering with any
special regalia.

"Ghost, Spear!" he shouted. "Come here! Come
right away!"

Maya froze. She couldn't move. The Mother Lion's
great green gaze paralyzed her, like a tiny bird before a snake. Behind her, Bud moaned softly.

The sound jolted Maya from her deathly inertia;
without another thought, she whirled and yanked
Bud.

"*Run! Run!*"

Bud stumbled as she hit the ground, but Maya
came down right behind her and grabbed her hand
and jerked her forward.

"*Run!*"

The two little girls stumbled into the tangle of
bush and bracken. Branches whipped at their faces.
Thick masses of leaves obscured their view. In an
instant they lost all sense of direction.

Maya's heart pounded. Her breath burned like fire
in her chest. Thin streaks of blood bloomed across
her cheeks where the branches scored her skin like
knives. She pushed Bud ahead, glancing in terror
over her shoulder. At any moment she expected to
see that terrible, sandy-colored shape explode through
the trees upon their trail.

Time slowed down. Though it only took seconds,
it seemed months, years to Maya before they finally
burst through the tangled undergrowth into a small
clearing.

The edge of the clearing was surrounded with
young hickory trees. Beyond, taller giants, their long
trunks slick as glass, loomed silently.

A hiding place! Maya thought frantically. She whipped
her head back and forth, searching for a small cave,
a hole in the ground, *anything*.

But there was nothing, only the trees and that

curious, deadly silence. She could hear her own breath rushing in her ears.

Meeeuuuoooooowwww . . . !

At first she ignored the low, mewling sound, not understanding. Then her frenzied gaze picked out the source, obscured against the background of darker brush: *two more!*

A tiny, calm part of her mind noticed that these two lions were smaller than the one on the log. Even so, they outweighed either of the girls by two hundred pounds.

Trapped!

Bud began to sob in terror. Maya glanced at her. The younger girl's face was white as a fish.

There isn't any time!

Bud screamed. The thin, whistling sound that came from her lips was hardly audible. Maya grabbed at a hank of her dark hair and pulled, hard. Bud's eyes popped wide.

"The tree. Climb a tree!"

Bud stared at her blankly. Across the clearing, one of the cubs rose slowly to his feet. He'd never seen anything like this before in his young life—and without his mother to show him what to do with it, he was puzzled.

"Urroouuwwww . . ." he called plaintively. Was this something to hunt? Or merely to toy with, as he did with his brother? He put one tentative paw down, the size of a small saucer, and gingerly stepped forward.

Maya took Bud by her shoulders and spun her around. She put her lips right on Bud's ear and screamed; *"That tree, Bud! There! Climb that tree!"* And shoved her with brutal force in the direction of a middling hickory that still had enough lower branches to make for handholds.

The combination of the push and the shouts woke Bud from her paralysis. She stumbled forward until

her hands had found the warm bark and, instinctively, she began to climb.

Maya followed. Her foot caught in something and
she half fell. Now the other cub came off his haunches
and joined his brother. Together, still tentative and
uncertain, they began to pick their way across the
clearing.

Maya came to her feet holding the dry branch that
had tripped her up. It was only a couple of feet long,
light enough that she could swing it. Not much, but
something!

She stood, her back to the tree trunk, and faced
the cubs. The one in the lead bounded suddenly
across the few feet separating them, and batted playfully at the little girl before him.

Maya shrieked in fear; then, as tears mingled with
blood on her face, she struck back with the branch.

The tip of it grazed the tender muzzle of the
young lion, who flinched back in amazement, hissing.

Maya flung down the branch and scrambled into
the tree.

"Climb! Climb higher! Come on, hurry up, climb!"

Mother Lion blinked. One moment the strange
things had been there, the next they were gone. Her
nose caught the fear smell which made them prey,
but she'd fed already today. They ran; they were no
threat, and she was lazy.

But a few moments later, her lassitude disappeared. In quick succession she heard the puzzled
mewling of her cubs, and then, a split-second later,
the surprised hiss of pain and confusion from the
one Maya had grazed with her stick.

Her eyes narrowed to slits of molten emerald fire.
Mighty slabs of sinew flexed in her thighs. One single bound took her the length of the log and well
into the brush beyond.

Her guttural roar filled the forest as she descended
like an avalanche of death toward the clearing,

where Bud and Maya frantically clambered like monkeys higher and higher into their refuge.

Old Berry stiffened in alarm. Other of the women halted their work and raised their heads. Mother Lion's enraged roar still echoed in their ears.

Old Berry shouted, "The children! *Where are the children?*"

The band of women leaped to their feet; eyes searched, voices called. Somebody was wailing loudly. Old Berry recognized the voice, if not the words—Blossom. It told her all she needed to know.

"Mayaaaaa! Where's Maya? And Bud! Bud's gone, too!"

Old Berry limped over to the hysterical woman and, without pausing, slapped her hard across the face. Blossom jerked back. Sanity began to peek through her glazed eyes.

"Shut up. Get yourself together! Now, *think!* Where were they when you saw them last?"

Snuffling, and with a thin trickle of blood from Old Berry's blow leaking from the corner of her mouth, Blossom screwed up her eyes in thought. "Over . . . there. I think," she said uncertainly, and pointed toward the ravine. "But they were just playing. . . ."

Old Berry snorted. "That girl!"

Now Blossom's eyes bulged. "I hear them! Can't you hear them?"

Old Berry could hear the sharp, girlish cries well enough. She could also hear a crescendo of snarling roars counterpointing the screams of terror.

"Yes, I can hear them. It means they're still alive." She gathered herself and turned to the other women. "You, and you. Take the other children back. Now *move!*" She scanned the ground. "The rest of you, take rocks. Pick up sticks, branches, anything. Come on, *hurry!*"

As the women scurried to do her bidding, Old Berry fought the fear in her heart as best she could. She, alone of all the women, had perhaps the best idea of what Maya truly might become. Old Magic had told no secrets, but Berry knew some of the old stories, too. Women, as well as men, passed down their secret songs from antiquity, and she knew more than she told.

If something happened to Maya . . . ! She cursed the weakness of her old bones, then pushed the momentary bleakness away. No time for sniveling! She would do as best she could, with what she had.

Quickly she gathered the remaining women into a small band. They bristled with poles, clubs, heavy rocks. "Come on!" she ordered, as she turned toward the ravine and the horrendous sounds that issued from beyond. She noted that Blossom had gotten control of herself, and now brandished a wicked pole almost as tall as she was.

"Let's go," Berry told them and, gripping her own staff more firmly, began to stump across the stony ground. Fearfully, the others followed, Berry at the forefront, her teeth showing in a frantic snarl.

Old Berry felt a thrill of pride as she led her motley army toward battle. The men, even armed with their terrible spears, would not have done it. Not even for two little girls. But these were women and, more important, they were mothers.

Old Berry knew a secret, and was reassured. Men were only men . . . but mothers protecting their children were the fiercest, most deadly animals on the face of the World.

"Hurry!"

Maya paused for a moment, her breath rasping in her throat. She clung to a branch perhaps fifteen feet above the ground. Just above her head, Bud sought purchase on an ever-thinning ladder of

branches as she fought her way higher into the
safety of the tree.

Their movements caused the hickory to bend
slightly. At its base the trunk was six inches thick,
but here it narrowed to less than four inches. Their
weight began to have an effect.

Maya glanced back toward the ground. Both lion
cubs sat at the foot of the tree, their green eyes
focused on the girls above. One of the cubs padded
forward and stretched to his full length against the
trunk. When Maya saw how far up the trunk his
forepaws extended—almost seven feet—she looked
up and said, "We'd better go higher, Bud."

The younger girl was hysterical with terror. She
whimpered and shook her head back and forth.
"We're going to *die*! They'll *eat* us!"

"No, they won't," Maya replied, as calmly as she
could. "We're safe up here, just keep on climbing."
But even as she spoke, she wondered if it was the
truth. Those cubs below looked like they could climb
as well as she could—even if, at the moment, they
were content with only watching.

Then her heart catapulted into her throat. A great
crackling noise sounded as Mother Lion bounded
into the clearing, her thick, warning growl thrumming like thunder. The huge cat skidded to a stop
at the base of the tree, never taking her eyes from
the two girls overhead. She butted at the cubs with
her wide, triangular muzzle, as if to reassure herself
that nothing was amiss. Then, satisfied, she gathered herself and exploded straight up.

Maya shrieked involuntarily as the great cat landed
on the trunk no more than three feet below her own
position. Huge claws flashed out as Mother Lion
scrabbled for purchase in the branches below. Her
hindquarters pumped and pumped again. Then, almost before she had gained a secure perch, Mother

Lion's forepaw lashed out in a lethal swipe at Maya's dangling feet.

Squeaking, Maya pulled herself up and ran smack into Bud's rear end. She put her shoulder there and pushed. *"Climb!"* she yelled at the top of her lungs, hoping to jar her sister from the mortal paralysis that had seized her. A moment later, she felt Bud begin to move at last. Still pushing, she forced the younger girl higher into the tree.

Mother Lion's momentum had carried her well up, but now she began to have trouble. The thin branches at this level wouldn't support her weight very well—some began to bend dangerously, even snap. Her first swipe had been more an extension of her initial leap than a well-delivered blow. Now she began to slip backward. She hissed her frustration, and concentrated on bettering her grasp on the tree trunk. For a moment the two terrified girls above her—now prey, for she was fully enraged—could wait. But she'd get them soon enough. There was no place they could hide from her wrath. She could climb, too.

Bud, once her paralysis had been broken, moved like a frightened squirrel. Within seconds she'd climbed another ten feet, almost into the crown of the hickory. Exhaling a harsh sigh of relief, Maya followed, conscious of the huge cat thrashing futilely below.

She finally stopped, clutching the trunk just below the top of the tree. Bud's legs, wrapped around the trunk for support, thumped into her shoulders. The trunk had narrowed; it was barely two inches across, and their weight caused it to sway back and forth with a sickening motion. They could go no higher, for above them the trunk disappeared entirely into a spray of delicate branches far too small to support their weight.

Maya looked down to where Mother Lion struggled. She hoped the cat wouldn't be able to climb up high enough to reach them, but she remembered the hideous length of forepaw that had narrowly missed her. Finally she simply stopped and waited, for there was nothing else to do. She watched Mother Lion warily, and hoped that Bud would continue to hold on. If either of them fell, it would be to the death.

"Hang on, Bud!" she commanded tensely. "Just hang on! I won't let it get you!"

Brave words. She had no idea how she'd stop the big cat if it got close enough, but somehow her own words of reassurance made her feel better. Sniffles answered her from above, but Bud seemed less frantic than before.

Maya opened her mouth as wide as she could. *"Help! Helllp!"*

Down below, Mother Lion finally had gotten a good grip on the trunk with her hook-like afterclaws. She paused; then with slow, careful movements, she began to hitch herself higher. Her eyes glowed with fearful lust.

Ever so slowly, like a great bow drawn by its string, the hickory began to bend.

"Help! Hellllp!"

Old Berry rammed her thick body through a screen of thorny brush, ignoring the pricks and tears in her flesh. Not far ahead the horrible sounds continued: childish screams, a counterpoint of mewing and soft growls, and most ominous of all, the thick, guttural coughing of a great cat.

"Hurry!" she shouted. Blossom thrust up to her side, her face wild. Her black hair was disordered, full of sticky burrs; her face, shiny with sweat, glowed red from exertion. She brandished her stick and forged ahead.

"No!" Old Berry called. "Wait for us!"

Blossom ignored the warning. In a moment she was gone. Old Berry redoubled her efforts. Now the women themselves began to shout and screech, hoping to frighten off the lion they could hear up ahead. Finally they plunged through a final barrier of shrubs and piled into the clearing.

Old Berry stumbled to a halt. Her aged eyes slowly looked upward, to find a horrifying sight. A sturdy young hickory stood on the opposite side of the clearing. Up near the top, two tiny figures clung with tenacious fingers to the very highest branches. Bud's legs had lost their hold on the trunk and she dangled loose, held only by the strength of her arms. Below her, Maya was still wrapped securely around the tree, but her white face was frozen with terror.

A few feet below, hissing and roaring, Mother Lion edged inch by cautious inch upward. Her weight bent the hickory into a great rounded curve. Bud's feet swung ever closer to the ground, where the two half-grown cubs, now enflamed by their mother's rage, leaped into the air, claws extended, trying to snare the morsel that drooped ever closer to their hungry fangs.

Blossom stood in the middle of the clearing, her mouth a round *Oh!* of rage and horror. A continuous, high-pitched shriek, so terrible it pained human ears to hear it, flowed from her throat.

She swung her pole in a wide, sweeping arc, and began to advance upon the two cubs, ignoring the howling mass of Mother Lion almost directly overhead.

"Rocks!" Old Berry shouted. *"Throw rocks!"*

Chapter Seven

The Green Valley: 17,990 B.C.

Maya felt the palms of her hands, slick with sweat, begin to slip from the soft bark of the tree trunk. Panic had turned her muscles into aching, trembling knots of agony. She could hardly breathe; her lungs seemed to be on fire. Still she kept on screaming for help, even though, half-blinded as she was by blood from cuts on her forehead, all she could see was the top of Bud's head and her arms, still wrapped tightly around the narrow branch a foot away.

A huge thrashing noise erupted near her own feet. Mother Lion moaned deep in her throat, as she tried to hitch her great body a few inches forward on the trunk. Her sudden movement shook the trunk like a child's stick, and the top sank a foot or so closer to the ground. The stench of the huge cat's odor filled Maya's nostrils. She didn't dare look around. Instead she tried to edge herself a few precious inches ahead of the flashing claws that could sweep her from her perch with a single deadly swipe.

The top of the tree was now almost parallel to the ground, Bud's tiny form hung straight down, and each frantic swing of her legs, as she fought to lever her small body upward, set off a new, hideous cater-wauling from the cubs leaping up from below. Then, as Maya watched in horror, Bud's left hand lost its grip on the slender trunk and dropped away. Now Bud was suspended only by the fingers of her right hand, as with her left she flailed blindly for a new hold.

"Hang on, Bud! I'm coming!"

"Aieeeeeee!"

Maya gripped the trunk tighter with her thighs and pushed herself a few more inches along the wildly swaying wood. Mother Lion began to lose her purchase and pistoned her huge hindquarters, seeking a new position for the long claws there. She coughed in her rage, then loosed a blood-chilling growl. One more time she swatted out with her right forepaw, but the killing stroke fell short by a hair's-breadth.

Maya extended her own right hand as far as she could, and tried to grab on to Bud's fingers. For a moment she thought she'd succeeded; Bud's fingers touched her palm, and she tightened her grip as much as she could . . . but then the sweat that coated her flesh broke the tenuous hold, and Bud's hand twisted away.

"My hand, grab my hand!" Maya shrieked.

Bud's eyes were locked shut by terror. Her entire world had shrunk to the single handhold she still maintained, with frenzied strength, to the limb above her head. Her short legs flailed and twisted; she heard nothing, not the grotesque snarls of Mother Lion, not the fearsome hissing and mewling from below, not the shouts as the women arrived, not even Maya's wild pleas from less than two feet above her head.

Maya bit her lip as she squirmed one more inch toward her goal; blood filled her mouth, but she didn't taste it. Her shoulders ached horribly; her thighs, locked around the trunk in a death-grip, had long since gone numb. Just a few inches more . . .

Got it!

Her right hand closed on Bud's slender left wrist. Maya gritted her teeth and held on for dear life, then began to draw Bud's fingers toward a new hold on the branch.

"I've got you!"

Mother Lion's hindquarters finally obtained a tenuous catch in the tender bark, and with a horrid explosion of power, drove her great mass forward. She yowled in triumph, but even as she reached for Maya's body with her claws her grip failed, and she began to slide away.

The movement shook the top of the tree like a mighty wind. Bud's right hand finally gave way; Maya held on to her left wrist, but Bud dropped straight down, suspended now only by the strength of Maya's right arm.

Mother Lion saw the movement; then, temporarily distracted, she saw the rest; saw the women, saw the strange thing with the stick advance, shrieking, upon her cubs. She gathered herself. . . .

Maya felt Bud's thin wrist begin to slide between her fingers. Too sweaty! She summoned up the last ounces of her strength, but nothing she could do would halt the inexorable slide; an instant later Bud slipped away, and dropped like a tiny acorn into the wrangling cubs below.

Mother Lion, hysterical with rage, fell like a sandy avalanche right behind her. Like the end of a whip, the slender branch upon which Maya clung lashed back toward the sky.

The men ran. When they reached Smoke Lake, they turned as one toward the appalling sounds of the broil in the forest. At their head, Spear brandished his namesake weapon. Ghost kept pace with him easily, even though he wore his full regalia of reindeer hide and skull. He carried a rattle in his left hand, and in his right a short, though wickedly sharp, ceremonial spear.

Skin and Stone and Claw and other of the men loped behind, their faces twisted by anxiety. They were hunters; they understood full well the import of the sounds they heard. Now the women's shrieks began to reach them, and a sudden cacophony of growls and snarls.

"Hurry!" Spear commanded. They lowered their shoulders and redoubled their speed, leaping over brush, clambering down the ravine, then up and into the woods proper.

A moment later they burst into the clearing.

Old Berry watched in stupefied horror as Blossom, waving her stick back and forth, advanced upon the cubs. "*Rocks!*" she screamed again and, finally, the women responded. The air above the clearing suddenly was dense with a hail of fist-sized stones. The missiles descended on the cubs, most without effect, but one jagged, sharp-edged projectile smashed into the left eye of the smaller cub. He howled his pain. Just as he did so, Bud fell like a shot onto his back. He arched in surprise, and the little girl tumbled to the ground. She lay dazed, half-stunned; the second cub sniffed at her, while the first danced over her body, trying to swipe the source of pain away from his eye.

Mother Lion fell into the squirming mass like a thunderbolt. Blossom screeched and rushed forward, her stick held straight out like a spear.

Mother Lion turned to face this new attack, her swordlike fangs fully extended, glittering in the sun. All her claws protruded, both front and hindmost; she didn't even notice when her after-claw slashed across Bud's stomach and spilled her intestines steaming upon the soft earth.

Blossom saw it, though; the death of her daughter sent her mad. Without another thought she lunged at Mother Lion . . . but her pitiful stave was no protection at all against the massive, slashing forepaw that almost tore her head off.

Now more rocks flew; the women set up a terrible, wailing cry. Mother Lion paused over her victims only an instant; her nose was full of the scent of fresh blood, but the advance of the women was too much. Her cubs came first!

She slapped one cub away; he understood and, with a single short bound, disappeared into the underbrush. A moment later his brother, blood dripping from one eye, followed.

Mother Lion crouched in place, hissing and growling dire warnings at the women. Then, finally, even she began to give ground, for the men had come crashing through the women and they bore the one thing Mother Lion truly feared: Fire!

Spear leaped toward her, his terrible weapon held straight out. On either side, Skin and Stone brandished torches. The flickering glow, the endless noise, these new things . . .

Too much! With a final, grating snarl, she turned and leaped for the safety of the dark trees.

Old Magic sat in the Spirit House, his eyes tightshut, the sacred stone, unwrapped, clasped tightly to his chest. He rocked back and forth and chanted a secret song. Smoke from the tiny fire filled his nostrils. After a time the World went away, and he hung suspended in darkness, dreaming Dreams.

He had no idea how long it took. Time had a way of behaving strangely in dreams. Sometimes he would wake after a very short dream and find that hours had passed in the World; other times, it was the opposite. So he simply waited, hearing his chant in the bones of his skull as a low, buzzing counterpoint to the dark.

She came, finally. Two eyes, one blue, one green. The eyes regarded him blankly. He didn't feel the numbing power of the Great Mother here; only the enigmatic gaze of Her handmaid. So he prayed to the eyes, over and over again.

Don't let her die!

After a time the eyes grew vague and shadowed. Finally they began to shrink, until only two tiny points of glittering light remained. Then they were gone.

Old Magic awoke with no idea whether or not he'd succeeded. He stared at the fire and, even though it was warm in the Spirit House, he felt a chill seep into his aged bones.

So cold . . .

The tree trunk, suddenly relieved of the weight of both Mother Lion and Bud, whipped up in a great arc. Maya had no time to think, to tighten her grip, anything. The trunk snapped back to perpendicular, like a great fishing pole. Maya felt her arms, her legs torn from the smooth bark and then, strangely, she was flying.

It only lasted a moment. Then she crashed to earth ten feet beyond the clearing. Something slammed into her head. She didn't feel it, though. She'd already lost consciousness.

Mother Lion's leap landed her well beyond the edge of the clearing. Her eyesight was terrible, but her sharp ears and even sharper nose told her the cubs were ahead, and safe. She lowered her great head and tore through the underbrush like a freight train, until the smell dragged her to a skidding halt.

There. She had no idea how it had gotten there,

but there it was. Her eyes glowed like fires as she silently advanced.

Maya opened her eyes and shook her head in confusion. The movement sent nauseating waves of pain rocketing through her small form. She reeled dizzily back against the rock that had halted her careening flight.

A long, nasty gash down her right arm had ripped away the coat sleeve and exposed flesh beneath. Bright crimson blood leaked sluggishly there, running down her wrist, dripping from her fingers.

At first she had no idea what had happened. Then a low, coughing grunt jerked her head up.

"Uh . . . *huh!*" She gasped in horror at the huge, triangular head less than three feet from her own face. Mother Lion's vast green eyes regarded her with utter calm.

Maya felt her heart try to explode from her chest as the great cave lion opened her jaws wide. A fetid stink emerged from those clashing teeth, hot and foul. Mother Lion's two huge fangs were streaked with blood—in that frozen moment, Maya could see it clearly.

She scrabbled with her injured arm for a rock, a stick, anything. Finally her frantic fingers closed on a bit of stone about the size of her hand. Slowly, she brought it up. Mother Lion didn't move.

She was puzzled. The blood spoor triggered every killing reflex she possessed, but somehow she couldn't bring herself to crunch the bones of this tiny, evil-smelling thing.

Then a fog descended on the red fire of her mind, and from the darkness a voice spoke to her in words she could understand. The voice was infinitely soothing, infinitely powerful:

"Your cubs are safe. You are safe. Go now. Back to your home. Go. I will be with you. Go."

Mother Lion shook her head. Her jaws slowly

closed. She eyed the tiny figure one last time, as it feebly waved the bit of rock. She no longer felt the bloody rage that had energized her before. In fact, she felt tired. She would see to the cubs, and then take a nap.

A nice, warm nap, on the rocks before the home cave where her family lived. But she would remember this strange one's scent. The others didn't matter. They were dead. This one, though, she would never forget.

"Meeeuuuu?"

But the strange thing didn't reply. Mother Lion's interest faded completely. She backed off a few feet, then turned and leaped in the direction of the sound of her cubs.

Maya collapsed against the stone outcropping. She suddenly felt too weak even to breathe. The stone fell from her fingers. Blood dripped on it where it lay.

Maya closed her eyes. Darkness came almost instantly; but the picture of Mother Lion, her huge sides heaving, her breath a hot stench, would not leave.

It would stay with her always.

Skin looked a hundred years old. He was no longer young by the standards of the People, but now he looked twenty summers more ancient than he had only seconds before.

He stood over the bloody mass of ripped flesh in the middle of the clearing and wept. Almost nothing remained of Blossom above her shoulders. The shattered bones of her skull peeped, like shy, bitter flowers, from the shredded mass of flesh and hair that had once been her head.

Oddly enough, Bud's small body had somehow been thrown close to her mother, and in the roil of the massacre, had come to rest on top of Blossom's right arm, so that the mother cradled her child in their final rest.

Horrible rest!

Bud's childish face was peaceful. Her eyes were closed. She looked almost normal, if you ignored the ruin of her belly, where shiny, tubular things spilled forth like devilish sausages.

The stench of blood filled the clearing. Already the women had begun a mournful wailing. Old Berry limped forward, her face ashen with grief.

Skin turned. "Mother, what happened here?"

She told him. When she had finished, Skin's face became as still, as hideously peaceful as that of his daughter at his feet.

"Maya. Her fault. She led Bud here." He spoke flatly, with no color or emotion in his voice at all.

Old Berry nodded.

Skin said nothing further. He knelt, and gently stroked Bud's cheek, then touched with trembling fingers Blossom's shoulder. Tears streamed down his cheeks. He seemed frozen, a statue, and Old Berry's heart went out to him. His first wife dead in childbirth, and now this.

The life of the People had always been hard, but this horror seemed more than anyone deserved. What had the People done, to bring this down on them? How had they offended the Spirits? What could be done to placate them?

These thoughts were roiling inside her mind when a new sound intruded. Some of the women called and pointed. Her eyes followed in the direction of their outstretched arms.

Maya staggered unsteadily from the underbrush and half ran, half stumbled across the cleared ground. Blood had begun to crust on her arm. A huge lump was plainly visible on the back of her skull. Her strange, multicolored eyes burned with a wildness that wasn't human.

Maya made a high, keening sound as she lurched forward. It never stopped, not when she sank down on Bud's body, not when she wrapped her skinny arms around Blossom's still chest.

That sound wouldn't stop for almost a day.

Skin looked down at her without expression. Then he turned to Old Berry. "I don't want her anymore. She's not my daughter. I don't want her."

Old Berry nodded. She understood.

A frigid wind whistled through cracks and crannies in the tent. The door flap hung partially open; Maya huddled in a pile of furs and stared at the fog that wreathed the hearths beyond. She coughed once, a low, hacking sound that filled her throat with bloody mucus; the tender membranes there were torn from the screaming of the day before.

She shivered. She'd never felt more alone in her life. Skin had not spoken to her at all. When she looked at his broken, stony face, it was as if he weren't there. He looked at her, but didn't see her.

What had she done? The terrible events of the day before were softening in her mind, becoming like the damp, gray fog that swirled outside. Low and muffled, the death chants of the women sounded like an ominous wind. Nobody remained in the tent but she; nobody would speak to her. Even Stone, her other father, said nothing. At first light everybody had simply left. They were bound for the place by First Lake, where Old Magic and Ghost would sing Blossom and Bud back to the Great Mother. She understood that much; the rest was an aching void.

Bud!

If only I could have held on, she told herself. She wrapped her thin arms around her chest and rocked back and forth. *If only I could have . . . If only . . . If . . .*

The thought came to her in a sudden flash of understanding: She *hadn't* held on. She'd enticed Bud away from the safety of the group, and she *hadn't held on.*

I killed her!

Sickened with the awful realization, she bent her head forward. A soft, strangled sound escaped her lips.

"Me," she said over and over again. "Me me me . . ."

"Maya."

She didn't look up. It seemed so much more comfortable this way, in the warmth of the furs, listening to the sound of her own voice as if it belonged to another. . . .

"Maya. What are you doing?"

Finally, the words penetrated the desperate mist that enshrouded her mind. She blinked. "Oh. Wolf."

Her brother dropped to his knees against her. His sturdy boy's frame felt comforting to her. They were the same age and had shared many of the same secrets, though in recent years, as he took up his new role among other males of his generation, they'd grown somewhat apart.

"Are you all right?" He touched her gently on the shoulder. Involuntarily, she flinched. Worry flickered in his black eyes. Unlike his sister, nothing about him was odd, different. Already he looked a great deal like his father, Skin. He was a handsome child, with strong cheekbones and shiny black hair. His brown face, permanently suntanned, had a cheery cast to it in normal times. He smiled a lot, and when he laughed the sound came from deep in his belly.

Maya loved him desperately.

"Oh, Wolf," she sighed. "Do you hate me, too?"

He shook his head. "No. You shouldn't have left

the women, but I know you. You can't help it, you do things like that. I wish I'd been there. . . ."

Fresh horror seized her. It had been bad enough, that what she'd done had ended in those ripped and torn monstrosities, left like broken dolls in the middle of the clearing. But to see Wolf like that as well . . .

She burst into tears.

Now the boy put his arm around her shoulders and pulled her to his chest. "Don't cry, Maya. Don't cry. You're safe now. I would have protected you," he said stoutly. His face, still fuzzy in outline from baby fat, bent close to her own.

After a while, she snuffled and wiped her nose on the sleeve of her coat. "Mother . . . Bud."

He finished the question in his own mind. The answer brought tears to his eyes, but he tried to hide them. "The Shaman is singing them to Her now. Can't you hear it?"

It was all she *could* hear, that doleful chant of mourning. It filled up her ears, her head, her heart like dull thunder. She could see the terrible picture in her mind: the People gathered in a great semicircle around two shapeless, still lumps wrapped in reindeer hide, resting on a bier of sticks and logs. Around the bodies would be gifts from the People: carved bits of wood, shaped stones, even weapons from the men. Things they would need, or could trade for what they needed, when they went back to the Great Mother.

She nodded. She looked up into his face. "Do you think—" She paused, shocked by the thought that had entered her skull. She licked her lips. "Will they go back to Her, do you think?"

Now it was his turn to feel shock. "Of course they will! Where else would they go?"

She had an idea, and it terrified her even more than what had happened the day before. "What if

She won't take them . . . because of me? What if their Spirits must wander, and She won't take them back?"

It was a terrible thought, but no less real for all that. She knew more about Spirits than she wanted to, right then. She'd sat at Old Magic's knee while he sang songs to her, while he chanted old stories to her, and almost without realizing it she'd soaked up a vast amount of lore. Her childish mind was not yet capable of analyzing it all, but it was there, a jumble of history and legend and knowledge. Spirits. Spirits surrounded the People like a haze—they lived in everything from the great animals they hunted to the tiniest bugs in the grass. There were Spirits in trees and flowers. Spirits of wind and light and thunder. Spirits of ice and fire.

Spirits of the People.

The Great Mother had created them all.

It was here that her knowledge snagged on cruel reality. "Wolf," she said, "do you think mama still loves me?"

The ways of the Spirits of the dead were far beyond Wolf's comprehension. He was a straightforward boy, more concerned with the games of his companions, the joys of the hunt, even the twisted paths of leadership he was only beginning to explore. Spirits were for the women, or the Shaman. "I don't know," he said at last. "Do the Spirits love people?"

Maya pushed herself closer to her brother and wondered if she would ever feel warm again. "I don't know either," she replied. "I hope so."

But as she listened to the mournful sounds from beyond the shelter door, she thought her hopes were vain. The Spirits she'd thought her friends had betrayed her. Perhaps her tormentors of early childhood had been right: She possessed an evil Spirit herself.

She hadn't spoken of her secret encounter with Mother Lion to anyone, but now, deep in the most hidden parts of her, she wished desperately that the great cat had taken her life, too. It would be so much easier to wander, even as a homeless Spirit, than to bear the guilt that weighted her down.

"Oh, Wolf, it was all *my fault!*"

He squeezed her shoulder and kissed her on the ear, but he didn't say anything in reply. He wasn't entirely sure she didn't speak the truth.

Finally he reached inside his coat and withdrew a small object. Wordlessly, her pressed it into her small hand. "Here," he said. "You keep it."

She looked down, then gasped in surprise. The tiny, carefully carved bit of ivory was Wolf's most prized possession. Stone had fashioned the figure himself. None of the other boys possessed anything so grand. It was the shape of a woman, with a tiny head and huge breasts, the image of the Great Mother herself. Many thousands of years later, archaeologists would discover these statues all over the world and christen them "Venus Dolls." The miniature carving was only a finger-length long— Wolf customarily wore it as a charm around his neck on a leather thong, for the protection its great magic offered.

The gift spoke more than mere words. It was the first thing since the disaster that had given Maya any comfort at all.

She looked into his black eyes. "Oh, Wolf, I love you."

He squeezed her shoulder, suddenly embarrassed. "I love you, too," he said.

The thick, greasy smell of burned human flesh hung over the Home Camp in a gloomy pall. Down by First Lake, the remains of the funeral fire still smoldered, tended by two of the younger women who poked up the embers with long sticks. They could no longer make out the shapes of the two forms that had rested there. Eventually, when the fire in the shallow pit burned out, they would push rocks and dirt over what was left. It didn't matter; the Spirits of Bud and blossom had already gone back to the Mother. The two young women found the duty cold and onerous. Everything important had already been completed, and they would miss the feast they could already smell roasting over the hearths—a counterpart to the dismal fire that was their own duty.

Berry and Magic sat inside the Spirit House across from each other, with the tiny fire between. As usual, it was quite warm inside. Berry had loosened her coat, so that her chest, with its sagging, pendulous breasts, hung open to the air. She fanned herself occasionally with a dried branch, upon which had been woven a pattern in softly tanned deer hide.

Magic seemed lost in thought, far away from her. She was used to it. The old man moved more slowly, thought more deeply, the older he grew. She had noticed such a change in herself, as well. It was as if great age conferred a new way of looking at things, slower, more thorough—she considered the future now, and the past. The present became more and more unreal, so that sometimes she felt she was a Spirit herself, moving silently among ghost-like People. If she felt that way, what must Old Magic know, who had lived with Spirits all his life?

It was the future—more specifically, *one* future— they met to decide this terrible day. Her nose twitched at the faint remnants of the funeral fire. The death of the woman and the child had been a disaster, true, but now they were faced with another. Old Magic seemed terribly worried, and she was unsure why. He'd never fully unburdened himself to her about Maya, although he'd given hints.

Somehow, the little girl was important. She knew that much. But the how and why of Maya's import was hidden from her. Perhaps that was about to end. She waited, fanning herself, for Old Magic to speak.

For his part, the old Shaman faced a terrible decision. He, more than any other, knew just what a turning was upon him. He bore the Secret. It was his duty to bring it to fruition. How would this horrible turn of events affect *that*?

"Do you think Skin has made up his mind? That he can't be changed?"

Berry considered. Finally, she nodded reluctantly. "You could order him to keep the girl—if the Spirits demanded it, he would obey. But I doubt if he would change his feelings about her. he's frightened, Magic. As far as he knows, she bears the mark of an evil spirit. Those eyes. And she's caused the deaths of both her mothers, and her sister as well. Unlucky." She sighed. "He's my son, Magic. But he's only a man."

Magic smiled faintly at that. At his age he was beyond sexuality, but it amused him to hear Berry speak of his sex like that—particularly since, in years long gone by, they had rolled under a few blankets themselves.

Yet he took her point. Men were less concerned with the doings of Spirits. To them, the invisible ones who shadowed the life of the People were of importance only as they affected the things men did—hunting, fighting, survival. Larger ideas, such as the import of the Spirits on the future of the People—those they left to experts like Magic himself and, for the women, Old Berry.

To a man, things were much more black and white. Men didn't much care for shades of gray. An evil Spirit could be identified by the work it did—men liked that notion. The idea that a Spirit might be both good and evil made them uncomfortable, for it meant that nothing could be predicted. They were aware of the fact of paradox, of course—fire could both warm and burn—but not of the concept. One took precautions, and left the rest to those who knew the deeper secrets.

I know a deeper secret, he thought suddenly. *I wish I didn't, but I do. Should I tell Berry?*

Magic's body grew weaker with the passage of every moon. He knew full well that, if the People had not discovered the Green Valley, he himself would have returned by now to the Great Mother. He could not have survived the rigors of the trek this long. But it was all of a piece: the Valley, Maya, the Secret. Events had conspired to trap him, and to lay a terrible duty on him as well. What if he went to sleep this night, and didn't wake up the next morning? What then?

The Secret would die with him. Not the force of it, of course, for that came from the Mother Herself. But Old Magic had noticed, during his many years, that many of the intentions of the Mother and Her Spirits were worked out only through the actions of the men and women who worshiped Her. She would help, but the People had to help themselves, as well. She might intervene occasionally—as when She'd spoken to the Mother Lion; although Maya thought that her own secret, he'd seen it in a Dream, and it had only confirmed what he already believed about Maya's unique destiny—but on the whole, what the People could accomplish for themselves She left to them.

He had his duty. His duty was to bring the Secret to full flower. He could do it, if he survived. But if he didn't, what then? Would the Mother intervene? What if She didn't? She had the whole World—perhaps the People would simply be cast aside, to perish forever.

He could try to provide protection against it. Berry was old, but sturdy, and younger than he. He guessed he had seven, no more than eight summers before Maya was ready. But already events had taken a turn for the worse. If Skin scorned his own daughter, what good would Magic's orders be? Skin might follow them grudgingly, but Maya's presence would be an ever more vexing thorn in his side.

Old Magic was wise in the ways of men and women. Accidents could happen—or be made to happen. If he forced Maya on her unwilling, frightened father, the result might be disaster. There must be another way.

He must take the first step now, though. He'd already noted Maya's absence from the funeral ceremony. A taste of things to come?

Probably, he decided. Maya could no longer stay with Skin. Now, the question was, how could he achieve that goal?

He opened his rheumy eyes and stared across the fire at Berry. She looked like some ancient carved piece of rock, steady and eternal. Her age-toughened strength warmed him. Perhaps the two of them would be enough.

Perhaps.

"I will tell you a Secret. . . ." he began.

Chapter Eight

The Green Valley: 17,983 B.C.

Maya left Old Berry, stumping along with her two sticks, far behind. The morning burned blue and clear above the valley. The highest days of summer approached; it was as warm as it ever got beneath the sheltered cliff walls, almost sixty-five degrees. Maya knew nothing of degrees or temperatures. All she cared about was that, temporarily free of the ancient woman's ceaseless supervision, she could take off her heavy coat, sling it under one arm, and run like the wind through the shadowy towers of the great trees.

She carried her moccasins, as well; up ahead, the path sloped down out of the forest to a small, hidden inlet of Second Lake; the tiny, sandy beach there was her favorite place in the whole valley. As she ran, her strong legs pumping, the crystal air filling her chest, she felt a twinge of guilt. It had been seven years since Bud and Blossom had died— seven long years of pain and rejection and guilt. Time had scabbed those wounds somewhat, but they festered still: in the way Skin still ignored her as if she didn't exist; in Stone's gruff disdain even when he taught her the secrets of his craft; in the way the other women and the girls her own age excluded her in small, hurtful ways from sharing in their own camaraderie. She had no friends beyond Magic and Berry, and though she loved both dearly, they were as distant from her as the primordial oaks and maples and pines under which her lithe brown body flashed.

Glints of light from the glassy-smooth lake ahead began to signal through the trees. Closer to the edge of the forest, where the sun was able to fight its way through the thinning crowns to the earth below, the underbrush grew more thickly and the path narrowed. Maya slowed and began to pick her way carefully, enjoying the sensation of the dark, soft dirt between her toes.

A moment later she reached the beach. She glanced once over her shoulder, but Old Berry was not yet in sight. No doubt, she thought, as she pictured the aged woman moving slowly through the shadows, birds squawking up at her approach, Berry would be along soon. But for a few blessed moments, Maya found herself alone.

She sighed and sank down to the sand. The good heat of it baked through the seat of her pants and warmed the muscles of her rear end. Second Lake stretched before her like a great mirror; the winds that ruffled its surface most of the year had temporarily died away.

She thought it seemed very quiet. It was a rare treat when Old Berry let her leave Home Camp, even though the People had spread out and new houses now dotted that whole end of the valley. Confined as she was, she could never escape the sounds of the camp: the shouts and cries of the children—so *many* children—the songs and laughter of the men, the chatter of the women as they worked. A fog of noise surrounded her constantly, so that it had become as much a part of her as the wind or the smell of smoke from the hearths.

Only now did she give a thought to the ever-present cacophony, by its absence. Slowly, as she lay back in luxurious solitude upon the sand, other, quieter sounds seeped into her ears. She heard the dry, woody chitter of squirrels scrabbling about the branches; the faint *slap-slap* of tiny wavelets lapping the rocks a few feet away; the sharp, high-pitched *reek-ka-reek!* of blackbirds and the deeper, throatier honkings of a few ducks bobbing safely in the center of the lake.

The sun felt good on her face. She closed her eyes and lay very still, trying to pretend she was the only girl in the valley. For a moment she was almost able to convince herself the dream was real, and that she wouldn't have to go back to the People, where it was always winter and the sun never shone on her face.

The first cramp took her by surprise. She groaned and rolled over onto her side, clutching her belly. Then a wave of pain looped her into a tight ball of muscle. When the seizure had passed, it left her limp and sweating and utterly terrified.

Was she dying? Perhaps, after all these summers, her childish wish had been granted. Mother Lion had spared her then; perhaps now the Great Mother had decided to take her back, to crush the evil Spirit within her.

She moved her legs and felt something warm and sticky down there. She put her hand down her pants and brought it back up, to stare at the bright blood which glittered on her fingers.

"Ahhh! I'm dying!" The sound of her own voice was distant in her ears, as if someone else spoke the terrible words.

Another surge of cramping brought tears to her eyes. This one was shorter, and when it was done she sprawled bereft, waiting for the Great Mother to appear and take her away.

"Dead . . ." she moaned softly. Somehow it wasn't a surprise. She felt her life ebbing away between her thighs. Tears sparkled on her cheeks. She wondered if she would see Bud and Blossom again.

"Ahhhoooo," she sighed.

"What's the matter with you?"

At first she thought the Mother had finally come. But it was only Berry, her gaunt, twisted form—she'd grown steadily smaller as she aged—looming over her like some gigantic blackbird, withered wings spread across her two crutches.

Wordlessly, Maya showed the old woman her bloody fingers. "I'm going away now," she whispered. "I'm going back to the Mother."

But Old Berry only shook her head and then, with painful slowness, lowered her creaking bones to the sand. When she was settled, amidst much sighing and wheezing, she said, "No, you're not."

"I'm not?"

"I think," Old Berry said, "it's time we had a little talk."

Ghost tapped his left hand against his knee in annoyance. Spear was late. Ghost sat on a log in front of his house—the *true* Spirit House, he thought of it now—and watched a spider the size of his little finger walk crookedly across the patch of packed earth in front of his seat. Ghost wore only leggings; his narrow, bony chest, marked with ritual tattoo scars, was bare to the sunlight that streamed down.

Once, his house had been on the far outskirts of Home Camp; now it was almost in the center. Much had changed with the People in the fourteen summers since they'd first come to Green Valley. The children who'd scampered behind their parents had grown and built their own houses; Home Camp had expanded with startling speed. Now a fresh crop of children—far more than he could ever have imagined—roiled and brawled and screamed all around. Further out, across the stream and First Lake, even newer houses had been built. Where the People had once numbered less than the hands of ten men, now double that number lived. The People were changing—he could see it clearly.

They were fatter, for one thing. A tribe of hardship, pausing only to gather strength for the next trek, the men and women had always shown their bones through their flesh. But here in the sunlight he could see the difference; the angular thrustings were gone, hidden away beneath new pads of fat.

Green Valley had done that. He was astonished at the bounty the People had been bequeathed in their new home. Gradually, as it had finally sunk into the collective consciousness that the Great Journey was over, there had been a slow relaxation, as if a great weight had been lifted from the bent shoulders of the tribe. It had taken a long time, though. Old Magic had told them, but at first it had been hard to understand. Though none could truly perceive the incredible period of time involved, the People had journeyed for twenty-five centuries. It was bred into them, the knowledge that nothing was permanent, that their home was always the next rise of the earth or distant range of mountains, barely visible beyond the horizon.

The People had become a tribe with the horizon permanently etched in its eyes. Now it was over. Ghost shrewdly guessed that the children squalling along the paths between the houses would have a different look to them; their limbs would no longer twitch with unconscious movement when the long winds howled, and brought news of places beyond the edge of their world.

He clicked his teeth together, his exasperation growing. Where was Spear? The hunter was nearing the end of his full strength, but still he led the hunts. He would be good for another few winters or so, Ghost thought, before he forsook active participation for a more sedentary post beside the sacred fires in front of the Mystery House. Ghost judged young Wolf, the son of Stone and Skin, as Spear's most likely successor. Though only fourteen the youth was fully fledged, and his skill at the hunt was already nearly legendary. Only a few moons ago, just after his initiation, he'd killed a full-grown bison, whose mighty horns were as wide-spread as Wolf's stripling body, with a single thrust of his spear. And he'd done it alone.

Wolf was interesting. Ghost had interesting plans for him.

Wolf's sister, Maya, was another matter. Ghost had interesting plans for her, as well. He hadn't quite decided how to implement those plans, but he had no doubt he would do so eventually. Old Magic couldn't live forever.

He licked his lips.

Where *was* Spear?

"Put the moss like this," Old Berry said. She'd stumped off into the forest and returned with copious handfuls of the soft gray stuff. Now, with practiced gestures, she showed her charge how to use it. After a while, Maya hitched up her trousers. A look of doubt passed across her face.

"Are you *sure*, Auntie?"

Berry sighed again. How had she neglected to speak with Maya about this before? Old age, she supposed. It sometimes seemed she remembered things from her forgotten childhood more easily than she recalled what she'd eaten for breakfast.

"I'm sure," Berry said firmly. "You aren't going to die, Maya."

Maya carried within her skull an incredible baggage of sophistication and naiveté. Jumbled in with years of lessons from Magic and Berry was an equally large freight of ignorance. Blood meant injury, meant infection, meant death. Though she tried to stretch her comprehension around the idea that women bled between their legs every month, and would for most of their life, it was hard.

She looked up at the older woman. "Why?" she said simply.

Berry's response frightened her. "I don't know," Berry said.

A new twinge from down there made her wince. It wasn't that Berry offered an unsatisfactory answer, it was that she admitted to having no answer at all. For half her life Maya had been accepted by only two people, both vastly older and more knowledgeable than she. Between them, they had always been able to quench her childish curiosity. Berry and Magic were the People's brain—their memory, their wisdom, their lore. Now, Maya felt her rock-solid faith in them shake slightly. Deep inside her something shifted, and on the new ground Maya moved with uncertainty. It seemed there were things even the old ones were ignorant of.

It was a frightening thought.

Old Berry could almost read her mind. "Don't be afraid, child," she said gently. "Even I don't know everything."

Hesitantly, Maya said, "Does Old Magic know?"

Berry frowned and shook her head firmly. "Maya. Old Magic knows even less of these things than I do. This is woman's magic, girl. He's a man." Her voice softened. "A very *wise* man, dear, but still a man."

These esoteric differences between the sexes tantalized Maya. "Do men bleed like that?" Wolf had grown even more distant from her, caught up in the woof and warp of hunting, weapons, fishing, but still, on occasion, he would talk to her; though it hurt her to see how furtive he was about it, as if, as he'd grown older, he'd come to accept the whispers and pointed fingers that marked her as different, perhaps even dangerous.

But he'd never mentioned anything about bleeding.

Old Berry chuckled. "No, child, men don't bleed. Only women." She paused, thoughtful. "That is what it means, you know. Now you aren't a girl any longer. You are a woman."

Maya touched her leg, felt the fur there warm in the sun. She didn't feel any different. So she was a woman now, because red blood seeped from the secret place between her legs? Somehow, that didn't make a whole lot of sense.

But it did allow a single ray of hope to break through the clouds of worry and uncertainty. If she was now, though she didn't understand why or how, changed somehow, perhaps other things could change as well.

"Then I can live with the young women, live in their house?"

Berry endured a long pang of sadness. How could she explain? She bore the weight of the Secret; Maya was forever marked, her life not her own, though she couldn't tell her so. Sometimes she cursed Old Magic, in the silence of her lonely nights, for having passed his burden on to her. She knew, with all the innate understanding women have for the weaknesses of men, that Old Magic had been helped by the sharing. The knowledge he'd given her had been a revelation; at first she'd not believed it at all. But he had shown her, spoken the hidden words as they'd been passed down to him, even unrolled the mammoth stone and let her see its soft golden outlines.

Finally she had accepted, knowing that as she did so she bound herself to the Secret, and hence to Maya, for as long as she would live. The burden was heavy, though inescapable. Pray to the Mother that Old Magic survived for a while yet. The weight was too heavy for two, let alone one.

As now. She couldn't tell young Maya the truth; only Old Magic himself, when he judged the time to be right, could do that. But she had to tell her something. Maya was strong, but Berry judged that she could still be broken. Loneliness was an insidious goad; hate a weapon, fear a curse. Maya lived her life with all these things; it was astonishing she'd turned out as well as she had.

"No," she said softly, "you can't do that. You have a different path to take."

The sun rose over Spear's left shoulder as he crawled slowly to the top of the buckle of tundra about six miles southwest of Green Valley's mouth. Behind him, Skin and Deer hugged themselves close to the stiff, dry tundra grass. Out here, away from the shelter of the valley, the wind moaned continuously, even in high summer.

Spear carefully tested the direction of the breezes and glanced back at the others, satisfied.

It had taken them almost an hour to worm their way to this isolated outpost. It wasn't that Spear was unfamiliar with this ground. Out front to their left, no more than a mile away across the grassland, flowed a river. Thousands of years later, the river would empty a great lake, and be wide and strong here. Now, what would someday be called the Ohio was merely a stronger stream than the one that emptied into it from the Green Valley. Spear had come the day before to search for spoor at that confluence. The great animals they hunted—bison, caribou, mammoth—no longer came into the valley proper. The stinks and noise of the People had frightened them away. But here, where the two waters flowed together in a bubbling froth, where the force of the water had ground a narrow, deep canyon with only a single path leading down, the great ones still came to drink.

It was coming on time to think of a hunt again. The mammoth mothers had dropped their calves almost three moons ago. Now the toddlers would be strong enough to follow, and the mammoths would slowly move. Later on small bands of them might join together, and, with luck and good tracking, Spear might drive them toward this spot, and their doom.

The journey from Home Camp to the river's joining had taken up most of a leisurely afternoon. When they arrived, Spear relinquished his leader's role to Skin, who still possessed his old skills at tracking and reading sign. They picked their way down the narrow, twisting path to river's edge, and Skin squatted in the mud there. After a time, he glanced up. His face was deeply troubled.

"Spear," he said, his voice unbelieving. "Come look at this."

"What?"

Wordlessly, Skin pointed to a series of small depressions in the mud. A few of them still showed traces of water that had not yet seeped away. Recent, then.

But that wasn't what had sent Spear's heart racing in his broad chest. It was the shape of the tracks. They were as familiar to him as the paths through Home Camp, for he saw hundreds of such marks there every day.

This spoor was not of mammoth or bison.

Then, hoarsely, Deer called from his spot at the top of the canyon wall. "Spear! Skin! Look to the north!"

Both men turned. It hadn't been there before, but now, as dusk slowly tinted the sky purple, it stood out like a thin, silvery spear.

The wind must not blow there, Spear thought. For the smoke to go straight up like that.

The night had been cool, but not uncomfortably so. Spear hadn't wanted to move far in the dark—he had a stronger fear of the dark Spirits than most—but he'd had no choice. Full of anxiety, he'd led them in the direction of the distant campfire.

At sunrise they'd begun their final advance, crawling through the dry, whiplike tundra grasses, careful to keep downwind, using every bit of skill they possessed.

Now Spear wormed his way a last few feet forward, and parted the screen of scrub that clung to the top of the low rise. Carefully he raised his head, slow as a snake sunning itself on a rock. He was supposed to meet Ghost later this day, but knew he would be late.

It didn't matter. His dark eyes widened at the sight below.

All thought of Ghost and his anger vanished completely. This was not for Ghost, anyway. Old Magic might be nearly paralyzed now, but Spear vastly respected what the Shaman still had locked within his mind.

He pulled himself carefully back, until he was certain his movement could not be spotted from below. "Back down!" he whispered.

When they'd reached the bottom, spear turned toward the distant valley. "We run!" he said hoarsely. "We run *now*!"

More than urgency lent them speed. Fear nipped at their heels as they loped tirelessly through the grass. They bore a dire message. Only Magic might be able to interpret it, for only the shaman claimed to have seen such things before.

Spear had never believed the old tales, but now he did. He'd seen with his own eyes.

The People were no longer alone.

                              *   *   *

Maya supported Old Berry as they walked slowly
back to Home Camp. Her bleeding had stopped,
and Maya felt much better. She was conscious of the
strange sensation of the moss between her thighs, but
even this novelty faded after a while.

Overhead a vee-shaped formation of ducks wheeled,
honking thinly in the afternoon sky. A few fluffy
white clouds sailed slowly across the blue. The woods
smelled damp, owing to the steam that rose cease-
lessly from Smoke Lake and eventually fell back to
the rich humus as a fine mist. Plants seemed to leap
from the ground here, green and sturdy.

Maya possessed no recollection of the life of the
People before they'd come to Green Valley. She took
the bounty which grew and crawled and flew and
scampered all around her for granted; she was of a
generation new for the People, for she had never
known a day of hunger in her life.

Old Berry seemed lost in thought, remote from
her. She'd often noticed the old woman in that state
in recent times. Not as bad as Magic, who spoke
less and less, even to her, as the years went by. But
the trend was obvious; she wondered, with a sharp
pang of sadness, whether one day they would quit
talking entirely, and she would be alone.

Sometimes, though, the old woman could be jollied from her reveries—and today, Maya felt herself
bursting with questions.

"Why don't the others talk to me?" she asked.

Berry grunted, and poked the ground ahead of
her viciously with her stick, but said nothing else.

"Have I done something wrong? I don't remember
ever doing anything." That wasn't quite true; the
scene of Bud's death would never fully leave her,
nor the way her mother's torn body had sprawled
in pitiful embrace with the corpse of her daughter—
but time had dimmed those pictures, and occasion-

ally Maya was able to convince herself they had little to do with her. She, like all the other People, had no concept of an "accident." Nothing occurred in their lives that wasn't governed by the Spirits, or the Great Mother working through Her Spirits. Everything was a gift, whether for good or evil, from the invisible forces which surrounded the People.

"Skin won't talk to me at all."

Now Berry snorted loudly. "Skin is a fool!" she said.

"He's your son."

"But still a fool," Berry replied. "He knows nothing."

Maya seized on the statement. Her mind was very quick. As often with children raised in the silence of elders, she had learned to snatch up every word offered her, to revolve those words in her mind and suck the last bit of juice from them. Maya took a full belly for granted, but not the simple kindness of a question. Or an answer.

"Is it a secret, Auntie?"

The old woman halted, startled. "What did you say?"

Maya repeated her question. Auntie Berry was sometimes hard of hearing. Usually when she was tired of answering questions.

Maya was reminded again of how piercing Old Berry's steady black gaze could be, when she really wanted to look at something. She waited patiently. Finally, Berry shook her head slightly, as if a bug of some kind had gotten stuck on her nose.

"What's Magic been teaching you lately?" she asked.

Maya was used to these subject changes. The Elders thought differently than she did. Things were never simple for an Elder. She considered. "Songs," she said at last.

"What kind of songs?"

"Mmm, about the Mother. And Spirits . . ." She

trailed off vaguely, for she didn't entirely understand Magic's recent instruction, if that's what it was. Of late, the Shaman had given off teaching her about special plants, and ways to make poultices, or how to find the will of the Spirits in the guts of a duck. Now it was mostly stories, but stories that made little sense to her. Magic sang of an endless journey, of great ice canyons, of a far place where another girl had once lived, a girl with one eye of green, and one of blue.

She'd found the idea that there had once been another like her comforting, but she didn't know how it had anything to do with her now. The People journeyed no more; intellectually, she understood how they *might* have once done so, but in all her short life the People had lived in Green Valley. The weight of experience was heavy; her own experience particularly so.

"He said that once upon a time there was a girl just like me."

Berry's eyes narrowed. This came perilously close to the heart of the Secret itself. What was Magic thinking of? Berry deferred to the old man's knowledge of spirits, but not as much as another more ignorant and younger woman might have. Berry knew something of the Spirits herself. She was more concerned, as far as Maya went, about other things. Solid things that went on two legs, and did terrible things out of fear.

She had been stunned when the Shaman finally told her the Secret. But she'd adjusted quickly, and her tough, practical mind had immediately searched out the problems, like a woman pulling bad seeds from a basket.

"Ghost," she'd said flatly, at the time.

Magic had nodded. He'd already given his assistant a great deal of consideration.

"Spear, too," Berry said. "He's terrified of the girl.

And Skin, of course. She frightens him, too, but he
blames her as well. He doesn't fear the Spirits the
way Spear does."

Magic had leaned forward and poked vaguely at
the tiny fire between them. "Spear is the leader,
when we need one. Skin is well liked, respected.
The People will follow them and imitate their ideas.
As for Ghost . . . well, Ghost is Ghost."

Berry pursed her lips. Ghost was more than
Ghost. Ghost would be the biggest problem of all.

Now, trundling along with the fourteen-year-old
girl—no, *woman*, Berry corrected herself—she remembered that awful day, with the smell of burning
bodies fresh in their nostrils, when the two of them,
already far too old for the task, had pledged themselves to somehow bring the Secret into being.

The one thing they had agreed upon then, and
still, as far as Berry knew, accepted today, was the
need for secrecy. Until the child-woman at her side
came into her full inheritance, she could be snuffed
out with sickening ease. And since they had no idea
just *what* that inheritance might be, they could only
wait, and teach, and protect her as well as they
could. Not an easy task, when to them Maya
seemed entirely ordinary, bored by the lessons her
Elders taught her, given to wildness and sudden
tears, even as the rest of the Tribe feared her as an
evil Spirit.

She sighed heavily. "Maya," she said slowly,
"someday you will understand everything. But not
yet. Your time will come, though. I promise you."

And then she tramped forward and would say no
more. Her eyes squinted in thought, Maya went
with her, supporting Berry's birdlike arm with her
own strong young shoulders.

Old Berry had said much that was strange, that
she would have to consider . . . but just as she had

begun to pick away at these strange new threads of thought, Maya heard the noise up ahead.

Berry quickened her pace. Maya wondered what all the shouting was about. No matter, she'd find out soon enough. Home Camp was now only a few hundred yards away.

Ghost turned on his seat, at the sudden cries from the hunters loping in from the north. That was strange. Usually Spear would return through the valley itself, but for some reason he'd taken a different, longer route.

Ghost *tch*-ed his tongue against his teeth, fully exasperated. Spear had little sense of time, Ghost knew—"late" to him meant little, and Ghost hadn't been entirely surprised at his failure to appear. Ghost understood time, from the necessity of spacing rituals in the proper way to appease each individual Spirit. Spear had no care for such things.

But now, although he saw Spear's eyes cut in his direction, the hunter seemed to have forgotten him entirely, for he wheeled aside and ran up the path toward the Spirit House. Toward Old Magic, who had come out of the Spirit House and now stood, painfully bent, leaning on his carved staff.

It must be something important, then. And somehow the old man knew of it, for although he didn't wear his great caribou robe, he bore the signs of his stature: the rattle, the dried snake, the ceremonial axe. Ghost had the idea that the Mammoth Stone was somewhere near at hand, as well.

As he walked with properly sedate pace toward the gathering crowd in front of the Spirit House, Ghost tried to quell the anger he felt growing inside him. By rights Spear should have come to him, but the old Shaman refused to relinquish his place to his successor. And as long as he did that, Spear and Skin and the others would go to him first.

The galling nettle of that truth was one that burned into his heart every day. That burning had begun to fester, although Ghost didn't realize it. All he was certain of was that he'd come to hate Old Magic, and his secretive, scornful companion, Old Berry. But the great bulk of his fury was fully reserved for another; once, he'd almost had Maya's life.

He regretted his failure to kill her for fourteen years. Now his features hardened as he saw them: the old woman and the young one, moving carefully up the path from First Lake.

Out in the forest, no doubt, speaking secrets. No doubt talking about *him*. He knew the old woman hated him. Probably the young bitch did now, as well. And yet, despite Ghost's subtlest efforts, Old Magic still held the girl first in his heart. He could not understand why. It was a secret. One of the many Ghost suspected the old man still kept from him.

He ground his teeth together, pleased with the tiny dart of pain the movement caused. Pain was good. The People needed pain, to keep them alert and strong, to weed out the weak and nurture the Spirits.

The thought gladdened his heart. Pain. Someday there would be no more secrets. And for one, the one he hated the most, there would be pain.

Greater pain than she'd ever known.

Old Magic stood before the Spirit House. His head was still full of a Dream, but he was coming to full possession of his senses.

"Spear," he said at last, "slow down! Quit yelling at me!" He paused, and waited for the hunter to quiet down. "Good," he said. "Start over. And slowly, this time."

"Shaman, we went to the hunting place by the river. You know this."

Magic nodded.

"We saw strange spoor. And then we saw smoke from a fire. We waited through the night, creeping up on the place where we saw the smoke. When dawn came, we crawled close and looked. Shaman, they were People, just like us!" Spear paused, puzzled. "Well, not like us, for they weren't the People. But they *looked* like us."

A dark knot of fear moved in Magic's belly. The Dream which had taken him earlier that day had hinted at danger, danger for himself, danger for the People.

Now he knew what the warning meant, and his blood felt like ice in his ancient veins.

Too soon!

He looked out beyond the small crowd gathered in front of him, now buzzing like flies over rotten meat, and saw Old Berry approach, leaning heavily on Maya's shoulder.

Coming from the other direction, Ghost limped rapidly along, his face a thundercloud.

In front of him Spear regarded him anxiously, and Skin was just behind, equally troubled. It seemed to Magic that, for a moment, the tableau had become a waking Dream, and in it, carefully balanced, were all the forces that conspired unwittingly in the Secret itself.

Ghost. The People. Maya. The Secret.

He felt suddenly too old, too tired. But that wouldn't do. Somewhere he must find the strength. Somewhere.

But where?

Maya's cheeks were flushed from the exertion of leading Berry carefully up the rocky path from First Lake. She glanced at the growing mob around the

Spirit House and saw Ghost, his face set like stone, striding rapidly toward the broil. For one instant their eyes met, and a dark spark jumped the distance between them.

Maya gasped. The contact was like a physical blow. She'd known for a long time, without knowing why, that Ghost hated her. But the apprentice Shaman had kept his true feelings well hidden, and had treated her with careful courtesy ever since she'd moved into a separate house with Old Berry and begun her true education.

Sometimes she sat in the Spirit House with Ghost, while Old Magic told them both of secret things. It had never occurred to her that this juxtaposition, this reluctant sharing, sent Ghost nearly mad with jealousy.

His dislike, which she sensed as a deep, thick undercurrent, didn't frighten her as much as it should have. Everybody disliked her, except for Old Magic and Berry—and after a time, she had managed to ignore the difference in the quality of Ghost's loathing for her.

To the rest of the People she was a familiar, if shunned, figure; the tribal distaste had become generalized over the years, the specific reasons for it grown fuzzy and indistinct with time. Even Skin sometimes forgot himself and nodded in her direction.

Ghost was different. He hated her personally. She knew he wasn't frightened of Spirits, the way the rest of them were. There was no reason for him to fear her.

But he did. This sudden lightning spark between them rocked her profoundly. It was as if somebody had drawn aside a tent flap, to reveal rotting horror within.

In that instant she saw a great deal, but what escaped her was the nature of the vision itself: deep, profound, terrifying.

On that day Maya dreamed her first Dream, if only for the tiniest flash of time. Then it was gone, and she turned to Berry.

"Can't we hurry, Auntie? Something's going on over there. Will you come with me?"

Berry had felt something too, though she didn't know what it was. "Yes, child," she said. She paused and stared into Maya's strange, glowing eyes. "Are you . . . all right?"

"Yes, Auntie, I'm fine," Maya replied.

Chapter Nine

Bison Camp, Northwest of the Green Valley: 17,983 B.C.

Black Caribou pushed aside the flap of his tent and stepped outside into a fine morning. He paused and stretched, feeling the luxurious pop and snap of cartilage in his shoulders and back, then slowly scanned the camp of the Bison People.

All appeared in order; there was a circle of round tents, ten of them, grouped about two makeshift hearths. The hearths had been constructed of round stones the women had brought back from the river's edge, a few hundred yards away. Little Rat squatted on his haunches at the nearest hearth and poked up the ash-covered embers as he fed sticks of dry kindling into the heat. The good smell of burning wood rose into the air, along with a thin stream of white smoke. Already the women were stirring; Black Caribou's nose twitched at the smell of fresh meat two of the girls were hauling toward the fires.

It was a haunch from the giant bison three of the hunters had speared the day before. The successful hunt was the reason the Bison Clan had stopped here; their kill weighed upwards of fifteen hundred pounds, enough to feed the forty men, women and children of the Clan for several days.

Black Caribou scratched himself beneath his furs as he surveyed the campsite with satisfaction. It was a good place to stop. The Clan had been on the move for several weeks now, following their namesakes as the great shaggy animals moved along the ice face and then turned to follow the river southward. This was all virgin territory; no other tribe, as far as Caribou knew, had penetrated this far into the great steppe.

"Little Rat!" he called suddenly.

The smaller man gave off his work at the hearth and looked up. "Ho, Caribou! About time you got your lazy carcass out of bed!"

Caribou chuckled. Rat was a funny little man, much given to cynical humor. He was also the most skilled of the Bison Clan's trappers, and Caribou thought the Clan would need his special abilities soon.

Off to his left, the river voiced a dull thunderous grumble as it poured over jagged black boulders. It flowed quickly here but the bank was shallow, and there were eddies, backwaters along it, where Caribou had seen fish with his own eyes.

Maybe Rat could design something for the women to use on the fish. He was clever that way. Rat, in fact, was clever in many ways. Caribou put one finger on his cheek and spat. Best not to forget that— in some things, Rat was entirely *too* clever.

Caribou grinned complacently. It was too good a morning to spoil with such reflections. He knew he was clever, too—perhaps not in precisely the same way as Rat, but in other, equally valuable areas. And if Rat got too far out of hand, well—he flexed the massive, humped roll of muscle across his wide shoulders—there were ways to deal with that, too. Rat was scrawny. Caribou knew he could break him like a dry stick across his knee, if it came to that.

He grunted with satisfaction. The women finished

tying the bison haunch to a long pole, which they extended out over the blazing coals after bracing it with a pile of crumbly gray rock. Now the delicious smell of roasting meat began to permeate the camp.

Life was indeed good. The bison seemed to be plentiful hereabouts, and there was water nearby. A good place to stop for a while, rest up, grow fat, before resuming their endless journeying. The Bison Clan had never known a permanent home, and never expected to. Not as long as the grass grew and the wind blew—and the bison ran between.

He hawked up another yellow gob of phlegm, spat, and walked over to where Rat stared up at him with bright black eyes. "I think we should send out hunters," Black Caribou said. "This is a good place to stop for a while."

Rat poked up the fire. A shower of bright yellow sparks flared up and sizzled into the curling fat roasting above. "A very good place," he agreed. "After breakfast I'll talk to Snow Rabbit and Summer Wind. We could leave today, if the Shaman says the Spirits are right."

Caribou nodded thoughtfully. The Spirit of Breath, the Father of All Things, would have to be consulted. But that was a problem for the Shaman, Broken Fist; Caribou suspected the news would be good. Broken Fist had a way of understanding what Caribou wanted, and most often the Father went along.

Amazing how it usually worked out that way.

Full of good humor, Black Caribou squatted next to the small man he guessed he'd have to kill someday, but in the meantime intended to use as thoroughly as he could. His stomach growled at him, loudly enough for Rat to hear it and grin.

"Hungry!" Caribou announced. "Poke up the fire, Rat! It's almost ready."

*   *   *

The smell of cooking meat woke Broken Fist from his troubled slumbers. At first, in the darkness of his tent, he blinked in disorientation; was he still dreaming, or not? After a moment the aroma of the roasting haunch made his mouth begin to water, and he decided the dreams were over. He'd been dreaming a lot lately; the Spirit of Breath was more active than He'd ever been before. *He is very hungry,* Broken Fist thought, as he crawled from beneath a mound of fur and rubbed grains of sleep from his eyes.

He broke wind and felt a long belch rise to his throat. The Clan had fed well the day before, and Broken Fist had himself eaten the brains and liver of the great bison the hunters had killed. Those organs were full of magic, but they gave him gas. He grinned sourly at this juxtaposition of the sacred and the mundane.

Broken Fist was a handsome man, nicely shaped, with a strong, athletic build. As a child he'd been a leader, along with Caribou and Rat, but the old Shaman had seen something more in him than merely another hunter. The Shaman had taken him before his tenth birthday and begun training him. The old man had done his work well; so well, in fact, that at the age of thirteen Broken Fist had no problem in brewing up the poisoned herbs with which he murdered his predecessor, just as the Spirit of Breath had demanded. That terrible Spirit sometimes hungered for even his most faithful servants, when His appetite grew.

The Spirit of Breath spoke directly to Broken Fist, most often when the Spirit was hungry. Breath was usually hungry; it was His most prominent attribute. He'd been quiescent for a while now, but if the dream Broken Fist had just wakened from was any indication, that time was drawing to an end.

Idly, he considered the possibilities of sacrifice. He

had no particular enemies at the moment. Twenty-five years old, he'd been Shaman almost half his life. After that much time, those who *had* been his enemies had somehow all ended up as sacrifices. Strange coincidence, that, but who was he to question the will of the Spirit of Breath?

There was Caribou, of course, but he was wary of the huge, thick-muscled man. Caribou would not go gently to sacrifice, and his influence was almost as strong as Broken Fist's own. Fist had some ideas about that, of course—perhaps Rat would help him, if he approached the smaller man properly. Rat would be a good leader—Fist knew that Rat could easily be brought to understand the necessity of co-operation between the Shaman and the Leader. Caribou sometimes forgot that, and these lapses of recollection were what now focused Broken Fist's attention on him.

He sighed. As for the rest, the signs were good. He'd examined the river bank not far away and noted obvious spoor; big game came here to drink. He'd even noted the broad, circular pads of a greater predator: Lions followed the game as well.

He raised his left hand and stared at the stubs of fingers and the crushed knuckles which had given him his name. It had happened when he was a boy, not long before the Shaman selected him. In a way, it was good the Shaman had taken him up—for the rock which had crushed his hand had also most likely crushed his chances to ever be the hunter he wanted to be. He'd been very lucky, though; the injury had been terrible, but no evil Spirits had come to it, to swell the flesh and make it rot. The Old Shaman had said it was a special mark of Breath's protection, and one of the reasons he'd settled on him in the first place.

Now it was only another of his hallmarks; Broken Fist ate everything with his right hand except the

Special Meat, the Sacrifice. For that he reserved the twisted ruin of his left, as a sign of the Spirit of Breath's personal favor.

He flexed the muscles of his back and arms until the kinks of sleep had gone out of them. His tent smelled of strange herbs and a cloying, sweet scent—bits of mostly dried flesh that garlanded the tools of sacrifice, which had been carefully constructed from the bones of other sacrifices. Outside he heard caribou's voice, deep and heavy, roaring with sudden laughter. The smell of food grew more intense.

He pulled himself up and thrust through his door, squinting at the bright sunlight beyond. It was a beautiful day, already quite warm. A few vagrant clouds meandered slowly overhead. The bright sunlight turned the hearth fires invisible, leaving only ghostly ripples in the air above the heat.

"Ho, Shaman!" Caribou called. "Come join us!" He waved a thick slab of half-cooked roast at Broken Fist. "Everything's ready!"

Not quite everything, Broken Fist thought. Soon enough, though. After the sacrifice.

The thought made his mouth water even more than the rich fat that was soon dribbling down his square chin.

After he'd eaten his fill—more than his fill; the taut muscles of his belly bulged painfully—Rat turned to the others and began to speak. His voice was thin but mellow; much of the tone of it came through his long, narrow nose. "Shaman," he said, "Caribou wants me to hunt. What does the Spirit of Breath say?"

Broken Fist put down the bone he'd been cracking between his teeth for the rich marrow. The ground around him was littered in a fan of debris—scraps of gristle and chips of bone, over which flowed a tide of black, shiny insects. Rat's voice was properly respectful, but Fist thought he detected an undercurrent of mocking laughter. But then, there was such an undertone to *everything* Rat said. Sometimes the Shaman thought Rat doubted even the existence of the Spirit of Breath. He smiled inwardly. It didn't bother him. He could manipulate doubters. It was the believers who were sometimes a problem.

Caribou, for instance, believed. But one of the things Black Caribou believed was that the Spirit of Breath had chosen him to lead the Bison Clan. In a way, Fist considered, it was true—but not in the way Caribou believed it to be.

He didn't answer Rat directly. Broken Fist never answered any question directly, if he could help it. He said instead, "I dreamed last night."

Both Caribou and Rat's interest quickened. He could see it in the way their dark eyes focused on him, became glittery and concentrated. Caribou licked his lips nervously.

That made Broken Fist want to laugh. *So, Caribou, there* are *things you fear, and my dreams are one of them.* But he knew that already, and so he continued. "The Spirit of Breath has given us great abundance," Fist continued, and made a wide, sweeping gesture with his crippled hand.

Caribou and Rat both nodded. A faint shadow of dread began to suffuse Caribou's blocky features. Broken Fist smiled faintly. "But Breath demands a sacrifice for His bounty."

. Now fear bloomed like naked dark flowers in Caribou's eyes. "But we did sacrifice, Shaman." He licked his lips nervously. "The liver, the heart, the brains of the bison—" He stopped as Broken Fist shook his head slowly back and forth.

"Not enough," the Shaman said. "The Spirit of Breath is hungry. It is why He gave the Bison Clan these gifts. He wants great gifts in return."

Even Rat looked shaken then. All of them knew well enough what sort of great gifts the Spirit of Breath demanded. It had been nearly two winters since the last Great Gift. Now, it seemed, there must be another.

Caribou's voice was thick, almost stuttering with terror. "Did . . . the Spirit of Breath name His gift?"

Broken Fist waited, savoring this evidence of his own great power, letting the moment stretch out that he might better taste the fear of his rival. Finally he nodded slowly. "Spring Flower," he said. "The Spirit of Breath demands Spring Flower."

Caribou groaned. But he knew better than to say anything. Even his own authority couldn't compete with the power of the Greatest Spirit. If Breath wanted Spring Flower, then He would have her.

There was no choice. Even though Spring Flower was his own youngest sister.

He was Chief. Broken Fist would eat her liver, but it would fall to *him* to devour her heart.

The Green Valley

Maya shivered with excitement. The news had gone through the People like a prairie fire. Other People! And not far away, either.

The information she had was jumbled and fragmentary. Old Berry had sent her to the house they shared, and told her to wait until she came back.

Maya sat on a stump before the tiny house and watched men and women gather in groups to talk quietly, their faces intent. More desperately than ever she wished she could join them, take part in their conversations, but she knew what would happen if she tried. No one would push her away but lips would close, eyes narrow, and somehow, as if by common consent, everybody would find some other place they needed to be. In less time than it took to swallow a few breaths she would find herself alone, surrounded by a space that no one cared to enter.

So she sat and watched and waited. She wanted to run to Magic's house, but Spear and Skin and Ghost and Berry were already there. She could just see the top of Old Magic's bald head, nodding slowly as somebody—she thought it was Spear, his hands moving as if making some point—spoke.

Finally, Old Berry broke away from the group and began to trudge heavily in Maya's direction. The girl sprang up and met her halfway, questions spilling out like water from a spring.

"Auntie, what is . . . Who . . . ? *Where . . . ?*"

"Hush, child," Old Berry admonished. "Go back to our house and make yourself ready. The Shaman wants to see you right away. Go now." She gave the girl a gentle shove—but as she watched Maya spin, her face alight, back toward their house, her ancient features were bitter and troubled.

Is this how it begins? she wondered.

Old Magic looked up when the girl came slowly into the tent. Although, as always, it was very warm inside, the Shaman's arthritis was giving him a lot of trouble; he felt as if his joints were full of tiny chips of ice, grinding together, wearing down cartilage and rubbing away flesh. But he hid his pain well, and smiled a welcome at her.

"Sit down, Maya," he said kindly.

Her face was glowing with good cheer. She sank, graceful as a young deer, into her accustomed cross-legged position on the other side of the fire. Although he'd seen her almost every day of her life, now he *looked* at her. She has become a woman, Old Berry had said. And a beautiful woman at that, Magic decided. Her nose, slightly flattened at the broad tip, neatly bisected high, hard cheekbones and almond slanting eyes. Her skin was the color of honey, and her long, straight black hair gleamed in the flickering light. When she smiled, as she did now, her teeth showed white and even, between sweetly curved lips.

Somehow, a part of him would always remember her as a tiny handful of flesh, darkly solemn, marked with traces of her own mother's blood. But she had grown and changed, even as the People had grown and changed. Today she'd entered her full estate. He'd not yet dreamed much about these strange People Spear had discovered, but he noted the coincidence between their discovery and Maya's transformation.

He didn't think it was coincidence at all, any more than he thought Maya's birth, just as the People had come upon the Green Valley, was coincidence. He felt the weight of the Mother's hand upon him like a stone, the terrible pressure of the Great Secret, the responsibility that had kept him living long years after his time had come.

In this smiling girl before him was the future of the People. He had no idea what that future might be like; he doubted very much if she did, either. How could she? He'd taught her much, as much as he could, but only he and Berry shared the Secret. Now, perhaps, it was time to end that burden for once and all.

But he quailed. What would happen if he told Maya what she really was? Would she understand? Would she even *believe*? She was adult now, a woman, but from Magic's vastly longer view, so young. So very young. And he had so little help to offer her.

All at once he felt his age, like a great soft fur enfolding him, muzzling him, binding him in sick helplessness. He'd done his best. He'd taught her as much as he could, as much as he thought she could understand of what he did, and what a Shaman represented to the People. He'd sung the old songs over and over, until at least the words were stuck inside her skull. Although she didn't know it, she carried most of what history he knew locked up in her memory. And she knew of secrets—small ones about plants and larger ones about Spirits. He'd seen to her training carefully; not knowing what she might need, he'd tried to give her everything. Spear had passed on his knowledge of the ways of stone, of how to chip and shape and burnish, and Old Berry had contributed her own wide-ranging lore as well. Maya could read a spoor, make a knife, sing a song, prepare a poultice. To her perhaps it was all a game, but Magic didn't worry much about that. Just that the knowledge was there, so that when the time came to use it, she would have it ready.

It was all he'd known to do, all he could do. He'd done as the Dreams had told him over the years. It had been a long time since he'd seen the Woman Spirit who looked so much like Maya—she came only rarely. But she sent her Dreams in a hundred different ways, although the message was always the same:

Teach her!

And so he had. There was only one final thing for her to learn, but it was the most important of all. She was barely fourteen summers old, but she had a destiny, and her destiny was greater than her own—it was the destiny of the People as well. He saw this, both from the faded, ancient chants he'd learned in his own youth, and from the shadowy urgings of the Dreams.

She was more than a Sign. He'd lied to Ghost when he named her that, although the lie had saved her life. Maya was a Sign, but also She The Sign Awaits.

Maya, in some way he couldn't comprehend, directly represented the Great Mother in the World.

He felt such a thing had happened only once before; perhaps it could happen only a very few times, and then only at the greatest of dangers, when the invisible road the People traveled came to the most critical of turnings.

He sensed a trembling in the moment, vast forces almost balanced in time and place. "Maya . . ." he began softly, ignoring the pains of his bones, his soft and sagging flesh.

"What?"

Her eyes seemed to shine with secret fire. *What is she thinking? This girl who is alone, so alone, and yet not alone at all.* He took a breath and plunged on, with the air of a man who casts a stone into a bottomless canyon and then stands waiting forever to hear the answering echo.

His old fingers plucked at the carefully made knots that bound the Mammoth Stone in its coverings of fur and soft leather. He got them undone and pulled on the mittens that protected the Stone from the touch of a male.

"Maya . . ." he said slowly, his voice quavering a bit as he lifted the Stone out and offered it to her, "take this, please, and hold it in your hands."

Bison Camp

Black Caribou waited until the Shaman, Broken Fist, had gone back into his tent. The Shaman had been smiling as he departed, but now that he was gone Caribou could let the careful, jaw-aching *blankness* fall from his own features. When he turned to look at Little Rat his dark eyes bulged a little, and sudden, bruise-like patches disfigured the soft flesh beneath.

Little Rat stared back, relief whispering like butterfly wings inside his chest. When the Spirit of Breath demanded His due, no man was safe. Nor had Rat been entirely blind all his life: He'd seen how those who mocked Broken Fist's deformity, or opposed him in other ways, somehow managed to excite the Spirit of Breath's hunger. Rat thought he'd concealed his own feelings well enough, but it was always a horrible, grinning solace when the bloody hands of Breath passed him over once again.

Not so for Caribou, though, and Rat wasn't all that surprised. He'd expected something like this for quite a while now. Caribou was a big, physically threatening man, who wasn't afraid to use his strength. Somehow, without anybody's fully realizing it, Black Caribou had been transformed into The Leader—Rat himself had only noticed the change recently. But once he had seized on the *idea* of it, the rest was plain to see. The men who tracked, who followed spoor, and the men who hunted, and those who searched for stones with which to make spears and knives—and their wives, and their children—somehow, all of them had begun, because it seemed so *natural*—to tell Caribou what they were doing. Or planning to do. Just to get his opinion. And equally often, if Black Caribou's opinion was that he didn't approve, or suggested a different way, well, then, that was the way it got done.

Rat doubted whether Caribou himself understood what sort of change had taken place—but he was sure Broken Fist had missed none of it. Now he was more certain than ever. He wondered who the Spirit of Breath might want next—and guessed that whoever it was, it would bring Caribou no joy.

He suspected that Breath wouldn't work up a hunger for Caribou himself, not any time soon. Not until Caribou had been so worn down that this strange new *leadership* role was chipped away to nothing.

Of course he said nothing of this to Caribou. Rat had a healthy respect for the idea of "every man for himself." If Caribou was too stupid to see what was happening right under his nose, then he deserved his fate. Rat certainly had no plans to enlighten him. Rat did have other plans, though. . . .

"It will be a great Sacrifice," Rat said solemnly. "The Spirit of Breath will be very happy."

But Caribou's own dark eyes were shadowed and miserable as he tried to force a brisk nod of agreement. "Yes," he managed. "Very happy."

The Green Valley

18 Maya came into Old Magic's tent feeling happy and nervous and curious all at once. Something had been different about Berry's face when she'd told her the Shaman wanted to see her—and though Maya hadn't looked very closely at that *difference*, she'd known it was there. She considered it as she'd changed her coat—she had two now, of leather cord she'd cured herself, both carefully stitched with her own hands, using needles of bone she'd rubbed long nights with a bit of smooth stone until their points could penetrate the fur of the coat easily. Sewing was only one of her many skills; there was so much she knew how to do, although, because she had little to do with the other women and girls, she didn't really understand how extraordinary this plethora of talents was. It all seemed so natural to her: Berry and Magic had taught her for seven years, and for seven years she'd learned from them. She knew her upbringing was different from the others', but then everything about her was different.

Now, another difference. She'd overheard fragments of conversation even from her perch, which the rest of the People unconsciously avoided—their steps just happened to wander around and about, as if there were a well-marked path only they could see.

But she listened. One of the advantages of being treated as invisible was that people tended, after a while, simply not to notice her presence. They said things they never would have if a real person had been about. And so, in this way, Maya had learned even more than she could have if her childhood and youth had been normal.

It was as if every event conspired to arm her further for the battles she would someday have to fight.

But what is wrong with Berry? She finished dressing and gave her coat a final smoothing with her hands. The caribou fur felt soft and thick beneath her fingers. *Berry is afraid,* she finally decided. But she couldn't figure out what Berry was afraid *about*.

The New People, probably. But Berry had already found out about them, first thing, when the hunters returned to camp. And that news hadn't frightened her. Only when she'd gone again to the Spirit House and talked for long hours with the Shaman had she come back frightened.

Somehow, Maya was certain, the old woman's fear had something to do with her. But she couldn't imagine what the real reason might be. And now in the hot, cinnamon-minty darkness of the Spirit Tent, with its low, moldy underscent of ancient male sweat, she saw it again. The fear. Magic was afraid, too.

". . . take this, please, and hold it in your hands."

In the dim light, she hadn't really noticed what he'd unrolled in his lap as he spoke to her. He was always showing her something, a bit of rock, a kind of dried leaf, the carving on a wooden stick used to command Spirits. The familiarity of the ritual of learning had become second nature to her. She leaned forward, feigning interest, while what she really wanted to ask was, *What about the New People?*

Then she saw the Mammoth Stone, and everything stopped.

Just like that, Old Magic went away. She couldn't see him anymore. She couldn't see the tiny, ever-present fire, nor could she see the shadowy piles of furs, charms, implements, leaves, berries, baskets that lined the curving walls of the Spirit House.

She couldn't see her own hands, nor the caribou coat she wore, nor the moccasins bound to her leggings as she bent forward.

It seemed she'd become wholly eyes, that all there was of her was what she could see, and all she could see was the Stone.

She was quite certain she'd never seen it before (she was wrong), but even so it was as familiar to her as Old Berry's seamed face, as the dry, lemony, decayed smell of Old Magic's breath.

She had stopped breathing for a moment, but she didn't know it. Somehow the Stone moved closer to her (or did she move closer to *it*?—she never knew for sure), and then it hung in glimmering darkness just beneath her eyes.

She could easily see every detail. The Stone was about the size of her palm. It was a mammoth, lovingly carved, softly polished, never touched. Time had softened its original ivory whiteness so that now it gleamed like dark gold. A single eye looked up at her. At the rear of the mammoth, where a tail should have been, was a strip of ivory that ended abruptly, on a weak angle. As if the ivory had been broken there, broken away from something else.

She wondered what the something else had been, but then that thought too went away, as if it were a question that didn't need to be asked. Not yet, anyway.

From far away, low and rolling and almost bell-like, words slowly rose up beneath the Stone like great, dark bubbles, each bubble bursting in a single event of sound.

Take . . . the . . . Stone.

"Yes," she breathed softly.

It was very odd. She knew that she was reaching out for the Stone (which hung suspended in . . . nothing at all), and that somehow her fingers were getting closer, closer.

She couldn't see them. Not her fingers, her hands, nothing. Just the feeling that she—that *her whole self*—was somehow enfolding, enveloping, *absorbing* the Stone into that place in her very center where, without knowing it, she'd been empty and cold and alone.

Click!

Like that. A tiny sound of fitting together. And she was whole.

She hadn't even known she was empty. . . .

"Ahhh . . ." she whispered.

The World came back.

Her senses snapped on, one by one. Smell: The furs in the Spirit House smelled dusty, as if they needed to be taken out into the bright air and beaten until great bluish-gray clouds puffed out of them. Taste: something in her mouth, thin and coppery— blood. Hearing: Old Magic's breath, a rheumy engine that gurgled and rasped in his sunken chest. Finally, feeling: The Stone felt slightly cool, but despite the shine of it, not slippery at all. Dry. Almost weightless.

She never wanted to let it go.

Wordlessly, she held the Mammoth Stone up to her face. She rubbed it on her cheek. She breathed on it, and sensed an answering reply, from somewhere far away.

She looked at Old Magic.

"Oh," she said. "Oh, oh."

"The Secret," he said simply. "Do you know the Secret?"

But she didn't. Not then. Soon, though.

Chapter Ten

The Green Valley: 17,983 B.C.

Somewhere a robin sang. Maya blinked. "What?"

"Do you know the Secret?" Old Magic repeated softly. His eyes bored into hers, like the tiny black beetles she'd seen digging holes in the soft dirt alongside the stream.

Secret? She had no idea what he was talking about. Sometimes the old ones were like that, would say or do things that made no sense to her, and in those moments she'd feel they had somehow slipped into a different language, even a different *world*. That would make her frightened; for if they left her she would be truly alone, and the thought of that was like listening to the winter wind howl above the valley in the night. But she felt his expectancy; though his voice was soft and his question slow, his eyes burned like hearth coals, and his shrunken, ancient body seemed to *push* forward, though he didn't move at all.

"I—I d-d-don't. . . ." she began, knowing her answer would not please him, and then, just as before, the World went away.

There are no secrets from Me.

Old Magic gasped. The change had taken only an instant, but now something that *was not Maya* sat cross-legged beyond the fire, facing him. The girl's amazing eyes had rolled back in her skull, so that their color was hidden and only blank, white skin filled the sockets.

A cold, greasy wave of fear sludged its way up his spine. He felt the flesh on the backs of his withered hands tingle. Had he been younger, his bones stronger, his muscles capable of responding, he would have uttered a short cry of absolute terror and sprung from the tent, screaming.

That voice, *that voice*!

Never in the World or out of it, in dreams or Dreams, had such a sound filled his ears. It still did, the long, slow intonations of it thrumming inside his head like the distant icy thunder which filled the valley every day. It went on and on, until he couldn't bear it anymore, and he covered his ears with his liver-spotted hands and, as tears ran down the cracked ravines of his cheeks, whispered, "Stop. Oh, please, stop."

Then a terrible thing occurred. After the space of ten heartbeats, as if his horrified plea had taken that long to reach its destination (just across the fire), the *thing that was not Maya* smiled at him.

It was a slow, twitching movement that had less to do with the girl's lips, the flesh and bone of her jaw, than did the expression that might cross the muzzle of a slaughtered caribou, hours after death. He thought of the way little children might play with such a trophy, pulling the fur this way and that, weaving the dead meat into shapes that sent them howling with childish laughter. But the worst thing about the smile was its distance; it had nothing to do with Maya at all, and very little to do with Magic. It was as if *the thing that was not Maya* had tried on a mask, something it thought might be pleasing to Magic's old eyes. There was a tentativeness to it, as if invisible fingers had pushed the

flesh of Maya's lips this way and that until it had
arrived at what it thought was a satisfactory
arrangement.

Shudders racked him.

The *thing* waited a moment, behind lips hanging
like strips of skinned meat. A thin string of drool
began to leak from the corner of Maya's mouth.
Those blank, white eyes burned into his heart, saw
through him and beyond him, as if he were a speck
hard to focus upon.

Then—and this was even more ghastly than before—those dead-meat lips began to twitch. The top
lip jerked to the right, but the bottom flapped up
and down, like hides hung up to dry in the wind.
A low, guttural, choking sound came from Maya's
throat; he could see her Adam's apple work up and
down, pushing against her larynx like an animal
trapped in a hole.

I have many Secrets, Shaman.

Old Magic did the bravest thing he had ever done
in his long life, or would ever do. He wanted to
shriek and shriek; instead, with an effort he would
never have dreamed himself capable of making, he
formed his lips, his throat, around words.

"Who are you?" he said.

A thin, high whine had begun to buzz in his ears.
He barely made out the reply over the insect hum
of it.

I am My gift to My People. Use Me well!

Maya's body jerked back and forth, but never far,
as if unseen cords bound her in that place and position. The skin of her face began to *shift*, as if hundreds of tiny animals struggled just beneath the
surface, pushing and poking and gnawing their way
to release.

"Ahhh," Old Magic moaned.

It stopped.

Just like that, *the thing that was not Maya* departed.

He knew instantly that it was gone. Inside his mind, he felt a great burning darkness fill with light, felt it *snap back* to wherever it had come from, even sensed the tiniest part of its struggle to make itself small enough to live within its chosen vessel. And he listened to the distance of it, the appalling empty distance it had traveled from *there* to *here*.

The stench of burning hair filled his nostrils. He looked down and saw that somehow he'd leaned over his tiny cook-blaze, and the hem of his robe had caught on fire. His face burned with heat where the narrow drizzle of smoke had coated his face, but deep within, there was no warmth. Only cold, an ancient, freezing cold, the chill of power beyond reckoning, the icy weight of the world beyond the World.

Once upon a time, when his understanding of the Secret had grown to full flower and he'd understood that the Power of the Stone, the direct communication between the Mother and Her Children, was forever denied to him, he'd been disappointed. The idea of seeing the Mother unclothed and naked had seemed a great prize.

Now he understood. Only the tiniest, most insignificant portion of *the thing that was not Maya* had entered the Spirit House, and the gargantuan force of it had almost killed him. But the ban had held, and saved him; he had not, and would never, see the Great Mother naked.

He closed his eyes and breathed the most profound prayer of gratitude he would ever make. Then, when he opened his eyes and looked at Maya's slumped form, pity clenched his heart in a fist of iron.

Thanks be to the Mother's mercy, he would never truly know Her. But for Maya, there was no such shield.

The Goddess was *within* her; for Maya, there would never be a place to hide.

Use Me well?

The child. The poor, poor child.

Maya awoke refreshed, as if from a long and deep sleep. The first thing she saw was Magic, slapping at a burning ember on the edge of his robe. How had that happened? She didn't remember anything. . . .

She shook her head.

Didn't remember anything. No, not quite true. There was something, but it didn't have anything to do with the oddly funny look on Magic's seamed features, or his frantic movements as he batted awkwardly at the singed patch of fur. She remembered a Light, the same kind of sensation she sometimes got if she placed her fingers across her eyes, turned her face toward the sun, and then, for the tiniest of instants, slipped her fingers apart so that the sun seemed to explode into her skull.

Like that, but much, much greater.

She remembered a Great Light, but somehow that didn't seem so strange. She was quite certain she'd seen the light before somewhere, but she couldn't quite remember where. Nor did it seem important, the Light. The Light just Was, and she thought it Would Always Be, and that it had very little to do with her.

Some, though. It had some little bit to do with her. More important, though, was Magic's question.

"I don't know a Secret, Magic," she said, her voice plaintive. "I'm sorry. Are you mad at me?"

And then, more practically, "Here. Let me help you."

She leaned forward to take Magic's robe and the Mammoth Stone tumbled, forgotten, out of her lap to the ground.

Magic *hissed*.

She drew back in alarm. What awful thing had she done now?

"Th-the Stone!" Magic spluttered, so terrified he could hardly speak. *"Pick up the Stone!"*

"What? Oh. Here it is." She rubbed it against the fur of her leggings. "See? It's not hurt at all."

Magic could feel his fingers tremble like frost-laden branches in a storm wind. Even beneath the warm fur of his mittens, his hands (he knew they would never be warm again) creaked and groaned an arthritic agony of protest as he accepted the Stone back into his safekeeping.

It took him several tries—the knots were the hardest—before he got the Stone safely wrapped up again. Maya watched this with twinkly interest, her vague memory of the Light already fading. "Are you going to tell me a secret, Uncle? Is that why you wanted to know if I knew one?" She looked down at her lap, her face suddenly sad and serious. "I *wish* I knew a secret," she continued, "but I don't."

Magic ignored all this until he had the Stone completely put away, back beneath its bed of cushioning furs, protected by its complicated web of cords and secret, intricate knots. The Stone had served his purpose; it had told him what he wanted to know.

More than he wanted to know.

But what to do about it? Never had the Secret pressed down on him so heavily. He knew, without knowing *how* he knew, that matters had reached a great turning point. It was, he was convinced, no coincidence that had brought blood between Maya's legs and new People upon the banks of the nearby river at the same time. For he had just witnessed the third factor with his own horrified eyes: The Mother had revealed Herself in Her Vessel. Maya did not belong to herself. She might not, he thought with a sudden twinge of terror, even belong to the

People, except in the most peripheral sense. She was a tool, no more and no less than the knives and choppers and scrapers the People used in their daily lives—but with one unforgettable difference. Her *user* was a Goddess.

Use Me well!

And those words had been spoken, not to Maya, but to *him*. The responsibility lay on *his* shoulders; he wanted desperately to cry out against it, but could no more do so than he could shout down the wind, or melt the mile-high wall of ice to the north.

He'd never felt older, or more tired, or more helpless in his life. But deep within him burned a flame, hard and bright and hot; it was the love he'd always had for his People, and in its own way it was no less strong than the terrible Mother Herself. As he turned back to face the girl who had become utterly *something else*, he reached deep into that ever-shining light and found, to his amazement, the strength he needed. He took off his mittens and discovered that his fingers had grown warm and supple, as if, by accident, that gift had been left behind for him.

He flexed his hands and stared at them with pleasure. Even Maya noticed.

"Uncle, your hands . . . they look different."

And so they did. The dark red liver spots had shrunk, almost faded away, and the bulbous, knuckly joints looked smaller, smoother. His hands had grown younger, and were throbbing with new strength.

Strong hands, he thought to himself. *I will need strong hands.* And he understood in that moment the nature of the gift *She* had bestowed on him.

The strength of the light, the strength to go on. The strength to do what was necessary. The strengthae0 to *Use Me well!*

In that moment of knowledge, the final revelation burst upon him like a thunderbolt from a black and roiling cloud. *This was Maya's purpose. This would be*

*her Power, to be the conduit, the Way Between, so that
the Great Mother Herself could intervene in the World.*

Again, pity took him in its obdurate grip. He
knew what happened to Stone's knives, after they
had been worn down by use. The went dull, and
broke, and were discarded.

That was the destiny of tools.

His mind skipped lightly over one other knot of
discovery, though: The Mother's first use of Her tool
had been to reveal Herself to him. He had been
changed, as well; now the two of them sat facing
each other, different than they'd been only moments
before, but still, in their varied ways, just as ignorant.

Outside, the hum of conversation grew more ur-
gent. He could picture the People gathering, waiting
for him to come to them with messages from the
Spirits.

He had his message. But it was one he could
never make them understand.

*The Great Mother is among us. She is with the People
now.*

Oh, oh, oh, and She is terrible.

"No, Maya," he said from the depth of his newfound strength, "I don't have a Secret for you. Not
yet. But I have something different."

Her clear blue-and-green gaze sparked with anticipation. "Oh, what, Uncle? What is it?" She thought
he had that air about him, that sly, funny expression
that never quite reached the surface of his face, that
she only saw when he was about to give her an
especially wonderful gift—a tiny bit of glittering
rock, or a small leather-bound bundle of sweet-
smelling herbs—and she forgot completely about
that strange instance when the Light had blinked in
the darkness of her center, and she'd been changed
forever.

"Tell me!" she pleaded.

And, knowing for the first time that what he was

about to do was right, absolutely right (*Use Me well!*), he said, "Would you like to live here with me? In the Spirit House? Would you like to do that, little Maya?"

Ghost stood for a moment outside his own house and watched a ladder of cloud move briskly across the bright blue sky, trailing a long pattern of shadow across the earth beneath. Just for a moment, as the shadow passed, his gaunt face looked a hundred years old.

Not far away, the turmoil was slowly dying down. Small groups of the People—he saw Spear in the middle of one, gesturing, explaining for the tenth or hundredth time where he'd gone, what he'd seen— still clumped together like balls of dirt, but even as he watched, pieces of the clumps flaked away, drifted off, just as a dirt clod in the stream would gradually wash away.

Dirt. Just like dirt.

Like him.

Old Magic had gone to the men's Mystery House, the long house built of bones and sod and heavy, half-cured hide, sunk halfway into the earth of the ledge above the stream. The Shaman had, for a few moments, frightened Ghost with the way he moved, the strength of his voice. Ghost had counted the months, the days for a long time now; the record of Magic's ever-growing weakness was a secret he held to his own shrunken chest like an ember of hope. *Can't live forever*, can't *live forever*, chanted the voice of that hope, but now, suddenly, the old Shaman moved like a man half his true age.

There was a new spring in his step, and Ghost noticed that his fingers, as he firmly grasped the signs of his office—the tall, carved staff, the rattle, the cord with which to bind Spirits—were less bent, less clawlike than before.

All the men had crowded into the Mystery House, until they sat shoulder to shoulder beneath a thick haze of silvery-blue smoke. Two small hearths smoldered inside, beneath holes cut into the roof, but with the door flaps tied shut, and the number of men there, not enough ventilation existed to push all the smoke out.

The smell of sweat, of damp hide, of dirt and moldy pine needles on the floor, of rotting meat and scorched rock from the hearths was overwhelming, but Ghost was so used to it he didn't even notice except to brush at his eyes once or twice in irritation at the smoky fumes.

The hide roof of the Mystery House glowed in the dim light with a thousand fantastic shapes. Up there frolicked mammoths with long, curving tusks; huge bison, their ruffs like shaggy bushes, their hooves broad and black; a pride of lions, leaping upon the backs of squealing, terrified caribou; and men, their spears long and sharp, dancing the mystery of their hunting magic around and through the painted Spirits of their chosen victims.

It was here the hunters came to prepare for the hunt; with feasting and fasting and herbs brewed by Magic or, more recently, Ghost, herbs which called the Spirits in Dreams that all shared. There was a spot, Ghost knew, not too far from where he now stood, worn by his rear end on a log. That was his place, where he sang the old songs and chanted the words that *called* the bison and caribou and mammoth to their doom. Old Magic had relinquished all of this to him, and Ghost had been well pleased. He had a sharp sense that in this, the mundane weave of life among the People, lay true power, and he wondered how Magic could have given it up so easily.

Somewhere deep inside Ghost still gibbered the small and frightened boy who had talked to Spirits as he lay writhing in the dirt, who was laughed at and spat upon and made the target of casual stones, but Ghost could no longer find him. The years had made the younger Shaman strong and confident; he could never do anything about his limp, or the unnatural thinness of his body, but none of that mattered anymore; his magic had brought game to the People, and the hunters respected him greatly.

He looked over the crowd and noticed Spear, in the center of the front row, gazing up at him. Spear in particular had become a friend, as much as two such different men could be friendly; Ghost recalled the day when that had begun to happen.

It had been going on fall, after the short hot brightness of summer. On the morning of the hunt, Ghost had risen from his house and stepped out into a world of chill and mist; gray clouds boiled and lumped overhead, their fat black bellies leaking thin drizzle that moved in fitful sheets before an erratic wind. The chill sliced at his bones, but he was dressed warmly enough in coat and leggings of soft caribou skin, and his great reindeer cape over all. Home Camp had seemed oddly silent; two fires smoked in the shelter of the overhanging cliff, their fumes rapidly disappearing into the mist. A few shadowy shapes moved around the fires; Ghost knew the women were already at work, making ready for the return of the men with the fruits of the hunt. He could hear the soft chinking sound of sticks poking at the coals.

He stretched and yawned; although the weather was foul he felt at peace, as if the mists enfolded him, making him more like his namesake. A Ghost, moving among the People, a Spirit walking the land.

He ate quickly, then found two of the younger men who'd stayed behind to carry his tools. They set off shortly after, and reached the River about three hours later. The Spirit Pole had already been implanted in its hole in the ground; it loomed out of the mist like a giant finger; its sides were slippery with damp.

Here, beyond the shelter of the Valley walls, the winds howled more strongly, tearing occasional holes in the fog which looped and swirled above the River. Spits of gritty snow rattled against the thickly carved wood, and made climbing difficult.

"Help me!" Ghost commanded the younger of his two acolytes, a slender youth with one bad eye who reminded him, though he didn't like to admit it, of himself as a boy. The youth, whose name was Gopher, came down, bent over, and placed his bony shoulder beneath Ghost's rump, as Ghost wrapped his own arms around the Spirit Pole.

Gopher grunted as he pushed, while Ghost hitched himself up. Finally, everything was ready. The young Shaman sat in his saddle atop the Pole, eight feet above the ground. He arranged his robe as best he could to keep out the damp and drizzle, then tied leather thongs across his lap to hold him steady. Finally, Gopher handed up a small drum made of hide stretched across a slab of hollow wood, the skull of a fox which had been filled with tiny, polished stones from the stream, and a small ivory knife. The last things Gopher passed up to him were the most important: a lumpy brown thing, and a miniature spear made of hardened hickory wood and tightly bound flint.

The brown thing was the heart of a Mammoth Mother. Ghost himself had ripped it, still beating, from her mighty body at the culmination of the Spring Hunt four months before. He arranged these things in his lap, except for the drum, which he hung from his shoulder by the cord attached for that purpose.

Finally, he checked the straps which held him to the saddle. It was important they be tight enough to hold him firmly, but not so tight that the circulation to his legs be cut off. He might have to perch here for hours. He fingered the knots and decided they would do; if they didn't hold him, he might be badly injured when he fell—and fall he would; for what was coming would take him from his body and leave it abandoned, a fleshy husk torn by the bitter winds.

Ghost supposed that what he did was normal enough—at least for one who spoke to, and was possessed by, Spirits. Old Magic worked his powers differently, but that was no surprise. Early on the old Shaman had told him the Spirits came as they wished to come, and what worked for him might not work for another.

Ghost never remembered just what it was he did when his own Spirits took him. That was part of the mystery; he had heard descriptions enough, but always from other eyes and lips. He himself had never the tiniest recollection of what he thought of as the Moment. Which didn't mean that he couldn't prepare for it.

He'd worked out his own methods, however, and they were just as effective.

In epilepsy, signals from certain parts of the brain overwhelm the functions of the rest of the brain; in effect, a part of the brain "explodes." Deep within the human brain lies a small, fingertip-sized bit of tissue known as the Reptilian Complex. This R-Complex doesn't *think* in any human sense, but is aware of the world around it as a shadowy universe of desire and fear; it is the snake brain, and from its hundred-million-year-old well come terror and aggression—the R-Complex is the cell-deep place where cold-blooded murder is born.

Should the signals from this ominous fragment of flesh explode to dominate the rest of the brain, then the human mind regresses instantly and becomes as much dinosaur as anything else, a roiling welter of hunger and death. That mind becomes hungry and terrible.

Ghost sat atop his Spirit Pole and waited for the hunt just as, without his knowing it, his brain waited for the hunger.

"Go find them!" he ordered Gopher.

About half an hour later the boy returned, panting from his run. "Close now!" he called to the Shaman. "Two mothers, three or four young ones. Can't you hear them?"

Ghost nodded. Though muffled by the wind and the mist, the thin cries of the hunters as they herded the mighty animals toward the river and Ghost's perch beside it had already reached his ears.

Deeper beneath the raucous shouts of the hunters, a sudden trumpeting squeal blared. Ghost nodded to himself, shifted the drum, and began to tap a beat with his left hand.

Boom ba-boom ba-boom.

Faster and faster.

Something huge lumbered by a hundred yards out, barely visible through the fog. Ghost stuffed his mouth with a wad of soft leather, let the ends of it hang out, and bit down hard. The drum, seeming to sound on its own, throbbed in his ears. Another shape, smaller, lurched into view, stampeded closer, bleeding from half a dozen wounds.

The young mammoth collapsed with a ground-thudding slam less than twenty yards away. Spear leaped atop the dying animal and plunged his weapon down with both hands, leaning his full weight upon it. Blood fountained up, splattering his face and chest and arms. A crazy grin split his face as he shouted triumphantly at the Shaman.

But Ghost couldn't hear him. He leaned slowly to the side, his jaws working mindlessly against the soft leather which kept him from biting his tongue in two. His drum had fallen silent.

Spear, down below, had a momentary, flickering vision that terrified him to his core. It seemed to him, through the mist of blood and rain which surrounded him, that he could see the top of the Spirit Pole, and that Ghost had disappeared. In his place coiled a great black snake, whose red tongue darted in and out and whose eyes burned with a cold, paralyzing fire.

Then the phantasm disappeared, as Spear turned to meet the frenzied, screaming charge of the Mammoth Mother who'd turned back to defend her child. He jerked his spear from the dead flesh beneath his feet and leaped to the ground, shouting for Skin to help him, but Skin was too far away.

Spear danced to one side and avoided the Mother's first crazed advance, but the great beast wheeled too quickly for him and he slipped on a muddy patch of trampled grass.

All the Mother could see through her two reddened, maniac eyes was a tiny figure, close by the fallen corpse of her daughter. She had her own burden of insanity, and now, as she advanced, all she wanted was to trample the offensive thing into a mush of red blood and crushed bone.

Ghost's upper body hung almost horizontal, held to the Spirit Pole only by its careful bindings. Spear saw only a flash, but one he would remember for the rest of his life, as he gathered himself for the only thrust he would have time to take.

It was hopeless—but in that flash he saw Ghost's hands, moving and twitching like small, slow animals. One hand held a tiny spear. The other grasped the lumpy, dried mammoth heart. The two came together as one hand plunged the spear into the heart, again and again.

He saw this only for the tiniest of moments, before a weird strength seized him and he plunged his own spear into the Mother's huge side. She fell dead next to her murdered offspring.

Later, Spear told Ghost of the moment. Ghost, of course, remembered nothing of it. He'd slept for ten minutes after the men had cut him down from the Spirit Pole.

He didn't have to remember, though. He knew what had guided Spear's desperate thrust. And he knew that Mammoth Mother had been dead *even before* that strike. For he had killed her with his magic.

Let the old Shaman match that! he thought, as he nodded faintly at Spear in the front row of the men. The hunter returned the motion just as Old Magic cleared his throat.

Ghost had no idea what the old man would say. He wasn't even sure he cared. Let the old fool ride his weird, newfound strength for a time. Let him play his strange and foolish games with the bitch-girl. So he would take her as his woman, eh?

When Magic had told him, almost as an aside, that Maya would be moving into the Spirit House, Ghost had gone almost mad with jealousy. But then, before his face could change at all, a coldness had welled up from a spot just above the top of his spinal cord.

The Snake Brain spoke to him and said, "All will be well. She is his. So she will be yours, along with the rest of his property, when he dies."

Ghost smiled to himself. Most of the men were looking at Old Magic now, intent on the words he spoke. But Wolf, Maya's brother, saw the smile flash across Ghost's face, and for no reason he could think of, he shuddered.

"Oh, Auntie, isn't it wonderful?"

"Isn't what wonderful?"

"I'm going to live in Uncle Magic's house and take care of him!"

The old woman paused in her work. She'd listened to Maya's ecstatic chatter for half an hour now, after the first explosion of news when the girl had burst into their house like a small, girlish tornado. "Maya, what did you talk about?"

Maya looked up from where she was bundling her second coat and leggings into a neat ball. She didn't have all that much to pack: her clothes, the gifts Magic had given her over the years, some herbs she'd just gathered. And moss—Berry reminded her to take moss. It seemed the bleeding probably wouldn't stop for a day or two, the old woman said. The thought worried Maya a bit; blood meant death. It somehow didn't seem right that she could bleed and not be harmed by it, though Old Berry assured her that was the case.

Now she heard a warning note in Berry's rough voice, as if the old woman were half-afraid of what Maya might say. Maya thought about it and decided it was just another quirk of the old ones, whose minds were still almost a complete mystery to her. She wanted to please the other woman—*other woman; I myself am a woman now*, she thought with a tiny thrill—but there really wasn't anything to say. Magic had shown her a pretty carving, and then told her she would come to live with him. That was all there was to it—wasn't it?

She couldn't remember anything else, and so she said, sounding diffident, "Nothing, Auntie. Just that I was to move into the Spirit House." A new thought struck her. "Auntie? Does that mean I'm Magic's woman?"

Maya was a curious mix of innocence and sophistication. She knew that the men of the People took women for their own. It was the natural way of things. Some men took only one, others had two or three. In some cases, as with her two fathers, Skin and Spear, there was an even looser, less-defined family structure, in which the men shared their wives but the women cleaved to their own children.

But she was unsure of these connections, and had no ideas at all about the underlying sexual nature of them. Neither she nor any other member of the People associated the sexual act with procreation. Sex was obvious: A man might parade naked, his member stiff and erect, proudly down the path toward his house, with his woman waiting for his arrival as naked as he was.

But what sex was, and what it concerned as far as other things, was as mysterious to Maya as the man in the moon.

As for Berry, she held her tongue and bit off her first, scoffing reply. Maya as Old Magic's woman? He was too old for the displays of the younger men. Old Berry guessed Magic hadn't known an erection for years. But what, then, *did* the old Shaman want with the girl? Already Berry and Maya did his cooking, took care of his House, tended his fire, and gathered the herbs and berries he needed for his work. Their house was less than ten feet from his own. Why was it necessary for Maya to physically occupy the Spirit House?

She guessed it had something to do with the Secret, although it was obvious now that Magic had changed his original intention of telling Maya about *that*. She had questioned her as carefully as she could, without touching on the heart of the matter, but the only Secret Maya could recall was the one Magic had asked if she'd known.

Yet the girl had held the Mammoth Stone. It must mean something!

"I don't know," Berry said at last. "Perhaps." She reached over and slapped Maya on her rump. "None of it will matter if you don't finish with that, girl. You may be a woman now, but you'll always be my little niece." She stopped, amazed to realize that was true. It had just fallen out of her mouth, but it was as true as anything in the World. Maya, her burden, had somehow become Maya, whom she loved.

She would have been mightily disturbed if she'd known Old Magic could give her no more coherent an explanation for his actions than Maya could. All he could tell her was that it *was right*, without understanding why it was.

He certainly couldn't tell of the vast and numbing power who had bent low over the Green Valley and, for one appalling moment, touched their lives with the tiniest tip of Her finger.

Nor could he speak of the Web which that Power had begun to weave twenty-five hundred years before. It wasn't that he wouldn't speak, but that he *couldn't;* he knew nothing of it at all.

Chapter Eleven

The Green Valley: 17,983 B.C.

Maya hummed softly to herself as she arranged her bed-furs on a pile of sweet-smelling pine branches. She'd cleared a small space for herself in the cramped confines of the Spirit House, a tiny place across the fire from Magic's own mound of bedding. She didn't know why she'd picked that particular location. Something told her not to bed down in the obvious spot, next to the old Shaman's sleeping place.

It was very quiet in Home Camp. She noticed it suddenly, her head coming up, her eyes soft and watchful. The familiar, everyday click and clatter of feet tramping by, sudden laughter, the joking calls of the men, the chip-chip *clack* as Stone worked on his tools—everything was silent.

She'd carried her bundles from Berry's house to her new home with a kind of bounding elation churning in her heart—but even as she did so, a part of her had noticed the ominous stillness, the air of expectant desolation, that hung over the village. For a moment she'd had the eerie feeling that everybody had departed, left her behind, and that she was completely alone with something else.

Furtively, feeling more than a little stupid, she'd

darted a glance over her shoulder. She couldn't explain why, except that for one awful moment she'd sensed the presence of something else there. But there was nothing, of course; merely empty paths and smoldering hearths, and thin wreaths of smoke rising lazily into the vacant air.

The men were all in the Mystery House; the women, forever barred from those sacred precincts, waited outside, some standing, some squatting, whispering to each other in soft, worried voices. That was why Home Camp seemed so forlorn, so empty. Of course it was.

Now she gave the arrangement of furs and boughs a final twitch; the sweet smell of resin filled her nose, and she smiled. With her bed made and her few possessions stowed in a neat pile next to it, the Spirit House suddenly felt homey to her.

I live here now, she thought suddenly, with a kind of happy wonder. *This is my home.*

She'd never really had a home before.

Bud, what happened? What really *happened?*

The power of that errant thought made her muscles jerk like the limbs of a deranged puppet. She gasped. Suddenly the silence, made even louder by the thin, distant honk of a duck flying low over Home Camp, seemed wholly ominous. Her eyes shot wide; she stared vacantly at the interior of the Spirit House, at all the familiar jumble, until, without conscious effort, her gaze settled on the neatly tied bundle beyond Magic's bed; that pretty carved stone was there.

She stared at the enigmatic package, and once again something called to her. She tilted her head, as if that sound were just beyond the range of her hearing, tantalizing but unapproachable.

Nothing. Silence, and the sound of her own breathing.

An ember popped in the ever-burning hearth at

the center of the Spirit House, and just like that the spell broke. She shook her head and waited until her rapidly beating heart had slowed down. But for some reason her fingers itched to untie those knots, to take out the small piece of carved ivory, to rub its warm, smooth surface against the soft skin of her cheek.

It was a bad thought. Magic wouldn't like it.

Yet her fingers still itched, for all of that.

"Dinner," she reminded herself. "No matter what happens, he'll be hungry."

The sound of her own voice shattered whatever remnants had remained of that strange interlude; she rocked back on her heels, slapped her hands down on top of her thighs, and pushed herself up. The women might all be at the Mystery House, but Maya knew she wasn't invited to join them. She would *never* be invited to join them. But she had meat and dried acorns and skill and a place in Old Magic's home.

Dinner and warmth and, at least for a moment, peace.

(*Oh, Bud, what* happened?)

She pushed beyond the door flap and stood up in the afternoon sun, listening to the rising hum of excited voices. The meeting was over.

She wondered what they'd decided, then thrust the thought away. Old Magic would tell her soon enough.

After all, she was Old Magic's woman now. Vaguely, she wondered if that meant the Shaman would stick his thing between her legs, down there where the blood was still slippery despite the dried moss. The thought made something flutter in her stomach; she couldn't tell for sure if it was fear, or happiness.

She bent down and tugged up a flap of hide from the hole in the ground next to the Spirit House where Magic kept his portion of meat. She rummaged in the foul-smelling stuff until she had found the lumpy, flopping carcass of a huge jackrabbit. She pulled it out and took one of the scrapers piled next to the hole, rubbed it against her thigh to remove bits of dried flesh, and began to hack the skin from the rabbit's body.

Some of those long, thick green weeds, she thought. *He likes soup made from greens. That will go fine with this.*

And maybe I'll grind up some acorns for the soup, she decided. *He'll like that, too.*

Northwest of the Green Valley

Spring Flower felt a slow, creeping numbness begin to tingle in her fingertips; it was sort of like when you stayed in one position too long and your foot went to sleep, and you had to dance and jiggle it until the feeling came back. But this was in her fingertips, and it was subtly different.

Everything was different. She didn't quite understand *how* it was different, but it was. Perhaps in the way her big brother, Black Caribou, slid his eyes toward her and then, when he saw her looking back at him, jerked his glance suddenly away.

Almost as if he were afraid to look at her.

"Go ahead, eat," Black Caribou said, and smiled at her. The smile was strained and showed too many teeth. It did nothing to make her feel better. If anything, it made her feel worse. Scared, almost. There was something wrong with her brother's smile, but she couldn't figure out what that wrongness was.

But he was her brother still, and she trusted him more than anybody in the whole World. He ruled their family, now that the dimly recalled figure of their father was gone, and she knew that in some way she also didn't understand, Caribou ruled the People as well. She had never questioned him before, and simply because the expression on his face was so odd, so frightening, was no reason to start now. After all, he loved her.

And so, smiling a little herself, despite the numb tingling in her fingertips—and now, she noticed, in her toes, too—she dipped into the woven-bark container full of red berries mixed with sticky honey and scooped another finger-full into her mouth.

The sweetness of the honey masked the sharp, bitter, acidic taste of the berries, and though her stomach grumbled a bit at the strange new treat, she ate willingly enough.

She was only eleven years old. She still trusted the big people in her life, especially her loving brother.

Black Caribou saw it in her eyes, that trust, and that was what made him want to cry. But he couldn't. The tears could only come later, and in private—Lest the Spirit of Breath be moved to seek yet another sacrifice—the next, perhaps, to be himself. And he wasn't ready to fight that battle yet.

No, he thought, as he watched Spring Flower slowly chew another mouthful of the gluey mess that was slowly anesthetizing her nerve endings, so that she might survive the proper length of time for the sacrifice to be pleasing to the Spirit of Breath— not yet. And for one terrible moment he wondered what was the *true* sacrifice, what it was that terrible Spirit found *most* pleasing: the death of his sister, or his own terrible agony at his part in it?

Someday, he promised himself. *Someday*.

Then he hid that promise even from himself, not knowing that the answer to his anguished question was simple.

Both. The Spirit of Breath craved both flesh and terror. Caribou, in his desperation, could not feel the vast, cold thing that hovered near, who sipped on his torment with a long, invisibly flickering red tongue . . .

. . . and found it exquisite.

Exquisite!

The Green Valley

Maya had chopped the skin from the rabbit carcass, working with quick, competent strokes—the rough blade edge of the scraper was sharp as a modern scalpel, and when it dulled a bit, she simply grabbed another piece of flint and chipped a new edge on the tool. She did this without thought; Stone had trained her well.

The flint-knapper had been inarticulately skeptical of the wisdom of giving that training—it had seemed improper to him, to impart his skills to a girl not yet even a woman—but for some reason Old Magic had wanted him to do it, and so he had. To his surprise he'd found Maya a willing, even talented pupil. Her eyes—those strange, disquieting eyes!—could spot the patterns of striking force in a piece of stone as well as he could; that was the secret, of course, the almost instinctive knowledge of how a chunk of hard, brittle rock could be coaxed, with a careful tap here, an abrupt pressure there, into breaking apart suddenly into long, thin slivers of naturally sharpened stone.

Somehow, in the process of her training, she'd almost won him over—she was certainly more talented than his other apprentices, two gawky boys, one of whom showed some signs of skill, but the other was as ham-handed as a berserk mammoth—and her cheerful, open disposition had warmed him even further. Almost, he was able to stifle the feeling that he was *doing wrong*—although Stone's sense of right and wrong had little to do with what such words would come to mean later.

"Right" meant that the People survived and prospered. "Wrong" meant that they starved and died. That was the basic, granite-hard shelf of reality beneath Stone's vague feelings. The Spirits never stooped to giving lessons on morality; had they tried, had Old Magic suddenly begun spouting such ethereal, meaningless nonsense, even his strongest supporters would have laughed at him.

The Spirits surrounded the People like a fog; they influenced every moment, every aspect of the People's lives; but even so, they remained *apart*. They could be influenced, certainly; that was Old Magic's—and now, to an ever-growing extent, Ghost's— job. But all that even the Shamans could do was to try to keep the Spirits, in the worst of their capriciousness, from destroying the People as mindlessly as a great bison might trample a fly. Sometimes, the Spirits could even be cajoled into bequeathing gifts; but again, there was no more concern for the People as individuals, or even as a tribe, than there was for the fly the bison spared, or fed with a juicy load of shit.

So Stone wasn't sure where this vague sense of wrongness came from; how could teaching his craft to this small, eager girl have anything to do with the People and their survival, let alone the Spirits?

He couldn't answer his own question, and so he continued on until Maya was almost as proficient as himself in the working of scrapers, choppers, blades. Finally, Old Magic had judged that she knew enough. Stone had given off his lessons with a relief he still didn't understand, although the feeling of wrongness had finally dissipated.

Maya, of course, knew nothing of Stone's feelings on the matter; the flint-knapper had trained her, and spoken carefully to her when he did so about nothing but her lessons. She had sensed no warmth in him, no change in her status as *outcast*, no matter how much she smiled, how happy she tried to be, how much she ignored the terrible cramps in her fingers and wrists as she struggled to hold the stones *just so*. Many times she'd gone back to her house and showed Berry bleeding scrapes on her palms, and only as Berry smeared soothing ointments on those wounds would Maya finally begin to sob from the pain and the misery of her aloneness.

No more than Stone did Maya understand why Magic had set her on the path of that particular knowledge. As far as she was concerned, although the skills she learned were interesting and, she thought, perhaps of value someday (though she couldn't imagine how), learning to work the flints was a skill that only made her more of an outsider. Now, not only did she bear the burden of all the other things that made the women mutter and turned the backs of the men toward her, but with her new lessons she became a girl doing a man's labor, and that upset some more than any of her other sins.

"Why do I have to do this?" she'd wailed to Magic, after a particularly infuriating session in which she'd almost broken the little finger of her left hand by slamming down on it the heavy striking stone, but Old Magic hadn't answered her. Not really; he'd only smiled and said, "Don't worry, little Maya. Someday, you'll know the reason why."

"I want to know *now*!" she'd burst out, fresh tears springing from her eyes,.

He had only grinned a toothless grin, shaken his head, and said, "But it's a secret, Maya."

Sometimes it seemed to her that everything was a secret—nor would she have been easier in her mind if Magic had told her the truth. He had no real idea why he'd sent her to Stone, beyond a feeling that he should do so. Even as he'd told her it was *secret*, he'd felt a twinge of disquiet.

The secret was from him, as well.

Now, as Maya finished with her work and rose to take the cleaned rabbit carcass down to the stream, the half-pain, half-pleasure of her lessons was almost forgotten. She thought no more of her skill with stone than she did of the other things Magic had insisted she learn. But in a diffuse way she was grateful—at least when *her* scrapers went dull, she could sharpen them immediately, without waiting for Stone to find the time to do it.

The chuckle of the stream, where it poured out from First Lake and splashed over a welter of boulders, buoyed her mood. She loved the sound of rushing water, loved the damp, clear smell of it in her nostrils, loved how the spray as she bent forward covered her face with cool mists.

She laid down the rabbit carcass and began to slop thick, dark mud on it, until it was covered in a coating as thick as two of her fingers. Then, pleased with her work—sometimes the mud was too wet, and didn't hold well—she got up and climbed back to the ledge.

Outside the Spirit House, Magic's hearth—now hers, too!—was a gray-powdered pile of embers almost two feet wide. She carefully placed her muddy parcel in the center of the coals, then used the fire-hardened stick next to the rocky ring of the hearth to push the coals over the crudely mummified rabbit. The heat would harden the mud, even as it baked the carcass inside to tender, juicy perfection. Her mouth watered as she imagined cracking open the hardened coating and watching the rich, red juice and thick, hot fat drip out.

Magic couldn't chew very well, but this meat would melt in his mouth.

He'll see, she vowed. *I'll be a good woman to him.*

And maybe if I am, somehow he can make the others—
Stone, Spear, even my father, Skin—love me.

Somehow.

In the distance, a sudden bibble-babble of voices heralded the end of the meeting in the Mystery House. Still smiling faintly to herself, Maya stood up and moved near the door flap of her new home. She would be waiting there to open it for the old man when he returned.

Something warm dribbled down the inside of her thigh. Earlier it had terrified her. Now it only widened the secret smile deep inside. *A woman*, she thought.

I am a woman now.

Northwest of the Green Valley

"Go on," Black Caribou said, "eat the rest of it." Tears were streaming openly down his sun-toughened cheeks now, but Spring Flower didn't seem to notice. She smiled a small, sweet smile, and wondered why everything had become so dim, why her head was full of whirling, spinning things. But she tried to do what her brother told her to do, even though his voice sounded distant and echoing, as if he called down to her from the top of a long, dark well. She tried, but she couldn't; her childish muscles no longer responded to her will but only twitched weakly, like the occasional, spasmodic jerkings of a slaughtered bison, who still kicks long after death.

Caribou inhaled at the pitiful sight, a long, sighing honk, and wiped the sleeve of his coat across the film of snot dripping from his nose. He held Spring Flower in his lap, supporting her back with his massively muscled left arm. She seemed to weigh nothing, no more than the tiny yellow flowers that were her namesake. Her eyes were half-closed, drowsy, their black pupils shrunk to the size of pinpoints; she was almost asleep, yet still she smiled that tender, trusting smile at him. He knew he should stop now, that if she passed out completely Broken Fist would be angry. The great sacrifice demanded its victims whole and aware, able to experience to the fullest the terrible pain to come, for the pain itself was the sacrifice the Spirit of Breath craved most. Caribou *knew* he should stop but he couldn't, and his fingers moved almost by themselves to scoop up a small portion of the sticky goo and gently—oh so gently (trembling now)—smear it on her lips and tongue.

He watched her try to chew, but the noxious stuff, red and tacky, slid slowly down her soft cheeks until he had carefully wiped it away.

Maybe it's enough, he hoped. He glanced at the bark container; it was almost empty, and a great longing seized him. *Let it be enough,* he prayed, and then he realized, with a fearful start, that he had no idea whom he prayed to. The abrupt epiphany froze him; his muscles locked up into hard, bulging knots. If he couldn't send his unspoken pleas to the Spirit of Breath, then *what was there*? He had no alternatives at all, nothing to ease the terror and desolation he felt as he cradled Spring Flower (the *sacrifice*) in his numbed arms.

"Brother . . . ?"

The small, sighing sound, a whisper so muted he thought at first it was his own imagination, nevertheless filled his ears with the sound of smoky thunder. He gasped and looked down at her small, heart-shaped face. A final moment of awareness flickered in the margins of her trusting eyes; her soft, dark brown lips moved faintly, and a thin dribble of saliva leaked through the red smudges on her chin.

Then she shuddered, a quite helpless movement, and closed her eyes.

Caribou began to cough. His mighty arms tightened on Spring Flower's limp, raglike body as the seizure took him. Dimly he felt her fragile bones grind together as he heaved and hacked, until finally his mouth was filled with a bitter, brown gummy substance that he spat in huge gobs onto the floor.

The convulsion passed; he felt empty. His belly ached abominably, and his cheeks and forehead felt slimy-cold. He tried to still the shivering of his thick, spatulate fingers as he gently touched the little girl's forehead. Hot there, dry as a hearthstone, burning up. But her eyelids didn't move, nor did the slow rise of her chest change its rhythm.

Broken Fist would be displeased. But Black Caribou, as the terrible thump of the log drums outside began to crescendo, didn't care about that anymore. His whole universe had shrunk to the small sleeping form cradled gently in his arms.

Her bones are like a bird's, he thought with sudden, forlorn wonder. The cartilage in his knees gave off two sharp, crackling pops as he rose to his feet. The drums beyond the tent walls hammered and thundered in his brain. Spring Flower's head lolled bonelessly—how her hair hung down, dark, like a fall of black water!—tilted back, the soft flesh of her throat exposed.

He hawked and spat a final time, grimacing at the bitterness that seemed to well up not from his body but from his heart. Then he bent his huge, brutal shoulders and pushed through the door flap into the gray light beyond. Just on the other side he paused, blinking. Something burned in his eyes. It blurred his vision. After a moment it passed, and he saw the ominous tableau awaiting beyond.

He shuddered, straightened, and stepped forward, bearing the weightless burden of his dreadful gift, out into the dead gray morning. No one looked at him. The chill strengthened him somewhat, brought a sudden flush of color to his ashen cheeks. As he half walked, half stumbled forward, it seemed that his eyes and ears and nose grew painfully acute. A thousand details hammered into his awareness, nearly overwhelming him with their awful power; all of the Bison People, men, women, and children, stood in their places around the reeking pit that belched greasy puff-balls of noxious black smoke into the leaden air. The stench of half-rotted meat clogged his nose—he noted the way the stringy flesh hung from well-gnawed leavings piled near the scatter of tents, rags of livid brown and purple, interlaced with stringy white tendon and the startling flash of tooth-polished bone.

Three men labored over the hollow logs; despite the chill, they were coatless. They labored with fixed intensity, the muscles of their arms shifting and sliding beneath brown skin slick and shiny with sweat, their lips drawn back in harsh rictus, their eyes wide and vacant, their teeth grinding pale against the rhythm of their song.

The drummers crouched alone on the far side of the pit, so that as the smoke rose it obscured them, and for a moment Caribou thought of them as ghosts, dead men drumming and drumming, and a new terror stabbed at his heart.

Except for the ceaseless movement of the drummer's arms, nothing stirred. To his right, the People—was that Rat, his jaw swinging vacuously wide, his red tongue lolling in slow, hungry lust?—stood like barren trees after a fire, black and empty.

Black Caribou suddenly realized what he felt like. He felt *dead*, or at least as much as he could imagine such a thing. The People had somehow become silent ghosts, just like the drummers, who, for some strange reason, he could no longer hear. And the

People—his friends, his family (two of his aunts stared at him with mute, empty eyes, small black pits in the center of their faces, just like tiny versions of *the pit*,) every one of them known to him all his life—now all stood *apart from him*, and he walked alone into the center of their ghastly, patient waiting.

Nerve endings nearly inanimate in the small bundle he carried—it helped him to think of it as a bundle, a thing, but the *thing* wouldn't let him do it—fired off a single pulse and muscles contracted slowly. The bundle *shifted* and he looked down, but Spring Flower had quieted (though now she'd become Spring Flower again, not a bundle, not a *thing*,) and Caribou saw there was no escape.

A narrow pathway extended from the door of the tent he'd just left through the gathered crowd directly to the pit—and there, his face painted white, his eyes two glittering smudges in that terrible blank expanse, waited Broken Fist, who had become a horror.

The Shaman's greasy black hair was pulled back tight from his broad forehead, so that the thin shape of his head resembled a skull. He stood naked, his taut, slender muscles, beneath their own dead-white coating, leaping out like leather cords. (*Like snakes.*) His penis was painted bright red, and dangled at his crotch like a devilish tongue. And hanging from tiny hooks made of fishbones, their tips piercing the flesh of his chest, his upper arms, his thighs and calves, were snake husks; long, gray, dry things, leached of every bit of flesh so that they were almost light as air, and gently moving in the faint breeze that gusted fitfully around him.

But the worst was his mouth. His jaws yawned wide to admit the head of a great snake, bleached and white, whose long, curving fangs arched out and down along the line of Broken Fist's chin. The illusion was startling; a part of Caribou's mind reminded him that Fist had no back teeth; they'd been chipped out long ago, to make room for the snake skull. But that shred of sanity vanished as quickly as it had come, faced with the appalling reality: Broken Fist had somehow *become* the Spirit of Breath, whose totem was the snake, and whose dominion was hunger and death.

"Agghhh. Aahhaagghhaa . . ."

The Shaman, his jaws horribly distended, could make no intelligible sound, only that ravenous, liquid grunting. But Caribou understood him perfectly well. The choked, gasping sounds were the voice of the Spirit himself, bidding Caribou to come forward with his burden (his *thing*), to bring to the Spirit of Breath the only thing that would still His hideous appetite.

Living human flesh.

Now the drums did fall silent, and Caribou heard the sound of his own footsteps, moist and crunchy. He was afraid to look down, lest he find that he walked across a field of bones still coated with blood.

"Aagghhaa . . ." sighed the Shaman, and raised both his arms in a gesture of incongruous welcome.

The dry rasp and rattle of snakeskins rubbing together filled the dank, chill air.

Caribou noted that Broken Fist's penis was now erect and throbbing, the red clay paint there glistening like fresh blood, the member twitching and jerking so that for a moment it seemed a snake had *crawled out of his belly* and now swayed there, observing the approach of the sacrifice.

Broken Fist nodded—snakeskins rasped together— and the drums began anew. Now Caribou was close enough to smell the sharp, acrid odor of the Shaman's sweat, mingled with the thin, high, coppery odor of the lines of half-dried blood that made a pattern across his white-painted skin, and he sensed the Shaman's displeasure as he saw Spring Flower's condition.

Unbidden, a thought burst in Caribou's skull like a great sheet of lightning: *I will kill you.* And for an instant he saw himself lower his burden, then reach forward with his arms like young tree trunks, his hands like the claws of a lion, and break the Shaman as a dry twig and throw the remains onto the smoking pit—but he did nothing.

It was as if something invisible had crept inside his body and *become* his body, so that his muscles were not his own but moved of and by themselves, and he carried her forward while something tiny and black gibbered at the bottom of his skull. When Broken Fist stepped aside to reveal the construction behind him, Black Caribou only nodded and then, with slow and gentle care, laid down his sister on her final gruesome bed.

Caribou had had no part in its making. He had helped with such things before, on the few occasions when a Great Sacrifice was demanded. But this time he had not, could not do it. No doubt Broken Fist had noted the dereliction, but Caribou didn't care. Yet as he laid down the tiny body—*so light, like a bird*—the details of its making marched through his mind.

They had found a stand of sapling pines down by the river. Young ones, whose trunks were as thick as a man's forearm, whose bark was smooth and silky, whose pale white insides bulged with so much clear golden sap that even the great heat of a fire would only cause them to bubble and smoke—at least for a time, a long enough time.

They'd lashed the skinned poles together at the corners and laid other poles across in a rude weaving, taking great care to soak the leather cords— even around the edges the bindings would still take heat, and must hold together until a rude litter or bed had been created. Then they piled rocks at the four corners of the pit to the height of a man's waist, arranging these pillars to hold the corners of the bed.

Atop the pitch-pine framework they piled a mattress of dried boughs, of sweet-smelling leaves, of faggots of desiccated steppe grass—tinder that would explode into flame at the first touch of a coal.

It was on this that Caribou laid down his sister. Something terrible, alien, still infected his muscles like an awful, wasting disease, draining his strength, leaving him only enough power to do what had to be done. Did her eyelids flicker just one instant? Did her lips move at all?

So soft, so vulnerable, dressed in her finest coat and leggings of white caribou fur.

Did she know?

"Aagghhaaaa!"

At the Shaman's low, guttural growl, the People began to come forward. Each carried something: a bit of fur, a bead, a small basket, a knife, *something*. And now, with a soft *pit-pit-pat* these pitiful gifts rained down on Spring Flower's sleeping form.

Caribou felt himself propelled backward; no hand touched him, no wind pushed against his face, but the thing inside him moved him like a big, shambling puppet.

After a time the shower of gifts ceased. Four men came forward and hoisted the four corners of the litter. The rhythm of the drums merged into a continuous rolling thunder as they positioned the rack over the pit, set it down, stepped back.

The wind turned sharply. Where before it had gusted up from the river in slow, occasional breaths, fretfully pushing wisps of fog and the stench of rotten mud before it, now it suddenly twisted and came down from the frozen ice-mountains of the north and blasted the pall of smoke away.

Beneath glowed a bed of coals, red the color of glowing scabs beneath a white, flaking crust, like skin breaking open to reveal the dark crimson meat beneath. Tiny yellow and blue flames began to dance across the hideous surface.

The first of the pine boughs caught.

Black Caribou stood as motionless as a rock. Not even his eyelids twitched when Broken Fist stepped forward and with a single thrust of his club, smashed open Spring Flower's skull—and it *was* a skull now, its soft flesh blackened and bubbling with yellow noxious juices—and scooped his fingers into the broken cavity and scooped out soft, gray, shining matter and raised it ceremonially to the snake head that grew from his jaws.

The rich, greasy smell of cooked meat filled the air. Caribou still could not move, not until one of the men—he thought later it was Rat, his eyes a strange mixture of pity and madness—had pressed his numb fingers around the haft of a stone knife and then pushed him forward, breaking the ghastly spell that had imprisoned him.

He leaned far out over the smoking, charred ruin that had been a trusting little girl only minutes before, thrust down (how easily the blade sliced through the tiny chest), ripped, reached inside, and drew out the dark, liverish-colored organ he found there.

Then madness finally took him in its merciful grip, and he never recalled thrusting the dripping thing— warmer than it had ever been in life—against his teeth, and biting down, and chewing the tough, rubbery flesh, and swallowing.

"Aagghhaaa . . ." growled Broken Fist.

And the People of the Bison, now crowding forward in mindless ecstasy, their fingers bent into hideous claw shapes, grasping, tearing, moaned in reply, until their mouths were stuffed with hot, steaming meat, and they could keen no longer.

Thus did the People of the Bison attempt to appease His endless, aching hunger when the Spirit of Breath, God of Snakes, first came to the Green Valley, to do battle with She who was His ancient nemesis.

The Green Valley

On that morning, the day after the great meeting at the Mystery House, when Old Magic had announced that he had spoken with the Spirits and they had commanded that the People make no effort to meet with these strange new People who were camped to the northwest, along the river, and that, in fact, the People were to douse their hearths and hold only a few coals against the time when the new People had departed and it was safe again to light the fires, on that morning Maya looked up.

Old Magic, his seamed face peaceful, chewed on the remains of the rabbit she'd cooked him the night before. He'd said little when he'd come back from the Mystery House, only thanked her for his dinner. She had thought he seemed tired, nearly exhausted, as if whatever electricity had galvanized his ancient body had all drained out. But he still looked different, younger.

He had eaten, rolled himself in his furs, and after a short time begun to snore. Finally Maya laid herself down, deciding that whatever else Magic might have in store for her, *it* wasn't likely to happen that night.

But now she looked across the fire and saw him looking back at her.

"Is something wrong, little Maya?" he said.

Wrong? She didn't know. How to describe the terrible sensation of a vast black door opening on an arid, stinking waste of fire and smoke? It had only been for an instant, and then the flash—like a memory, but *not* a memory—was gone. it frightened her badly, but she had no mental signposts, no way of measuring it, no way of describing it to him.

Something new had come into her secret world, something alike but subtly, horribly different from that flash of blinding light she no longer consciously recalled.

She shook her head, puzzled. "No, Uncle. Nothing's wrong. Would you like another rabbit for dinner tonight?"

Magic had felt it too, but even more diffuse, like the rags of a bad dream you can't grasp upon awakening. He stared at her for one more heartbeat, then smiled.

The rabbit had been delicious. "Yes, Maya," he said. "Rabbit would be fine."

Chapter Twelve

The Green Valley: 17,983 B.C.

Maya stared at Ghost in disbelief.

They sat on the far bank of First Lake, with the afternoon sun beating down on them—the clouds of the last week had cleared away, like a thick, soft blanket turned over to reveal an endless well of blue—side by side on a fallen log, their bare feet almost touching the gently moving, icy waters.

Summer was fast giving way to bitterly short fall, but for a time the weather would be as fine as it ever got in the Green Valley: lazy, hot days and crisp, cool nights, and the smell of water and grass and dry, fallen leaves in the air. One thing was missing from the rich olfactory stew, however: The hearths were cold and silent. Fire had carefully taken coals from each hearth and secreted them within tiny balls of clay lined with dried moss, which he kept in a shallow cave in the vast overhang of the cliff wall. He fed the dimly glowing coals as if they were tiny, fragile animals—a bit of moss, tiny twigs—and husbanded them against the time when he would bring them forth and transform them back into the glowing pits that it was their birthright to be.

"No, it's true, Maya," Ghost said softly. "I want to be your friend."

She licked her lips and stared at him. The words, the precious, wonderful words! How long had she waited to hear them? She had lived in a cold place for so long that her heart had become glacial, so long that she had feared nothing would ever bring a spark of warmth to the chill waste of her insides. Yet to hear them at last from Ghost, of all people, jolted her to the core of her being.

She stared at the young Shaman as if seeing him for the very first time, struck dumb by the enormity of his quiet words.

He had found her in front of the Spirit House, where she'd sat humming a simple tune, her eyes bright and sparkling as she sorted through a basket of acorns left from the previous fall's harvest. She had hardly noticed his approach, so silently had he come, and so when he first hunkered down and said "Hello, Maya" she'd started and spilled the basket into her lap.

"Oh, my!" Color rushed to her cheeks as she fumbled for the scattered bounty.

"Here," he said, "let me help."

Together, silently, they recovered the tiny brown nuts—Ghost's fingers seemed as supple, as quick as her own, and she was very conscious of his smooth brown skin rubbing gently against her shoulder as they worked—and when they were done Ghost said, "Little Maya. Can you come with me a while? I want to talk to you."

It was the longest speech he'd made to her in five years, and certainly the kindest. Kindness, simple courtesy . . . these were not things she associated with Ghost. Cold, distant concentration that made her feel like one of those black beetles helpless in the light of an overturned log, perhaps, but not courtesy.

And recently, of course, he'd had nothing to do with her at all. When their paths did cross, his flat, black gaze had flicked over her as if she were something he barely comprehended, a shadowy blip that annoyed his vision only for an instant before disappearing entirely.

Ghost had, over the past year or so, made her feel like a disgusting, dead thing, so insignificant that she purposely avoided him now, in order to avoid the hopeless dread he made her feel. Worst of all was the knowledge (and it seemed stronger whenever she got too close to him) that Old Magic would not live forever, and that when he returned to the Great Mother, Ghost would take his place in fact as well as function.

And what would happen to her then, in the dead gray glaze of his regard?

Thus his simple statement, as they sat together on a log beside the water, burst like a thunderbolt into the morass of her weltered thoughts.

"I know," he went on slowly, softly, "you think I hate you. Isn't it true?"

He smiled at her, and she was amazed at the sunny warmth that filled his narrow face then. Almost, she could sense a longing there, and though she could never know of a small, skinny, outcast boy who'd tasted agonies at least as terrible as her own, she responded to it. She couldn't help herself. Those buried feelings called across the gulf of adulthood to her, and she answered without thought.

"Oh, no, Ghost, I never—"

Slowly, he raised his right hand. "You don't have to lie, Maya. I know what you think. And you would have been right. Once, I did hate you. But not any longer, I don't think."

This new revelation sent quivers of confusion racing up and down her arms, her belly. Ghost saw it, and reached over and touched her shoulder. The weight of his hand was a new thing—none of the People beyond Ghost, Berry, and Wolf had touched her so in all her recent memory. (Once she'd been loved, once there had been Blossom, and Bud, and even Skin, but that was long ago, and hidden behind a screen of blood. Long, long ago, and almost forgotten.)

She felt something hot and wet begin to trickle across her cheeks. She licked her lips again and tasted salt.

"Don't cry, Maya," Ghost said. He leaned forward and peered into her face. She could smell the cinnamon heat of his breath. "You have beautiful eyes, did you know that?"

These words nearly sent her tumbling off the log in a blue funk—her *eyes*!

Nobody had ever said anything like that about her eyes, the hateful colored orbs that were her ultimate badge of some deep shame she could no longer remember, but that reminded her every time she stared into a clear pool of her essential difference— *I am not of the People!*

Beautiful?

She burst into tears and bowed her head as long, honking cries ripped from her throat. Then the strangest, most terrifying, wonderful thing occurred. Something warm and heavy curved around her shoulders and gently squeezed her close to another, stronger heat; the heat of Ghost's body, the warmth of another human, a warmth she thought she'd lost forever.

Ghost hugged her close and waited until her cries had subsided. Then he began to rock her slowly back and forth, as if she were a child. He put his lips close to her ear and whispered, "It's all right, Little Maya. All right. Everything will be all right."

After a time he said, "Come walk with me, Maya.

The forest is pretty right now, isn't it? And it's a beautiful day for a walk."

He stood up and took her hand and tugged gently. She rose as if in a dream—but a *splendid* dream, a dream she hoped suddenly with all her heart would never end—and followed as he led her to the path, its soft brown surface marked by thousands of passages, led her down the path and into the cool, green cathedral of the woods.

The smell of pine enfolded them, and the thick, rich decay of rotting leaves, and the good, crisp scent of water bubbling in the stream; clouds of golden midges hovered in the slanting rays that pierced the tall canopy overhead; robins sang and bright bluejays cawed harshly, and from somewhere up ahead a single duck honked a plaintive cry. Their bare feet—Ghost wore pants and leggings, but no moccasins—made soft *shh-shh* sounds in the warm dust of the path. A thin film of sweat burnished Ghost's shoulders, so that his skin looked as if it were carved from warm brown ice.

She felt her own breasts—they'd grown much larger recently—sag and bounce gently against the arch of her ribs, and the sensation stirred up a new welter of feelings, emotions somehow tied up with Ghost but *not*, not really. . . . Yet she was acutely aware of his presence, of the *physicality* of him, of the way his muscles moved and slid, moved and slid, of the tiny pulse in his slender, corded neck, of the way his head tilted just so as he strode along, of his hand around hers, soft and dry and warm.

Could it be possible? Had she been so totally mistaken about him? Something so weak and painful she'd thought it forever gone pierced her then, broke her laboriously constructed defenses like so much flimsy cloth, something all others took for granted but for her it was like a brand-new language, a fruit never tasted.

Maya's heart broke like a badly made dam before the most uncomplicated of assaults: an act of simple human kindness.

She had no defense against it.

She followed Ghost blindly and hoped it wasn't a dream, or if it was, that it would never end. And so eventually they came to a sandy place surrounded by the hiss and bubble of hot springs, and sat down and stared out across Smoke Lake, where the waters belched up long threads of stream and the mist hung low in the afternoon like a fog made of silver.

Here Ghost put his arm around her once again and said, "Maya, we must be friends now. Magic is old. Someday he will be gone. And who will take care of you then?"

She looked up into his face, so gaunt, so serious. "I . . . don't know."

He nodded gravely. "I will," he said.

She could only blink and turn away, and look out on Smoke Lake, and so she couldn't see his eyes then: wide and black and staring, the smoke from the Lake reflected there in tall, silver columns, blank, empty, hot.

The night after the day when Spring Flower had spilled her brains upon the glowing coals of *the pit*, Ghost awoke shuddering and covered with sweat. His tongue burned in his mouth. He rolled over, spat, and tasted the copper-salt of his own blood. Not truly awake, he raised his fingers to his mouth and touched the surface of his tongue and felt a deep gash there—painful to the touch!—and realized the Spirits had taken him in his sleep. A thrill of fright shook him. The nighttime visitations were the worst, for he could not prepare for them as he did for the seizures he induced himself. This time he'd been lucky: He hadn't bitten his tongue in half. Nor had he swallowed it, as he'd done once, and only chanced to revive from his convulsions a moment before a deeper darkness had taken him.

Ghost lived with the secret knowledge that his own body might murder him at any time. It gave him a different outlook on things than that of those whom the Spirits never favored with such *personal* attention. The Spirits might raise him up or cast him down, but whichever they did he would have utterly no control. Ghost had grown up with the knowledge that, in the end, he was nothing but a puppet—and, more terribly, that those who pulled his strings cared not a whit for *him*. He was only a rag, a vessel to be filled or emptied by whim, a *thing* to be *used*.

It made him crazy, of course, far crazier than even Old Magic in all his unease had ever guessed. Ghost could only view the rest of the World as the Spirits viewed him—as *things*.

The People had no true reality for him. They slipped in and out of his awareness as easily—and as trivially—as water sliding over rocks. Only as they impinged on his own existence did they exist for him. Old Magic was marginally more real to him than, say, Skin, since he judged the Shaman to have power over him. Magic could possibly *hurt* him, might even be able to *kill* him (although, since Ghost possessed no conception of his own life, his conception of death was necessarily fuzzy), and therefore, in the possibility of pain, the old man assumed a greater *presence* within the inchoate mass of Ghost's interior existence.

Later Shamans, of whose far-future existence Ghost had not the slightest inkling, would have had a field day with Ghost, debating endless scenarios of Nature and Nurture. Was it the epilepsy that had created Ghost's peculiar, deadly state of mind? Or was it the horror of his childhood, the bedrock fear of his own difference that had done it?

Ghost would of course have rejected both theories as, first, speculative, and second, irrelevant. He *knew* what had created him—the same ghastly thing that had created everything else.

She Whom He Hated.

He thought those words as a single word, Shewhomhehated, a long, slobbering sound of pure malice. Shewhomhehated had far more reality to him than any of the pale shades with whom he lived his gray empty life.

She had made him what he was, for *She* had made everything. She was the terrible Mother who had borne him, spat him out from Her horrid loins into a World that meant nothing at all to him, for in Her awful Making She had left something out of him.

She'd left *him* out of him, and there was nothing in his deepest center but a chill and swirling void where nameless things gibbered in the night.

He was the husk that walked like a man, but that was his secret, the thing he could never reveal, for if those ghosts who swirled around him, shadowy things with names like Magic and Berry, were ever to discover how stunted, how empty, how truly *different* he was, then they might rip the husk away and discover . . .

. . . nothing.

Nothing at all.

It had taken him long, slow years to discern the meaning of his own existence, to finally understand that he *had no meaning* beyond that which was occasionally infused into him in the growling, twitching times he couldn't remember after they were ended. But even *things that were used* could learn to use other *things*. And so he had, had learned to manipulate and deceive, to chuckle at jokes and sing songs and use his magics just as if they were his own and not the pitiful leavings he knew them to be.

Once, some years before, he'd noticed that many of the People—Spear in particular—often glanced at his face and then turned away, peculiar expressions of distaste pulling their lips down, wrinkling the skin of their cheeks. As if they smelled something bad.

He'd wondered about that, for it frightened him. And so he'd observed the People (*things*) carefully, searching for clues. Finally he thought he had it— the People responded in a certain way to one type of facial expression.

It involved the narrow baring of teeth, the stretching of lips so that they curved into an upturned curve.

The expression was called a "smile." He thought about it a while longer and realized that it was only when he tried to smile that Spear and the others looked at him with something very much like fear. Finally he began to trek down to Third Lake, to a place where a backwater right by the shore was always still and calm, and in the still calmness there he could see his own face.

He began to practice. He pushed his skin up and down with his fingers, stuck them into his mouth and twisted his lips this way and that. It took him months of secretive practice before he began to get the hang of it, and many more months before he could finally *smile*. After a time, he could even suppress the desperate need to scream at his own reflection.

Perhaps it was the other thing that had helped. Occasionally he still thought about the other thing, at times when the world seemed particularly cold and gray. The other thing warmed him a bit, brought wan flashes of color that flickered over his thoughts like the blaze of dying embers on a night fire.

It had happened simply enough. He'd been down by the water, twisting his skin like flaccid clay, when he'd heard a thin crying. *Back in the woods*, he thought, turning in surprise. *Yes, definitely the woods. Growing closer now.*

He crawled over until he was hidden behind a large, crumbling boulder, and there he waited, an odd expectancy growing in his belly.

When the little boy toddled out of the trees, his feet stumbling on the path, tears streaming down his cheeks as he wailed, Ghost felt strangely let down. Only one of the brats—he didn't recognize this one, of course; it was hard enough for him to keep track of the adults who did matter—and he felt mildly annoyed that his important practice time should have been thus interrupted. He supposed he would have to drag it back to Home Camp, squalling and hiccuping all the way.

He stood up.

The little boy—no more than three years old—saw him and stopped. He sniffled twice, knuckled at his reddened eyes, then made a small, happy sound and lurched forward.

Ghost stepped away from the boulder and waited, his arms folded across his chest, until the child had reached him, flung his arms around his knees, and held on as if Ghost were some weird but totally welcome tree.

"Let go!" Ghost demanded, but the child only squeezed tighter. Experimentally, Ghost reached down and tapped the boy lightly on the top of his head. The childish hair was thin and fine; he felt the tiny bones of the skull beneath.

That was mildly interesting. It made him think of . . .

. . . different kinds of dreams he sometimes had.

A new thought struck him. The child had obviously wandered off from the women. And the women, he knew, were havesting nuts and berries near Home Camp. The boy had wandered a long way. He was lucky to have stumbled over Ghost at all, instead of stumbling into marsh or quicksand, or even a roaming cave lion.

The thought tickled at the top of his spine. Almost as if the boy . . .

. . . had been sent.

It seemed very quiet in the forest then. The boy finally released Ghost's legs, staggered back, and sat down.

Plop.

Ghost noticed that it was smiling at him now, a happy little smile, trusting.

Smiling.

Maybe that was why he'd stumbled here (been sent), to this spot, at this time.

Ghost leaned over and scooped up the tiny form, turned, and went back to his place by the water. He sat down cross-legged and placed the boy in his lap. It squirmed happily there. The pressure of the boy's body reminded Ghost again of the different kind of dreams.

Hot dreams.

The child smiled at Ghost.

Ghost smiled back.

Its face changed as it began to cry. Now it thrashed against him, the screeching noise from its distended mouth rising into an irritating series of shrieks that hurt Ghost's eardrums.

"Hush! Be quiet!" Ghost said. He tried another smile, but that only made matters worse. Now the little boy beat against Ghost's chest with tiny fists, his face gone red and ugly.

Ghost put one big hand over its mouth. It bit

down hard on the meaty flesh of Ghost's palm, and Ghost withdrew it with a muttered curse.

Still, Ghost found the twinge of pain interesting. It made the little thing seem more *real* to him. Experimentally, he put his hand back, waited for the tearing feel of those baby teeth.

"Ouch!" Ghost said, though he really didn't feel all that *much* pain this time.

The child was frantic now, shrieking and burping and thrashing about. Then he wet himself. Ghost felt the hot moisture dribble into his groin.

Hard down there, just like in the different dreams.

The heat began to rise out of his crotch, spread into his belly. He couldn't seem to hear *it* now, though *it* was obviously still making noise.

He pushed one finger into the soft flesh of its neck, watched the tiny mark there slowly fade.

He raised his hand and stared at the marks of teeth on the flat of his palm, at the thin drops of blood. He looked down at the brat, and what he did next seemed entirely natural to him. It had holes in it, and out of those holes came noise and moisture. Ghost thought that maybe he should plug those holes. Fill them up, so that nothing, not noise, not liquid, could leak out.

Perhaps mud would do it. He scooped up a little and tried to stuff it into its mouth, but it spit it out.

No, mud wouldn't work.

Fingers?

But it bit down on the fingers, and though Ghost still found the pain of interest, he decided that fingers weren't the answer, either.

Perhaps . . .

Later, after he had finished and the sheet of colors he'd felt, tasted, smelled had faded to a dim gray glow, Ghost had flung the battered, torn remnants far out into Smoke Lake, watched them float for a time before finally sinking beneath a red, filmy scum.

He washed his hands in the warm water, and when they were clean he was surprised at how *good* he felt. He leaned over the still, faintly pink water and, contemplating the colors he'd felt for the first time in his life, smiled again.

Not bad. Not bad at all.

Later that night Home Camp had been in an uproar. Something about a lost child. Ghost paid no attention, even when they came to him for magic. He worked a ritual, but it came to no effect. The boy was never found.

Ghost wasn't surprised. They would never find it, because it had never existed. It had only been a ghost, a poor ghost.

Poor, sad Ghost. And who could ever find a Ghost like that?

But this was all lost in the misty past when he awoke in the night and realized that the puppet ak1master, Shewhomhehated, had ridden him again, though She'd only wounded him somewhat.

As he lay their in his dark misery, for one moment something came to him. A memory that wasn't a memory, more as if something had been *planted* inside, something wholly alien, not him at all, but somehow attached to him. Clinging to the thin blister which was all that kept the void inside him from bursting out and swallowing him whole and screaming.

It was as if a vast door had opened, and something had *come through*.

For a moment he thought it might have been Her. But even as he thought of Her, Shewhomhehated, such a revulsion seized him that he flung over on his side and puked until nothing more came up but a thin green spittle.

Somehow, as he lay in his desolation of pain and

vomit, he didn't think it had been Shewhomhehated
who had ridden him that night. No, not at all.

Something else, though.

After a time, he went back to sleep and dreamed
of snakes. It was well he slept alone. Nothing
human could have borne the ghastly burden of his
smile that night.

Berry joined them for a cold meal of bread made
from acorn flour and dried strips of the bison Spear
and Skin had killed north of the cliff wall two weeks
before. They sat in front of the Spirit House, on the
well-worn logs placed there; the hearth in front of
the logs, normally a cheerful bowl of warmth, now
lay barren and dark. Inside the Spirit House, resting
in the smaller circle of stones, lay a clay pot which
sheltered coals from that fire. Unlike the dimly glowing hearts of other fires, which Fire kept safe in his
cave, these coals remained apart; this fire was sacred, and Magic would not let it out of his keeping.
Maya had already checked the soft, charred quilt of
moss on which it fed; the tiny coals glittered like hot
eyes when she lifted the lid and looked inside.

The normal sounds of the village were muted, as
if the level of life had lowered with the dousing of
the flames; it was already dark. Overhead, stars glittered like chips of ice, cold, remote; a horned moon
was just rising over the shadowy barrier of the cliff
wall, its wan light picking out hushed, slow-moving
shapes. But it wasn't chilly; at least the heat of the
fires wouldn't be missed. Maya knew that many of
the People would sleep outside tonight, their beds
turned feet-first toward the overhang, which leaked
heat stored up in the black rock during the day. She
would not, of course; her place was by her man,
even though Old Magic had displayed none of the
manlike tendencies she'd wondered about when
she'd first moved in.

Actually, Magic hadn't changed his relationship with her at all. The only difference resulting from the move was the quality of noise she had to suffer in the long marches of the night. Berry had snored in long, gulping, wheezing gasps that sounded almost like coughs. Magic snored a deeper tone, with less whistling, but he farted a great deal, so that by morning Maya was happy to fling the door flap wide and let in a bit of fresh air.

Otherwise, she still slept in a small house with a very old person; only the sounds and stinks had changed, and she was slowly coming to the idea that perhaps that was all that would change. Magic certainly showed no more sexual interest in her than had Old Berry.

In a way, it was a relief. She stared into the soft, warm, moving darkness of Home Camp, chewed thoughtfully, and considered the startling developments of the afternoon.

Ghost had walked her back to Home Camp. The trek had been idyllic; she'd felt herself almost float along, her legs matching his own stride for stride, though Ghost did limp a bit. He'd even held her hand again, and the warmth, the touching, had awakened deep wells of longing.

But she was utterly confused. Enough of her sharp, lonely intelligence remained to question, even as they swung down the path, what Ghost's motives might be.

Why now? she wondered. *Why after all this time . . . ?*

For she trusted her own instincts, and despite the upheaval of the afternoon, she knew that only a short time before Ghost hadn't liked her at all. As she chewed the stringy meat (at first, when you bit down on it, it tasted a lot like bark; only after much jaw-cracking labor would it begin to give up its juices), she tried to fit his mind-bending change of heart into the familiar, everyday weave of life she already knew.

Then it came to her: the blood. It was the blood between her legs that had done it!

The signs had been there all along. She simply hadn't noticed them, or understood what they meant. Now all those mysterious things came flooding into her mind as if she'd never seen them clearly before, but under the hot new light of her fresh womanhood they glimmered stark and revealing.

Sunflower.

She thought of Sunflower, a girl a year older than herself. No particular reason an incident involving her should have sneaked into her thoughts, at least no surface reason, for the incident had been painful. It had been another failure, one that had cemented her more firmly into her matrix of loneliness, although Sunflower hadn't known it at the time.

Sunflower, born with an oddly twisted right foot that made her walk a stumbling, clumping series of half-falling lurches, was almost as much an outsider as Maya herself. But she had a sweet, shy disposition, and made as much of her infirmity as she could; she always tried to go with the rest of the girls, even though the long hikes were an agony for her. But she was given to disappearing for hours at a time, and she didn't romp or play with the rest. She liked to weave necklaces of flowers to wear across her shoulders, blossoms of white and blue and delicate pink. Every once in a while, in her own wanderings, Maya had seen her from a distance, surrounded by wild, luxurious shrubs, bending over, delicately picking the luscious blooms one by one, her calm, flat features distant and soft.

Because Sunflower was so shy, many of the adults thought her stricken with a Spirit that made her stupid, as sometimes happened, though Maya divined the streak of sharp intelligence which actually did exist beneath Sunflower's silent, withdrawn exterior.

Maya had even dreamed about becoming friends with Sunflower, they shared so much of loneliness and rejection. But then something had happened. Abruptly, Sunflower was no longer an outsider. At least not with the boys, who began to flock around her like big, gawky birds, their eyes bright with some secret excitement.

And Maya, with the questioning view of the eternal outsider, noticed other things. While Sunflower still had no friends among the girls, the women began to take note of her. They would nod, or speak, or even on occasion help her with her tasks. It was as if something had touched Sunflower, something invisible but potent, and changed her, though Maya could see no outward transformation.

Sunflower began to smile more.

Maya watched all this with silent wonder, and with the secret hope that whatever had transfigured Sunflower might also work its magic on her. Sunflower took to disappearing for longer periods, usually during the afternoon, but this time with a difference. She no longer returned garlanded with petaled necklaces of her own creation. Instead the brown, slender arms of boys would be resting across her shoulders, and the two—sometimes three or four—of them would be laughing.

It was a puzzle.

The puzzle deepened one somewhat chilly, gray spring day when Maya heard a thrashing in the bushes beyond the small clearing where she was gathering acorns fallen during the winter. It was a solitary occupation, and for a moment the noise frightened her; then she relaxed, because, amidst the sound of cracking branches and sliding leaves, she heard a voice.

"Ouch!"

Maya's first instinct was to pick up the soft leather bag she carried and move on, but then a flare of anger seized her. She had come here to work. Let whoever approached find their own place! And she knew they would, once they saw what pariah it was they'd stumbled upon.

She'd arranged her features into a fierce, forbidding scowl, knowing the expression would hasten the unwanted visitor on their way, but when she saw Sunflower stump into the clearing, she relaxed and faced the girl.

"Oh," Sunflower said. She blinked. "I didn't know . . ." She turned to go back the way she'd come.

"No—wait!"

"What?"

"Don't leave. Please." Suddenly Maya thought that maybe this was the time. They were safely alone (always alone), with no one to see if Sunflower broke the circle of silence that surrounded Maya.

Reluctantly, the older girl paused. Something held her to the clearing. Maya thought perhaps it was herself, though she was wrong.

"Well . . ." Sunflower said. Two small, uncertain lines had appeared over the bridge of her nose. She glanced at Maya with almost petulant irritation. "I didn't know you were here."

Maya ignored the whiny hesitation in Sunflower's voice, too thrilled at the knowledge that, for whatever reason, she was having a conversation with *someone else*. She cast frantically around for something that might help her to continue the small miracle.

"Do you . . . come here a lot?" she asked. "There are lots of acorns, and . . ." She paused, considering. "Right over there, those bushes, they grow beautiful purple flowers, as big around as your two fists put together."

Despite all the changes that had come over her in the past several months, Sunflower still loved her blossoms. Her eyes widened with new interest. "Really? Where?"

A few moments later both girls were chattering happily, each for the moment conveniently ignoring the strangeness of their conversation.

"My father says you have an evil Spirit," Sunflower announced at one point, as she dumped a handful of acorns into Maya's bag.

Maya, eyes twinkling, replied, "Old Berry says you're stupid."

And so they compared their respective deformities, two girls alone in the woods, until Sunflower's head came up as the new sounds cricked and scrutched toward them.

"Don't be afraid," Maya said quickly, and placed a comforting hand on the other girl's shoulder. "It's not animals, I don't think."

But Sunflower shook the hand away and said, "I know it's not animals."

"What is it?"

"It's Young Bison and Turtle."

Maya blinked. "How do you know?"

"They were supposed to meet—" Sunflower stopped speaking, a new, sly expression passing across her face.

Maya didn't notice the change, or she might not have asked her next question. "Those two boys? But why are they coming here?"

"Not *boys*," Sunflower said suddenly, her voice low and intense. "Not *boys* at all," she continued, as if speaking a secret only she knew.

"What are they, then? What do they want with you?"

Two bright patches of red bloomed in Sunflower's cheeks. Her expression slanted down into something almost ugly, jealous. It was as if she had noticed Maya for the first time that day, and was sorry she had.

"*You* wouldn't understand." Almost unconsciously, Sunflower's right hand dropped to the joining of her thighs and began to rub slowly. "You're still a baby."

"A baby? I'm *n-not!*" Maya sputtered, her stomach sinking at the sudden rejection.

"Oh, yes you are!" Sunflower called over her shoulder, for she was already plunging toward the brush, toward the thrashing noises there. Maya saw that her eyes were glittering with some emotion Maya didn't yet understand. Sunflower tipped and lurched along, and then she was gone.

Maya had stood alone in the clearing, wondering what had just happened. That was a long time ago.

Now, sitting on the log, the sour taste of chewed meat in her mouth, she understood. Sunflower had begun to *bleed*. She'd become a *woman*. And when she had, despite her club foot, despite all the awful rumors about her, the boys (*men*) had discovered her anew.

Maya had no illusions. Men liked to stick the snake thing between their legs into the hole women had between *their* legs. She didn't understand why, but she knew it was true. So evidently blood and womanhood could change almost anything.

Perhaps, she thought, hope catching in her throat as she remembered the strange, warm sensation she'd felt when Ghost had hugged her, perhaps the blood could change even her own exile.

Ghost said it could. He wanted to be her friend. Perhaps he wanted even more. Perhaps he wanted to stick his snake into her hole.

The thought sent a tiny shudder racing up and down her spine. Then, suddenly, she was afraid. She was Old Magic's woman. What would *he* think?

She looked up. Magic was speaking in low tones

to Old Berry, who chewed, nodded occasionally, but made no reply. "Magic?" Maya said at last, having a hard time getting the word around the lump that had grown in her throat.

He blinked and turned toward her. "What, little Maya?"

"Ghost talked to me today. He said he wanted to be my friend."

Without the fire, it was too dark for Maya to see how Magic's white, twisted brows suddenly arched like a pair of snowy caterpillars. "Really?" he said. "Tell me about it."

Magic was old and terribly experienced. None of his sudden worry showed in his voice. But Berry flinched at the strength of his grip as his fingers tightened on her shoulder, with power she would never have guessed he possessed.

Not at his age. Not unless he was very, very frightened.

Chapter Thirteen

The Green Valley: 17,983 B.C.

In the cramped, gloomy interior of the Spirit House, Maya sensed an electric tension spring up. Magic stared at Old Berry, whose face had taken on a questioning, I-told-you-so expression.

Finally Old Magic sighed heavily and turned back to face Maya across the small, cold hearth. "My dear," he said, "I think it is time for you to understand a few things."

The tension did not abate; if anything, Maya sensed a strengthening of the electric feelings that seemed to buzz inside her ears like invisible honey bees. "A secret, Uncle?"

He smiled faintly. "Yes, child. A Secret." He sighed again. "Perhaps a Secret that shouldn't have been secret—at least not from you."

Maya had no idea what the old man was talking about. All her life she'd struggled with secrets—the hidden things that Magic and Berry had taught her, of plants and animals and spirits, and other, darker riddles; her eyes, those frightening, inexplicable marks of her difference; the terrible, shameful things she *must have done* (though she didn't understand them, either) that had made even her own father avoid her like a demon; the unspoken agreement among the People, which shut her forever into lonely silence. All secrets. Her life had been entirely shaped by secrets into a thing of terrible solitude, and now that Ghost, for the first time, had demonstrated a willingness to give her the gift she craved the most, Magic was babbling of secrets again.

She made up her mind. "Uncle, I don't want to hear another secret."

He started. "What?" It was the first time Maya had shown any inclination to question him. A little throb of warning began to tick at his forehead. He stared at her as if she'd tried to bite him—and in that moment made his first great error, the one that would lead to all the rest. He saw in that instant all his plans march before him, the visions which had sustained him from her birth, the old songs, the stories, the awesome magnificence of the burden he'd carried all his life—and he grew angry.

How dare this chit of a girl who thought she was a woman defy him? Didn't she know what he'd done for her? How he'd saved her life—no, not just once, but many times—taught her, trained her, *prepared* her for her role? Didn't she realize how much agony he'd expended, in the dark, painful reaches of many long nights? How he'd *sacrificed* himself for her, and for the People who would soon need her desperately? (*How* will they need her? *How*?) Didn't she understand *gratitude*?

And so, as his irritation swelled into anger, he ignored the tiny voice inside his skull which answered all those questions. *No, she doesn't know, because you've never told her.* Instead, he forgot what she truly was: a girl barely a woman, a lonely child but strong, willful, as capricious as any girl her age.

So he spoke to her briskly, strongly, his anger peeping around the edges of his words like a bright flame.

"Maya. *You will listen to me.*" (Didn't she *understand*?)

He ignored the sullen notes which infused her slow reply, ignored the way her eyes turned down, the way her lips slowly pursed into a puffy, stubborn pout. "Yes, Uncle," she said. She looked down into her lap and refused to raise her eyes to him as she spoke. Instead, she watched the way her fingers began to twist against each other, like a small nest of . . .

. . . snakes.

For Old Magic was angry, yes, but then he understood his own anger; it came of fear. If Maya rejected him, she rejected The Mother—or so it seemed to him, who had confused his own mission with one far greater—and the survival of the People hung in the balance. He paused; dimly he perceived the importance of the moment. *She must understand.* (And Ghost . . . Why did the thought of Ghost bring the shakes to his newly strong fingers, sweat to his seamed brow?)

Ghost was dangerous!

The thought came to him just like that. His apprentice was somehow behind all this, turning her from her path, somehow breaking the tenuous cord that had bound the girl to him and to her destiny. And because he feared Ghost, he swallowed a great gulp of air and did the only thing he could think of to set things right, once and for all.

She must understand!

He turned, reached behind him, and brought out the wrapped bundle of fur. Silently he undid the secret, sacred knots—ignoring the uneasy stirring of Old Berry at his side—until the burnished surface of the Mammoth Stone glowed dimly in the murky light.

"Here," he said gruffly, thrusting it across the dead hearth. "Take it."

Maya reached for the offering instinctively. Though

the only thing she *thought* she wanted to do was go back outside the Spirit House, find Ghost, and simply *talk* with him, something made her reach for the Mammoth Stone. She couldn't help herself.

And when she took it, she felt the thinnest of vibrations sink into the flesh of her palm, and course steadily up her forearm. She stared at the Stone, puzzled. It wasn't doing anything. But still she felt that quiver, as if the Stone were pregnant with some unknowable power, trying to give birth right there in her fingers.

She became aware that both Old Magic and Old Berry were staring at her with eyes as hot as dusty coals. Unconsciously, her fingers closed around the Stone and drew it close. She didn't realize that as she spoke, she brought the carving close to her chest, to her heart. "What?" she spoke into the waves of expectancy which pounded out from the old ones' glowing eyes. "What is it?"

"Do you feel anything?" Old Magic asked.

She shook her head. What did he want? What were the two old ones *waiting for*? Again, a surge of rebellion welled in her chest. They were always full of mysteries, these old crones, become so alike in their age and wrinkles and silence that they were almost indistinguishable from each other. And she was *tired* of it, yes, their expectations and their secrets and their unspoken riddles. She looked down, surprised to find the Stone pressed hard against her breasts. "I don't feel anything, Uncle. Just like before."

Magic's breath leaked out of him in a long, slow shudder. He slumped back, and for a moment Maya thought his head looked just like a skull, bleached, empty, eyes like vacant pits.

"Ah," he said softly. "Ah. I see."

Then he told her. He began in words so whispery

she could barely make them out, though she sat only a few feet from him, but as he continued his voice grew stronger, took on the singsong chanting rhythm she'd known so well all these years, and finally she realized what she was hearing. The greatest of the Stories, the Memory he'd guarded all his life, the Secret that had been handed down a misty line of Shamans like him stretching back and back into times so ancient she could barely conceive of them.

The Stone felt warm against her flesh. Without noticing, she brought it to her cheek and rubbed it gently.

Now Magic's voice reminded her of the log drums the People sometimes played, at times of triumph or despair. His words *rolled* off his tongue, each one clear and quivering with hidden strength.

". . . and you, Maya, the Stone is *yours*," he said. "Only *you* can wield it for the People, only *you*. You are She Whom We Have Waited For; you, *you*, YOU!"

Her mouth fell open and she stared at him in profound shock. This wasn't a secret, it was a *revelation*. It changed *everything*. It explained *everything*.

(Of course you, *you*, YOU are different. . . . You are She Whom We Have Waited For, you are The Goddess, you are—).

She burst into tears.

"Someday," Magic went on inexorably, ignoring her wild sobs (*She must understand!*), "you will take my place, Maya. Not Ghost, but you. Yet it is still a Secret, and Ghost must not know. The time is not yet. *Do you understand me?*"

And though she didn't understand him, no, not at all, she nodded her head yes, because she had agreed with him all her life, and he was her man, and he wanted it. . . .

"Yes," she snuffled. "Yes, Magic, I understand."

But she didn't. And all that would come later sprang from this, Magic's terrible mistake.

Bison People River Camp

After the sacrifice of Spring Flower, Broken Fist retreated to his tent for a night and a day. When he came out, he pronounced the omens good. The Spirit of Breath had been pleased with the sacrifice. So had Broken Fist, for he had marked well the anguish of Black Caribou, his enemy. If Black Caribou and Rat and the others would hunt now, the results would be bountiful.

So Broken Fist spoke into the blue morning, and the men began to prepare. Caribou moved like a man in a dream. He refused to look at the Shaman, and Rat tried to jolly him.

"Huh, Caribou, we will make a great killing! Many bison, perhaps, much meat!"

But Caribou, who stood looking over the slate-gray waters of the river, as far as he could get from the still smoldering pit where he'd eaten the heart of his beloved sister, would not be jollied. He merely grunted, and turned away.

"Go without me," he said.

"No. You must come. You are our strongest arm, our greatest hunter. How can we hunt without you to lead us?"

Caribou stood as unmoving as his namesake, testing the air of the endless tundra. A low, biting wind gusted along the tops of the silvery-green grass, tugged at his coat, polished his cheeks. It seemed to him that voices called to him from the wind, and perhaps they did. The Spirits lived in the air. The Ghosts walked there.

Spring Flower.

He shuddered. Perhaps he should hunt. Should do something, anything, to wipe the grotesque memories of the sacrifice from his mind. Suddenly the thought of clean breezes, empty horizons, the concentration of stalking—even the spearing and the blood—seemed immensely attractive. He moved his shoulders in a slow, massive shrug.

"Very well," he said. "I will hunt."

"Good," Rat told him.

They began to make ready.

The Green Valley

Maya kept the secret to herself for three whole days before she told it to Ghost. She hadn't meant to . . . exactly. It just came out.

When she'd stumbled from the Spirit House three days before, Ghost had been watching, his eyes as perfectly empty as the vast expanse of glacier to the north. He'd wondered what had occurred to upset her, though he thought he knew. Ghost was a shrewd judge of humans—although he never thought of them as fellow humans, and so was able to study them as dispassionately as he would a curious rock, or some tiny squirming variety of newfound wildlife. And as he watched her move blindly down a path toward First Lake, he knew that something momentous had happened to her. Most likely she'd told Magic about her newfound friend.

Ghost had no illusions about Magic—he suspected that the old Shaman would immediately do his best to stamp out the burgeoning "relationship." Ghost didn't know exactly why Magic was so wary of him, but he knew when that wariness had begun, and once again he regretted that he hadn't been able to end Maya's life at the beginning, with a simple clean stroke of the spear he'd carried that day.

Yet, perhaps because he lived his own secret life so far from the mundane world of the People, he saw things that Magic had not noticed. He saw Maya as the young woman she was, isolated, lonely, yearning for the same friends and companions and acceptance Ghost had wished so fervently for, in the long-gone days of his crippled, outcast youth.

He'd been a victim then, and so, he judged, was she now, tender and vulnerable. Magic might order her, command her, instruct her, but he couldn't befriend her, not in the way she craved. Ghost never practiced his smile anymore; he'd even learned new expressions, and the People didn't turn away from them either. He thought his mask near perfect; not flawless, of course, but good enough.

Good enough to fool a frightened, lonely girl.

So he got up from his seat and followed her, and after a time he walked with her out into the woods, ignoring her sudden distance—"Ghost, I can't talk with you anymore"—and he nodded, and *smiled*, and patted her on the shoulder and said, "Well, then, you can walk with me, can't you? After all, I'm your friend. Friends don't have to *talk*."

Maya's skull was a turmoil. Magic had been clear enough: This smiling male who wished to be her friend could become her enemy. The old Shaman had explained that *she* would be his successor, not this one. And he'd told her that Ghost might not like that at all, might no longer wish to be her friend. She could understand that, in a vague, shadowy way; she equated it with the idea of someone stealing one of her few precious possessions—the shiny blue rock Berry had once given her, or the perfectly white rat's skull Magic had polished until it gleamed like the moon. If someone stole those from her, she would *hate* them. She'd told Magic this, and he'd nodded.

"Yes, Maya, like that, but worse. Much worse. You must be careful of Ghost. And you must keep the Secret. The Secret is for you, not for him."

The Secret!

The Secret had stunned her. It sat in the rushing stream of her thoughts like a great black boulder, impenetrable, immovable, so that her mind roiled and jumbled around it in huge, splashing confusion—and, like a boulder, it was indigestible. She couldn't swallow it. She kept returning to it, poking at it, testing and tasting it, trying to make sense of the new world it represented.

I am She Whom We Have Waited For. I am part of the Great Mother. I am the savior of the People. (From what, pray tell?) I will be Shaman. I will be—

She couldn't. She simply couldn't absorb the idea that she, a rejected outcast, a small and lonely girl, represented the culmination of a great legend that had its roots in the beginning of the World.

It was silly. Particularly that part about the Mammoth Stone. Now she understood why Magic always asked if *she* felt anything when she touched the soft, warm ivory. And what could she reply? *Yes, Magic, I feel great things, surging power, the Mother Herself.*

For she didn't. A little warmth, a soft vibration, quickly felt and as quickly gone. It was pretty. She liked to hold it. But that was all. The Stone gave her nothing of She Whom We Have Waited For, no hint of vast power, nothing to guide her through this incredible revelation.

It was only a stone, just like the boulder that jammed up her mind now. She wasn't even sure she liked where the Stone was now—bundled up again, but under her own bedding, for Magic had given it to her.

"It's yours now, Maya. You must keep it and guard it, until the time."

The time for what?

She had no answers. In a way she was even more of a freak than before, because there had always—in her own mind—been the chance that somehow the People might change their regard for her, might at last relax and accept her into their community. But there was no accepting this! Old Magic—and Berry, nodding uneasily at his side—had convinced her well enough of that! She was She Whom We Have Waited For, and nothing, not in the World or out of it, could change that awesome judgment.

"Yes," she'd said, glancing up at Ghost's smile and feeling a little less alone, a little warmer, "you can walk with me."

And Ghost had nodded, and smiled, and said no more. He was content. He could wait.

He repeated his own secret mantra. *The old fool can't live forever.*

In time, she will be mine. Her secrets will belong to me. She will belong to me. And then I won't have to smile anymore.

His tongue darted in and out once, like a snake's, but Maya didn't notice. He didn't speak, but he took her hand and they walked on.

Now, three days after the silent walk, when she'd occasionally looked up at him as he stumped along, even started to speak a couple of times, and he'd smiled, smiled, they sat together on a log near Spirit Lake, listening to the *plop-plop* gurgle of boiling mud paint a soft whisper on the hazy afternoon. Far out over the lake a loon uttered a single plaintive cry.

What can I do? Maya wondered. *He's so kind.* For Ghost had not pressed her at all, not asked why she couldn't talk to him, why she must break off their budding friendship. At first she'd tried to avoid him, but that seemed impossible. Wherever she went there he was, silent but smiling, perhaps brushing accidentally against her as they passed each other on a path. Always there, and she wanted so very much to hold his hand again, to sit and talk.

What did Magic know, anyway? She still couldn't believe all she'd heard—and now, after three days of settling, the boulder remained as huge and black and indigestible as ever. She Whom We Have Waited For? What sense did that make? She didn't feel like the Great Mother (whatever *that* might feel like), and Magic's desperate effort to *make her understand* had only left her feeling small and weak and helpless.

I don't want to be the Shaman, she thought suddenly. *I don't want the responsibility.*

All I want, she thought with sudden wonder, *is for somebody to love me.*

"Ghost?" she asked softly.

"Mmm?"

"Can I tell you something?"

He shifted around on the log and faced her. He wore only leggings and a jacket that hung open to his waist. She noted the fine thin curve of his chest, so unlike the bulky, fat-padded shapes of the rest of the men.

He's different, she thought. *Like me . . .*

"Of course," he said. His voice was soothing. It seemed to melt without trace into the background of humming insects and slow water lapping against the shore of the lake, and the hiss and burble of the mud.

He smiled at her.

She made up her mind. The Secret was too great. She had to share it with somebody, and there was only one who might understand, might help her to bear the awful weight Magic had shifted to her shoulders. She bit at her lower lip. Then she said, "Magic told me that once, a long time ago . . ."

And Ghost nodded and smiled as she began, in a beginning that would shape fairy tales forever more—*Once upon a time*—the oldest tale of all, the story of the gift from the gods.

When she'd finished, her voice little more than a whisper, she turned her head away from him, as if she feared what he might say. (*Don't hate me, Ghost.*) He touched her shoulder gently.

"Don't worry, little Maya," he told her. "It's all right, don't worry. Everything will be fine."

And he smiled.

Ghost went to his house after Maya had returned to the Spirit House. His muscles danced with the tension of controlling his own rage; it had been close, but he'd managed to keep from slipping his long fingers around her slender neck and squeezing until the cartilage and small bones there snapped like rotten sticks.

Instead, he had smiled until the expression felt like invisible fingers stretching his skin into shapes never intended for a human face.

It was the hardest thing he'd ever done, harder than enduring the insults and agonies of his childhood, harder than the blank, silent holes that filled his memory when Shewhomhehated took his mind and rode him like an animal. At one point he'd felt himself slipping into that abyss, and by sheer grinding force of will had pulled himself back.

If there had been a door on his house, he would have slammed it. As it was, he ripped off his coat and raked his chest with his fingernails until long, ragged streaks of blood dripped down his rib cage. His eyes bulged, and the muscles of his jaws creaked to release low, gagging sounds from his swollen mouth.

After a time the seizure passed, leaving only cold madness behind. At least he could think.

So the old fool has planned to betray me all along!

He'd suspected something, but never this. Not after all this time. And his successor was to be the girl he'd almost killed.

His hand reached out and found the ceremonial spear among his other tools. He closed his eyes and began to drive the blade into the soft earth of the floor, again and again, imagining great gouts of blood welling up from the earth itself. Spittle leaked from the corner of his mouth. He gulped and panted like a dog and sucked it back in, then spat it forth again, all unknowing.

Finally he sank back. The frenzied striking movements of his arm slowed, then stopped. Snot began to drip from his nose. He didn't notice. His jaws ground together in hideous rhythm; ripples of unhurried movement coursed through his muscles. He drew himself up into a fetal position, knees against the blood drying on his chest, and shuddered.

"Ugh. Ugh a-hugh, a-hugh."

It wasn't a human sound at all.

When Ghost awoke two hours later, his mind felt as clear, and as cold, as the ice that formed on Second Lake in the wintertime. *It's simple*, he thought. *She is the key to everything, she and that Stone. But I can't do anything about the Stone. The Stone belongs to Shewhomhehated, and if I touch it, I will die.*

That seemed completely obvious to him. Plain as his ruined knee and the limp that had resulted from it, open as the hate and fear he'd been shown as a child, stark as the horror he felt after ShewhomIhate rode him and tossed him aside like a wad of shit-smeared leaves. It was Her, always *Her*, and this was simply still more of the plot She wove about him. In a way, he wasn't surprised at all; She'd always hated him (*Why?*), and having failed to destroy him already, had sent an emissary. An evil spirit named Maya, whose very eyes proclaimed her danger to him.

Paranoia is not the idea that everybody is out to get you. It is, rather, the idea that you are so hugely important that you are *worth* the attention of everybody else. But what do you call the notion that the *Gods* are after you?

Dimly Ghost understood that corollary, and his equally dim answer was simple.

Why, I must be a God, too.

The thought burst in on him with the stunning force of a flash of summer lightning over Green Valley. It seared the soft, runny insides of his skull into a crackling mush. It was *so obvious*.

He began to chuckle—because, in that same blinding instant, he saw the answer, and it was *so obvious* too.

He armed the spittle from his chin. His lips twitched. For a moment, he smiled. Then he folded up the grotesque expression and put it away.

Tonight, he thought. *Tonight will be a good time.*

Maya sat for a while after taking Old Magic's evening meal in to him, plopping down on the log in front of the Spirit House. She listened to the soft call of the wind, and stared blankly at a sky full of stars. She felt, for one of the very few times in her life, completely at peace. It seemed that in telling Ghost the Secret she had somehow nullified its power. The boulder that had dammed her thoughts had magically dissolved into gravel, been swept away, and now her mind flowed as cool as the light from the green and twinkling lights overhead.

Faint shadows moved about Home Camp. She heard soft cries, laughter, the beginning of a song from the direction of the Mystery House. Yet something was missing from the familiar, comfortable scene: the sweet smell of burning wood, the tang of roasted meat, the dull, warm glow of the damped fires. For the hearths were still dark and cold, until the men Magic had sent out to watch the New People came back and said it was safe for Fire to rekindle his namesakes in their black and stony homes.

But even without the cheerful heat of the coals it was nice just to sit, she thought, sit and think about nothing, and watch the stars glittering and winking overhead like a million cat's eyes. Not so comfortable a thought, but she pushed it away; Mother Lion was now long ago and far away.

The quiet *scritch-scrutch* of feet upon the soft soil of the path brought her head slowly down, to stare at the form resolving out of the night.

"Hello, Maya," Ghost said. He kept his voice low, almost a whisper. She knew he did it so that Magic wouldn't hear, and was grateful for it. He understood—that was the best thing about him. He understood her, her confusion, her loneliness, the way Magic's story had torn her terribly. Nor did he condemn her for having fallen into this quandary, or tell her she was being a bad girl for not obeying Magic in every instance, for questioning, if only in her own mind, the life the ancient Shaman seemed to have mapped out for her.

The gratitude she felt at this was overwhelming in its pathetic purity. Had she thought about it at all, she might have wondered how Ghost could have changed so quickly and completely. But she didn't ask that question, because she was no more capable of refusing friendship than she was of refusing the air she breathed. Unlike the young Shaman's knee, her wounds were invisible, but no less dark, deep, and badly scabbed for all of that. Had she asked herself to explain Ghost's sudden change of heart, then she would also have had to question his friendship, and she simply wasn't capable of it.

She had, in fact, sacrificed the only treasure she had—the coin of future power offered her by Magic—on the altar of that friendship, because what Ghost offered was real, not some dream of distant tomorrow that might—or, if her experience was any guide, most likely might not—come true. And so she felt a thrill of joy at the sight of him, at the way his teeth flashed in the dark, at the low, husky sound of his voice.

"Can you walk?" he whispered.

She held up one hand, silencing him. Then she strained her ears. From the Spirit House behind her she heard a long, low series of snorting sounds. Another might not have heard them at all, or mistaken them for something else, but she'd lived with them for a good time now—long enough, at least, to recognize them almost without thought.

At least he wasn't farting yet . . .

"He's asleep," she replied. "For a little while. I can't stay long, though."

He shook his head. "No, just down to the other side of First Lake. Far enough away so we can talk. I've been thinking about what you told me today. I think there's an answer. Do you want to hear it?"

She looked up at him, at his slender face, at his smile, and at that moment she wanted whatever he had to give, with an unquestioning sort of lust that was fearful in its intensity.

"Oh, yes," she breathed. "I want to hear it."

On the far edge of the small lake, away from the heat baking off the high rock wall that sheltered Home Camp, it was a little cooler—but the wind which whooshed over the rim of the cliff missed the lake completely, leaving a pocket of perfectly still air which smelled of damp moss, of sweet mud, of late summer. Fireflies winked here, tiny yellow lamps.

They sat so close that their shoulders touched, and Ghost put his hand on her knee. She trembled at the light touch, and at the way his warm breath puffed on her cheek as he spoke into her ear.

"It's the Stone, Maya," he began.

Her trembling grew more pronounced. He felt it, and squeezed her knee gently. "Don't be afraid of it, Maya. It's only an old piece of bone. Magic's crazy, you know."

Maya started. The statement was so unexpected she completely forgot about the hot, humid feelings Ghost's fingers sent ratcheting into her belly. "What?" she whispered. "What did you say?"

"Oh, yes," he went on in that soft, calm voice. "An evil Spirit, maybe a ghost from one of those new people. Haven't you noticed?"

He paused a moment and then, as if understanding that she wouldn't answer, continued in the same pleasant tones. "Well, perhaps not. But to me, it's as plain as"—he chuckled—"as the nose on your face. Look at him. His hands—did you see how they've changed?"

She had; oh yes, she had.

"And the rest. He tells us to put out the fires, to hide from the new people. Doesn't that seem strange to you? How long can we go on like this? Soon our dried meat will be gone. It's hunting time, but he won't let us hunt. What are we supposed to do? Starve until these people go away? What if they don't?"

They were, she had to admit, perfectly reasonable questions. They'd even crossed her mind, as she'd rummaged in the bottom of the storage pit next to the Spirit House, noting how little meat remained and wondering if they could gather enough nuts and berries to make up the difference. She considered this, and was able to ignore another voice that whispered to her that something was *wrong*, that something terrible was abroad in the balmy hush of the evening.

"Old Magic isn't crazy," she said. *Yes, he is. He must be. If he's not, then I will be, and soon, too.*

Ghost paused, as if tasting each word he would speak, accepting some, rejecting others. "Well, perhaps not exactly crazy," he said. "Something has hold of him, though. Some kind of Spirit. Maya, I knew all about the Mammoth Stone. He told me when I was a boy, in the first moons of my training. It's only a carving—he made it himself. I . . ." Inspiration struck him. *"I watched him carve it, Maya."*

"Y-Y-You did?" Now she was totally confused. She had seen the Stone, touched it, even hidden it beneath her furs. Old Magic said it was old, very old, but the lines cut into it had been sharp and clean. Not old at all. Oh, the color had turned a bit, but mostly the tiny figure looked as if it could have been made yesterday. Certainly not hands of hands of summers ago—a figure that made no sense anyway.

None of it makes sense. She hadn't felt anything when she'd held the carving, had she? No, of course not. *(Oh, yes I did.)* Nothing at all. *(Light.)* But why would Magic lie to her? Why would he want to make her miserable?

She couldn't find an answer—at least, not one any more plausible than what Ghost offered her as his long fingers massaged the flesh of her thigh.

Her clear, starlit equanimity of only a few moments before vanished like the smoke that had once hung over Green Valley. Now *everything* became confused, blurry. Thoughts twisted in her skull like dancing shapes just out of reach. Magic . . . Ghost . . . his fingers . . . The Stone was only a stone, and she wouldn't have to become something awful, something *totally alone*. Ghost could help, he could drive the Spirit from Magic's body. . . .

(His hands!)

. . . could make all the pain and fear and confusion go away.

Could he? *If only he could.*

But *could* he?

"Ghost?"

"What, Maya?"

"What should I do?"

Smiling and smiling, he told her.

Chapter Fourteen

The Green Valley: 17,983 B.C.

Maya accomplished the deed quickly, before her newfound resolve could fade in the light of morning. She left Ghost at the lake and went back to the Spirit House and rolled into her blankets. But then she lay wide-eyed, staring into the darkness, listening to the sounds of Magic's ancient body. She lay unmoving for what seemed like hours, until the chill seeping into the Spirit House told her the longest hours of the nights were nigh. Then, as quietly as she could, she rolled over and, working mostly by touch, removed the bundled Mammoth Stone from its hiding place beneath her furs.

Only for a moment did she pause then, because it seemed that the small bundle throbbed in her hand, like a tiny animal. But then even that sensation passed, and she thought she'd probably imagined it.

I don't know . . . she thought. Something nameless struggled against her intention, but it was so formless, so vague, that she was finally able to brush it aside. Ghost had indeed been persuasive.

"I think it's the Stone itself," he'd said. "Magic made it, but somehow a Spirit has gotten into it, and from it into Magic. These things happen, Maya.

The Spirits are strange. We can never know truly how they work. But there are things we do know—I *know*—about Spirits. How to drive them away."

He'd paused, as if marshaling his thoughts, and she'd waited breathlessly. If he could do what he said—lift the horrible burden Magic had charged her with—remove that endless, empty doom, then perhaps she might, at last, know a real future. She didn't think of it in precisely those terms, of course; it was more a balancing of her revulsion at the thought of following the path Magic had revealed, and the betrayal she felt at disobeying his instructions.

Carefully, sensing her quandary, Ghost had added as much weight as he could to his side of the scale. He'd touched her thigh again, and allowed his elbow to brush against her breast. She shuddered faintly. "Bring me the Stone," he'd said. "I will drive the Spirit from it. Then you can take it back to Magic, and he will forget this craziness. Can you do that?"

For what seemed the longest time she'd simply sat and stared into the firefly darkness, listening to sounds only she could hear; the sound of stillness, perhaps. The silence that had enveloped her all her life.

"Yes," she'd whispered at last. "I can do that."

And now her moment of paralysis broke; she stepped across that last ledge of indecision, and tumbled over into the abyss. She had no idea she was falling, though. To her, it seemed that all she did was creep silently from the Spirit House, a soft, furry bundle with a terrible heart wrapped inside clutched to her breasts.

The night sky had turned cold. The stars glared down on her as she made her way silently up the path. Just outside Ghost's house, a shadow grew suddenly from the dark to meet her.

She jumped with fright. "Oh!"

"Shh. It's only me, Maya," Ghost whispered comfortingly.

She moved toward him.

"Did you bring it?"

Wordlessly, she thrust the bundle forward.

"Here, take it."

"Ahhh."

When she had finally handed the Mammoth Stone to Ghost, it seemed that two things happened. Once again, just as when she'd told him the Secret, a huge weight rose softly from her shoulders. But at the same time, she felt a sudden sense of loss—of something absolutely precious given over, of some ghastly, final mistake.

Almost, she reached to take the Stone back, but Ghost moved slightly, and somehow he now faced away from her, and she could no longer see the bundle.

"Ghost?"

"What?" *Was that a new note in his voice? Harsher, but triumphant?* She was so confused she couldn't tell.

"Will Magic be all right now?"

"Oh yes, Maya. Don't worry. Magic will be *fine*."

They spoke a few more words, but Ghost seemed in a hurry to leave. Finally he said, "Maya. I have to do the thing as soon as possible—it will take time. I need to start right away."

She shrugged. "Will I see you tomorrow?"

He didn't reply.

"Ghost?"

"Mmm?"

"Will I—"

"I heard you. Don't worry, Maya. We'll be seeing a lot of each other. As soon as I'm finished, then we can be together as much as we want. Go, now."

He turned, and so did she, and as she walked slowly back to the Spirit House, which now loomed out of the darkness, its shape for the first time dark and frightening, she wondered what she had done.

She thought she'd done the right thing. Why, then, did it feel so *wrong*?

Ghost paused at the door of his house and watched Maya's figure retreat down the path, grow vague, disappear. His lips flickered once, into a *smile*. Then he stooped and ducked around the door flap into the waiting darkness inside.

Darkness.

He *liked* the darkness. It was secret, it *hid* him. He didn't much care if the fires of the People were ever relighted. He'd discovered a strange feeling of power when he walked the silent, empty night. He would slip between the dark, humped shapes of the houses, his feet barely whispering in the much-tracked dust, hearing the faint sounds of sleepers, their grumbles and cries, and a wild sensation of *mastery* would suffuse his veins like hot honey. *I hold them in the palm of my hand! All their pitiful little lives. I move like a ghost!*

The inside of his house was chilly. His breath puffed out in faint silver clouds as he squatted down and finally, by the thin starlight glowing through his open door, looked at the precious bundle he held.

There was really nothing to see. He'd seen it before, anyway. Nor did he wish to unwrap the fur and expose the Stone to light again. *She* was in there. He knew it with the same bone-deep certainty that also told him *She* would kill him if he touched her trinket.

He had no intention of touching the Mammoth Stone. No intention at all—but he did have a plan.

He chuckled silently. Finally he placed the Mammoth Stone in his pack, straightened his furry coat, and crawled back into the blazing night.

Home Camp seemed utterly silent, empty and vacant, as if the People had departed on some new and endless trek, leaving him behind. For an instant the chill of the night struck to his heart, and he shivered. But then, like a ghost, he began to move, following the main path toward First Lake.

By the time the sun had peeped over the rim of the cliff wall, he was nearly to the wide mouth of the Green Valley. He tramped along briskly, the sun beating down on his shoulders, his momentary qualms forgotten. Mosquitoes buzzed in his ears. A squirrel chittered off in the underbrush, and in the hazy distance he thought he heard the guttural cough of a hunting lion. But he paid no attention to all of this. Even the lion brought him no fear. He was exalted now, a ghost walking the World, and nothing could touch him.

Up ahead a great blacksnake slithered across the faint trail, and he laughed aloud without knowing why.

Soon enough everything would change. Soon enough, the old fool would regret his treachery. Soon enough the girl would be his—and he wouldn't kill her; oh, no, not *kill* her at all.

He had other plans.

He strode on, looking neither right nor left.

He knew exactly where he was going.

Black Caribou raised one thickly muscled fist— even his *fingers* bulged with thick tendons—and brought the small band to a halt.

"There," he said.

It was their fourth day out and so far, despite Broken Fist's encouraging words, they'd found no game. A few jackrabbits, but without snares they were helpless against the bounding rodent's quickness. Their heavy spears might bring down caribou, bison, even mammoth, but the jackrabbits only laughed at the clumsy weapons.

They had followed the river down, searching for watering places, for the characteristic tracks of the great beasts they hunted, but after three days they'd turned back. Oh, they found spots, all right—places where the high, crumbling river bank, worn away by rushing water so cold it would freeze a hand in a minute, had crumbled into natural pathways down—and in the late summer heat, perfectly preserved prints of hooves and broad, flat mammoth spoor. At one place even a pile of shit, not yet dry, but no sign of the animals themselves.

Now they trudged in a small group, seven men, their heavy spears slung carelessly over their shoulders. It wouldn't be the first time the Shaman had been wrong, nor would it be the last. Broken Fist's errors of this kind were easy to understand—he could speak only of what the Spirits told him at the time he spoke—and the Spirits, particularly the dark and ominous Spirit of Breath, changed their minds as quickly as the shifting wind.

But Caribou didn't mind. The hunt had eased him greatly; somehow, in the vast bowl of blue sky, beneath long, fish-scale clouds, the winds rolling across the empty steppe like huge, invisible boulders had cleansed him.

His memories of the sacrifice had faded. The terror of that day almost seemed like a dream now, a terrible nightmare that might have happened to somebody else. He could no longer recall—nor did he try to—the way Spring Flower's tender, trusting lips had moved to breathe his name as he fed her blood-colored poison. Even the ghastly sight of her flesh cooking, crisping, burning from her bones had gone to some other place in his skull, some locked place where it might gibber in his dreams, but he no longer saw it in the light of day.

In fact, about the only thing he could remember

now was the sound of the drums, and even that was fading.

"Hey, Rat!" he called.

The smaller man came up to him, shading his eyes against the slanting fire of the sun. "What, Caribou?"

"Look over there."

Rat turned in the direction of Caribou's gesture. At first he saw nothing—nothing out of the ordinary, anyway. They had just topped a low rise. On their left the river bubbled and churned in its bed, uneasy and swollen with summer ice-melt. On the right, clear to the horizon in the direction Rat now searched, stretched mile upon rolling mile of brown, sere steppe grass, like the smooth back of some vast dun animal. Rat squinted. He was proud of his far sight, as good—maybe better—than any other in the tribe. "I don't see anything," he muttered.

"There," Caribou said. "Not in the center; follow my hand."

Rat glanced at Caribou and adjusted his field of vision slightly. The sun was past overhead, casting a stunted puddle of shadow at his feet, and farther out, nearing the horizon, the view was further muddled by the distorting effect of the sun's rays. He stiffened.

Very faint, very far away. Something.

At first he thought it was a patch of low clouds, almost like fog. But not quite. He bit at his lower lip, and tried to concentrate. More like . . .

. . . smoke.

Yes, that was it, but hard to make out; something darker there, a patch of color that stood out faintly, like a bruise against the tan of the prairie.

"Mmm. I see it."

Caribou grunted. "Looks like smoke."

Rat nodded. "Sort of. But it doesn't rise like smoke."

They stared at each other. The odd sighting made

both of them curious, but they'd been out four days now and the "smoke" was very distant. They'd grown up on the steppe, so that the odd quirks of distance and light held no mysteries for them, and without thinking much about it Rat quickly estimated the enigmatic "smoke" as being at least a day's trek distant. Unless they hurried, and they had no reason to hurry.

Caribou shrugged. "What do you think?"

Rat shrugged in return. "Don't know. It's not mammoth. Or dust from bison."

Leaping Snake, a young man with a twisting scar running from his forehead down through a blank left eye and across his cheek, pushed up. His eyesight wasn't nearly as good as either Caribou or Rat's, but his tracking sense was extraordinary, as if nature had compensated for his injury by developing his sense of smell and taste. He could put a bit of trampled mud in his mouth and tell you, almost to the hour, how long it had been since the beast had made its mark.

He said, "I smell bison."

Both older men turned to stare at him. Snake nodded eagerly. "The wind turned just now. It was coming from across the river, and now it's blowing from upstream. Can't you smell it?"

Snake's nose almost twitched with eagerness. His single good eye, a dark, dark brown, glowed with excitement.

Rat, who found Snake's sensory skills as extraordinary as Snake did Rat's own eyesight, couldn't smell anything. But Snake was rarely wrong.

"How far?" Rat asked.

Snake cocked his head. "Not far," he said. "Remember that place where we found the bones?"

Rat glanced at Caribou. Not far upstream, on their trek down, they'd come across what was obviously a well-used watering place. They'd discovered bleaching

piles of caribou and bison bones, well gnawed with
the familiar grooving, splintery characteristics of cave
lions. In the jumble, and the subsequent destruction
wreaked by lions and other, smaller scavengers,
they'd missed one other telltale sign: the slanting
fractures caused by human tools of stone.

"Yes," Caribou said. "I remember it."

"I think there," Snake told him.

"How many?" Rat asked. His voice was terse, but
a growing excitement underlay his words.

Again Snake cocked his head, a peculiar, animal-
like questing motion. "Many," he said at last. "I
think many."

Rat nodded. "What do you think?" he asked Caribou. On the hunt, Rat deferred to the huge, hulking
man, as did everybody else. The real platform of
Caribou's growing power was his skill as a hunter—
alone of all the Bison People, he'd once killed a
mammoth with only a single spear in mortal combat.
It was from this almost supernatural ability as a
hunter that his other, more shadowy authority had
grown.

Caribou grunted. Snake was wrong, sometimes,
but not as often as Broken Fist and his predictions.
Something inside him warmed to the idea that it
would be human skills, not divine, that led them to
meat.

She didn't have to die, then, did she?

He made up his mind. "Upriver," he said. "And
quickly."

Rat nodded, and adjusted the balance of the two
heavy spears he carried. "Let's go!" he called, and
set off, moving in a long, deceptively easy jog. The
others followed, loping along behind Caribou and
Rat. The ground-eating run didn't look very fast, but
the men could keep it up for hours on end.

For several moments the day was full of the soft,
thumping beat of their heels, then the sound died

as they crested the rise and descended. In a moment they were gone.

Nobody looked back, toward the mysterious dark smudge and the smoke that wasn't smoke. That would come later.

Not much later, though.

Ghost came to the place of bones by the river at noon. He'd moved quickly, hoping to finish the deed and return to Home Camp by dusk. The wind had pushed at his back all day, speeding his steps, as if the huge spirits there wished to aid him in his task.

The Mammoth Stone, still wrapped, bumped at his hip in the light skin pack he carried. Its weight was inconsequential—sometimes he was almost able to forget it was there. Other times, without warning, the load would suddenly feel like boulders; he could *feel* the burden pulling him down. Then that sensation too would pass, and he would once again become Ghost, strider of the wind, whom the Goddess cared enough about to despise.

All through the blue morning his thoughts remained a glowing, formless blur. Later, he would barely remember the trek. He felt exalted. Although he hadn't eaten for almost a day, his flat stomach made no protest, nor did he regret, even as he sweated beneath the sun's heat, that he'd forgotten to bring a clay water jug.

He came to the river in a glare of light, a tiny brown stick-figure almost lost in the slow-rolling, endless steppe, and paused at the edge of the cut leading down.

He had chanted great animals down here, seen much bloody slaughter from the top of the Spirit Pole. Sometimes it seemed that the only time he truly *lived* was when he hung from the top of the pole with the wind in his face, singing songs of power, drawing the great beasts to their doom. *But that will end soon*, he thought. *Her* charm rode his hip now, taking its final journey—a trip out of the heart of the People, to . . .

. . . where?

He stood a moment at the lip of the defile, staring down at the gray, slow-humping water of the river. It looked smooth and powerful, like a vast, translucent snake, endless, no head or tail, just a body. *The body of the snake*, he thought, momentarily transfixed by the force of it.

Throw it in. Be done with it forever!

He licked his lips. The river pounded down its rocky track with a dull, muted roar. Tiny bits of glittering spray fluffed up from the jagged rocks that stuck out like broken teeth at its edge. Other than the sound of the water the noon was silent as night.

He moved forward one step. Bits of dried mud flaked beneath his feet, tumbled down the sharp incline with a dry, scratchy hiss.

Throw it in!

His vision wavered. For an instant he saw two rivers, one flowing next to the other. But one was red, and looked like blood. The banks of that river were bones, huge, scattered piles of bones, and for the tiniest eye-blink of time, it seemed to him the bones were human. Mounds of whitened, bleached skulls, their eye sockets empty and accusing, tumbled racks of cracked and desiccated skeletons beneath, rib cages shattered, arm bones and leg bones broken as if beneath a mighty weight.

He shook his head. A low, itchy, humming noise began to vibrate in his spine, and for a moment he thought *She* would ride him again, right there on the river bank. Then the vertigo passed as if it had never been. He blinked.

A vision, no doubt. Ghost had no fear of visions. His dreams had been far more terrible than this vision of bones and blood. He dreamed of absolute emptiness, of the loss of his body, of the endless wanderings of ghosts.

Throw it into the water!

He sighed.

Visions weren't usually much help, either. The waking kind, at least. They were enigmas, seeming to say much without saying much of anything at all. So he saw a river of blood, coursing between banks of bone. What did it mean? Where had it come from? What thing had sent it to him? *Whose blood? Whose bones?*

The Spirits, as usual, were playing at their paradoxical games. He took another step forward, and his pack thumped smartly at the place where his thighbone joined his pelvis. Strange. The Mammoth Stone felt heavy again, as if it wished to drag him down. Down to the twisting, hungry water. Down to the bones. To the blood.

Mesmerized, he scrambled forward, his glazed eyes on the river. The long, thrumming roar of it filled his ears, louder even than the complaining groan of the ice wall to the north. He reached level ground at last—his feet made sharp, sucking sounds in the mud there—and started forward.

Stopped.

Footprints?

The depressions were many, and still contained a faint level of water. Recent, then. And not of the People.

A shuddery thrill twitched up his neck, into his skull. These were the Others . . . and suddenly he knew the meaning of the vision.

He glanced to his right, where a scatter of huge bones marked the graveyard of mammoth, bison, even caribou. Some had died of natural causes, others he'd sung to their death himself. The ivory, picked clean by time and tiny teeth, gleamed in the hot sunlight.

The sunlight that filled his brain now.

Footprints. Headed downstream.

But the camp Spear had sighted was upstream.

The visitors would return, then.

And when they did . . .?

He *smiled*.

The Mammoth Stone seemed to jump inside his pack, like a panicked rabbit. Its weight tugged his shoulder down, but he ignored the feeling. Moving like a zombie—or a ghost possessed—he stooped over and began to gather rocks. It took him only a few minutes to build a cairn, flat-topped, reaching barely to his knees.

When he was done, he stared at the small monument. It seemed fitting to him, and no traveler who came this way could miss it. Moving slowly (he could hear his bones slide against each other, hear the *click-pop* of cartilage, hear the rush of blood in his veins), he slipped the pack from his shoulders. Set it down, opened it, and, grunting with effort— the Stone was so *heavy* now—took out the wrapped bundle of fur. He placed it on top of the plinth, and as he did so, in the distance, a long, trumpeting cry split the rumble of the river.

He snapped his head up; his eyes felt on fire. Mammoth. Beyond the distant bank, invisible to him. The cry of a great animal, angry and triumphant.

No more fear, he thought wildly. *No more!*

The tightly wrapped bundle glittered in the noon, each strand of fur seeming to absorb light and throw it back a hundredfold. It grew so bright he couldn't look at it anymore. He turned and began to make his way back up the path. His feet slipped once on broken bone, but he didn't notice.

Finally he regained the top of the decline and a fresh wind, rising from the east, smote his face. It was cold and filled with a hint of damp. A million miles away, at the bowl of the horizon, dark gray shapes began to hump up.

Storm, he thought. *Have to hurry.*

He moved away from the river, out onto the vast rolling waste of the steppe. He didn't look back. There was nothing there anyway. Nothing *he* wanted to see, at any rate.

When he was gone, shrunk to a tiny dot and at last invisible, the river still hissed angrily, like a great gray snake cheated of its prey. On the small rock monument, the bundle waited silently for its destiny to come to it.

The bones did nothing at all.

Leaping Snake was the first to reach that spot on the river he had named "The Place of Bones." He came over the dark lip of bank and was silhouetted there by the long, slanting rays of the sun as it sank in a ball of red-orange fire to the west. He was facing the sunset, and for a moment he had to squint to make out the downward path.

His nostrils fluttered delicately. *Too late*, he thought. *There was game here, but now it's gone.* Then he froze, his head snapping up like that of a frightened fox. His skull came all the way up, paused, then began to swivel slowly on his neck. He closed his eyes, both the good and the bad, although the lid over his sightless eye only partially covered the dry, collapsed orb there.

Snake was blind in one eye and nearsighted in the other. He was nearly helpless in the action of a hunt, as likely to be trampled by accident or tumble over a cliff as to hit anything with the single spear he carried. But he didn't care about that. His value was different, but no less important. The accident that had blinded and disfigured him—a fall, for even as a child fully sighted he was already clumsy—had occurred early enough for his other talents to develop fully. He didn't understand why everybody couldn't do what he did. At first he'd thought it entirely unremarkable that he could taste a leaf, or a blade of grass, and distinguish a hundred, a thousand different sensations. The green of a leaf; the clear silver of the water in the leaf; the hint of dead gray smoke from a long-gone fire; the brown crackling dryness around the edges (if it was fall and the leaf drying); the heavy, musky odor of mammoth, or the hotter, saltier spoor of bison; even the thin, acrid taste of some small insect that had roosted on the veins of the leaf for a moment before passing on.

The world he "viewed" through his nose was even more spectacular, a gorgeous melange of odors and scents impossible to classify. If Snake had any real problem, it arose when he tried to describe that incredible panoply to those who were forever unable to know it. To him scents not only *smelled*, they had color and taste and a *feel* he could know inside his mind.

His hearing was only slightly less potent than his other hyper-keen senses. So as he stood at almost precisely the spot where Ghost had stood only a few hours before, he could, without opening his eyes at all, understand more of what had happened here than Caribou or Rat could ever know, with their sharp eyes and dull noses, tongues, and ears.

As he stood in his own comfortable darkness, he read the surroundings like a book printed in a hundred different languages. The mammoth had come here, four of them: a Mother, a young bull, and two calves from the spring birth—he could easily distinguish their individual smells. They had paused to drink, shat (two big piles, three or four smaller), then made their way upstream a hundred yards or so to the shallow ford there, splashed across, paused again on the far side, then ambled away, leaving clouds of stink in their wake.

But something else had come later. The subtle, bitter odor lay on top of— No, that wasn't right. More *in between* the heavier, more bountiful smells of mammoth. Snake smelled man. But not of his People, and he wrinkled his nose. This new stench was different from the smells of the People he knew. This was Other.

Eyes still closed, he began to quiver faintly with excitement. The smoke smell, the cured-hide smell, the sweat smell caused by diet were all similar, but subtly alien. An *Other* had come here—and not long ago. Just after the mammoth had departed, in fact.

Once he'd established all this to his satisfaction, he opened his eyes again. Then he dropped to his hands and knees and crawled forward, his nose close to the ground, until he'd reached the bottom of the incline and found the first muddy, water-brimmed footprint.

He leaned forward, stuck out his tongue, and tasted the moisture there.

A preposterous number of impressions welled up from his nose, his tongue, his mouth. He could never explain it to his mates, but he *knew* this Other. He was still frozen in this position, shaking slightly, when Caribou and Rat crested the low ridge somewhat in advance of the others.

The two hunters stopped, glanced at each other, then started down.

"Snake!" Rat called. "What is it?"

Snake reached the mud flat a few steps ahead of Caribou, but it was the hulking leader who saw the cairn first. He stepped around Snake's crouching form and advanced upon it, his eyes wide.

He unhitched one of his spears from his back and let it fall into his right hand. He glanced uneasily from right to left. Animals hadn't built this thing, nor had animals tied the complicated knots that restrained the furry bundle. He moved slowly, carefully, advancing on the strange construction with more than a little fear.

He knew magic when he saw it.

The People of the Bison had not crossed the path of another tribe for almost twenty years. Caribou dimly remembered that crossing, and what had happened shortly thereafter. He'd been too young to go with the men when they'd gathered up their spears and clubs and crept out into the night. Broken Fist hadn't been Shaman then, but the Spirit of Breath had spoken just as easily through the old Shaman. The God of Snakes had been as plain, and as hungry, as he always was.

That tribe of Others had been small, less than ten, and weak from long journeying. They'd tried to resist the sudden night attack, but the Bison People had been strong and lucky—two of the other hunters had been killed, and the rest brought back tied in a long human chain with ropes of cured hide.

The Spirit of Breath had fed well in those days. Caribou could still remember the avid, pinched look on his friend Strong Fist's features. Strong Fist would soon become Broken Fist, though nobody knew that then. But Caribou thought now, in the clear, limpid vision of hindsight, that Fist's future had been plain for anybody who wanted to see it, in the humid lust that had twisted his lips as the sacred smoke rose into the waiting, invisible maw of the Spirit of Breath.

Those thoughts flashed through his mind as he approached the mysterious pile of rock and its small, furry burden. The People of the Bison had no reason to trust strangers, and very good reasons to be wary of them. The Spirit of Breath was always hungry— Caribou occasionally wondered what might happen if they ever met a *large* tribe. Would the God of

Snakes send them hunting for his meals anyway, until the People of the Bison themselves became his sacrifices?

He shivered. Overhead, painted rusty red by the sinking sun, long, curling fingers of cloud stretched out across the sky. Behind these bloody banners a mighty range of black-green thunderheads was building. The sharp electric smell of storm was heavy on the still air. The dying wind was another bad sign.

A shadowy pile of huge bones loomed on his right hand. For a moment, Caribou found it hard to breathe. He sensed Spirits here, clustering invisibly like gigantic, slow-moving flies come to feast on a corpse.

He blinked. He realized he'd stopped moving, though he didn't remember any intention to do so. Behind him, Snake was coming to his feet, whispering rapidly to Rat, who was nodding and starting to come forward himself. Caribou didn't have to turn and look to know this. The soft scuffing noises, the muffled words, told him all he needed to know. As did Rat's sudden sharp intake of breath, and a scrabble of stones kicked into muck when Rat jerked forward.

He'd seen the pile too, Caribou understood. And, suddenly, he didn't want Rat to get to it first.

Caribou lowered his head and bulled forward through the gathering gloom, ignoring Rat's soft question.

"What's that?"

Caribou jammed the butt of his spear into the soggy earth beside the flat-topped stone pyramid, leaned over, and brushed his fingers across the surface of the bundle.

Just fur. Soft, gleaming, well-kept fur, and hard little knots. He picked it up, turned it one way, then the other, as Rat loomed suddenly at his shoulder.

"What is it?"

"Don't know," Caribou said.

"Open it up." Rat's voice sounded strained, as if he were frightened and trying to hide it. But eager, too. *Hungry*, almost.

Caribou shook his head. His big, lumpy fingers worked at the cords, pushed at the knots.

Impatiently, Rat said, "Here, let me. . . ."

He reached forward, but Caribou turned and shoved him back. "No."

He worked at the knots again, finally realized he would never fathom their secrets and, holding the bundle in his left hand, jerked his spear from the mud. It came out with an ugly, *splutch*-ing sound. He brought the razor-sharp chipped edge of the long spear blade down and inserted the tip of it beneath one of the cords. He sawed back and forth. The cord popped loose. It took him a few moments to cut the rest of the taut bindings. When he was done, part of the fur folded away of its own accord. He could feel a hard lump in the center of the soft hide.

For one instant Caribou thought he saw a sudden flash of fire, off across the dimly rolling river. *Just the sun*, he told himself.

He looked down at his left hand, then turned the rest of the fur away and said, "Ahh."

Rat said nothing, but he pushed up close against Caribou's side.

The small figure glowed up at them with amber clarity. Slowly, slowly, Caribou brought one big, callused fingertip down onto the smooth surface.

Warm, he thought.

Why should it be warm?

Rat made a low, coughing noise. he turned, spat, then turned back.

"It's a magic thing," he said at last.

"Yes," Caribou agreed. "But not our magic."

Rat thought a moment. "We should take it to Fist."

But hadn't it actually been two *flashes of red? Like* eyes?

"I guess," Caribou said at last, as dusk fell and the first long tendrils of storm began to rise around them. "I guess we should."

Snake said, "Footprints. They go in *that* direction."

Chapter Fifteen

The Place of Bones: 17,983 B.C.

Caribou, still holding the Mammoth Stone, turned and looked at Snake whose myopic eyes blazed darkly, blindly where he knelt over his newest find. He was facing away from the others, toward the broken scrabble of rock they'd just descended. "Look," he mumbled eagerly. He brought his right hand to his lips, tasted, nodded.

"Not very long ago," he said. "He was here—then he went back the other way. I can smell him, too," he added.

Caribou glanced at Rat. Obviously, from the piece of carved bone Caribou still held in his right hand, *someone* had been here. Snake said it was the man, and they had no reason to doubt his talents on the matter. Caribou stared at the small tracker, huddled like a shaking wolf over his spoor.

"Not one of us," he ventured. It was always possible another party had come down the river from camp after their departure. But Snake shook his head. "No. Other," he said.

"That place, where the smoke doesn't look like smoke . . ." Rat ventured.

Caribou nodded. He glanced down at the Mammoth Stone he held. Something had changed there.

279

He couldn't quite figure it out—the color was different, faded perhaps. He shrugged, wrapped it in its furs, and thrust it into his pack. "Come on," he said to Rat.

Together they climbed to the lip of the ravine. Both men shaded their eyes and gazed off over the rolling steppe. Finally Rat shrugged. "Can't see anything."

Caribou nodded in agreement. Far out on the rolling dun plains danced smaller precursors of the mighty storm they could see building above the horizon, hiding vast swatches of grass behind shifting veils of rain. The unseen visitor could be behind any of them—nor was the mysterious place of smokes visible any longer, either. The steppe looked empty and forbidding, beneath the larger backdrop of the great storm hard on the heels of its smaller progeny.

Caribou shivered.

"Let's get back," he said.

Rat nodded.

A moment later, the Place of Bones lay empty; only a single crude pile of rock, already beginning to darken from errant splatters of rain, showed that anything had ever happened here at all.

The Green Valley

The gigantic storm had heaved its lightning-shot bulk over the ramparts of Home Camp as dusk faded into night. Old Magic sat alone in the Spirit House, staring fixedly at the open door flap, beyond which hissed and roared a solid sheet of water. The high wall of the rock cliff sheltered the Camp from the worst part of the storm, but Magic wasn't thinking of the storm at all. To Maya, the old Shaman looked frozen. His eyes glittered blankly in the occasional shattering blasts of lightning which crackled all around the Camp. She wasn't particularly worried; she'd seen him enter deep trance before. Usually he warned her, but sometimes he just slipped away. She went on with her preparations for dinner, only slightly uneasy at what she'd done the night before.

She'd been out and about until just before the storm had broken—working quietly near First Lake, casually wandering the paths (but always somewhere near to Ghost's tent, though the young Shaman was nowhere to be found).

Finally the rain had driven her back to the Spirit House, where she found Magic already withdrawn, his eyes like two flat husks of flint. He'd not spoken, nor given any indication he knew she was there.

Now she finished with a cold mush of ground acorns, mixed with the last of their dried meat and a few shredded greens. The thick gray paste looked unappetizing, but it would nourish him. If she could get him to eat it.

"Magic . . . ?"

No answer.

She sighed. Sometimes he would stay like this for hours. She would just have to wait. She drew her fur jacket more closely around her shoulders, then wrapped herself further in one of her bed furs. *It's not there anymore.*

The absence of the Stone was like a tiny hook pricking at the furthest edge of her thoughts. It was very cold inside the tent. She wished she could kindle the fire, but Old Magic had said nothing about it. All through Home Camp, and the outlying clusters of houses, the People sat huddled close together for warmth.

She exhaled softly, her breath making a thin silver plume in front of her face. Then the most exquisite agony she'd ever felt seized her muscles, her bones in its galvanic grip. Her teeth snapped together. Her face twisted suddenly, the muscles pulling against each other. One arm—her right—shot straight out, palm up, and hung there, quivering. Slowly, her head began to tilt backwards, straining against the column of her neck, where thin tendons made an audible popping sound.

Old Magic's eyes shot wide. For a moment sanity returned to them, but only for a moment. By the standards of his time and place, the Shaman was incredibly ancient. The slightest illness, the most trivial injury, could have destroyed him with no more effort than the closing of a fist on an ant. But he had survived, even prospered, for many years beyond his natural span. Part of it was the nature of his life, in many ways less strenuous than the lives of his people. Part of it could have been his own will, his refusal to *let go* while his task remained uncompleted. But part of it might have been *something else*—that vast, unknown and unknowable *thing* which had energized him for so long and which, at the very instant of his final moment, drained away into the unknowing flesh of Black Caribou, far away beside rushing waters.

Caribou had felt nothing beyond a slight warmth. But at precisely the same moment as he stared down at the small, exquisite carving and ran his fingers across its smooth surface, the muscles of Old Magic's eyelids jerked wide. Deep inside his skull capillaries burst like tiny rotten dams, spilling a flood of pulsing blood into the interstices between the cells. A great and growing bubble of blood burped behind his staring eyes; a star-shot scatter of veins suddenly appeared in the whites there, and a broad, purplish bruise disfigured the flesh around his left eye.

He felt nothing. It was entirely painless. To him, it seemed that a broad, red curtain had slowly descended across his vision.

He could see Maya across from him, her features

twisted in silent agony. He wanted to reach out to her, to help her, but it was too late.

Too soon, but too late!

"Maya . . ." he groaned.

Then the curtain descended fully, and Old Magic entered the waiting dark. Somewhere off in the distance, tiny but growing, a light appeared. He moved off toward it, and his concern fell away. Everything fell away, as he moved toward the Light.

She heard his final cry, though she herself was paralyzed with terror. The darkness yawned for her, though it was neither kind nor accepting. It was merely empty, the darkness of the pit she'd created for herself.

When she finally had been released, she stared at the old man where he lay, toppled face-forward into the cold, empty ring of his dead fire.

The sound of his last word rang in her ears, as loud as the thunder which raved outside.

Her name. Her name, and nothing else.

Slowly, she brought her hand to her mouth, felt her lips quiver in cold horror. "M-M-Magic . . . ?"

But of course he didn't reply.

Then, "Oh—*Mother!*"

But She didn't answer either. *How could She?* Maya wondered, her terror fresh and absolute. *I gave Her away, didn't I?*

There was no answer to that, either. She closed her eyes and, silently rocking, waited for Ghost to return.

Bison People River Camp

Broken Fist turned the object over in his hands. The small carving seemed flat and lumpy, grasped in the mangled ruin of Fist's fingers. His blank, empty eyes regarded the thing thoughtfully; he sensed a turning point.

Caribou faced him across the smoky fire inside his tent. The exit flap in the roof had been tied down to prevent rain from entering, but a few drops still found their way inside, to hiss and spatter in the small bed of coals across which Caribou and Fist faced each other.

"Is it magic?" Caribou asked softly. He had felt a momentary pang when he'd turned the Stone over to the Shaman, almost as if the Stone hadn't wanted to leave his keeping. But if it was magic the Stone belonged in Fist's keeping, for only the Shaman was equipped to understand it—and to deal with it, if it was some sort of trap laid for the Bison People by the mysterious Others. Thus Caribou had had no hesitation in relinquishing the Stone, even to one whom he thought of as an enemy, when he knew the good of the Tribe as a whole might be at stake. It was one of the things that made him a natural— and in Fist's shrewd eyes, a dangerous—leader and a worthy foe.

Broken Fist looked across the fire at him then, his eyes suddenly quizzical and merry. And dangerous. "Yes, it's magic. I can feel the magic on it. Weak, though . . ." And still he stared at Caribou, as if daring him to say something.

In a way, of course, he was. Fist understood magic, and more important, the *symbols* of magic, and the power of those symbols. This small carving was only a symbol, of course, but it was dangerous in a way different from that of the powers of the God of Snakes. It was *alien* magic, and Fist, who was aware of the turmoil hidden beneath Caribou's stolid features, was extremely curious: Just what did the mighty hunter think he'd found here? A tool? A weapon, perhaps, against Fist himself?

For Broken Fist knew that Caribou was trapped

within the cage forged by the Spirit of Breath, as long as Caribou's world remained that of the People of the Bison. Fist had already proved his supremacy—and at the same time, the omnipotence of the Snake God—when he'd forced Caribou to eat the heart of his own sister. He hadn't missed the daze in which Caribou had wandered afterwards, nor had the fact of Caribou's renewed strength escaped his attention. Caribou had left to hunt, a broken man—now, returned, he was rejuvenated—as if the sacrifice designed to destroy him had never happened at all.

Was it this carving, this *symbol* of alien, unknown magic, which had given him hope? If only by its existence, which reminded that there were other powers out there, other magics which might be stronger than those of the Spirit of Breath himself?

Broken Fist waited for Caribou to say something.

Caribou, for his part, couldn't seem to take his eyes from the Stone. "Weak, though . . . ?" he muttered.

Suddenly Broken Fist knew exactly what he must do. This tiny chink in the barriers of his own fortress of power must somehow be filled in, and the best way to do that would be to rob the symbol of its power entirely, by stamping out, at the very beginning, any *belief* in the power of the Stone.

He shrugged. "*Very* weak. Here. You can have it. Make a nice trinket, maybe." And he tossed the Mammoth Stone back to Caribou, who caught it easily, as if he'd been waiting for the surprise gesture.

Broken Fist narrowed his eyes as he watched this display. He searched for any signs of triumph, for any conscious knowledge that Caribou might display about the Stone. And he saw nothing. Caribou only grunted softly, then slipped the Stone into his pack, as if it were the worthless trinket Fist claimed it was.

Broken Fist slumped backward a bit, though his

questing eyes never left Caribou's face. "So," he said. "Tell me how you found it. Everything. And also, about that smoky place you saw, you and Rat."

As Caribou obligingly recounted everything he could remember, Fist nodded and clicked his teeth to show appropriate interest—though he had little concern for the actual details. What had fully engaged his entire concentration was simpler, and much more brutal.

There were Others near!

And already, stirring with the restless, voracious lust of a ball of writhing snakes, the hunger of He Who Is Always Hungry was coming awake again.

The only question remaining was how best to feed Him.

The Green Valley

Maya heard soft footsteps, heard the door flap whip open, felt the sudden inrush of cold, damp air, but she didn't move. She sat as she had for perhaps an hour, staring at the top of Old Magic's bald head. It was an interesting skull—she'd never really *looked* at Magic before, but now that he was dead, she found him the most fascinating—the *only* fascinating—thing in her entire universe. There were lumps and bumps in the gray flesh there, and a short, thickly ridged scar beginning high above his right eyebrow and meandering backwards to the crown of his head. The scar looked very old; normally it would have appeared faded to the point of invisibility, but now its twisty path stood out in high white relief against the spreading purple blotch that disfigured half of the top of the old man's head.

"Maya . . ."

Ghost froze. It was quite dark inside the Spirit House, and at first all Ghost could make out was the huddled form of the girl and, across the dead fire, a slumped, almost boneless shape. Then a sudden strobe of lightning threw the interior into harsh, blue-white illumination, and etched the scene upon his mind forever.

"He's dead, Ghost," Maya said dully. "Old Magic is dead."

Which Ghost could see perfectly well for himself. He just wasn't sure he believed it. In fact, he was pretty sure he *didn't* believe it. No matter how much he'd craved Magic's death, no matter how many times he'd chanted his private mantra to himself (*The old man can't live forever*), no matter how long he'd waited for this moment—*he had to be certain!*

He launched himself forward on his hands and knees, scattering the dull black coals of the tiny fire pit, banging his knee painfully on the ring of stones there. His blackened hands found Magic's withered head and lifted it. He stared into the ruined face, lighted again and again by what seemed a continuous shattering fusillade of lightning bolts.

The face had become a mask, a horror. Magic's mouth hung loosely open, revealing his few remaining yellowed teeth, like stones in an arid field. His tongue, swollen and purple, lolled from his desiccated lips. The whole top half of his face was the color of dried blood, from the spreading bruise of the massive stroke which had claimed him. One eyelid drooped shut, the other, frozen into a grimace, revealed an eyeball that looked like broken glass, so starred with exploded veins it was.

That eyeball stared at nothing, and Ghost shuddered and let go of Magic's head. It fell back with a soft, hideous *plupping* noise. Dead.

Dead, *dead*, DEAD!

"*Ahhh!*" A great scream of absolute joy belched into his throat. He threw back his head and expelled the awful sound from his lungs, his throat, for if he'd tried to keep it inside it would surely have exploded him like a rotten fruit.

"*AYEEEEEEEAAAHHHH!*"

Maya moaned faintly and put her hands over her ears. She closed her eyes.

"*AAAHHHGGGHHH!*"

"Ghost . . ."

Thunder swallowed her plea as if it had never been. Ghost might have continued for hours, crouched over Magic's shrunken husk, the muscles of his neck and throat straining to release the terrible sounds within, but even the thunder and lightning couldn't entirely mask his joy.

Somebody pushed inside the Spirit House, a bulky figure dripping with rain, stinking of matted fur and sweat and smoke.

"What's going on? What's happening . . . ?" Spear tried to make out the scene, but, momentarily blinded by the cascade of flashes beyond the door, could only swivel his head back and forth and sputter incoherent questions.

"Ghost, is that you? Maya! What . . . ?"

The lightning crackled again. Spear saw Ghost crouched over Old Magic's corpse, like a wild dog guarding its prey. The young Shaman's hands were bent into claws, and his eyes glittered with a demon light of their own. But when he spoke, his voice was soft and reasoned.

"Old Magic is dead," he said calmly. He glanced down at his fingers, seemed surprised at the shape they'd twisted themselves into, and visibly forced himself to relax. Seemingly of their own accord, his hands found Old Magic's head and settled it into a more natural position. "I sang my grief, Spear. Did you hear it?"

The horrid sounds which had come from the Spirit House and had brought Spear—and others—on a dead run, hadn't sounded much like grief to the hunter, more like the guttural, triumphant shriek of some giant carnivore exulting over its kill. But Spear was in no mood to question the new Shaman.

For that was who regarded him across the old Shaman's body. Whatever Ghost might once have been, he was now Shaman of the People of the Mammoth, and the hot, mad light in his eyes belied the calm of his narrow face.

"I heard, Shaman," Spear said softly.

"Ghost . . ." Maya whispered again. She seemed helpless to say anything else.

Spear glanced at her. "She was with him?"

Ghost heard the revulsion, even the fear, in Spear's voice when he said those words, and suddenly he understood that his victory was complete. To Spear, this was the girl-woman who had caused the deaths of her own mother, her sister, her foster-mother, and now she had evidently witnessed—at the very least—the death of the Shaman who had befriended her.

"Yes," he said, his voice as flat as Maya's own solitary plea.

"Kill her," Spear said.

Ghost *smiled*. "Oh no, Spear," he replied. "I am Shaman now. Trust me to deal with . . . evil Spirits."

Once again Spear's eyes flicked toward the girl, then rapidly away, as if he feared even to look at her. "Whatever you say . . . Shaman."

And he was gone.

"Ghost?"

The new Shaman let Magic's head drop again, with that same sickening sound, and hunkered back in Maya's direction. "Don't worry, little Maya. It's all over now." He paused and licked his lips, savoring the triumph he'd half believed would *never* come.

But it had. Oh yes, it had.

He *smiled*.

"It's *all* over now," he repeated, and Maya, at last fully understanding the horror she'd created for herself, began to cry.

Bison People River Camp

"Find out where the trinket came from," Broken Fist said.

"Yes, Shaman," Caribou replied.

The Green Valley

The storm had passed on, walking and stalking the night, and now, as Ghost led the miserable, terrified girl forth from the Spirit House which had been her home, stars began to peep forth from the ragtag haze left in the wake of the deluge.

It was nearing morning. A faint gray rime lay upon the top of the cliff where eventually, she supposed, the sun might rise again. But not for her. For her there lay ahead only darkness, the empty bleak vacuum of the pit. No Light there. She had no Light, for she'd given it away.

"Come, Maya, hurry along!" Ghost insisted. He tugged at her shoulder. A curious sensation had come over him as he'd wrapped Magic's corpse in his furs, preparing the ancient Shaman's body for the coming fire. Old Berry had helped him, her seamed face shiny with tears, although she hadn't sobbed openly. Ghost knew she grieved—he had a better understanding of the relationship between the two old ones than most, having studied it with nearly insane jealousy for years.

But even Old Berry accepted the change. Death was no stranger to the People—the bedrock of their existence was a constant struggle against death, and one that they always, eventually, lost.

"Are you sad, Berry?" he'd asked, as they finished arranging Magic's furry shrouds.

She'd grunted something unintelligible, but nodded. He'd glanced over the body at her, noted the way her eyes slid from his face. "I am Shaman now," he told her softly. It was a challenge, and both knew it.

For a moment her eyes had brightened, and she'd stared at him full-on. But then it was as if she couldn't bear to look at the expression on his face and, once again, she'd dropped her eyes in submission.

She spoke her only words of the long night then: "Yes, Ghost. You are the Shaman."

In the capitulation of that admission, Ghost saw the last of his enemies vanquished. And of the fire of that victory was born a strange feeling: mercy for the vanquished.

He could afford it. Who could oppose him now? Not Berry, evidently, and certainly not Maya, no matter what bizarre plans Old Magic might have been weaving for the girl. In fact, Ghost thought, he'd have to step both quickly and carefully to keep Spear—perhaps even Skin, her own father—from murdering outright the woman they regarded as an evil, threatening Spirit.

Spear would be no problem, he decided, nor would Skin. Even Wolf, Ghost thought, Maya's brother, would not wish to interfere. He knew Wolf still harbored tender feelings for Maya, but as the years had passed and Wolf's stature had risen, the young man had grown more and more distant from her. Wolf might be a problem, but not over Maya. Not if Ghost was careful, and he certainly intended to be that. Had not care and planning been the hallmark of his entire life? No, wreaking terrible revenge on Maya might upset Wolf, and at the moment

Ghost wanted nothing to becloud the glorious visions he meant to make realities.

Besides, Maya was fully beaten now. With Magic gone, Ghost saw more clearly that her power had been from, and through, the dead Shaman. Without him she was nothing, certainly no threat. Yes, he could afford to be magnanimous.

Best, though, that she understood precisely how her world had changed. He remembered the swell of her breasts, now invisible beneath the shaggy, sodden furs she wore. His breath quickened.

"You are my woman now, Maya. Do you understand that? You belong to me."

She hadn't looked up. Perhaps some small sound had escaped her lips, which were blue with cold and quivering visibly in the growing gray light of dawn. Perhaps not.

"What did you say?" he asked, and jerked hard enough on her shoulder that she stumbled a bit.

"Yes, Ghost," she replied, clearly this time. Her eyes sought his. To him they seemed empty and dazed, the eyes of a small creature in an inescapable trap.

Which, of course, she was.

"Good," he said.

Maya slept. She had dreams, but she wouldn't remember any of them. There wasn't much to remember—just great, empty fire-shot vistas of desolation and doom, and once a huge snake, scales glittering, rising endlessly from a pile of burning bones.

There had been no Light.

"No . . ." she mouthed silently. *"No . . ."* And she'd awakened to hard bars of yellow light streaming in through the open door flap of an unfamiliar tent.

No, not unfamiliar. She blinked. She lay wrapped

in furs just inside the door, facing another pile of furs across the gently flickering fire. The tent was warm. The smoke hole had been tied open and the gray smoke rose straight up, through the bars of light, which turned it to purest white in shifting layers.

She watched the smoke for what seemed a very long time. Nothing went on in her mind. It seemed there was nothing inside her mind but smoke, either. After a time the wavery veils began to dissipate. She heard sounds, and was surprised to find that they were coming from her own mouth. Sobs, low and choking. Tears filmed her vision.

She was in Ghost's house. After a time she quieted. She wondered what she would do. Nothing, most likely. There wasn't anything *to* do. Magic was gone. The Light was gone. She'd seen the way even Old Berry had looked at her, a mingled expression of disgust and disappointment, as if somehow *she'd* been the cause of Old Magic's death.

There would be no help from the ancient herb woman.

Or from anybody else, either. Only from Ghost, who *smiled* at her, and told her she was *his* woman now. dimly she understood that it *was* all her fault. She'd thought that giving the Mammoth Stone—that *hateful* symbol of her endless servitude—to the young Shaman would free her—and indeed it had.

Certainly Old Magic would no longer plan her future for her. And the Stone was gone, wasn't it? She had no idea what Ghost might have done with it, but she had no doubt whatsoever that the Mammoth Stone was no longer with the People. She couldn't explain that knowledge, not even to herself, but she was as certain of it as she was that the departure of the Stone had somehow killed Old Magic.

Which meant *she* had killed Magic, just as she'd somehow been responsible for the deaths of everybody else who'd ever loved her. Suddenly, for no reason at all, the memory of the deaths of Bud and Blossom rose up to haunt her. She remembered then in grisly detail that awful day: the hot, fetid breath of Mother Lion, scrabbling ever higher in the tree; the caterwauling of her cubs below; the screams; and the way the tree had suddenly rebounded, flinging her like a tiny stone through the sky.

Almost, then, she knew something of importance, but try as she might, she couldn't decipher the meaning of it.

Then, once again, she saw the torn and bloody bodies of her foster sister and mother—and now, in her fevered vision, their eyes were open and staring at her accusingly.

"You!" they seemed to shout. *"You did this! You killed us! Monster! Demon!"*

"Demon . . ." she whispered. Yes, that must be it. It was all her fault. She must be punished. No doubt, Ghost would see to it. She read her punishment in his terrible *smile*, in that expression that seemed to promise all the pain she could bear.

Very well, she thought dully. *No Light left now. All alone. Darkness.* She wanted to cry again, but she couldn't. She had no tears left.

She had reached the bottom of the pit, and she'd done it all by herself.

"Oh, Mother . . ." she whispered.

But there was no reply, and all she could think of was snakes. Huge, black snakes, red-eyed, hissing triumphantly.

Snakes.

He had intended to be gentle in victory. Somewhere, deep inside the wasted desolation that was Ghost's true interior, there still wandered a lost little boy, sobbing in fear. Sometimes, in moments of triumph, that little boy's voice could even be heard—

those moments were as close as Ghost could ever come to empathizing with another human being. But even the feeling he knew at those times wasn't true empathy, in the sense of actually feeling what another person feels. It was more a mathematical exercise: Ghost himself had once been a person—a lost little boy—and these others might also think of themselves as persons—though they weren't, not really—therefore there must be some sort of connection between the two.

Not a connection he could really know, however, and thus even when he tried to bridge that distance it was always a tenuous bridge, easily torn down by the mildest of breezes.

He'd returned to his house after supervising the building of Magic's pyre. There would be a great burning, and he would sing a great song of return for the old man. Whether he believed anything he would put into the song didn't matter at all—they, the others, would believe, and that was all he cared about.

Nevertheless, the physical act of laying out stones, of piling on what dry tinder they could find after the storm, of layering weaves of heavy green logs onto the structure, these tangible evidences of his final victory had put him into an excellent mood.

He'd returned to find Maya lying on her back, still wrapped in her furs, staring dry-eyed at the roof of his house. She'd allowed the fire to smolder down to coals, which irritated him somewhat, cut through the veneer of good cheer he'd been feeling.

The fires could burn now, of course. That had been some crochet of Old Magic's—Ghost doubted whether the instructions to douse the hearths had come from the Spirits anyway. More likely, he guessed, Magic had simply feared the presence of the Other People for reasons of his own, and hoped to escape detection until the Others moved on.

Ghost didn't care. He'd listened carefully to Spear's reports—the camp of the Other People was small. They would have no chance against the much greater numbers of the People of the Mammoth, and already Ghost was beginning to have some ideas about *that*.

Yes, let these invaders find the People. They might be sorry if they did—oh yes, sorry indeed.

"Maya, you let the fire go out."

Mutely, she stared up at him. Her eyes—that alien mixture of blue and green—seemed unfocused, as if they saw him but didn't *see* him, as if somehow he wasn't there.

A stab of fear lanced through his chest. *Those eyes.* But he held himself in and crouched down, until his face was very close to hers.

"Get up now, little Maya. I'm hungry. I want you to cook for me."

She acted as if she didn't hear him, as if she were completely alone in the tent. Her eyes never moved as he spoke, and suddenly his cheerful temper vanished. How *dare* she ignore him, Ghost, who was her complete and total master? She must be (*punished*) made to learn.

"Maya!"

Still the waxen skin, the empty, staring eyes.

Fury twisted his features. He reached out, grabbed a handful of fur, and ripped her blankets away. The force of his gesture rolled her over on her side like a doll—and like a doll she lay there unmoving, mindless, *ignoring* him!

He couldn't *stand* it!

It was only when he tore away her coat in a single huge motion that he realized his penis was throbbing and erect. Like a snake ready to strike.

All his feelings of victory, of magnanimity vanished before the huge well of hate and anger which began to pump behind his eyes. As he sank down on her he grunted, and as he buried himself in her lifeless form, he groaned.

It was only after the blood had begun to flow and she had finally started screaming that he *smiled* again.

It was, after all, only the pain he'd wanted.

Needed.

This he thought as he rode Shewhomhehated, down into the grinning dark.

Chapter Sixteen

Near the Green Valley: 17,983 B.C.

They had come on the heels of the storm, loping into the dawn with tireless stride. Snake had led the seven of them, following Ghost's spoor even after the cleansing rain with animal ease. The Green Valley's mouth had opened before them like a shining mystery. Caribou led them to the nearest wall, as far from the stream which led out of the mouth as he could get.

"I think we should go up," he said.

Rat nodded. It made sense. If there were Others here, as seemed likely, they would live in the valley, not above it. If they were careful, they might be able to approach entirely unobserved—and if they *were* discovered, they would hold the high ground, from which they could throw rocks with terrible effect.

The smaller hunter, his bright eyes reflecting the vast blue light of the empty sky overhead, gestured at a series of ledges which seemed to offer an easy way to the canyon's rim. "That way?"

Caribou nodded thoughtfully. Part of him ached to explore this incredible find; the Green Valley made him long to see its strange trees, to smell the mysterious silvery puffs of smoke-that-wasn't-smoke clearly visible above the forests. But he had his mission. *Find out where it came from*, Broken Fist had said. He wasn't here to explore. He had come to discover the home of the Others—those who already lived here. A shudder of jealousy gripped him then: *already possessed*. The Green Valley could never belong to the Bison People, for the Others had already claimed it.

Can never be mine, he thought, *unless . . .*

But that was for Broken Fist—and the Spirit of Breath—to decide. For once in his life, he hoped the God of Snakes might truly be hungry. That would be one desire he could support wholeheartedly.

But first, they must know what they faced. And there was only one way to do that. "Up," he said. "Quietly."

He followed the rest of the band, his huge spear at the ready. He thought he'd heard the cough of a hunting cave lion somewhere back the way they'd come.

Home Camp, the Green Valley

Maya hurt. Oh, how she hurt.

The sun was approaching its zenith when she finally dragged her bruised and broken body from the bloody tangle of furs on which she lay sprawled like a castoff doll.

Every movement was an agony. Twice she fainted, just trying to sit upright. Finally she managed to prop herself on her right arm. Dimly, through the red fog that kept creeping up on her, she understood that her left arm wouldn't hold her—it was broken, and every time she tried to use it jolts of pain shivered through her dislocated shoulder into her teeth, which would grind together seemingly of their own accord.

"Ughhh . . ." she moaned. The sound came muffled between cracked teeth, between obscenely swollen lips. Below her waist was only a huge, sticky well of anguish. Vaguely, she thought she might still be leaking down there. Surely her lifeblood was flowing out now, not like the slow gush which came with the moon, but a longer, throbbing discharge, a river of blood on which she might soon—mercifully—float away.

When she tried to open her eyes, at first nothing happened. Finally, with an adhesive, sucking sound, her left eyelid managed to break its seal of dried blood, and she saw the interior of Ghost's house through a pink haze. Her right eye wouldn't open at all.

She stared around with dull concentration, trying to piece things together. Not much came—shock and terror and loss of blood had wiped her memory clean. She remembered him falling on her, and then a great, tearing agony between her thighs, and then . . .

Nothing.

Her one good eye stared fixedly at Ghost's blanket pile beyond the smoldering fire. He would come again, she supposed. The thought brought no fear with it—whatever it was in her that allowed fear had been overloaded, short-circuited. In fact, it seemed to her that *everything* inside her had been destroyed. She felt nothing but pain, and a wish . . .

. . . a wish to die.

"Ugghh." She forced her legs beneath her, came up into a kneeling squat. Her head whirled crazily. For an instant she thought the darkness would claim her again, but then the vertigo passed and was replaced by a kind of hard, glittering calm. The calm of purpose.

The purpose of death. The only way out, the only way to end this terrible emptiness. Even existence as a ghost—she supposed that was what would become of her—even that pale and lifeless subsistence as a shade would be better than what she had now.

Now she had nothing but pain. Ghosts didn't feel pain, did they?

"Uggh."

It took her almost an hour, but when the human mind concentrates fully on a goal it can accomplish wonderful things; the sun was just past noon when she finally wobbled upright onto the flat, dusty space in front of Ghost's house. She took a deep breath and tottered forward, down the path to First Lake, toward the trails which led out of Green Valley into the vast, empty steppe. Through her pain she was dimly aware of others, mostly as faint crimson shadows that shied away from her in horror. But nobody said anything, nobody moved to help, nobody impeded in any way her stumbling, lurching journey toward oblivion.

Dusk was falling hard when Caribou motioned them to a stop just beyond the last downfall of the wings of stone that sheltered the green valley. They'd moved quickly; it had only taken a couple of hours to locate the Home Camp of the Mammoth People, snug beneath the shelter of the mighty cliff wall.

Caribou had been shocked at what he'd seen then. This was no straggling band of wanderers; the houses of these Others covered nearly all the open space on the broad ledge between the cliff base and the small lake beyond—and there were more houses there, alongside the water, even hidden back in the fringes of the forest.

People beyond counting! They filled the paths, men, women, many children. There seemed to be a lot of young ones—most too young to matter, but the youths of hunting age were many as well. He spotted the Mystery House for what it was, a gathering place for the men of the tribe, and was appalled at the huge size of it. These People were as numerous as the leaves on the trees; you could drop all of the Bison People into their midst and they would be swallowed up as completely as a stone dropped into a lake.

But Caribou was a great hunter, and he'd known fear before. He quieted the excited whispers of the others, motioned them to lie still in their positions overlooking Home Camp, and gestured Rat forward.

"How many?" he asked softly.

Rat's normally sparkling black eyes were narrow with thought. "Too many," he replied, equally softly.

He's afraid, Caribou thought absently. *Well, so am I.*

"We have to warn Fist."

Rat nodded, though it was obvious that warning the Shaman wasn't uppermost in his quick mind. All Rat wanted to do, Caribou sensed, was get out of there before someone discovered them. But Caribou was the leader and he couldn't allow it, although he sympathized greatly with Rat's desire.

"Cut a branch," he told Rat.

Rat hesitated, then nodded and belly-crawled backward until he was no longer visible from below. Then, crouching, he used his knife to saw and hack a branch from a stand of low shrubs. Sap leaked wetly from the shredded cut. He returned, and handed both the branch and the knife to Caribou, who jerked his head to signify that Rat should retreat again.

What came next was the most dangerous part, and as such, Caribou reserved it for himself. He pulled himself forward until he had an unimpeded view of the activity below. The top of his head was in plain sight, should any of the Others glance up in his direction. He hoped the glare of the sun overhead would be some protection, but he couldn't count on it.

Then, perched precariously, he began to slice a thin cut into the branch for each new Other he saw. He worked as quickly as he could, frozen and uncomfortable. He hoped the single length of branch would be enough.

Now, safely miles distant from that boiling swarm of the People, Caribou motioned them to a stop. After he'd counted as many as he could he'd pulled his men well back, then marched them along the rim-top until they reached a way down near the middle of the valley. This time they'd descended; Caribou still meant to discover the meaning of those strange smokes he'd seen before. He thought this might be the most dangerous part of the journey; but if the mysterious smoke puffs signaled an even larger gathering of Others—ominous thought!—then he, and Fist, had to know about it.

Whatever he might think about the Shaman personally—and they had once been friends—Broken Fist's role in the life of the Bison People was crucially important. Caribou had not yet come round to a full comprehension of his own growing importance—though he sensed that was the reason behind Fist's ever more obvious dislike—but even if he had, he would have understood that the two of them must work together, especially in situations like the present one, where the Bison Tribe might be faced with real and imminent danger.

So he did his duty, although the trek through the looming forest of strange, lushly green trees, with the chatter of squirrels and the screech and chirk of birds in their ears, sent them all along with anxious expressions on their broad, flat faces.

The Lake of Smokes had been another marvel, though Caribou had felt vast relief that the smokes

were natural, and not the vapors from an encamp-
ment even larger than the one at the head of the
valley.

Snake found a trail easily enough. His nose assured them that the path was little used, and not
recently; had he been closer to the lake, he most
likely would have picked up the bloody scent of
Maya's passage, but the two paths wouldn't con-
verge until they became one almost at the valley's
mouth and veered sharply west toward the river.

They halted just before exiting the valley proper,
stars beginning to prick like silver eyes from the
black canopy of night. The men were shadows to
each other; only Caribou, by virtue of his huge bulk,
was distinguishable from the rest.

The sound which froze them, still and watchful,
was terrifying; the deep, guttural roar of a cave lion,
unmistakable in the last of the twilight, and near.

Very near.

The remnants of the path stretched out toward
the gently undulating steppe, now a sea of darkness
stretching toward an almost invisible line, above
which glowed the bright green evening star.

Caribou hefted his massive spear and looked
around uneasily.

"Snake?" he said.

The tiny, doglike man was almost quivering with
excitement and fear. "There!" he hissed. "Right over
there! And . . . something else."

"What?" Caribou was in no mood for vagaries—
lions were bad enough, lions hunting in the dark
potentially disastrous. Long chills of unease rippled
up his spine. There was something very bad about
all this. Cave lions never hunted at night. But the
choking growl had been unmistakable—*something*
was hunting out there.

"Blood," Snake whispered.

Caribou felt a sudden stab of terror. Who knew

what strange and frightful spirits might guard this tribe of Others? Had he managed to arouse them, whatever they were? Was it Spirits hunting now, not lions?

He grasped his spear more firmly, and wished that Fist had come along. Spirits were for the Shaman to deal with, not a hunter, no matter how strong. But Broken Fist wasn't here. The hunter, somehow, would have to deal with it.

"Snake, stay with me. Rat, bring the rest up right behind. Let's go."

Moving together, their eyes glinting white against the rising moon, the small band moved forward along the path.

Nearby, something big yawned.

Maya staggered along the paths, fading in and out of consciousness, though never actually collapsing; even when the darkness overtook her, her legs still somehow managed to keep her moving. Her legs were the only things that moved, however; inside her head only a cold, black silence lay, like a frozen pond, chill and motionless.

After a period of time she would never be able to recall, her aimlessly pumping thighs—so slick and hot down there, so . . . *empty*, brought her to a halt. The overstrained muscles there simply would not support her any longer and, with a low, liquid groan, she sank to her knees and then toppled bonelessly over.

She lay on her side. Her swollen left arm shrieked pain at her, but the pain seemed distant, far away. It had nothing to do with her. She was nearly blind now; her good eye had begun to stick shut, no matter how much she tried to blink intermittent trickles of blood from it; the deep gash above her eyebrow would break open every time she brushed her arm across it, trying to clear her vision.

Dusk began to fill up the silent world; she knew she was farther away from Home Camp than she'd ever been before, but that moaning, querulously demanding voice inside her whispered implacably that it wasn't far enough. Vaguely, she understood that she was still inside the relative safety of the Valley, and her goal was farther away than that. She wanted *outside*, out on the vast empty plain, with the chill winds cutting into her, cooling the restless heat that burned from the inside, until at last she could simply blow away on that wind, a ghost, a shade, the Spirit of evil everybody said she was.

"Uh-*ougha*!"

The low, horrible sound penetrated her fog as perhaps nothing else could have. She knew it well; it shadowed her nightmares.

Mother Lion came a-hunting. Almost, then, she smiled, as much as she could, through broken teeth and swollen lips. Perhaps this would be a better way than even the empty steppe; there was a certain fittingness about death by tooth and claw that appealed to her.

The gelid mass inside her skull shifted slightly as ancient memories came bubbling to the surface of her awareness like poison gas. For her it had all begun then, in the clearing on that hot day. She'd been too young to remember the death of her real mother, but not so her foster mother. Mother Lion had spared her after the grisly dismemberment of Bud and Blossom. Maya's strength hadn't been enough to save them. It wouldn't be enough to save herself now.

Gratefully, she stretched out her right arm. "Guh," she whispered. "Come."

The movement cracked open raw scabs, and fresh blood—the same blood that had summoned the great beast from her jumbled caves not far away—

bloomed its scent into the night. Mother Lion tasted the seductive reek of helplessness, and came.

When it happened, it happened so quickly that even afterward, Caribou was never sure exactly what had occurred. All he knew was that all at once, almost at his elbow, there came a mighty thrashing as something dark and heavy burst like an avalanche through the scrub bordering the path. He saw one of his men go down with a wailing shriek, saw the huge, onrushing shadow, and had barely a moment's time to set the butt of his spear firmly into the soft surface of the path. He was still kneeling down when Mother Lion, a spitting, wailing maelstrom of death, impaled herself upon the flinty point of his weapon.

The shock of her insane charge slammed him backward, but even as he fell he heard her die; it was a low, liquid gurgle and a sighing hiss, as blood rushed into her bellows-lungs and hot, fetid air rushed out.

His spear tip had wreaked havoc inside her, puncturing her right lung before slashing her great heart nearly in half. She was dead even before the weight of her own attack forced her writhing carcass further down the haft of his spear, ripping it from his hands.

He fell beneath her corpse, all the while pushing out wildly with both his hands and his feet, as her rank, muddy fur choked his nose and mouth and the sheer bulk of her blinded his eyes.

They crashed to the ground together. Caribou continued his struggle for several seconds before the realization that she was dead managed to penetrate his screaming awareness.

"Ulff!" he grunted, and shoved once again, the muscles of his shoulders and chest bulging out with the effort. Mother Lion's dead weight shifted slightly, and he managed to get his head out from beneath her stifling carcass.

"Help me!"

He heard rustles in the brush, faint whispers, then Rat's voice, low but clear.

"Caribou?"

"I'm all right!" he called back. "It's dead, the lion is dead, now *get it off me!*"

Suddenly the night came alive with noise. Rat made a sharp, crowing call of triumph. Snake laughed insanely. The others joined in, and Caribou had to shout to make himself heard over the din.

"Be quiet, you fools! We aren't alone here. Be quiet!"

Gradually silence fell, broken only by muffled snorts of effort as the rest struggled to heave the bloody corpse from Caribou's prone form. After a minute of sweaty work Caribou felt the great bulk roll off him, nearly crushing his ribs in the process. He slid his right leg away and pushed himself to his feet. When he looked down, he saw that the lion's limp corpse came nearly to his waist.

Huge, indeed. But a lion, not a Spirit, though it was the largest lion he'd ever seen. He'd been more than lucky this night. Silently, he breathed a prayer of thanks to the Spirit of Breath, who had surely watched over him.

Only after this had been done did he allow himself a moment of thought. It was more than strange, this—all he knew of the mighty saber-toothed beasts told him they *never* hunted after dark. But this one had. Moreover, the cave lions generally avoided man. Yet this huge beast had charged them all. Why?

He would never know the answer to his question, never discover that Mother Lion, over the years, had lost her fear of man; familiarity—the times she'd tasted human blood—had indeed bred contempt. For this was, indeed, the Mother who'd disemboweled

Bud and all but beheaded Blossom and, later, carried away two small children of the People of the Mammoth who'd wandered away from their mothers and never been found again.

She'd become a man-eater, and it was the scent of man-blood and prey that had drawn her, for she'd sensed Maya's helplessness as easily as she might have gauged the exhaustion of a caribou or bison, out on the steppes that matched the color of her pelt so well.

But Caribou would never know, and so he could only shake his head in puzzlement while he waited for his heart to quiet in his chest. The others crowded round, their mouths dark *Ohs!* in their shadowy faces, awed at the monster their great hunter had slain with a single thrust.

Now he shook himself, then bent, grasped the shaft of his spear, and began to rock it back and forth as he pulled it from the mighty carcass.

Rat said, "Breath, that was—close."

Caribou nodded.

"It must have been crazy—or ridden by an evil spirit."

Caribou couldn't say anything to that. The idea paralleled his own uneasy thoughts too closely. His spear came loose with a long, sucking *slurp*. He knelt and wiped the flint head clean on the lion's fur.

For a moment he considered trying to bring a trophy with him—the head would do nicely; he could see the faint white flash of sabered tusks as long as his arm, gleaming in the starlight—but decided they didn't have enough time. Sound carried well on the still night air; who might have heard the sounds of this struggle?

"Let's go," he said, when he'd finished with his weapon.

Grumbling faintly, the rest of the men gathered

round. They wanted trophies as well; great potency lay in the dead body before them, and claws from the beast would take only moments to remove.

But Caribou wouldn't give them that time. He was still not entirely convinced that nothing supernatural had motived the huge beast's attack. And he decided he'd feel a lot better when this mysterious—and fearsome—valley was well behind them.

They'd just begun their trek toward the welcoming emptiness of the steppe when Snake said, "Over there. Don't you hear it?"

Caribou stared at him.

"Something breathing. And . . . blood."

Which was how Black Caribou, Chief of the People of the Bison, discovered Maya, of the People of the Mammoth, and forces of which neither was aware came together once again in their endless battle above and below the World.

Maya woke to find herself floating bumpily along, her face turned toward an overturned bowl of stars. It was the pain that had awakened her and convinced her that, somehow, Mother Lion had spared her one more time.

As for where she was, that was beyond her. She tried to sort out impressions through a prickly fog of hurt; something held her behind her thighs and across her shoulders. The feeling was so unfamiliar that she had to grope back to early childhood to find something similar: *carried*. Someone was *carrying* her. Once she had that part straight, she could piece together the rest. The arms that buoyed her up were big and thickly muscled. Massive lungs labored next to her ear; she tried to open her eyes, but they were still glued shut by dried blood and swelling. Her left arm dangled loose, each movement there playing a carillon of agony across that side of her body.

"Mmmahhh . . ." She tried to speak, but it came

out as a soft moan. The bouncing movement stopped immediately. Dull, booming sounds, rhythmic but incomprehensible, filled her ears. *Words*, she thought dimly. Someone was speaking, but she couldn't make sense of any of it.

Caribou looked down at his burden. He was having more than second thoughts about her. The moon had come up and turned the steppe into an undulating silver plain, but even his sharp eyes couldn't make out fine detail; he'd seen enough, though, to know that this strange young woman had been terribly injured. The dark shadows that marked her face, and the soft swellings he felt there, as well as the odd, loosely bent shape of her left arm, made him wonder if he wasn't carrying little more than a corpse-to-be.

At least the lion hadn't gotten her. The coincidence seemed providential to him. What had she been doing out there, far from her people, broken-limbed and fainting? Perhaps it was an omen, or even a gift from the God of Snakes. Whatever, he couldn't simply leave her there. Better to bring her to Broken Fist, and let him worry about it. He'd scooped her up and bones had ground together in her ruined arm, loud enough for him to hear the faint, scratchy sound. She'd uttered one sharp yelp, then gone entirely limp. *Better for her*, he'd thought at the time.

He'd carried her across miles of steppe. Carrying her had caused him to go more slowly than he'd wished to, but they'd made good time anyway. Nothing seemed to be following them, though in the dark it had been hard to tell. Now, as the moon lowered toward the horizon, a flat gray sheen was beginning to light up the horizon behind them— false dawn, soon to be followed by the real thing.

She twisted weakly in his arms, making soft, mewling sounds. "There, little woman. Soon you can rest," he rumbled, in what he hoped was a soothing voice.

He could just barely see her lips move, see her tongue creep slowly between them, and he understood. "Rat," he said. "Soak a bit of fur in your water."

Rat came up and handed him a piece he'd torn from the corner of his jacket and dipped in his water bag. "Put it in her mouth," Caribou instructed.

Wordlessly, Rat obeyed. Caribou could sense the smaller man's disquiet, but he ignored it. He could deal with Rat. The woman tasted the moisture and grunted softly. Her lips—he could tell they were swollen—moved over the supple fur, sucking at it. She quieted then.

Caribou sighed. "Let's go," he said.

She was light as a bird. Once again, he wondered what had happened to her. Time would tell. If she lived, perhaps she would tell him herself.

For some obscure reason, the idea pleased him. Carrying her brought back good memories of happier times with his sister.

Snake, who had been running point, darted back. His teeth were a broad line in his dark face. "Not long now," he announced. They'd been paralleling the river, heading north, for some time.

Caribou grunted. His arms were beginning to ache, though he had no intention of surrendering his burden. Already he'd begun to think of her as his.

His find. His . . . woman.

His.

Home Camp, the Green Valley

Ghost thought how nice it would be to curl the fingers of his right hand into hooks, slide his fingernails into the soft space beneath Spear's eyes, and rip down, tearing the flesh of his cheeks away from his skull like the skin of a slaughtered caribou. He almost could *see* the pattern of raw red meat and shiny white tendon that would be revealed. He quivered faintly with the beautiful thought of it, but Spear didn't notice. His stony features remained disapproving.

"She went down the path toward the forest," Spear said flatly, as if describing the fall of turds from the asshole of a bison.

Ghost had spent most of the day in the Spirit House, readying Magic's body for the fire the next day. Whatever he thought of the Old Shaman, certain things had to be done properly; the powerful spirits which had guarded the old man must be appeased, if only because their anger would be sure to fall on the new Shaman. Moreover, Ghost knew that other eyes would watch him, eyes searching for any lapse in the correct burial rites—Old Berry might have submitted to him outwardly, but she remained an enemy and she still retained her most potent weapon: the gossip of the women.

So he had done all the correct things, though they had taken much time; the preparation of the body itself, the long, dolorous chants, the supervision of the building of Magic's pyre. Finally, at dusk, he'd returned to his own house to find Maya gone.

And now this great hulk of a hunter was telling him that half the village had seen her go, but nobody had thought to stop her, or even to inform Ghost of her leaving.

Yes, it would be very nice to flay Spear alive with a dull scraper, then scoop out his guts and stuff them down his screaming throat. Slowly.

Ghost drew in a shuddering breath and *smiled*. Spear looked away. "Very well then, Spear. When did she go?"

Spear told him. He had watched her stagger away, of course, and thought at the time, "Good riddance." Now he sensed he might have made some sort of mistake. Rage was baking off Ghost in almost visible waves, and Spear was only now coming to realize that Ghost was considerably more upset than he expected him to be.

Which puzzled him. Why was Ghost so angry? Anybody with eyes could see that the new Shaman had always hated the girl. For years he'd treated her like the dirt under his feet. Spear thought, with good reason, that had Ghost been able to circumvent Old Magic's protection of the girl, Maya would not have survived a week. But now, all that seemed changed.

It made him surly and stubborn. "She went at noon. Why do you care, Ghost? She was an evil Spirit. Even you said so. Why do you want an evil Spirit in the home of the People?"

For the first time, Ghost felt the full weight of the Secret. He knew what Maya was, and why he had to have her. She was Shewhomhehated, made powerless, and she must be *kept* that way. But she'd escaped somehow. He felt a ripple of terror—was it an accident? Or was the Terrible Mother at work again, hatching Her plots against him?

But he could say nothing of this to Spear. The Secret must remain secret. Almost then, he felt a flicker of sympathy for what Old Magic must have undergone, in his own stewardship of the awful legacy.

He forced himself to slow down, to make his voice sound calm and reasonable. "Spear," he said, "Maya was indeed ridden by an evil spirit. But I am Shaman, and I know how to deal with such things. You saw her?"

Spear nodded truculently.

"Spirits must be driven away. I was doing that."

Spear recalled Maya's blood, her sickening bruises, the loose, flapping slant of her arm, and shivered inwardly. If *he'd* been an evil spirit, he certainly would have abandoned such a broken vessel. "Yes," he said.

"Well, then. I hadn't finished. No doubt the spirit led her to escape. Now it's out there somewhere, free. We must find her, catch her, bring her back. So I can finish my work, and destroy this threat to the People forever. Do you understand me?"

Reluctantly, Spear nodded. He did understand, no matter how much distaste he felt at bringing the doomed girl back.

"Good," Ghost said, and *smiled* again. "Will you get some men together? She shouldn't be hard to find. She can't have gone far, not the way she was."

Again, Spear nodded his head. No, she couldn't have gotten far. Most likely, she was dead by now. The thought didn't displease him at all. Yes, that was the likeliest outcome; and if they could find her corpse, then perhaps Ghost would calm down. Spear didn't like the way the Shaman was smiling at him. There was a fever behind his dark eyes, and his teeth seemed way too big.

"I'll get Skin. And Wolf," he decided. "That should be enough."

"Good. Get going," Ghost said. He paused. "But wait for me. I'll come with you."

The first stars were coming out when they loped off down the path. But they didn't find her. Not that night. In fact, not for a long time. And when they did, many things had changed.

Chapter Seventeen

Bison People River Camp: 17,982 B.C.

Spring came early that year. By the end of the fourth moon the river ice sheets were breaking up with great, booming cracks, choking the rushing waters with jagged icebergs and sending up tall plumes of white spray.

Caribou led out a party of hunters and returned three days later, carrying huge packs of meat from the kill only half a day's journey beyond the river. The women had gone out and joyfully retrieved enough food to succor the Bison People for many hands of days.

The omens were good, although they hadn't seemed so at first. When he'd first returned from his foray into the Green Valley, Caribou had been afraid that terrible things were in store for the Bison Tribe, but it had not been so.

The first seemingly bad omen had been that they'd lost Squirrel in the darkness of the battle with Mother Lion. By the time they'd discovered his absence, it was too late to go back for him. The second bad omen had been the woman herself. Caribou had feared she too would die—viewed by the cold light of day, her injuries were terrible. She'd drifted in and out of consciousness, while Broken Fist set her broken arm and anointed her wounds with magic salves. Caribou himself, with a single, jerking twist, had pushed her shoulder joint back into its socket— the woman had fainted again when he did it, and he'd thought for a time she might never awaken again.

Yet, somehow, the woman had survived. Fevers wracked her, and she wasted away until her bones showed through her skin like sticks, but she never quite drifted away. Finally, after three weeks, she awoke clear-eyed for the first time.

The cuts on her face and the swellings around her eyes and broken jaw were gone by then; two of her front teeth were broken out, but when she smiled up at Caribou he thought she was beautiful.

Her eyes, for one thing; the Bison People were not as homogenous a stock as the People of the Mammoth; eyes other than black were not completely unknown, and there was no automatic spiritual proscription against them. Caribou thought Maya's green and blue gaze odd, but attractive. It caused little comment otherwise, except among the women, to whom it was obvious that Caribou had taken a wife. But even that jealousy waned with the onset of winter, and when Maya fell sick again, coughing and spitting up glistening ropes of saliva, the women nursed her without complaint.

Once again Caribou thought he might lose her, but as before, some force inside her wouldn't let Maya die. The fevers and coughing lasted almost a week, and she was listless and dull for two more weeks, but after that she began to gain weight and take an interest in her new surroundings.

The first storm of winter had howled down on the River Camp in the night, and when the People awoke their world had turned to white. But they had chosen their site well, and the rocky banks of the river protected them from the worst of the weather. The hunters had been lucky, and much dried meat was laid away. If they wanted water, they only needed to hack an opening in the river ice; a small stand of trees a bit upstream provided wood. All things considered, Caribou thought, the Spirit of Breath had done well by his people.

And by me, too, he thought suddenly, as he gazed at the thin, quiet woman who sat on a log in front of his tent, quietly sewing a patch on his fur jacket.

"Maya" was her name. He knew that now. In the long, dark silences of the cold time, he had patiently taught her to speak the language of the People. She'd taken to it quickly, though sometimes her tongue still slipped on an unfamiliar shaping of sound. Nevertheless she spoke easily, and there were times when Caribou almost forgot how she'd come to him in the first place.

She speaks easily, he reflected, as the first rays of spring sunshine washed over her dark hair, turning it red in places as she bent to her work. *But she doesn't speak much.* He sensed a darkness in her that he was reluctant to probe. She claimed to remember nothing of how she'd come to be on the path that night, nor did she recall what had happened to cause her injuries.

In fact, Maya claimed to remember very little even about her own people. Broken Fist had spent much time, at first, quizzing her about the camp Caribou had discovered. But Maya, in slow, halting speech, hadn't offered much help. The People are the People, seemed to be the extent of her knowledge. Where they'd come from, how many of them there were, which Spirits ruled them—all this was a mystery to her.

Fist hadn't believed her protests of ignorance at first, but Caribou had taken him aside. "Remember how she was when I brought her in? The lumps on her head, the cuts and bruises? I think a Spirit has stolen her memory."

Fist had looked thoughtful at that. It was, he supposed, entirely possible. He'd seen such things happen before. He didn't entirely give up then, but his interrogations became fewer and farther between, and finally tailed off entirely.

Winter deepened into ice-locked hell, but life remained snug and comfortable in the camp of the Bison People. It was, Caribou thought, one of the best winters he could remember, and gradually, his sense of ominous foreboding began to leave him.

Now, with spring breezes bringing the smell of green grass to his nose, his thoughts turned to his own future, and to hers. He supposed they would be moving on soon—the few moons of summer were the best time for travel—and though a part of him regretted leaving the mystery of the Green Valley, another part looked forward to the trek, to the long hunt, to new places and sights.

Also, Maya's belly had begun to swell. Not much, though; it would be many days before she dropped her child, and he guessed the People would be safely in their new winter camp by then.

As soon as Maya's health had returned, Caribou had raped her as a matter of course. She'd neither fought him nor protested, merely submitted with dull resignation. But later, rape had turned to pleasure or so it seemed. She'd begun to respond, at first in tiny ways, later with more enthusiasm.

She was a full-grown woman. And although neither of them made any connection between the sex act and pregnancy, she was healthy enough. Now there was a child growing in her womb, and she knew it. The other women had finally understood that her knowledge in the area was deficient, and had been happy to fill in the gaps—not even her bouts with morning sickness, when she would suddenly be overcome with nausea, bothered her much anymore.

Maya glanced up from her work and saw Caribou staring at her with a slight grin on his face. She smiled back. Caribou made her feel comfortable. He made her feel happy, in fact, and that was the hardest thing to get used to.

She had no idea how she'd come to the People of the Bison, beyond what Caribou had told her. There were long black swatches of emptiness inside her skull. The last thing she remembered clearly was Old Magic, though she had a vague intimation that the ancient Shaman was somehow departed. She remembered nothing of his death, and even the existence of Ghost had been wiped from her recollections as if he'd never been.

Without knowing it, almost all of her old miserable life had gradually slipped away. She might occasionally remember flashes of Wolf, or Bud, or Blossom, people whom she'd loved, but only snatches, without context. She didn't mind. Without a past she must live in the present, and she found her new life remarkably fulfilling.

The other women treated her well. Foggily she thought this was a new thing, but she didn't understand why. And so she accepted their friendship as her due, since nobody seemed to find it strange. She even, when she began to understand it, gloried a bit in their admiration; for she'd finally deciphered that Caribou was a man of importance to the Bison People, and as such, she shared his stature.

Again it was a new feeling, but one she willingly accepted. Only in her dreams, which on occasion awakened her in the night with muffled screams, did she sense the tiniest fraction of the pit that had been her previous life. But with the morning light even those half-recalled horrors would fade, and the dreams themselves seemed to occur with less and less frequency.

"Caribou," she said. "You need a new coat." She lifted the much-worn fur garment and shook it gently. "See. It's all patches. There's nothing left for me to sew."

"I like it," he told her. He moved next to her and squatted down, a small grin wrinkling his blocky features. "Do you want to make another?"

She shrugged. "If you bring me the skins . . ."

He nodded. "The caribou will begin to move soon. They are dropping their calves now, and when the young ones are old enough, the great herds will gather." He lifted his head and gazed off across the river, at the long, rolling waves of fresh green grass. "We'll leave this place then—to follow the herds. Caribou and bison. Have you ever seen them, Maya?"

She glanced down at him. His massive shoulders were hunched, his big forearms crossed over his knees. He was still gazing at the steppe, his eyes shadowed and distant, and she sensed that he saw the herds now, thunderous and vast, in his mind's eye. She couldn't imagine what they might be like.

"No," she said softly, "but I'd like to."

They sat like this for several minutes, her fingers working of their own accord, he lost in his thoughts, comfortable. The sun, still thin and watery with spring, warmed them; she could hear the sounds of the camp—the thin, high laughter of the children, the women calling to one another, an occasional shout from where a group of hunters were casting spears at a distant bush—and for one instant wished it would never end. Though Maya had few memories left in her poor, raddled brain, what she did recall was enough to make this moment seem even more burnished. *It's peaceful*, she thought. *That's all it is, peaceful.*

She sighed and touched Caribou's shoulder gently. "Here comes Fist," she said.

Caribou's eyes refocused on the approaching Shaman. Broken Fist was naked to the waist, the sun gleaming on his slender, muscular chest and back. He was smiling as he approached.

"Ho, Caribou!" he called.

Caribou raised his right hand in greeting. "Fist," he replied.

The medicine man came up and squatted down next to Caribou. He nodded at Maya, but didn't greet her personally. She still felt a little afraid of him—his first interrogations hadn't been very gentle, and at the time she'd been completely unable to withstand his shouted questions. Later, after he'd begun to lose interest in her, a new relationship had formed. Now, she understood, he regarded her simply as an extension of her man, and therefore paid little attention to her.

She didn't mind. Broken Fist still frightened her a bit. She wasn't sure why. Perhaps it had more to do with *what* he was—a Shaman—than who he was. Maya didn't think she liked Shamans very much, though she had no idea why.

"A good day, Fist," Caribou said.

The Shaman rocked back and forth on his wiry haunches, nodding agreement. He obviously had something on his mind. Caribou waited. Finally Broken Fist clapped his hands together once, an oddly formal gesture.

"I want you to go back to the Green Valley," he said. "Take some of the hunters—Snake, perhaps, and Rat. Go look, then come back and tell me what you see."

Caribou stared at him. "Why?"

"I have spoken with Spirits," Fist replied, surprised at the question. "There are things I need to know."

"To know about what?"

Fist curled his fingers into fists and twisted them back and forth. "I'm not sure," he said at last. "I've had dreams. Perhaps we will move to the Green Valley, instead of traveling down the river." He stopped, then glanced brightly at Caribou. "The Spirit of Breath wishes it. When will you leave?"

Caribou, though his mind was suddenly boiling with surprise, kept his expression blank. *Move to the Green Valley? What can Fist be thinking of? But it doesn't really matter, does it? If the Spirit of Breath demands it, what choice do I have?*

"Tomorrow, with first light," he said, after a few seconds' thought.

"That's good," Fist said. He stood up, spared one further glance for Maya, and said, "Make sure your man has a warm coat for the journey," he told her. Then, graceful as a hunting cat, he turned and walked away.

Maya glanced at Caribou. "What does he want?"

Caribou rose. "I don't know."

She carefully placed the finished patch job on the log beside her. "It's ready," she told him. He picked up the coat, examined it, nodded, and grinned at her.

"Be careful," she told him.

"I will," he replied.

The Green Valley

Ghost picked his way slowly along the nearly deserted paths of Home Camp, the spring sunshine glittering on First Lake and casting bright, painful barbs into his eyes. Those few of the People out and about in the early morning—mostly women—avoided him, their eyes downcast.

He clambered down the jagged, boulder-strewn

embankment that led to the water, and seated himself on a handy rock. Across the tiny lake, a single stream of smoke rose like a white exclamation point from the huddle of houses set back into the trees there.

Only one, he thought. Once, the Camp would have been full of hustle and bustle, the women about their tasks, the men telling stories, the children laughing and tumbling about. Now there was only a hushed, fearful silence, and a single strand of smoke.

He wondered how long it would take for the remaining People of the Mammoth to find enough courage to kill him. Not long, he judged. The disaster was nearly complete; soon enough, he thought, it would come to its inevitable end—with his own death. Only the mystical power of his position had saved him thus far, and that power was sadly eroded now.

He hunched forward, to wrap his scrawny arms around his shins and rest his chin on his knees. Beyond the forlorn group of empty huts yawned the dark mouth of the main path that led on to Smoke Lake. He squinted at the opening and remembered the terrible night which, as far as he knew, had marked the beginning of the catastrophe that was now slowly winding to its inevitable end.

He, Spear, Skin, and young Wolf had set out in the dark, expecting to find Maya wandering aimlessly through the forest or perhaps collapsed on the path itself. But they hadn't, not right away, and when the path forked in two—one trail leading down through the marshes around Second Lake, the other meandering off through the darkened forest— Skin had spent long moments before finally deciding "There." He'd pointed toward the left-hand way, which led toward the water of Second Lake and, finally, Smoke Lake.

But Maya had neither been near Second Lake nor, as far as they could tell, had she wandered from the trail into the bogs and quicksands that bordered it. Skin led the way, pausing frequently to squat, sniff, and feel. He was ancient, but the People had no better tracker. Ghost marked down the growing reluctance he sensed in the older man to Skin's obvious distaste for anything dealing with the subject of his renounced daughter.

But they'd gone on, moving through the eerie dark—Ghost could *smell* the Spirits drifting, clacking dryly, in the shadows beyond the path—until they saw the spectral plumes of steam rising from Smoke Lake on their left.

Spear had brought them to a halt. "Do you think she could have gotten this far, Ghost?" he asked uneasily. "She . . . didn't look like she could."

Ghost paused, listening to the long sigh of wind through black leaves, to the chitter of the Spirits. They'd seen no sign of her, beyond a few footprints Skin had picked up from the jumble of the path, and even those had disappeared far back. Could she have gotten this far? Ghost was amazed she'd even been able to rise from her furs. But she had, and now she was gone. The thought made him want to tear his hair in rage.

It wasn't Maya who had escaped. It was *Shewhomhehated*, his rider, whom he'd finally conquered—or had he? The terrible Goddess rode *her* now, and She was capable of *anything*. And if he couldn't find Maya, then She would triumph once again.

"Yes," he grated. "She could have come this far. Even farther—the evil Spirit within her is very strong." He made up his mind. "Let's go," he said. "We'll find her."

Spear nodded, thinking that Ghost was more than a little crazy—the girl *couldn't* have reached this point, not the beaten, broken, shambling girl he'd seen—but then, Ghost was the expert on Spirits. Perhaps a Spirit—an evil one—could have brought her this far. He shrugged.

"We'll go as far as the Lion Caves," he decided. "I don't want to roam around there too much, not after dark with only four of us."

Ghost nodded. He wasn't frightened of lions. But he was terrified that Maya might escape once again. "Good," he said. The party moved on.

They'd progressed perhaps another mile when they heard the mewling shriek of Mother Lion as she impaled herself on Caribou's spear. The sound froze them. They stared at each other in the growing light of the stars. "What was that?" Ghost whispered.

"Hunting lion. Something got it," Spear said tersely.

Then Skin raised his hand. "Listen," he said.

The sound was faint, but after a moment of concentration, all of them heard it clearly enough. A male voice, screaming in terror.

"The Others!" Ghost hissed.

Spear looked unhappy. "Yes," he agreed.

"Let's go," the Shaman urged.

But Spear put one big hand on his chest. "No," he replied. "No further. I don't know who—or what—is out there. We'll come back in the daylight. With more hunters," he said.

His voice was adamant, and even Ghost had to admit Spear was right. Chasing off into the dark, now that they knew invaders had penetrated the Green Valley, was madness. Even through his own madness, Ghost could see it.

Then a thought brightened him. Perhaps Maya had gone this way, only to succumb to the spears of the Others. It was certainly a possibility, and even crazed as he was with lust for her death, Ghost didn't look forward to running into that party of trespassers, in the dark, with only four of them.

The heat in his chest began to cool. Finally he

shrugged. "All right. We'll go back. But we return tomorrow, with the rest of the men. Agreed?"

Wolf said, "What about Maya?"

Ghost remembered—sometimes he forgot—that Wolf's feelings about his sister weren't always as hostile as the Shaman would have liked. Why had he brought him along, anyway?

He pushed the thought away. "Her, too," he snarled. "We'll find her in the morning, too."

There was little more to say. Another round of shouts—first of triumph, then of anger—stiffened their backs. They stared at each other, eyes rolling whitely. Then they turned back the way they'd come. After a time, all returned to silence.

And so Caribou had carried Maya's battered form far out onto the steppe by the time the great party of hunters—all the able-bodied men Home Camp had been able to muster—finally discovered the huge, flyblown carcass of Mother Lion lying in a sticky puddle of her own blood. But it was Skin, trying to decipher the welter of tracks around the huge sabertooth, who discovered Darting Squirrel's body, and called Ghost over.

"Shaman! Over here!"

Ghost had left off his dour examination of the big cat, and limped over to the smaller scout where he crouched back in the bushes. "What? Oh . . ."

Skin squatted near the dead man's head. He looked up. "I don't know what got this one," he said. "Wasn't the lion."

Ghost nodded, and knelt down for a better look. The face of the Other man was composed in death. His open eyes stared glassily. A thick, cracking coat of yellow mucus coated his upper lip and trailed off down his cheeks. Bloody froth had dried at the corners of his lips. But the plague germs in that blood were still active enough.

Ghost reached out and touched the skin. Cold,

and already going soft in the morning heat. A huge green fly buzzed down and began to walk across the dead man's right eyeball.

Ghost licked his lips. There were many subtle differences about this Other—his garments were sewn in an alien manner, the seams done differently than those of the Mammoth People. In one gnarled hand this hunter still grasped his spear—Ghost noted that the spear head was larger, clumsier than those carried by the People. Nor did this one have a spear-thrower in his kit.

There were many things Ghost would have liked to ask squirrel, but the Bison man was dead. Ghost sighed. He turned to Skin. "Maya?" he said.

Skin shrugged. "Can't tell. The ground's a mess here, all trampled. There were six or seven men stomping around—and the lion, too."

Ghost looked at Darting Squirrel's corpse again. A mystery. The dead cave lion, felled with a single mighty stroke, but undefiled. No trophies taken. No Maya anywhere to be found. And this one, dead, of no discernible cause.

What had happened here? He began to think he might never know.

The wind shifted, turned ponderously from the north, and rose, moaning as it swooped low over the canyon rims. Far out over the steppe clouds were forming, painted gold and purple by the light. The clouds had low, heavy bellies, full of darkness.

Winter coming, Ghost thought. It made him feel lonely, and very frightened. Something had happened here, but he didn't know what. He guessed it didn't bode well, though; not for the People, and not for him.

He wasn't wrong.

Now, he stared blankly at the spring-freshened waters of First Lake, and the desolate huddle of houses beyond. Even in his wildest dreams, he could not have guessed the extent of the disaster to come.

Nor had it taken long to make itself known. Less than three days after the discovery of the slaughtered cat, one of Skin's women had come to the Spirit House where Ghost now lived. Old Magic was only two days in the fire, his memory still fresh, but Ghost hadn't waited. He understood the value of symbols. Whoever lived in the Spirit House was the Shaman—therefore, he would live there.

The woman had crept up quietly, and waited until Ghost had finished grinding up a dark blue powder between two smooth stones. When he was finished, he looked up at her. "What is it?" he asked.

"Skin," the woman said. "Something's wrong with Skin. A Spirit, I think. Can you come?"

He'd easily heard the undercurrent of terror in her voice. Skin was old—but whatever was wrong with him was more than old age.

"Give me a minute," Ghost had told her. "I'll be there."

Skin didn't know him when he arrived. The tracker was already delirious. The heat which baked off his forehead was almost too hot for Ghost to touch. And Skin coughed, long, racking sounds, and sprayed sticky tentacles of snot from his nose and mouth. Already the glistening, clear stuff was showing hints of pink.

His women were gathered round, the three wives he still shared with Stone; their black eyes were worried circles in their faces. Stone himself came in, looked at his old friend, then at Ghost.

"Is it an evil Spirit?" he wondered.

"Perhaps," Ghost said abruptly. "Everybody get out. I must do things."

Willingly, they emptied the tent, leaving the Shaman alone with the dying man who would be the first test of his new authority and skill.

Ghost emptied his medicine bag, took out a small arrowhead, a rattle, the rest of his tools. He closed his eyes, searching for a path to the Spirit which possessed Skin, which was sucking his life out right before his eyes. After a time he took up the rattle, shook it, and began to chant.

His song was low and tentative. Already he felt doom hovering over his shoulders, looking down, grinning at him.

Doom took the form of a woman.

Almost as if She were riding him.

Ghost shuddered faintly, and kept on with his efforts to banish this new, evil Spirit.

Twenty-four hours later, when Skin hacked up a huge, bloody chunk of grayish-white lung, expelled the thin, sour contents of his bowels, and died, he knew that he had failed.

It would be the first of many failures.

In fact, he thought, as he stared over the flowing ripples that marked First Lake, *I was lucky to save any of them.* Ghost believed in Spirits, but in a strange way. Since he knew what it was like to be ridden by Shewhomhehated, he couldn't deny the possibility of other Spirits sinking their deadly claws into their own chosen victims. But since he didn't comprehend the basic humanity of those victims, his comprehension of their possession was equally weakened—Spirits eating spirits was as close as he could come. He believed, but he didn't Believe—nor did he think Magic had believed, either. Not in anything but the Great Secret.

But that was destroyed, wasn't it? He picked up a pebble and tossed it far out over the waters, where it sank with a soft *kerplunk!* into a widening circle of tiny ripples. The Secret was gone, broken, its pieces scattered to the rivers, to the winds, to . . . wherever Maya had gone.

Dead, no doubt, he consoled himself. She had

been terribly wounded. He knew it, he had done it, beaten her with cold glee even as he'd raped her again and again, shattered the arm she raised weakly to protect her face, then broke out her teeth and scarred her face, all the time perfectly aware of what he was doing, all the time *smiling*.

He should have killed her then, he knew, but he'd wanted time to enjoy his victory. The same old mistake.

No, of course she was dead. He clutched his knees and rocked back and forth and told himself again that yes, she was dead, the Secret was gone, all was well.

He rocked faster and faster, repeating his own words to himself until his eyes became slits and his teeth ground silently together and, finally, he almost tipped over.

The seizure passed as quickly as it had come. He sat perfectly still then, feeling his own sweat cooling on his back, tasting the copper of his own blood in his mouth.

Finally he sighed and dragged himself to his feet. There was a chance, perhaps. If he was quick and persuasive. He would have to deal with Spear, but he thought he could. Spear and Wolf. For some reason, the Spirits had left them alone.

In the chill aftermath of his convulsion, he finally accepted the truth he'd denied ever since Maya had stumbled, battered and broken, from Home Camp into the dark.

Shewhomhehated still lived.

In the winter, from the time she'd disappeared until now, with spring cracking and bubbling about, fully three-quarters of the People of the Mammoth— the very old and the very young first, then, gradually, even the strongest of adults—had hacked their lives out onto their bloody chins.

Shewhomhehated still lived, and Her revenge was terrible.

He wondered if he had enough time left.

"The evil Spirits come from the Others," Ghost said. He kept his voice low and firm. He sat inside the Spirit House, all the totems of his power and authority ranged about him. Spear and Wolf squatted across from him. Spear's dark eyes were flat and hostile. Wolf only nodded, his features blank.

"They took Maya and her demon with them. Now they work magics against us." He raised his eyes to glare at Spear. "You let her escape, Spear. See what you have done."

It was an ancient ploy, this resettling of guilt, but Ghost knew he had to try it. Spear was essential— what authority still remained with the shattered People rested on his burly shoulders. His and Wolf's.

The charge rocked the older hunter. "I didn't know what you were doing! How can you blame me?"

"You were *afraid* of her. That's why you didn't stop her. If you had, then"—Ghost shook his head in mock despair—"none of this would have happened. But I forgive you, Spear. And I offer you a chance to make good your mistake."

Spear chewed at his lower lip, absorbing this. He had lost both his wives and all his children. He was alone, and fearful. Privately, he had his own understanding of events. Ghost might rant and rave about the disappearance of the girl as the beginning of the winter of terror, but Spear remembered another event that had occurred at the same time.

Yes, Maya had disappeared, but so had Old Magic. Spear wondered if that was a coincidence. He didn't think so. Nothing like this had happened as long as the dead Shaman had been there to make his magic. The Spirits had been good then. Only after his death and replacement by the younger man across from him, whose cheeks were sunken and whose eyes burned, had the disasters begun.

But he couldn't be certain. And Ghost was exactly right; he hadn't stopped Maya because she *had* frightened him, as she lurched bleeding and vacant through the Camp like a bloody specter.

He thought some more. Already he had considered a plan; murdering Ghost might be a dangerous thing, for it would leave the tribe without a Shaman. The foolish boy whom Ghost had taken in training was nowhere near ready to assume such a role. But if the Shaman was the cause of all their misery, then perhaps having no Shaman at all would be better than their present plight.

Yes, it was an appealing idea: simply plunge his spear into Ghost's body, then gather the remnants of the People and lead them away from this demon-ridden valley forever.

But if he was wrong? Then he would be leading those who were left to their deaths.

He didn't know. And so he decided to wait, to test one final time the strength of their magic man. After all, his spear would have grown no duller in a few more days.

"What do you want me to do?" he said at last.

Ghost nodded, as if he'd expected no other reply, though inside, his rapidly beating heart had begun to slow. "Take men and find the camp of the Others. If they have the devil woman, I have to know about it."

Spear glanced at Wolf, who shrugged. Maya was becoming dim in his memory. Somehow he thought she wasn't dead, but with equal certainty, he thought she was gone. Gone forever, perhaps.

"Yes," Spear said. "We will do this."

Thus did the two Shamans, each unbeknownst to the other, sow the seeds of war in the springtime of the world. This they shared, and one other thing: their dreams, which were full of fire and the snake that lived within.

The Snake whose eyes glittered with red hunger, in the darkness of their nights.

Chapter Eighteen

Above the Green Valley: 17,982 B.C.

Caribou crawled to the brink of the overhang and looked down; the group of several men behind him were crouched as they had been before, on the first journey. Overhead the sky flared perfectly blue beneath a blazing white sun. Caribou kept his head low and hoped to blend into the ragged lip of stone. He discovered immediately that he needn't have worried.

No one below looked up at the sky. Those few who dispiritedly walked the paths of Home Camp kept their heads down. He saw three women carrying baskets around the fringe of First Lake, where before he'd seen twenty. The women moved slowly, and picked their way like sleepwalkers.

He glanced at the men's Mystery House. Two men sat on a log there; they looked like lonely birds perched on the solitude of empty benches. As he watched, one of the men poked at the small fire that filled only a quarter of the huge hearth in which it sat.

Something terrible had happened to the strange People. Was this what Broken Fist had meant? Had the Shaman known of this, or only guessed?

Caribou pulled himself back and whispered softly to Rat: "Take a look."

The smaller man hitched himself to the brink, peeped over, then froze in concentration. He lay like this for almost five minutes, then nodded to himself and retreated. "Where did they go?" he asked.

Caribou wrinkled his forehead. "Go? I don't think they *went* anywhere. Did you see all those piles of burned branches, those pits?"

Rat nodded and licked his lips. The People of the Bison knew about pits. "Dead . . . ?"

Caribou nodded. "I think so."

Rat shook his head. "So many? What could have happened?"

The chief shrugged. "I don't know. Maybe Fist does. He sent us."

Rat's eyes widened. "He *must* have known," he said. Awe filled his voice. If Fist had known, could he have *done* this? Rat recalled the Shaman's startling prediction: that the Bison People might move to the Green Valley instead of trekking downriver. Fist must have known, or suspected, *something* like this.

"We should get back. He'll want to know right away."

"Yes," Caribou said. He considered. "I want another look," he said. He crawled forward again. This time he saw the wide door flap of the Mystery House open and three men emerge. Two of them were older hunters, the third young and in his prime. Something about the young one ticked a cog of memory, but Caribou couldn't chase down the errant hint. The three men paused. They seemed to wait for something. After a moment, a fourth man came out of the House.

Caribou licked his lips. This was a new one, one he'd searched for on his previous visit but had not been able to locate. The newest arrival wore a headpiece made of caribou antlers, and a long, beautiful coat. He carried a small drum, which he began to beat with the fingers of his right hand.

The Shaman of the Other People. Caribou noticed he limped. He thought of Broken Fist's deformity. The drumming ceased, and the Shaman began to speak rapidly to the three men. He seemed to exhort them. Finally the oldest of the three, a hulking man almost Caribou's size, replied. There was a flat, brutal quality to the way the big man gestured; his hands chopped once, then again.

Whatever it had been about, the conversation ended. As one, the small group turned and loped down the path toward first Lake. They carried spears and packs, but Caribou thought they were too small for a hunting party. There was a purpose to their steady pace that the chief recognized. These were men setting out on a trek. Caribou thought he could guess what their journey's goal would be. He pushed back from the brink again.

"Quickly," he whispered. "And quiet. Back along the cliff tops. I want to get to the valley mouth before they do."

"Who?" Rat asked.

"Three of them," Caribou told him. "I think they're looking for us."

Spear, Stone, and Wolf had broken straight north, angling across the steppe toward a point above the Other People's river camp. They moved quickly, a small band beneath the huge sky, and had reached the waters which still boiled with ice melt by nightfall. They camped rudely, sleeping in their furs, and didn't light a fire. Morning woke them chill and sluggish; Wolf went down to river's edge, crouched on damp stone, and lifted a palmful of water to his lips.

"Cold," he said. Spear, squatting next to him,

said, "Hurry up. I want to reach their camp before the sun crosses the sky."

Wolf nodded. Stone, gathering up the last of his breakfast scraps, went about his work silently. A crow cawed harshly above them, disturbed at their presence. Wolf glanced up and shivered. The black bird swooping above their heads seemed an evil omen.

"Do you think she's there?" he asked.

Spear cocked a grizzled eyebrow. "Your sister?" He didn't seem happy with the thought. "Could be, I guess. We never found her. Though that doesn't mean much. There are bogs in the valley. Or a lion could have dragged her off."

Wolf finished his ablutions. "I hope she's there," he said.

"Why?" Spear hoped the opposite. The Shaman's obsession with the missing girl was evidence to him of Ghost's failing influence. What could one girl, possessed of an evil Spirit, have to do with the disasters which had befallen the People? She might have even caused them, through her long stay with the tribe. *If she still lives,* Spear thought, *I will kill her rather than let Ghost bring her back to us.*

Wolf shrugged. "She's my sister."

Spear nodded. It was a motive he could understand, at least, if not approve of. Ghost's motives were beyond comprehension, though Spear suspected he wouldn't approve of *them*, either.

He said nothing of this. Wolf was a mighty hunter. Spear liked him a lot. He hoped this ill-fated journey wouldn't make enemies of them. So he only grunted and said, "Let's go, then. The quicker this is done, the better, I think."

Wolf nodded and rose smoothly to his feet. Within ten minutes the small party was heading downriver, hugging the base of the high banks as much as they could in order to conceal their presence. They left nothing behind to mark their camp.

Shortly after they had left, Snake squatted where they had slept, thoughtfully licking a shard of black stone. "They slept here," he said. "This spot."

Caribou nodded. He'd kept his own party well behind, in order to avoid spooking his prey. He knew Snake would spot their campsite easily enough. Now, as he scanned the area, he noted the efforts they'd gone to in order to conceal their presence.

They were spies, no doubt. Or were they? Perhaps they were something worse.

"We'll keep to the high ground," he told Rat, who nodded agreement.

"They'll hide close to the river," he replied. "They don't want anybody to see them."

Caribou hefted his spear. "We see them," he replied. A few minutes later, sweating as the heat of the sun grew on their shoulders, they set off.

"What will we do when we find them?" Rat wondered.

"Maybe kill them," Caribou replied. "Maybe not."

Rat nodded. The Spirit of Breath was always hungry. He didn't mind appeasing that appetite with foreign meat at all.

Above Bison People River Camp

Spear wiggled on his belly to the sparse shelter provided by a low heap of rocky scrub. He peeked over, then motioned Wolf and Stone close.

"I don't see her," he whispered, as he pushed a tuft of soft green grass out of his vision.

He lay unmoving for several moments before he understood that something was wrong. He raised his head, alarmed at the sudden silence. He managed to turn halfway and caught a glimpse of Wolf, flat on his back, with Rat's spear at his throat. Then the biggest man he'd ever seen brought the butt of his weapon down on Spear's forehead, and Spear saw no more.

Bison People River Camp

Broken Fist stepped close to Spear and smiled. Spear hung from a pole set into the ground next to the cold fire pit, his brawny arms jerked back and up by the leather thongs pinioning his wrists. Likewise his ankles and knees were also tethered. He was naked and shivering in the sharp afternoon breeze. A thin trickle of dried blood extended down from his matted gray hair into his salt-and-pepper beard. His dark eyes snapped furiously, but he remained silent. He'd been hanging like this for two days.

"Why did you come to our camp?" Fist repeated softly. He turned and glanced at Maya, who stood next to Caribou, watching the scene with hooded gaze. "Go on," Fist said, "ask him."

"Why did you come to the camp of the Bison People?" Maya said.

Spear stirred. He brought his head up. His lips worked and then he thrust his face forward and spat a huge, glistening gob at her. "Demon!" he snarled. "Animal! Murderer!"

"What did he say?" Fist asked.

"He called me a demon, an animal."

"Oh." Fist turned back to the hunter. He eyed him with speculation. Then he brought the razor-sharp blade down and sideways in a lightning motion. As if by magic, a long red line appeared in the curly hair of Spear's chest. Spear arched his back but didn't cry out. The wound blurred as blood leaked onto his skin.

Stone and Wolf, similarly bound, watched the scene a short distance away. Stone kept glancing uneasily at the huge, vacant fire pit. Wolf stared proudly straight ahead, as if all this had nothing to do with him. His slender, muscular form gleamed in the sunlight. Unlike the other two, he had very little body hair—Maya glanced at him and wondered why his skin was so smooth, like that of a tiny muskrat.

Fist wiped the blade on Spear's hair. Then he reached down and touched the tip of it to the older man's testicles. "I'll cut them off if you don't tell me why you came," he whispered. "I'll put them into your mouth and choke you with them."

Spear didn't understand the Shaman's words, but his actions were unmistakable. His lips moved as he tried to work up another defiant mouthful of spit, but Fist only laughed, stepped back a pace, and smashed his mangled left fist, hard as a club, into Spear's nose with a sound like crunching celery. Fresh blood spurted red; Spear gasped and thrashed against the pole like a hooked fish.

Maya watched the scene with a calm face, but Caribou could feel how tense her muscles were, how she flinched slightly as Fist battered at his helpless captive. Sweat mingled with blood on Spear's face, chest, and arms as the medicine man hacked and slashed at him with the knife, never wounding too deeply, but slowly, and with evident malice, flaying Spear's skin from his bones as he dangled helplessly. Finally, after an hour had passed, and Spear finally slipped into limp unconsciousness, Maya uttered a small, mewling sound.

"I want to go to the tent," she whispered to Caribou.

He looked down at her and saw that she was pale

as ice beneath her ruddy complexion. She kept licking her lips as if they were dry, and she swallowed repeatedly. He leaned close and said into her ear, "Fist will notice. He'll think you favor your former people."

"I don't care. I don't want to watch any more of . . . this." She put her forehead against his upper arm. "I feel sick."

Caribou saw a way out. "Come, then," he said, loud enough for Fist to hear and leave off his sport, "if the heat is making you sick, you don't have to stay here."

He glanced over the top of her head at Fist, whose eyes had narrowed in suspicion. Caribou shrugged. "She's carrying my son," he told the Shaman. "That one isn't going to say anything." He tipped his head in Spear's direction.

The captured hunter looked like a caribou when the woman had finished butchering it. The white lips of innumerable cuts crisscrossed his upper body, showing pink, moist flesh beneath. Blood, both dried and sticky, coated every inch of him, even his legs. His tongue lolled from his mouth and his head dangled bonelessly forward on his neck.

Caribou doubted he would survive another hour of torture; it was evident to his eyes that Broken Fist didn't much care. The medicine man, naked and painted, was far gone in blood lust. The Spirit of Breath hungered within him, for the only food the God of Snakes desired: blood and pain.

As always.

Fist shrugged. "Take her, then. But be ready, for the next one."

Caribou nodded. "Come, Maya," he said gently, and led her away.

Maya heard a high, shrill scream from beyond the tent flap and closed her eyes. She couldn't have explained to Caribou why she was so upset; she wasn't certain herself. Something in her rebelled against the torture, but that revulsion conflicted with a deeper feeling of dark joy. A part of her had always wanted, she realized, for that hulking hunter to know agony. She had no conscious memory of Spear, but somehow she recognized him, and knew that he had hurt her in the past. The other two captives were more complicated.

The one named Stone called up recollections both ugly and sweet, though the memories were formless, more feeling than detail. And the young one, the third, bothered her most of all.

He'd stared at her when Caribou had dragged the three of them into camp, prodding at them with their spears and laughing uproariously. Wolf was his name; he'd told them that much. He'd spoken to her, only a single sentence, but had called her by name: "Maya, why do you look at me like that?"

She twisted restlessly on her furs. Nausea gripped at her stomach, but it wasn't the baby. Memories hidden inside her were trying to get out, and she was afraid of them.

Her injuries had done a great deal of damage; but beyond the initial amnesia, she'd had no reason to try to recall what was lost. In fact, she'd fought to remain inside the comforting gray cloud that shrouded the time before her discovery by Caribou. But these three new ones threatened all her hard-won comfort—she was certain that her life before had been horrible, but she didn't want to know the specifics. Yet she had no choice, it seemed. Fist would no doubt sacrifice all of them to the Spirit of Breath— she suspected it would be a horrible sacrifice, though no one had ever described such a thing to her—and she would no doubt be called on to translate again.

Why hadn't she forgotten her language along with everything else? Then Fist would have left her alone.

She sat up, filled with a restlessness that made her fingers itch to do something. Anything. She glanced around the dim interior of the tent, so familiar. The bedding she and Caribou shared. The small hearth, set precisely beneath a carbon-blotched smoke hole. The pile of their belongings—his, really. Knives and scrapers. Two hide packs, containing a host of tiny things: beads, carved bits of bone, lengths of thin leather cord, chips of flint.

She grunted and crawled over to one of the packs and upended it, vaguely intending to clean things, rearrange, perhaps discard any useless junk.

A soft, furry bundle clunked out at her knees. She stared down at it. She didn't remember having seen it before, and then she understood. This was Caribou's hunting pack she had emptied and generally he carried it with him. It was full of a hunter's tools: spare blades, thongs, a chunk of dried bison meat wrapped in several thicknesses of leaves, an extra pair of leggings. And the bundle.

She sighed, settled back on her haunches, and began to sort. As she worked, whimpers of agony drifted in from the outside. She shook her head unconsciously and hunched her shoulders, as if to ward off a blow.

The chipped blades had gone dull. In her mind's eye she could see how to fix that: A few sharp blows with a shaped wooden form would restore the edge in moments.

She blinked. How had she known that?

She stared at the knives for a long time, hefting them, feeling their balance and weight, admiring the skill of whoever their artisan had been. Finally she wiped them clean on her furs and set them aside. Sharpening them would be something else she could do, to keep her mind off—

She shook her head again. Better not to think. The youngest one, who knew her name . . . She picked

up the fur-shrouded bundle and felt the hard shape
of something small inside.

Only a single thong held the package closed. The
knot was loose, as if Caribou had wrapped it carelessly, and placed little importance in the contents.
Without thinking about it her fingers nimbly undid
the knot, and the fur fell open to reveal the Mammoth Stone.

As she stared down at it, barriers came crashing
down inside her skull with hollow, booming sounds.
After a while she began to shake.

Caribou watched the torture proceed with half an
eye. He was worried about Maya. The capture of
the three spies—for he was certain that's what they
were—obviously had stirred painful memories for
his woman. He alone was aware of how little she
remembered of her previous life, and that blankness
suited him perfectly. Sometimes she would dream,
but upon waking she never recalled whatever it was
that had disturbed her sleep. Caribou wondered
who "Magic" was, and "Bud" and "Blossom." Those
last two names he knew well enough, for her worst
dreams were evidently about them—at least, it was
their names that would send her bolting up, eyes
wide and unfocused, covered with sweat. But when
he asked her in the daytime who they were, she
would only shake her head and say she didn't
know.

He hoped the inevitable deaths of these interlop-
ers wouldn't foster more nightmares, but he was
afraid they might; not only because of the mere presence of the men, but because of what would happen
to them. Eventually Fist would tire of his sport—
already Caribou saw the signs. Then the fire would
be laid in the pit and the glowing coals made ready.
Maya had never seen a Great Sacrifice; if such a
thing made Caribou sick and weak with disgust,

who had known the horror of them all his life, what might it do to his poor woman?

Especially if the victims were those she might have known once. Would the shock be too great, and bring back the memories he thought were mercifully hidden?

Maybe they could escape, he thought, and glanced once again at the trio. An idle thought, and now that he looked more closely, probably a futile one. The first man, the big one called Spear, was near death already. He swung limp and unconscious, coated with his own blood.

The second, whose name Maya told him was Stone, wasn't much better off. Fist hadn't brutalized him for as long as Spear, but he'd made up in ferocity for what he'd lost in time. Two of Stone's fingers were gone, his teeth were broken out, and one eyeball had started clear out of its socket and lay on his cheek. He, too, lolled in unconsciousness.

And Fist was beginning with the third one, the young man whom the Shaman had purposely saved for last. Caribou doubted he would damage this one much, for the big hunter knew how Fist thought about things: The youngest captive would make a good sacrifice, living for a long time while his flesh melted from his bones and his screams ascended to the God of Snakes like precious gifts.

No, they won't escape, he thought. *Not even with my aid.* He wondered if he could somehow keep Maya from witnessing their final destruction, but guessed shrewdly that Broken Fist would allow no exceptions. If Maya was to be fully admitted to the People of the Bison, she would have to partake fully of all their life—including those rituals that brought such pleasure to the terrible Spirit who ruled them.

The torture had been going on for so long that most of the People had lost interest. A few women stood close, their eyes avid, and Caribou thought

once again that women were more terrible than
men. He knew, from the glassy, hungry look on
their faces, that if given the chance, the women
would do far more damage to the captives than Fist
would.

The Shaman knew it, too. He turned and made
shooing motions at one woman who had ventured
too close, brandishing a piece of jaggedly broken
shell with ferocious gestures.

The men, for the most part, had drifted away.
Caribou saw Rat down by the river, soaking a long
piece of leather thong. He had just turned in that
direction, intending to chase away his misgivings
with some desultory conversation, when the painted,
howling figures poured over the hills that led down
to their camp. A spear, thrown with such incredible
force by some strange attachment Caribou didn't understand, pierced the neck of the woman with the
shell and burst through her throat in a gout of crimson blood.

She fell to her knees, her mouth twisting in a silent scream, and the battle was on.

Maya heard a confusing jumble of shouts and
screams, but it was as if the noise came from another
world. It had nothing to do with her. The only thing
that mattered now was the tiny carved figure she
held in her hands.

At first it hadn't meant anything. She'd stared at
its soft, glowing warmth for a moment, not understanding the weird, inexorable pull it exerted on her
attention. She couldn't look *away* from it. Then, as
she began to shiver, her lips moved faintly.

"Wolf," she whispered. "Oh, Great Mother, *Wolf!*"

Caribou automatically tried to raise his spear,
then realized he wasn't carrying it; the weapon still
leaned against the front flap of his tent. His eyes

slid in that direction, then he realized there was no time. He cast about for a replacement. Another moment brought him to the edge of the pit, where branches and cut logs had been piled. He hefted a chunk of wood as long and thick as his leg. It made a perfect club. With a snarl on his face, he turned to the fray.

The invaders poured down the edge of the decline, some casting their spears with that strange, stick-like mechanism, others holding their weapons forward as they ran. At first he'd thought there were many of them, but now the first wave was across and he saw that there were no more coming.

Four hands of hunters, maybe six. Several of the Bison People were down, transfixed by sharp spear points. A low growl bubbled in Caribou's throat. He rushed forward, dodging projectiles; the spear-throwers, now unarmed, had begun to pick up rocks and hurl them at the Bison warriors.

Rat rushed to his shoulder, wielding his own spear. "Let them come closer!" he shouted over the rising din. "Go to the side!"

Caribou nodded. Rat was a quicker thinker than he; the smaller man had already spotted the small number of attackers, and was putting together a flanking movement. Other hunters scurried up. Caribou brandished his club and shouted, "That way! Over that way!" He led them toward the north end of the camp, past the three captives.

As they thundered toward the cutoff point, Caribou saw a strange and terrible thing: The biggest captive, the one called Spear, awoke. His eyes glittered madly. His muscles bunched, relaxed, bunched again. Blood poured from his wounds in streams as, with a superhuman heave, he wrenched from the ground the pole to which he was bound. A twisting motion of his thighs snapped the leather thongs from his ankles. He raised the long pole like a battering ram and screamed as he charged forward, directly at the approaching group.

Caribou, in the lead, dodged to one side. Behind him, Rat wasn't so lucky; Caribou's massive body had prevented Rat from gauging Spear's path correctly. The huge pole caught him at shoulder level, smashing him to one side like a fly. Caribou heard the bones in Rat's shoulder crunch sickeningly as the smaller man fell. Without thought, Caribou scooped up Rat's spear; he felt better with a proper weapon.

Spear's charge had run out of steam. Now he stood in a circle of Bison hunters, spinning around, thrashing with the pole. He chanted as he moved. The hunters tried to penetrate the circle of death, but without success. As Caribou watched, two more fell; one was only bruised, but the other man's head was split open and his gray brains splattered on the ground.

Caribou shot a glance over his shoulder. The invaders had reached almost to the center of the camp. The women scattered before them; only a few of the Bison men had managed to mount a defense, and they were falling back before superior numbers.

Meanwhile, too many were occupied with Spear. *"Leave him!"* Caribou shouted. His booming voice grabbed their attention. He gestured toward the main body of attackers. "That way! Stop them! I'll take care of this one!"

The group around Spear fell back, then wheeled toward the main battle. For a moment the big hunter was left unmolested. His chest heaved as he stood alone. He reminded Caribou of a great Mammoth, wounded unto death but still dangerous. *This hunter is very brave,* he thought. He lifted his spear and stepped forward.

"Come, hunter!" he called. "I will kill you!"

Spear didn't understand the words, but he understood what Caribou was about. Summoning up one final frenzy of effort, he raised his pole again and lurched at Caribou. Pink foam coated his lips as he shouted incoherently.

Caribou waited until he was certain Spear was committed to his charge. Then he flung himself to the right, just before the tip of the pole could reach his belly. He felt a deadly breath pass him by. Then Spear, unable to stop his charge, rushed on by; Caribou whirled and plunged Rat's spear into the hunter's back with all the force he could muster.

The massive point cut Spear's spine in half and the big man arched, shrieking in agony. Then, boneless as a child's doll, he fell forward.

Caribou spared him only one sympathetic glance. *A very brave man*, he thought. Then he raced toward the main battle. He saw that more of the Bison hunters were rushing up from the river now; the group he'd sent down to reinforce the first defenders had arrived, and the first rush of the attacking charge had slowed.

Rage filmed his eyes. He raised his spear on high and shouted, "With me! Follow me! *Kill them all!*"

Maya staggered weakly from the tent. She felt light, as if she were floating. She held the Mammoth Stone in her right hand. Scenes of carnage greeted her. She saw the maimed corpse of a woman whose left arm had been sawed off at the shoulder, lying on the path a few feet away. The arm was nowhere to be seen. The woman had staggered that far before her blood ran out. Maya could see a long, glistening trail leading away from the body.

Further down, toward the center of the camp, lay more bodies; spears protruded from some. Others had smashed skulls. A few still moved, their limbs twitching like crushed insects.

Near the pit, she saw Spear lying facedown, a

huge wound in his back. Rat sat next to him, his face white and twisted with pain as he clutched at his ruined shoulder.

Shouts echoed from a final conflict near the base of the hills, where the Bison hunters had driven the remnant of the attackers. As she watched, two more of the Mammoth people fell; then the remainder threw down their spears and knelt in surrender.

A movement at the top of the hill caught her eye. Two figures, silhouetted black against the blue sky; her mind buzzed with memory. The Stone felt hot against her flesh. She recognized them both. Ghost, and the scrawny form of his apprentice, whom she remembered as a younger boy. As she watched, Caribou raised his spear and gestured to her. Relief flooded her; Caribou had lived!

Everything she'd blocked, every memory she'd thought lost forever, had returned when she'd touched the Mammoth Stone. She didn't know whether to be grateful or terrified. But with the rush of memory had come fear—for herself, for the People of the Mammoth, for Caribou—and for Wolf.

A trio of Bison hunters charged the top of the hill. A moment later they started back down, their two captives safely in tow. Ghost limped as they pushed him before them with their spears.

Everybody was near the edge of camp now. The women, sensing victory, crawled back from the rocks where they'd hidden and converged on the spot, waving sticks and carrying stones. Maya looked at the third pole and saw Wolf gazing stonily back at her.

He was unharmed! Thanks be to the Mother!

She ducked back inside the tent and came out a moment later, carrying a small knife from one of Caribou's packs. The shouting had died down, but the area around the pit was deserted. She hurried over, concealing the knife against her thigh. She still clutched the Mammoth Stone as if it had become a part of her flesh. Perhaps it had.

"Wolf!" she whispered as she came up to him. He watched her warily. "Don't be afraid! I'm going to cut you loose!"

As she spoke, she sawed at his bonds. First the thongs around his ankles, then the thicker ties at his wrists. "Run!" she told him fiercely. "They're busy now, you can get away!"

His dark eyes were sad as he shook his head. "Maya," he said softly, "what have you done?"

But two strands of hide still bound him when Maya felt strong fingers close over her wrist. "Ah," Broken Fist said as he plucked the blade from her fingers. "A traitor. More food for the God." He grinned down at her terrified face.

"Good," he told her. "He is always hungry."

Chapter Nineteen

Bison People River Camp: 17,982 B.C.

"You mustn't try to run away," Caribou said to Maya in their tent. He shrugged. "It wouldn't do any good." A thought struck him. "There isn't any place to run," he added, as he tried to make his voice sound kind.

In truth, he was worried. Fist had dragged Maya to him in the aftermath of the battle and told him what she'd tried to do. He'd wanted to tie Maya up and leave her with the rest of the captives, but Caribou had pledged she wouldn't try to escape.

The Shaman had regarded him with a piercing eye, but capitulated. He had more captives than he knew what to do with, and already visions of the greatest sacrifice in the history of the Bison People were smoldering in his brain.

Moreover, Broken Fist knew his politics. Caribou had become a mighty hero to the Bison People. Many had seen him slay the deranged giant, Spear, with a single thrust. And it had been Caribou who had rallied the hunters when the battle was in doubt. He had plunged into the melee like a demon, slaying right and left. When it was over, the huge hunter had at least a hand's worth of heads to hang before his tent.

So Fist had shrugged and said, "See that she doesn't escape. She is a traitor, Caribou. We'll speak of it later." Then the Shaman had turned to supervise the binding of the few remaining invaders. Caribou took Maya's hand and led her back to the tent.

"Why did you *do* it?" he had whispered harshly. "Fist will try to kill you now!"

She had stared at him. For the first time he had seen how clear her eyes had become. One green, one blue, they both sparkled like smooth stones under clear, running water. "He is my brother," she'd said simply. And that was how he'd discovered that her memory had returned.

Now, a day later, Caribou paused to give thought to his plight. As he walked through the camp, men and women came up to speak a few words, or simply touch his shoulder. Wide-eyed children trailed after him, whispering in awe.

The aftermath of the battle was better than he'd expected. Twelve of the Bison People—five women—had died in the first murderous onslaught. In the battle following, several more had been wounded. He knew some would die. He feared his friend Rat would be one of them. The small man's shoulder was a crushed and leaking mass of broken bone and torn flesh. Fist applied salves and made a magic chant, but Rat became feverish and incoherent. Caribou had seen others in his condition. None of them had survived.

But the Bison People had reason to be cheerful in their victory. Caribou had no way of knowing that the mightiest of the enemy's warriors, men whose intelligence and bravery could have given them, even with their depleted numbers, at least a chance at victory, had already been captured—though he suspected Spear had been one such, and was glad that Spear had been weakened by torture before he'd had to face him.

Without their leaders, the men of the Mammoth People had followed Ghost's strategy, and it had been a poor one. Rather than take advantage of the greater range supplied by their throwing sticks, Ghost had simply sent them down in a frontal charge that deprived them of what little hope they had. They fell quickly before the larger weapons of the Bison People. Now less than two hands of them remained alive, tethered together in a long chain of misery. Fully half their number were gone. Caribou suspected that back in the Green Valley, none but women and young children remained. The Valley was theirs for the taking.

That thought cheered him not at all. He saw another confrontation coming. Fist wouldn't let him bask in his recent glory. The Shaman was jealous of his power. He couldn't allow a rival to grow too strong without trying to strike him down. And Caribou knew how the blow would come.

Through Maya. He recalled how he'd submitted to Broken Fist's authority another time, even though it had cost him his beloved little sister.

Yes, he saw well enough what Fist would try to do. The question was, what would he do about it this time?

What *could* he do?

There was one possibility, but it was so frightening even Caribou, the greatest hero the Bison People had ever known, could barely bring himself to think about it.

Instead he said to Maya, "You remember everything now?"

She nodded. In the folds of her coat the Mammoth Stone lay hidden close to her heart. She hadn't told Caribou about it. Nor had she mentioned how the sight of it had sent a lightning bolt of memory crashing through her fogged mind. She knew he wouldn't understand. She wasn't certain she did herself, though she knew many things now that she hadn't even suspected before.

She simply sat, a small woman with her arms folded around her knees, and wondered what she would do. She wished she'd never re-discovered the Stone—the anguished memories it revived had haunted her dreams the night before.

But now she remembered Bud and Blossom; not only their deaths, but their lives, and the way they had loved her. She remembered Magic, too, and Old Berry. Of the four, only Berry might still be alive, though she had been afraid to ask the captives. Fist had set a guard on them, and Caribou told her she was forbidden to approach the barrier of thorny branches which enclosed them.

And so she remained in her tent, sunk deep in thought, wrestling with the responsibilities she had fought all her life to escape.

"You will save the People of the Mammoth," Old Magic had told her. *"You are the Great Mother come among us."*

She'd been a child then, a million years ago. Now she was a woman, and she could see at least part of the terrible frustration of that prophecy. Caribou had finally told her what he'd discovered when he'd visited the Green Valley a second time. "I think all their men are here," he'd added. "Only a few left, and Fist will probably kill them." He'd shaken his big, shaggy head and said, "Your People are almost gone, Maya. The God of Snakes is always hungry."

She didn't fully understand what he meant, but she could guess. Something terrible, something fatal for the few remaining remnants of the tribe which had driven her out, but for whom she still bore a responsibility she could never escape.

And Wolf. She remembered how he'd given her trinkets and, when he could, love. Now he huddled with the others, for Fist had ordered him cut down.

Stone as well, though the man who had once been her father was dead when they loosed his bonds. A stray rock had smashed his skull.

"You will save the People of the Mammoth!"

Easy enough to tell a little girl, who had no idea what the old Shaman was talking about. But what to do now?

"Caribou," she said softly, though her eyes glowed with a weird incandescence as she spoke, and Caribou suddenly, for the first time, felt a twinge of fear, "I can't let them die."

She squeezed her knees together and looked him straight in the face. He saw no weakness on her strained, unhappy features. "I *won't* let them die."

He sighed. She was only a woman. He didn't care about the others. He only cared about her—and the child she carried in her belly.

"Very well, Maya," he said at last. "I understand. They are your People. But you are mine, and I won't let you die, either."

Their eyes met and locked. When he finally looked away, shaken by the intensity of her stare, he almost believed she would find a way.

A way for both of them.

Ghost folded his arms across his chest and stood naked, facing the Shaman of the Bison People. Broken Fist, in full regalia, stared coldly back. The two men were alone inside Fist's Spirit House—Ghost had known the summons would come and it had, just after sunrise on the second day of his captivity.

"You are the Shaman of the Other People," Fist said.

Ghost shook his head. The tongue of the Bison was foreign to him. He replied in his own language. "I don't understand."

The two men stared at each other. Finally Broken

Fist sighed. "Do you speak the tongue of the Spirits?"

The words came out singsong, like a chant—for the Spirit Tongue was sacred, used only to communicate in secret rituals with the ghosts and demons and shades which ruled all People.

Ghost's eyes widened. His own voice took on the lilting quality. "I speak to the Spirits in their own language, yes."

Now Fist smiled. The other Shaman's words were subtly different, but he could understand. He'd been afraid he might have to use Caribou's woman to translate, and he didn't want to do that. "Good," he replied. He gestured to the furs piled around his medicine hearth. "Sit, then."

Ghost, whose hands were bound in front of him, but whose legs were free, nodded and squatted down. After a moment, Broken Fist did likewise. After he'd settled himself, he took a moment to gather his thoughts. He wasn't entirely certain of his goals but he thought this alien magic man, whose shadowed eyes held a dark anger he thought he recognized, might be bent to his own purposes. Though he'd originally intended to kill the enemy Shaman in front of the Bison People, in order to demonstrate the superiority of his own magic over that of the Other, now he gave thought to further possibilities. Mentally, he shrugged. If nothing presented itself, he could always carry out his original intention.

"Who are your People?" he began.

Ghost, for his part, discerned a similar potential for cooperation. Their People might be enemies, but Shamans were Shamans. Among those who dealt with Spirits, there was always the possibility of common ground.

"My People are of the Mammoth, and the Great Mother," Ghost began.

Fist listened attentively to the older man. When Ghost was done, he nodded formally. He said, "My Spirits are stronger than yours. The Spirit of Breath, who rules all People, has shown His power over you. My hunters have seen your houses empty and your people gone. Now your men are mine. What do you say to that, Shaman?"

Ghost lowered his head. He was afraid Fist might be right. Everything, all his hopes and plans, had dribbled away after Magic's death. *Curse the woman!* Shewhomhehated had finally won Her battle with him.

Yet he discounted Fist's ravings of the Spirit of Breath's power. He'd felt the lash of the Mother, and he knew She could sweep this prattling magic man before Her like a tumbleweed in a storm. But She'd withheld Her force in order to bring him down. Never mind that She'd brought down the People of the Mammoth as well. The Great Spirits were capricious. Ghost doubted they cared much for the welfare of their charges when their own interests were at stake.

But maybe there was a way. The more he considered, the more it seemed possible. First, he would have to convince this babbling medicine man. He *smiled* to himself and looked up. "Your Spirit of Breath didn't prevail," he said softly. "Our Great Mother deserted us . . . because we harbored an evil demon." He licked his lips while Broken Fist stared at him without expression.

"This evil Spirit destroyed us. She will destroy you, unless you let me kill it. And make no mistake, only I know how to rid you of the demon."

Fist chuckled, but there was no humor in his words. "Rid *me* of the demon, Shaman? There are no demons among the People of the Bison."

"Oh, but there are," Ghost replied. He hadn't seen her, but he *knew* she was here. He could *smell* her. "Her name is Maya," he continued. "And as she brought down the Mammoth People, so will she threaten the mighty Spirit of Breath." He paused. "And you, Shaman. She will destroy even you."

The silence held for a moment. Then, betraying nothing, Broken Fist said, "I will listen."

He did. When Ghost had finished, Broken Fist nodded a final time. He put little credence in the other man's lurid tale of possession. He'd seen the woman. There was nothing inside her but broken things. Yet Ghost had just given him a key with which to solve his own thorny problem. Best of all, the enemy Shaman would achieve the solution for him—he need not dirty his own hands in the slightest!

He took a breath, and allowed himself a brief, greedy thought of the slaughter to come. But his voice was calm as he replied. "We have the woman you speak of. Perhaps she is possessed. I have noticed strange things about her."

Now the carrot, to bait this pompous magic man. "Perhaps, if you can do what you say, I will let you live."

And the stick. "But only if you can destroy her." He shrugged. "Otherwise, you will be the first to feed the Spirit of Breath."

Ghost nodded. He'd expected nothing more.

That night, Caribou held Maya close. Outside, the pounding of log drums had begun, as smoke swirled and billowed about the river camp.

"Do you hear the drums, Maya?" he whispered.

"Yes." Her voice was soft, and steady enough. *She has no idea*, Caribou thought, and shuddered. He remembered feeding paste the color of blood to his shy, trusting sister.

"Fist is making ready for the sacrifice." He paused,

because he didn't want to continue. His own terrible choice loomed just ahead of him.

She didn't say anything, only snuggled closer to him. She took one of his big, callused hands and placed it over her warm belly. He fancied he could feel the baby stirring there.

He sighed. "Fist told me to bring you to the pit in the morning. I think he will sacrifice you to the Spirit of Breath then."

She asked the question he'd dreaded. "What will you do, Caribou?"

He closed his eyes. "I don't know."

She placed her small hand over his. "Don't worry," she said. "It will be all right."

But it won't, he thought. *No matter how it turns out, it won't be all right.*

When he began to snore, Maya rolled away from him and lay on her back, staring up at nothing. Gradually her right hand crept to the Stone, which lay near her heart. When she touched it, she felt a tiny itching sensation. The moment, she knew, had come.

The moment to choose.

She closed her eyes and gripped the Mammoth Stone more tightly. After a while her breathing grew steady, and she slept.

She Dreamed.

. . . walking.

At first there was nothing but darkness. She walked through a void. Then came Light, at first a spark, then a flame, then an inferno.

She walked through Light, and found herself on a long, rolling plain. In the distance, mighty peaks thrust up gray shoulders of stone. She continued, though now she was terribly frightened. There was nothing here to frighten her, but her fear grew more oppressive with every step.

It seemed she walked for days, though perhaps it was only a little time. Time, here, she thought, had little to do with the World.

Then she saw them, a small clump, hard to make out, gathered in the mighty green distance. As she approached she began to make out shapes. A woman stood at the front. Hulking behind her, a great Mammoth Mother. Next to her, her fingers entangled in its flowing fur, Mother Lion. Maya recognized the lion, and smiled faintly.

Now I know why you spared me, she thought.

There was a huge Bison Mother as well, pawing at the grass, a Caribou Mother, and a host of others. Trembling, she approached them. When she was only a few paces away, she stopped.

The woman stepped forward. She looked familiar, too. *It's her eyes*, Maya thought. *The same as mine, green and blue.*

This woman's hair had streaks of gray in it, but her face was calm and strong. around her neck, suspended from a leather thong, hung a Mammoth Stone. It looked subtly different from the one Maya now touched, but she knew it was of the same power.

The woman's lips moved. Her words came out a distant whisper, ominous. "Now you must choose, Daughter," she said.

Then she stood silent and waited.

Everything waits, Maya thought. Even the mountains seemed to hunch toward her, as if listening for her reply.

All my life I have avoided this, she thought. *I've run from it, hidden from it, pretended it didn't exist. When Magic told me of it, I forgot. When I Dreamed of it, I wiped it away. And when the Stone came to me, I gave it to my worst enemy. And why? Because I was different, and wanted to be loved. I wanted to fit in. So I fought that which was always inside me, and tried to destroy the destiny which was mine at birth. And finally, when the pain and betrayal became too great, I tried to forget everything.*

Because I was afraid.

Slowly, she withdrew the carving from her coat. In the strange gray light of this place—which was not, she knew, of the World—the Stone glowed like warm gold. She extended it on the palm of her hand.

The woman before her said nothing. It seemed she could wait for the rest of eternity.

She can, Maya understood in a flash. *She can wait forever if she has to, for there is a Choice, and it's real. I can turn and walk away, and that is a Choice. Nothing will happen then, except the People will die, and I will not have saved them.*

She looked down at the Stone in her hand, remembering. All the times of her life paraded past: the hurts, the agony, the beatings and rejection. Her own father had disowned her. The Shaman had almost killed her. The People had cast her out.

Choose.

What did she owe them, her own People who had done these things to her?

Choose.

The answer, when it finally came, was utterly simple. She owed them life, for that was what the Stone was about. It was about Life.

Her shoulders sagged, then straightened, as if something invisible and heavy had just flown away. She stepped forward, sank to her knees, and held up the Stone to the woman who stared down at her with glowing eyes.

Above her, Maya saw something vast and cloudy coalesce. In it rumbled thunder. "I am who I am," Maya said, as the bonds that had constrained her fell away as if they'd never been. A fierce joy filled her. "I choose You, Mother! I choose Life!"

Overhead, a bolt of lightning shivered the boiling clouds. In her hand, the Stone glowed with an answering Light of its own. Maya looked up at the woman and said, "Take me, Great Mother. Use me as you will."

Smiling gently, the woman extended one hand and touched Maya's hair. "Not me," she said. "*Her*."

And Maya's eyes opened finally to see She Who Steps Down From Clouds, She Of A Billion Names, extend Her own mighty hand.

"*Welcome!*" boomed the thunder. "*Welcome home at last, Daughter!*" shrieked the lightning.

"*Welcome!*"

The sun glittered in a sky the color of still river water. Only a few wisps of thin, gray smoke rose from the bed of smoldering coals that filled the sacrificial pit. Next to the pit stood the bed made of green wood, on which the victim would lie on the fire. Caribou led his woman from his tent and blinked at the blaze of light which filled the world.

All the People of the Bison were gathered round the Shaman, whose hideously distended mouth, full of the teeth of snakes, slavered grotesquely. Even the captives were ranged about, tethered and guarded by a contingent of strong hunters.

He paused for a moment, unsure, but Maya said, "Come, husband." Then, to his amazement, it was she who led *him* down to the burning pit.

The People parted before them in silence. The drums rolled to a crescendo, then stopped. Their sound seemed to ring in the emptiness which followed.

Maya, still in the lead, halted in front of Broken Fist, who stood rigid before her. He stared at her, a thin trickle of drool leaking down his chin. Her calm demeanor angered him. He raised the rattle he carried in his left hand and shook it in her face.

"Evil Spirit!" he shouted. "Demon, begone!"

She said nothing, only smiled at him as if he were a child.

He stopped his capering. He turned to the guards and motioned with his head. They led Ghost forward. The captive medicine man wore his fine cape of caribou, but Fist had not allowed him any other badge of office. He had no intention of granting Ghost any more legitimacy than he had to.

"Do you know this woman?" Broken Fist said in a language of the Spirits.

Maya understood perfectly. Old Magic had taught her the same words in her childhood. Only she'd forgotten, until she'd remembered.

"She is a demon!" Ghost replied. He was *smiling* now, and even Broken Fist flinched a little before the madness revealed. He decided Ghost would be sacrificed after all, as soon as he finished with this demon.

"You said you would destroy the evil Spirit," Fist chanted. He gestured with the knife he held in his right hand.

"I will do this thing," Ghost replied, and reached out for the knife. Maya felt Caribou stir beside her. In his right hand, Caribou carried a great spear. He had made his own decision in the night, and Maya loved him for it. But she touched his shoulder lightly and shook her head.

Broken Fist handed Ghost the knife. "Then do it!" he howled, and moved away to give the other Shaman room. Inside, he was filled with glee. He hadn't missed Caribou's small movement. But Caribou's anger must be directed toward Ghost. Ghost was the threat. Whichever way it came out, Fist couldn't lose. If Caribou murdered Ghost, then he would have profaned the sacrifice. If he didn't, then once again Fist would have demonstrated his power over the big hunter. Moreover, though Fist was nowhere near as wary of Maya as Ghost was, the fact remained that only after her departure had the Mammoth People been broken. Perhaps there *was* some power within her—if so, best it were demolished now.

He grinned savagely, the snake jaws inside his mouth glistening with saliva, and waited for his plan to unfold.

Ghost weighed the knife in his hand. He glanced a final time at Broken Fist, and then his own madness seized him. His eyes burned as he turned toward Shewhomhehated. It had been a long road, but he would annihilate Her now. Triumph sang a sickly song in his veins as he moved toward Her, the knife raised over his head.

Maya faced him unmoving, a faint smile on her lips. Then, just before Ghost brought down the knife, she raised her right hand. In it glowed the Mammoth Stone.

"You want it," she said softly. "Then take it."

Ghost froze, his arm extended high over his head. For one long moment he did not move. Then his face changed. The muscles beneath his skin warred with each other. It looked as if worms burrowed there, humping and writhing. Slowly, his arm began to drop, though obviously he hadn't intended it to. The muscles in his shoulders bulged with the effort he expended to push the arm back up. But to no avail. Lower and lower his arm fell, until it extended horizontally. The knife fell from his fingers.

Maya looked almost sad, Caribou thought, as she brought the Mammoth Stone down to touch Ghost's flesh.

Ghost screamed.

The storm broke.

Afterwards, Caribou tried to forget the storm. It had come up out of a perfectly clear sky, out of nowhere, a rage of boiling black clouds and screeching wind and lightning so thick he'd felt his hair stand on end and sparks sizzle from his beard.

The gathered crowd had scattered for shelter, but Caribou, leaning on his spear for support, had stood firm. So only he had seen what happened next, and even he didn't see *all* of it.

It is said by modern Shamans that epileptics feel no pain during a seizure. No one knows whether this is true, for epileptics remember nothing of the dark time when lightning explodes inside their brains.

What Ghost felt was a crawling wave of energy that extended from the Mammoth Stone to his fingers, up his arm, across the neuronal paths to his spine, and thence to the soft gray matter inside his skull.

The brain controls all. Frantic collisions occurred in Ghost's mind, connections that should not, could not, have been made. Electricity sizzled down his nervous system, ordering muscles to push and pull in ways they'd never been intended to.

He could no more stop what was happening than he could will himself to fly. Slowly, before Caribou's horrified gaze, Ghost's muscles began to pull his body apart.

The small bones in his wrist snapped first. Then his jaw, grinding slowly, brought his teeth in and down, and he chewed off his own tongue. Both his shoulders dislocated themselves with audible pops—and then his right leg snapped as the long muscles of his thighs jerked against each other.

His stomach bulged, as if full of snakes. His head jerked one way, then the other on his neck. Even over the roar of the storm, Caribou could hear the flat bones tearing away from cartilage there. Ghost's mouth opened, and his severed tongue fell out. Then, finally, his head came down, while his arm came up to meet it.

Maya stood as silent as a rock while she watched her enemy of old gnaw his hand off at the wrist. Still Ghost didn't fall; it was only after both his knees had been wrenched apart that his dying muscles could support him no longer.

He fell with a soft, boneless thump and lay on his back, sightless eyes wide open to the rain. Caribou saw clear droplets bounce on his eyeballs, like water spattering a pond.

Broken Fist bulled forward, his hands hooked into claws. The wind rose into a hurricane and pushed Caribou backward. Lightning flared so brightly it blinded him, and he turned away, deafened by thunder.

He never saw the rest. Nobody living, except Maya, did—and that, perhaps, was for the best.

It wasn't Broken Fist who moved toward Maya that day. The Shaman had seen more than enough. Ghost had been right. And this was a Spirit he had no stomach to face. Had he been able, he would have turned and run as far and fast as his legs could carry him. But he wasn't able, for his body was no longer his own. He whom he worshiped had finally entered the fray.

Maya saw it, though. She felt the World tilt, as something unimaginable wedged itself into Broken Fist's body. Fear stabbed her heart, but at the same time an eagerness welled inside her. This was what her life was for, this confrontation.

It has been so long, she thought, and she knew the thought was not her own.

She raised the Mammoth Stone into the hell of thunder and lightning that hid them. "I accept You!" she cried. "Come through me now!"

With force unthinkable, She Who Gives Birth To All heard her plea, and granted it.

* * *

Ah, Son and Father. We meet again.
Hello, Old Woman. Do you come to contest My will?
In this time, in this place, I do.
Begin, then.

In the maelstrom that surrounded her, Maya stood firm. She felt her feet rooted to the earth, and from the earth flowed strength she couldn't begin to measure. Things invisible and omnipotent lumbered in the air above her. She sensed a strain so great she thought the rock beneath her might be cracking apart.

The Stone in her hand burned with a fire the lightning couldn't dampen, while behind Broken Fist the coals of the sacrificial pit, untouched by the rain that fell like an avalanche, flared an inferno of reply.

She saw snakes dancing in those flames.

There must be a balance, she thought. *If the balance is broken, it must be restored. Neither Death nor Life alone, but both, together.*

Slowly, Broken Fist began to give ground. The snake teeth fell from his mouth. His eyes rolled back in his head, and showed only blank white. His legs moved without his knowledge.

Wavering tendrils of Light emanated from the Mammoth Stone. To Maya they resembled soothing fingers, which now helped the shaman to his final bed.

In the end he lay down on the coals, flat on his back, his arms outstretched. After a time, his eyeballs began to bubble in the cookpot of his skull.

She heard doors as vast as the World itself creak ponderously together, closer, closer . . .

Closed.

The feeling of strain was gone, along with whatever had vanished behind those doors. Her muscles, taut with tension, relaxed suddenly. Her hand, with the Mammoth Stone in it, fell to her side. Her shoulders sagged.

Not the People, but all people. Something had been decided. For a time there would be a balance. Mother, Father, Daughter, Son. As always, when the Powers finished a debate, They discarded Their tools.

The Light went out of the Stone.

Maya fell to her knees, the stink of Broken Fist's burning flesh strong in her nostrils. She barely noticed the storm ending as quickly as it had begun, or Black Caribou lifting her up and carrying her back to their tent.

She slept for a night and a day, and woke clear-eyed. She did not dream, nor did she Dream. He was there when she awoke, his face drawn and anxious.

"Are you all right, Maya?"

She touched his features, and knew her life would be with him. "I'm fine," she said. For the first time, she felt the baby kick. "And so is he," she added, bringing his hand down to feel the new movement.

"He . . . ?"

Maya smiled. "Yes. He. You will have a son, Caribou."

His fingers moved against her belly. Then, slowly, they both began to laugh.

Chapter Twenty

The Green Valley: 17,981 B.C.

Caribou dandled his son on his knee as he sat on a log outside his new house, beneath the towering cliff of Home Camp.

"He's hungry, I think," he said doubtfully, as the baby, called Young Wolf after his uncle, sucked vigorously on one huge fingertip.

Maya rummaged in the basket of dried meat she was pounding together with berries to form a paste. "Here," Maya said, "let him chew on this."

Young Wolf uttered a delighted coo as his father gently inserted the tidbit into his tiny mouth. "Spring will be full on us soon," Caribou said.

Maya nodded.

"The bison will gather."

She nodded again. She knew what was running through her husband's mind. She'd seen it coming. In truth, she felt itchy and restless herself.

"Will you lead a hunt?"

He was silent a moment. Then, slowly, he said, "I wish I could follow them." *There.* He glanced at her. *It is out in the open now.*

"Follow them?" she said. "You mean leave the Green Valley?"

He looked down at the goggling bundle in his lap.

"The child is young yet, but he's healthy enough." He paused, then raised his head. "Wolf is a good leader," he said.

She nodded. "What about the others?"

Caribou considered a moment. "Not many would want to leave, I guess. Rat would go, and his woman. A few others." He sighed heavily. "Most would stay here, though. This is a beautiful place, Maya. It's good for the People."

She'd saved Rat's life. Caribou had thought he would die, but Maya had found herbs and salves that drove the Spirits of Heat from his wound. The small man couldn't use that arm, but his other arm was still strong and his wit as quick as ever.

He idolized Black Caribou's wife. She smiled at the thought. Much had changed since the strange and terrible occurrence at the Bison river camp. The remnants of the Mammoth hunters had returned to Green Valley. A short time later the Bison People had joined them, filling up a portion of the empty houses beneath the cliff.

It would be a long time, though, before Home Camp was as well populated as it had been before the plague. "I don't know if Muskrat is ready yet," she said thoughtfully.

"He's smart, you said. Isn't he learning what you have to teach?"

"Oh, yes, he's fine that way. But it isn't easy, making a boy a Shaman. Ghost never taught him much, I guess. There's so much for him to learn."

Indeed there is, she thought. Until her memory had fully returned, she'd never understood just how much she'd known. How much Old Magic and Berry had taught her over the years. Trying to cram all that knowledge into Muskrat's young skull was sometimes a trying experience. Especially since he seemed so eager to learn, though the prism of awe through which he regarded her sometimes got in the way.

"A few more moons," she said. "He'll be ready then."

Caribou still looked preoccupied. "Maya . . ." he started, then trailed off.

"What is it, husband?"

"Would . . . you go with me, if I went away from here?"

She smiled down at her work. "Yes, Caribou. If you wish to go, I will come with you."

His huge shoulders sagged with relief. "You wouldn't miss . . . your People? Your brother? Old Berry?"

"Of course I'd miss some, husband. But my People, your People, they've changed. They're becoming one People, one tribe. Besides, it's a little hard, being a Goddess on earth. I'm not sure I didn't prefer it better when I was an evil Spirit. At least they weren't all afraid of me then. They just hated me. It was . . . easier. Now they expect me to solve every little problem that comes along. I don't want to be Shaman here. I never wanted that, even though I think that's what Old Magic had in mind."

Caribou digested this. Maya spoke calmly, but he understood what she was really saying. And he wouldn't mind having his wife back, rather than the awesome Goddess who'd slain Gods and Shamans in the midst of storm, which was how most everybody regarded her.

Nor did Caribou much like what he was becoming, either. The battle at the river and the plague had stripped the Mammoth People of most of their strongest men. Only Wolf remained; he was a likely youth, and they'd become fast friends. But even Wolf deferred to the mighty Black Caribou, who had slain Spear and a hand of others.

Just as my wife doesn't wish to be the Goddess, neither,

Caribou thought, *do I wish to be the Chief. What I want to do is hunt, and follow the bison as they thunder south, into the great empty plains.*

"I don't know if there would be enough willing to go," he said at last. "Hunting is hard. It takes many men to kill the bison or the mammoth."

Maya placed the basket to one side. She reached over and hoisted Young Wolf to her own lap. He was a smiling, happy child, and his eyes belonged to his father. Deep, dark brown eyes. She thought he would be handsome when he grew up.

"Maybe not," she said. "Let me think about it."

Caribou was accustomed by now to these brief hints of mystery. His woman was mysterious by nature—and he had his own secret memories of the day by the river. He'd seen what he'd seen, though he never talked about it. Not even with her.

"I'm going to find your brother," he said. "We should discuss it."

She jiggled the baby, who cooed with delight. "That's a good idea." Then, almost as an afterthought, she said, "Tomorrow I will go into the forest for a day. Old Berry can cook your food for you."

"Don't you want me to come? There are still lions at the rocks near valley mouth."

She shook her head. "No lion will bother me," she said.

She sat in the sun-dappled clearing beneath the tree from which Bud had fallen, where Blossom had died so long before. She hummed to herself and stared up, remembering.

For a moment, perhaps, she Dreamed. But when she awoke, with a little shake of her head, the remnants of the vision still danced before her eyes. She recalled how the tree had bent, and bent further, until its leafy tip almost touched the ground. And when Mother Lion, spitting and squalling, had tumbled down, and the tree had snapped back and flung her through the air like a bird.

She fumbled in her pouch and withdrew a long cord of toughly cured hide. She didn't know why she'd brought it, just that it had seemed a thing to do. She rummaged further and found a chopping stone, a knife, and a scraper. Still humming, she stood up and walked a few paces into the forest. There were, she decided, many likely saplings to choose from.

Caribou whistled in surprise as he let the string snap on the tall bow Maya had carried out of the forest. He had no idea how she'd come to make it, but nothing Maya did could ever surprise him.

She said it was a gift from Mother Lion.

The arrow he loosed flew far out over Second Lake. He hadn't aimed it—he'd not yet developed that skill—but the arrow, falling wild, pierced a duck which floated in the center of the lake.

Caribou set down the bow and reached for another arrow. It was a crude thing, simply a very small knife blade lashed to a long, notched stick.

With this mighty weapon, even a few hunters would have no trouble prospering. He lifted the bow again. He wanted to make sure he knew how to use it, when the time came. And the time would come soon. Summer approached.

The arrow made a high, whickering sound as it flashed through the air. Caribou smiled, and bent for another.

In the heart of high summer, the small band gathered at the mouth of the Green Valley. They milled for a while in the bright, hazy morning, speaking softly.

Wolf came to his sister and wrapped his arms

around her and squeezed. "You're sure about this?" he said.

She smiled. "I'm sure."

He nodded, and stepped back. "The Great Mother go with you, then."

"And stay with you," she replied. "She will, Wolf. She loves the People."

Wolf tried to smile. It was hard. "I love you, Maya," he said.

"I love you too, brother."

They regarded each other silently. Tears brimmed in Maya's eyes, but they were tears of happiness. Old Berry stumped up. She thrust a heavy pack into Maya's hands. "Make that hulking man of yours carry it," she said gruffly. "Things you will need. Herbs, grasses. Things."

Maya took the pack. "Thank you, Berry. I'll miss you."

The old woman scowled. Then her wrinkles shifted into the widest smile Maya had ever seen. "Go well, daughter of mine. Go well."

Maya touched her cheek gently. "And you, my mother. You, too."

Caribou called from where he and Rat were supervising the loading of the travel poles, on which they would drag all their possessions. "We'd better start, Maya. We'll have to hurry, to reach the river by dark."

Maya waved at him. Out beyond the small group an ocean of green grass curved softly toward the horizon. In the far distance, a great gray cloud hung low to the earth. She imagined she could hear, beneath the endless groanings of the northern ice, the sound of the bison as they thundered steadily south.

But the ice still ruled. Its noise would only grow stronger, as it continued the retreat begun thousands of years before.

"Wolf?"

"Yes, Maya?"

She reached into her coat pocket and took out the Mammoth Stone. "Here," she said. "For your daughter. Its home is here, with her."

Trembling, Wolf took the Stone. "You're sure?"

She nodded. Wolf's daughter had one green eye, and one blue. "She's so young," Wolf said.

"It doesn't matter. If she needs it, she will understand when the time comes."

Wolf stared at his sister one final time, his steady gaze drinking in the sight of her. He thought it was the last time he would see her, and he was right.

Maya touched his shoulder. "Tell her this. When she returns to the Mother, the Stone is to be buried with her ashes."

Wolf nodded. He didn't understand, for what she ordered was a new way of sending spirits Home to the Mother. He didn't say anything, but she sensed his question. "It's all right," she told him. "It will be needed. Later. For now, though, I think its task is almost done."

They embraced a final time, and Maya turned away.

And that was the way Wolf remembered her, her face toward the steppe, as she joined her husband and walked slowly out of the lives of the People, whom she had touched and changed forever.

He watched for a long time, until the small band had dwindled and disappeared in the ocean of gently moving grass, across which their descendants would travel until they filled every part of the new land.

At last he could see no more. "Come, Berry," he said, and took her arm. "Let's go home."

Thus did the Mammoth Stone end its long journey, in the morning of the World.

Don't miss the sequel to *The Mammoth Stone*, coming soon from Signet—

KEEPER OF THE STONE

by Margaret Allan

On the day of the confrontation, Maya dressed in a robe cut from the skin of an albino caribou and decorated with drawings of power. Around her neck she draped a necklace of teeth from the jaws of a mother lion. From her wrists and ears she dangled treasures carved of mammoth tusk. With a grimace—for it was hot and heavy—she donned a headdress fashioned from the skull of a doe caribou. Finally she unwrapped her most prized possessions—a rattle carved out of an unblemished length of maple and a mammoth sculpted from a bit of pink quartz.

When she finished she looked through the slit at the edge of the door of the Spirit House. Her nostrils twitched at the smoke from the herbs burning in the Sacred Fire. She listened to the hum of conversation as the Tribe gathered at the hearth. She gave her robe a final shake, tilted her head back, and inhaled deeply. She was terrified.

I will die soon, she thought. Her fingers curled at her sides. They itched for the Mammoth Stone, but that was gone long ago. The pink quartz figurine she had carved to replace it was beautiful, but its power was weak.

She no longer dreamed the Great Dreams. At first, that had seemed a blessing—it had meant freedom

and a future for her and Black Caribou. Now the
future had arrived, and she missed the Stone desperately.

What will the Mother do? she wondered.

If the Mother turned away from her, who would
help her save her people? Perhaps it was already
too late. How could she know the Mother's intentions? She hadn't seen Her in thirty full turns of the
seasons.

The rhythm of the drums quickened. She watched
the drummers, young men naked but for hide
clouts, their sweaty faces vacant as they pounded
the magical cadence.

She sighed. Soon all questions would be answered. Would she still be Shaman? Or a pariah,
cast out to die alone, while Buffalo Daughter wore
the robe of white caribou?

Oh, Mother!

She paused, but the Mother made no reply. She
had abandoned Her daughter. As Her daughter had
abandoned Her?

The carving was slick in her palm as she pushed
through the door. The sunlight smote her like a
hammer. She blinked, straightened her shoulders,
and marched toward the Hearth of Testing. Voices
fell silent, then resumed in whispers after she
passed.

The Mammoth Stone!

But it was too late for futile regrets. She walked
to face this judgment alone—for the Mother was
fickle, and worked Her own purposes. *Never my purposes,* she thought. *How had I forgotten that?*

She stopped at the fire, her face grim, and glanced
at those gathered to watch the challenge. Most of
them she had counted as friends. But as she examined their features with the newfound clarity of
dread, she saw their fear and understood why this
testing must now take place.

Lines marked the faces of the adults, sunken bellies disfigured many of the children, and hungry wailing sounded from the infants. She knew they blamed her. The Shaman was the health of her people, and their tribulations were her own.

It had been a moon since the hunters had killed a stringy bison whose meat was barely enough for soup. Since then her magic had remained barren. Her people were hungry and frightened. Never in all the years of trekking had they gone so long without fresh meat.

A stir beyond the fire drew her attention. At first she couldn't see Buffalo Daughter for the crowd that surrounded her. Buffalo Daughter's extended family was by far the largest in the Tribe. It seemed all of them had chosen to support the young woman by escorting her to the challenge. Maya saw her own family—Black Caribou, her mate, along with Young Wolf and Little Caribou, her two sons, and their wives and children—gathered a few feet away, watching her. Black Caribou offered a nervous smile that didn't come off.

She understood. Caribou remembered too much. Though he never spoke of it, she knew he had seen the truth on that day she had defeated her enemies, the Shaman's Ghost and Broken Fist. Her spine shivered as she recalled the appalling force the Great Mother had channeled through the Mammoth Stone into the destruction of the two Shamans. She knew that if she held that Stone today, she would have nothing to fear from this confrontation. But the Stone was gone. She must face Buffalo Daughter's challenge alone.

She stared across the fire at Buffalo Daughter. So be it, then. If the Mammoth Stone was denied to her, it was also denied to her challenger. They would meet on equal ground, without the aid of the great Powers who ruled the world. She, born a vessel for those Powers, understood Them better than anyone still living. Sometimes, when pity for Ghost stole into her thoughts, she was grateful that the Stone had been left behind. Ghost's terrible fate reminded her of the destiny of vessels, after their usefulness was over.

"Ho, Shaman!" the woman's voice called sharply. "Are you Dreaming now?"

Maya smiled. "No, Buffalo Daughter, I am not. I awaited your arrival." She glanced at the shadows which had lenghtened past high noon. "You are late, I see."

"Perhaps you should not be in such a hurry," Buffalo Daughter replied.

The woman who stood beyond the fire was about Maya's height. She possessed a full, rounded figure. Her hair and eyes were black as chips of obsidian.

Maya regarded her silently, her thoughts envious. *She has never known the pain of difference. She was never mocked because of the way she looked. She grew up loved and cared for.*

Once again Maya felt loneliness, as she recalled her own childhood, so full of fear.

Does she know? Does she understand what it is she seeks so fiercely?

Buffalo Daughter wore a robe like Maya's, but made from the skin of her own namesake. It fell in soft folds from her shoulders to her feet. She had pounded a mixture of dried berries and certain roots into the cured bison hide, so that her garment was red as blood. She had etched magical runes of power on the skin with charcoal. A rack of antlers topped Buffalo Daughter's head. On her face she had smeared a mask of red clay, which made her eyes flash like coals at the bottom of a fire.

Altogether fearsome for one so young, Maya thought, and decided, with grudging admiration, that Buffalo Daughter had learned her lessons well. *I taught her everything she knows. But did I teach her everything I know?*

Maya spread her arms. "Buffalo Daughter, why do you come to face me now?" She spoke slowly. Her words quieted the crowd. The drummers paused. Into the silence came only the hiss and spit of the fire.

The younger woman stood proudly erect. Her red clay mask remained rigid as she spoke. Only her lips moved. The effect was eerie, as if Buffalo Daughter had become a doll, controlled by something else.

Perhaps she is, Maya thought.

"The great animals disappear," Buffalo Daughter said. "Your magic no longer finds them or calls them. The hunters return with empty hands. The People cry out with empty bellies. Soon the children will begin to die. We are cursed with evil Spirits. Why have you not driven these Spirits away? Have you lost your magic, Shaman?"

There it was. The challenge, finally spoken aloud, hung in the air between them. She felt the weight of her people's gaze on her as they waited for her answer.

It was true. She had sought in the half-world of Dream for the Spirits of mammoth, caribou, and great horned bison, but for many moons she had found nothing. In the gray light of worried mornings, she had asked herself the same question. Her people depended on her for their survival. If she could no longer guarantee their safety, perhaps it was better to find out now—to lay down her burden and pass on to the fate that awaited a fallen Shaman. She sighed. In a way, this confrontation was a relief.

"I have not lost my Powers, Buffalo Daughter," she said. "If you choose to match your Dreams against mine, you will know the truth. Do you so choose?"

Buffalo Daughter didn't flinch. "I do."

Maya nodded. "Very well. Make ready."

A murmur swept across the crowd. Buffalo Daughter intended to overturn their history. Only Black Caribou among them had ever seen magic faced against magic, though the battle he had witnessed was far different from what would now ensue.

And a good thing, Maya thought. At least this contest would not involve the cold Powers which ruled them all. Or so she hoped.

She watched as Buffalo Daughter spread out a rug made of the skin of her namesake. On this the woman settled herself and arranged her robe around her.

Maya gestured, and her youngest son's second wife, White Fox, spread out a mammoth hide, its fur combed into softness. Maya sank down, wincing at the pains in her knees. She was too old for this. Why did she have to face such a challenge at the twilight of her life? Hadn't she served the Mother faithfully? This should have been a time to cherish her children and grandchildren, not a time of sorrow and hunger and fear.

Oh, Mother, why me? Why now?

But she knew the answer: The Mother used Her tools as She chose—She did not ask permission of them. *And that is all I am*, Maya thought. *All I ever was—a tool.*

It was a desolate thought.

"Are you ready, Shaman?" Buffalo Daughter called.

Buffalo Daughter's image shimmered through waves of heat above the fire, so that the younger woman seemed to float above the earth.

"I'm ready," Maya replied. "Let us begin."

Buffalo Daughter lifted a clay bowl and scooped out a fingertip's worth of yellow paste. She put the finger to her lips, licked, and swallowed. Then, carefully, she replaced the clay bowl at her side.

Maya opened the pouch at her waist and took out a handful of dried brown berries. They tasted sharp, bitter. Each woman used her own elixir, but the effect would be the same. A gateway to Dreams.

Dream was to be matched against Dream—to the more powerful Dream, victory. When this contest was done, the People would still have a shaman. Only the name of that shaman was now in doubt.

Calmly, Maya gazed across the fire at her challenger. As if sensing her attention, Buffalo Daughter's own eyes locked with hers. Maya felt the dark current pulsing between them.

Everything stopped. Maya smelled the herbal essence of the fire, tasted the bitterness of the berries she had swallowed, heard the sigh of the wind, felt the hard earth beneath her buttocks, and looked into Buffalo Daughter's dark, burning eyes—growing larger, larger. . . .

The Dream took her and the world fell away.

In the darkness, Maya saw two points of light—the eyes of Buffalo Daughter, locked in confrontation, sharing the same Dream. It was true, then. This battle was ordained. Two could share a single Dream only by the leave of those Spirits who ruled the Dream World. For an instant all hung motionless. Then, slowly, the dark began to clear.

Maya's mind convulsed in shock as the Dream World sprang into existence around her. She stood on a vast and rolling green plain. Nearby a grove of trees bent to the breeze. The air sparkled like clear water and made the range of white-topped mountains in the distance seem near enough to touch.

She knew where she was, though she hadn't been here in more than a hundred seasons. It was a Great Dream, for she had returned at last to the World of the Mother Herself!

Triumphantly she faced Buffalo Daughter, who

stood a few steps away. "Now you see my Power," Maya said. "This is the World of the Mother I have brought you to."

But Buffalo Daughter's lips curled into an enigmatic smile. "You have brought *me* here, Shaman? I think not." The younger woman raised her right hand toward the trees. "Look, Shaman! Your doom approaches."

Maya turned. At first she saw nothing. Then, slowly, the figures began to resolve in the gemlike light. Again there were the huge, almost forgotten beasts: a mammoth mother, tall as a tree; a great caribou; and pacing alongside in perfect harmony, the gigantic mother lion Maya remembered so well. Yet something was different. In the forefront walked the old woman who was the Mother's handmaiden. She led at the front of the pack a mighty golden buffalo.

The group approached, slowed, halted. The Mother's servant took hold of one of the buffalo's long, curving horns and led her away from the main group. Not once did the old woman turn her varicolored eyes on Maya. Instead, without hesitation, she guided the huge beast to Buffalo Daughter's side.

"Here, Daughter, is your sign. Mount up and ride." The old woman's voice shivered with the sound of suddenly rising wind. For an instant Maya felt the awesome electric presence of the Mother Herself, like the tremorous aftershock of a bolt of lightning.

Buffalo Daughter vaulted onto the mighty animal, which received her patiently. Once settled, the younger woman gazed down at Maya's face. There was a whisper of regret in her next words.

"This is my Dream, oh Shaman, not yours. And this is my Power, as well. Do you doubt it?"

Maya stood dumb, unable to answer. Buffalo Daughter sat atop the great mother buffalo, at whose head waited the woman who served the Mother in all things. Maya stared at the ancient handmaiden. An unspoken plea moved her lips.

"Your time is over, Daughter," the old woman said. Maya heard pity in her voice, but iron decision as well. "Now another will take your place." The old woman looked up at Buffalo Daughter and smiled. "Welcome, Daughter," she said.

"*No!*" Maya was startled by the harsh cry, even more startled to realize it had come from her own throat. Yet she couldn't stop herself. The words tumbled heedlessly in a jumble of outrage. *"I have served faithfully!"*

Maya felt her cheeks burn with shame, with rage, with helplessness. *"It isn't fair!"*

The older woman waited patiently until she was sure Maya was done. Then, as if nothing had been said, she turned back to Buffalo Daughter. "Go with Her blessing," she said softly. Once again, Maya felt the harsh lightninglike quiver that signaled the nearness of the Great Mother.

Chill bleakness seized her heart. She wanted to grab Buffalo Daughter and shake her, make her realize how meaningless such promises were. To tell her how once the same promise had been made to her on this same gentle plain. And how false that promise had become, now that her own time had ended. But it was futile. The younger woman, who had never felt the essence of the Mother, the endless raging well of Power, would not—could not!—understand. Only time would teach her, as it had taught Maya, that the Gods could not be trusted. The Gods—for the Mother didn't rule alone, something else Buffalo Daughter would someday discover—used Their tools however They would, and when They were done with them . . .

When They were done.

"The Dream is over," Maya said softly.

With infinite compassion the old handmaiden regarded her. "Yes," she replied. "It is."

Maya bowed her head and let the dark sweep her away.

"Maya!"

It was Black Caribou. It took her a moment before she recognized the voice and felt his hand on her shoulder. She opened her eyes.

"Yes, Caribou," she said. "I'm here."

Worry colored his voice as he whispered in her ear. "Maya, what has happened? Look at Buffalo Daughter!"

Maya glanced across the fire. The sacred flames had burned down to coals. Buffalo Daughter stood silently, staring at her. There was a new majesty to the younger woman, evident in the straightness of her spine and in the way her nostrils flared as she held her head high, waiting for Maya to awaken.

"Yes, Caribou." She patted her husband's hand. "I know. Here, help me up."

She grunted as Caribou lifted her. She swayed only a moment. Then, knowing what remained, she faced her nemesis.

"Maya," Buffalo Daughter said.

Hushed exclamations erupted from the crowd. No one missed Buffalo Daughter's use of the Shaman's name without her title. But this was nothing to the uproar that swelled up when Maya replied, "Yes, Shaman?"

Buffalo Daughter's smile told the rest of the story, but the ritual had to be completed.

"Do you yield your power to me?"

"I yield, Shaman."

Buffalo Daughter paused an instant to savor the moment of her ascension. Only a few terrible words were left, to seal her new office. Yet before she spoke them, her black eyes flickered.

Does she see her own future? Maya wondered.

Perhaps Buffalo Daughter saw *something,* for her voice lost its iciness, and quavered a bit.

"You are cast out, Maya. You must leave the People, for another serves them now!"

Caribou's breath-squeezing hug about her waist startled her, but she managed to reply, "Yes, Shaman."

A stir at the edge of the crowd turned heads. Men pushed their way to the fire, their voices full of joy, their eyes alight.

"Buffalo!" one shouted. "A small herd, less than half a day away!"

All eyes swept from Maya to the new Shaman, whose power was now made convincingly evident. Maya felt something gritty in her left hand. She opened her fingers and looked down. A handful of pink grains were all that remained of the tiny quartz mammoth. They fell in a glittering shower to the ground.

"I will leave tomorrow," Maya said.

So began the last journey of the first Daughter of the Stone.

He slid his fingers from her ponytail to the back of her neck and urged her closer.

Her fingers splayed against his chest. She murmured something against his lips. He barely heard. His head was full of sound. Full of pulse beats and bells.

She murmured again. This time not against his lips.

He frowned, feeling entirely thwarted. "What?"

She pulled back yet another inch. Her fingertips pushed instead of urged closer. "Do you want to answer that?"

It made sense then. His cell phone was ringing.

Don't miss
Cowboy in Disguise *by Allison Leigh,*
available June 2021 wherever
Harlequin Special Edition books and ebooks are sold.

Harlequin.com

From #1 *New York Times* bestselling author

LINDA LAEL MILLER

comes a brand-new Painted Pony Creek series.

A story about three best friends whose strength, honor and independence exemplify the Montana land they love.

"Linda Lael Miller creates vibrant characters and stories I defy you to forget."
—#1 *New York Times* bestselling author Debbie Macomber

Order your copies today!

HQNBooks.com

PHLLBPA0521

Love Harlequin romance?

DISCOVER.

Be the first to find out about promotions,
news and exclusive content!

Facebook.com/HarlequinBooks

Twitter.com/HarlequinBooks

Instagram.com/HarlequinBooks

Pinterest.com/HarlequinBooks

ReaderService.com

EXPLORE.

Sign up for the Harlequin e-newsletter and
download a free book from any series at
TryHarlequin.com

CONNECT.

Join our Harlequin community to
share your thoughts and connect
with other romance readers!
Facebook.com/groups/HarlequinConnection

HSOCIAL2020